CHARGED

BY JAY CROWNOVER

The Saints of Denver Series
Charged
Built
Leveled (novella)

The Welcome to the Point Series
Better When He's Brave
Better When He's Bold
Better When He's Bad

The Marked Men Series
Asa
Rowdy
Nash
Rome
Jet
Rule

Coming Soon
Honor

CHARGED

A Saints of Denver Novel

JAY CROWNOVER

WILLIAM MORROW

An Imprint of HarperCollins*Publishers*

HarperCollins books may be purchased for educational, business, or sales promotional use. For information please e-mail the Special Markets Department at SPsales@harpercollins.com.

FIRST EDITION

Library of Congress Cataloging-in-Publication Data has been applied for.

ISBN 978-0-06-238597-0

16 17 18 19 20   OV/RRD   10 9 8 7 6 5 4 3 2 1

Dedicated to the one person that has held my hand through all my worst decisions and cheered me on through all my amazing ones . . . this book and this story about bad decisions leading to the best things in life is for you, Mom.

You're just the best, and every mistake I've ever made, every bad choice I've blindly made, you've been there to pick up the pieces afterwards.

Luckily, I do indeed have some pretty awesome stories to tell after everything is said and done, and all the storms have passed. But nothing makes me happier than knowing that none of those tales of wonder and of woe would have had a happy ending if I hadn't been able to share them with you.

INTRODUCTION

She's immature.
   She's a brat.
She's annoying and not very nice.
Why is she getting a story?
Whenever I have a character that seems like they *shouldn't* get a story or like they might not deserve some kind of happiness, they are inevitably the characters that I most want to turn it all around for. I want to know their stories more than anything, and I want to dig into why there might be more to them than we initially see. It happened with Asa, and it happened with Avett from the minute she touched the page. I always knew I wanted Brite's daughter to get a story, but I had no clue how layered, complex, and difficult that story was going to be. She's a hurricane all right, and watching the storm break on the shore has made for some of my most favorite writing to date. I never start out with a character determined to make the reader like them, but I do hope that by the end of the journey, the reader understands the character and maybe even sympathizes with them a little bit . . . and hey, if you do end up liking that character you were so sure you hated . . . score one for me. <3 (Looking at you, Melissa Shank!)

I think Avett is the character that speaks the most to the person I was at the same point in my life. As I was writing her I kept cringing and thinking, yep . . . been there and done that, and now I definitely have a story to tell about those choices and the consequences they led to. Sometimes the story is the best part of screwing up, and really, no matter who we are or where we've been in life, we all have a story to tell. I feel that for all my characters, but for some reason it really, really rang true with Avett and Quaid.

When I was twenty-two I made a lot of questionable choices: about men, money, school, and my future in general. I had to be rescued (by family, not a handsome fella, which was a total bummer for me!) and one would think I learned my lesson because I was sure that was as low as I was ever going to get. Flash forward to my early thirties when things once again fell apart because of my bad choices and my foolish stubbornness. There I was for the second time in my life needing to be saved with more stories to tell and harsh lessons learned. (That story involves *Rule* getting published and my whole life changing, so even though it starts with heartbreak, it ends with a dream come true.)

So go out there and screw up. Have experiences so that you have stories to tell, and do it without an apology.

Memories and mistakes are both beautiful and important in their own ways.

Love and Ink,
Jay

All things truly wicked start from innocence.

—Ernest Hemingway

CHAPTER 1

Avett

*D*on't worry, Sprite, bad decisions always make for good stories . . .
I could hear my dad's gruff voice, lightened with humor, in my ear as he told me those words every single time I got caught doing something I wasn't supposed to do when I was growing up. I was always doing something I shouldn't then and now, so I heard those words a lot from him. Unfortunately, as an adult, my bad decisions resulted in consequences far worse than a scraped knee or a broken wrist from falling out of the tree in the backyard he warned me repeatedly wasn't sturdy enough to climb. And sadly, my dad reassuring me in his firm and gentle way, while calling me his little Sprite as he kissed my boo-boos, wasn't going to help my current situation at all.

This boo-boo was big-time.

This boo-boo was life-changing.

This boo-boo was anything but a good story waiting to be told.

This boo-boo very well could be the end of me, the end of the rope where my patient parents had dangled precariously for years, and it very well could be the end of any kind of future

I may have had. A future I was well on my way to letting a lifetime of bad decisions and even worse choices screw up. At barely twenty-two, bad decisions had sort of become my stock in trade and were as familiar to me as my own face. I was almost legendary, at this point, for putting all my trust in the absolutely worst kind of people. If there was a wrong path to take, I was going to skip gleefully down that road and not look back until I ended up exactly in the kind of situation I found myself in at the moment. It wasn't like this was even a new dead end; it was the same one I ran into over and over again. No matter how hard I tried, I couldn't get myself turned around, and the longer I was circling this dead end, the darker and more wicked it became.

I knew better. I really did, even if there was a boatload of evidence contradicting that fact.

I wasn't stupid, naive, immature, or senseless. I might appear that way to anyone on the outside looking in, but I had my reasons for being a consummate failure and lifelong loser. All of those reasons had nothing to do with me not knowing better and everything to do with me knowing exactly what I deserved.

For a long time now I had been spiraling out of control, whirling, falling deep and deeper into a pit of really awful actions and consequences, each seemingly worse and more painful than the last. I also hadn't made any kind of effort to try and pull myself out of the tailspin, so logically I knew the only place I was going to end up was right here, right at the lowest part of rock bottom. I never imagined the landing would be so jarring.

I had been in need of rescue for a long time and now I really needed it because I was facing a very real prison sentence, and a very real attorney dressed in an immaculate suit, while I sat there shivering, locked in handcuffs, and choking on fear. I never in a million years would have imagined rescue coming in the form of a man like the one sitting across from me. He looked like temptation and ruin, not salvation and redemption.

I wasn't guilty of what they were saying I did, but I wasn't exactly innocent in all of it either. Sadly, that was the story of my life. I was always the girl that wasn't quite good, the one who was just bad enough to be trouble, and the man seated across from me looked like he didn't have the tolerance or patience to deal with any of the chaos that I always seemed to be drowning in.

I laced my tense fingers together, and fought not to wince, or even worse, break down into sobs as the handcuffs snapped around my wrists, knocked loudly on the metal table that was separating me from the man that was supposedly here to save the day . . . and me. He told me his name, but I couldn't remember it. I was a mess of nerves and confusion, and he wasn't helping put any of my anxiety to ease. I was also sleep deprived, and terrified of what was waiting for me after this meeting was over. My future had always been uncertain, resting on shaky and unstable ground on a good day. Right now, I was longing for that wobbly foundation, and scared shitless that my latest bad decision had finally landed me in a spot that I couldn't lie, cheat, steal, or manipulate my way out of.

The stoic and startlingly good-looking lawyer seated across from me didn't look like any white knight I had ever seen. He was too slick for that, way too calculating in the way he looked at me while he silently judged me. No, this guy wasn't the good guy riding in to rescue the damsel and prove himself a hero; this was the guy that the villains paid megabucks to in order to keep them out of jail. In all that I had done, I'd never considered myself a villain. I knew I was a bad guy (or girl), but I wasn't a corrupt, amoral criminal with the actual intent to harm anyone other than myself. However, under the scrutiny of this man's unusual gunmetal-blue gaze, which held not even an ounce of warmth or reassurance in it, I was starting to reconsider my stance. He made me feel like I was well on the road to corruption and disgrace, and he had yet to utter a single word. I'd never done anything bad enough or stupid enough that I required a professional to defend my actions before now, and I was having a hard time believing this guy gave a single shit whether I was innocent or not.

All I wanted to do was cower away from him, and pretend like I was anywhere else in the world but in this tiny room with a metal table that was bolted to the floor between us. I moved my hands again, and couldn't hold back a flinch and a tremor as metal scraped across metal. Rock bottom was going to leave more than bruises if I ever managed to pull myself up and dust myself off. This was going to scar, deep and vicious, and I hated that I deserved every single stinging mark.

"I don't want your story." His words were sharp and to the point. I blinked at the rough sound of his voice in the sterile room.

"I don't want to know if you knew what your boyfriend was up to or not. I don't care. All I want to know is if you understand what you're being charged with, and how serious those charges are. If the answer is yes, all I need to know is if you are willing to do whatever I tell you to do moving forward."

Did I understand how serious the charges were?

Was this guy fucking kidding me right now?

I was hooked up in cuffs. I was wearing an orange jumpsuit, and had on rubber shoes that squeaked across the floor when I walked. I hadn't slept in two days because, after everything went down the night I had been arrested and booked, I'd been locked up in a cell with one woman who was so strung out she kept seeing little gremlins coming out of the floor and, as a result, kept jumping up on the rigid bunks suspended from the concrete cell wall, barely missing stepping all over me. The other woman in the holding cell was there because she had tried to run her cheating husband over with the family minivan when she found him in bed with their next door neighbor. He had been in the family's dining room at the time, so not only was the woman fighting mad about the affair, but she ranted and raved well into the early hours of the morning about how her unfaithful spouse better be on the phone with the insurance company to repair the damage she'd caused. She was a bag stuffed full of crazy, and the more I tried to ignore her, the more she seemed determined to tell me her entire life's story.

Yeah, Legal Eagle, I had a pretty damn good idea how serious the charges were, and I was scared shitless about what would happen to me if I was going to be found guilty of them.

I lifted my chained hands in front of me and let them fall back on the table to make a noisy and unmistakable point. The man didn't bat a single, ridiculously long eyelash at the motion, but his mouth tightened a fraction. It was a pretty mouth. All of him was pretty, in one way or another, and I wondered if when he walked out of this industrial meeting room he shook himself off like a wet dog to rid himself of the feel and taint of crime, sleaze, and bad decision making. He looked like the type that had never, ever took a wrong step. He oozed confidence, self-assurance, and arrogance like it was an expensive cologne that was crafted and bottled just for him. It should be reassuring, should make me feel like he had this all handled, like I would be home safe and secure in my own bed in no time, but instead it made me bristle and feel even worse than I already did. I was a train wreck and that was bad . . . but having a witness to the wreckage, a witness as put together and unflappable as this man seemed . . . Well, that made the fallout from my latest bad move seem a hundred times worse.

This guy wasn't the type to chase bad choice after bad choice. In fact, he made his living riding to the rescue for us poor slobs that did. A very nice living if the Rolex on his wrist and the Mont Blanc pen he was tapping against the file in front of him was any indication.

"I understand how serious the situation is." My voice was quiet and tiny in the empty room. I cocked my head to the side as we continued to size one another up. "My dad hire you?"

I wanted to hold my breath while he answered, but I couldn't get my lungs to work. I couldn't get anything to work.

I was a screwup. I was a failure, a flunky. I was a loser, a manipulator. I was one hot freaking mess on top of another, and through it all my parents, more often than not my dad, had always been there to pick up the pieces. He forgave me. He excused me. He cleaned me up and gave me helping hand after helping hand. He loved me when I didn't want to be loved. He was always there, but not this time.

Bad decisions make for good stories, Sprite.

Dad's words chased themselves around in frantic circles in my head as I felt myself slip a little farther, fall a little deeper and realized *this* . . . this point was actually my rock bottom, as the man who claimed to be my defense attorney shook his tawny head in the negative. "No. A former client actually contacted me and asked me to represent you. He paid my retainer in full and told me that any bills that are incurred while handling your case should be handed over to him. I was hired before the police had you booked and taken to lockup."

My dad wasn't here to kiss the boo-boo this go-around. He wasn't waiting in the wings to dust me off and tell me everything would be all right. Not this time. This time I had gone too far and a miserable, uncomfortable night with a drugged-out weirdo and a psycho, suburban mom had nothing on the ice cold fear that climbed up my spine, vertebra by vertebra, at the thought that I had finally done something Brite Walker couldn't forgive. I knew it was coming. I knew that even my big, badass, former Marine, Harley-riding father had a breaking point. I pushed and pushed to reach that point my entire life. I always figured when the fracture happened it would come with a giant boom. I expected an explosion that would level Denver. The fact that it was barely a whimper, a whisper of sound that indicated a good man's heart was breaking, made me feel even worse than I already did. I had no idea how it was possible, but I sunk even lower than rock bottom. This was what a torrent of misery and despair felt like and I was submerged neckdeep in it.

I blinked back tears and tilted my chin up at the attorney. "Who's paying for you to be here?"

My mom loved me. She had a huge heart that was made of marshmallow, but she had reached her point of no return with me much earlier in my life than my father had. My parents divorced when I was in high school, right on the heels of one of the most defining moments of my youth. My dad rallied like he always did and tried to make the separation as easy on me as possible. My mom went from being distant and confusing to actively pushing me away. I was never sure if she forced the distance between us because things were so easy between me and my father or because they were so hard between her and me. Either way, the strain in our relationship did nothing to help the rapid descent that started to engulf me when I realized exactly what kind of person I was.

A harmful one.

A guilty one.

A selfish one.

I could even be considered a dangerous person, if you asked the right people, and they weren't necessarily wrong. It was amazing how hazardous doing nothing could be. It had even more disastrous results than doing the wrong thing . . . at least, it had up until now.

The lawyer's cultured and smooth voice startled me out of my dreary thoughts. "Asa Cross. He was one of the victims of your boyfriend's armed robbery attempt. The other was an off-duty police officer. So it's no surprise that they booked you and locked you up with almost zero lag time. The DPD protects its own so no one is looking to do you or your boyfriend any favors."

I winced when he brought up Jared.

Jared, the boy who had come along and convinced me he loved me. The boy that assured me we were so much alike we couldn't fail. He was as screwed up and unhappy as I was, so we were bound to be together forever.

Jared, the boy that had hid from me the fact he was not only an addict with a serious problem but also deeply involved in the city's drug trade until I was so far in, with what I thought was love for him, to pull myself out.

Jared was the perfect punishment for a girl that couldn't get it together and deserved nothing more than exactly the kind of guy he really was.

Jared was also the boy who had run off with his supplier's stash and money, leaving me behind to pay the price for his dishonesty and to pass along the message that his connections weren't happy with him. He was also the boy that managed to convince me the only way to help him to help us, was to steal from the one place that had always been home no matter what. He convinced me that petty theft made no difference, that it was money I was owed anyway since my father had handed over his bar, his livelihood, without a thought as to what that meant to me. Jared was good with words when he wasn't high, and like always, I couldn't do the wrong thing fast enough. Only, the handfuls of cash from the register barely put a dent in the amount he owed.

Like I said, I wasn't stupid or naive, so I should've known when he told me he needed to swing by the bar my dad used to own and where I used to work that he was up to no good. Jared was always up to no good, and more and more frequently that no good left marks on my arms and legs. He'd learned pretty quickly that even though I constantly disappointed and let down the people that loved me, they still cared, they always cared, and they didn't appreciate me walking around with black eyes and swollen cheeks. He hadn't slapped me across the face again after Church, the new bouncer at the bar, followed us out to the car one night and gave a few crystal clear hints about what would happen to Jared if I showed up looking roughed-up again. Addicts were unpredictable, but they knew how to hide the things they were doing that were wrong, the things they didn't want other people to know about. So Jared still did bad things to me; he just got more skilled at hiding the evidence, and I pushed harder at the people that cared so I didn't have to make excuses. I could never explain why I stayed or why I thought a guy like Jared was the kind of guy I was supposed to be with. I knew why, but that didn't mean my reasons would go over well with them because, despite everything, they cared about me, even if I knew I didn't deserve it. The lawyer didn't want my story . . . That was fine because it felt like I would be torn in half every time I was forced to tell it.

"Why would Asa hire you to represent me? He hates me." And rightly so. I had given the gorgeous southern charmer a thousand really good reasons to loathe me in the short time we had known each other. I couldn't imagine why he would go out of his way to help me out. He wasn't exactly the warm and fuzzy type, even on a good day.

The attorney lifted a gold-colored eyebrow and leaned back in his seat. He put his expensive pen down on the file in front of him and considered me through narrowed eyes. This guy had silent interrogation and intimidation down to a fine art. I felt like he could tell exactly what made me tick and exactly why I did the things I did simply by looking at me. I wasn't used to that kind of perception from anyone, especially not from a guy that clearly came from a different kind of world than I was familiar with.

"Considering your current surroundings, shouldn't you simply be grateful that he did?"

I bristled a little at the censure in his tone. "I'm just confused."

"Good. That's what I want you to tell every single person that asks you anything about what happened that night. You were confused. You didn't understand what was happening. Your boyfriend coerced you and lied to you. You had no clue what his plans were that evening."

I shifted in the rock-hard seat and all the chains attached to me rattled again. "That's all true. I didn't know what he had planned that night. I never would have gotten in the car with him if he told me he was going to rob the bar." But I knew as soon as I recognized where we were headed, something bad was going to happen, and I did nothing to stop it . . . again.

I could have slid into the driver's seat and left. It would have been so easy. I could have put the car in drive and kept going and going until I ran out of gas and ended up somewhere far away from the nightmare I was stuck in now. I could have climbed out of the car, walked inside that bar, and begged Jared to stop. I could have picked up my cell phone, called the police myself, and told them that my junkie of a boyfriend was tweaked out, owed some bad people a lot of money, and was currently trying to stick up the bar that had saved my dad's life and that had always been a safe place.

So many good choices, so many right things I could have done, and yet all I did was sit there in the car and wait. I knew it was going to go bad. I knew someone was going to get hurt and I had done nothing. Nothing was the worst choice of them all, so of course that was the one that had settled around me like a lead blanket. I was suffocating on all the things I could do, should do, but it was the nothing that won. It was the nothing that defined me. It was the nothing that owned me, ruled me. It was the nothing that haunted me, chased me. It was the nothing that I spent my entire life trying to repent for and live beyond, but nothing always won.

Moments later, while I was still fighting through the nothing of the past and the paralyzing nothing of the current moment, I found myself facedown on the asphalt of the parking lot in front of my father's legacy, being arrested for accessory to armed robbery and, according to the very angry cop that shoved me in

the back of his patrol car, looking at anywhere from three to five
years in prison if convicted.

"I told you I'm not interested in your story. Your boyfriend is in
the hospital with a bullet wound but he's already singing a pretty
little tune that points the finger at you as the mastermind behind
the robbery. He's painting you as a vindictive daughter, angry that
the family business was passed on to someone other than you.
He's claiming you used your relationship to manipulate him into
robbing the place, to teach your father a lesson. Considering he
has a five-mile-long criminal record and a history of drug-related
charges, he's not exactly credible, but then again, neither are you."

He tapped the file in front of him with his index finger and
all I could do was sigh. That file held a lifetime of poor decision
making on my part. It was all laid out in black and white, every
flaw, every terror, every mistake . . . right in front of this too-
pretty man and his chilly and unwavering gaze.

I don't think I'd ever been this exposed, this unprotected and
bare, before anyone. It wasn't a pleasant feeling and it took every
last scrap of self-control I had not to squirm guiltily in my seat.

"I've had a few hiccups here and there, but I've never been
in jail before now." I sounded defensive and infantile. I didn't
understand how he wasn't getting up and walking out of this
room without looking back. I thought that was probably what
I would do if I was in his shoes . . . not that I would ever be able
to afford his shoes. The guy was the complete opposite of everything I had ever known. I don't think my dad even owned a suit
and the only time I saw him in a tie and shoes that weren't boots
was when someone was getting married or buried.

Those golden eyebrows danced upwards again and the
corner of his mouth pulled down in something that would

have been a frown on a less extraordinary face, but on him it looked more like a practiced expression of displeasure. I wanted to kick myself for noticing anything about him other than his credentials, considering the circumstances. He was distractingly good looking and it was annoying because I needed to focus on my impending doom, not his perfectly straight teeth and his disarmingly sharp blue eyes. "Multiple tickets issued for underage drinking, public intoxication, a recent DUI, a citation for shoplifting, a citation for trespassing, more than one basic assault charge . . . should I keep going?"

I gave my head a little shake. "No. I understand that it can't be my word against Jared's because we're both equally untrustworthy. Neither one of us is running around with angel wings attached to our backs."

That had his frosty demeanor thawing enough that the corners of his mouth kicked up and I felt my breath catch and my eyes widen at how the slight expression turned him from outrageously handsome into something so otherworldly attractive that my simple human mind couldn't compute it. I wondered if he won all his cases because the female jurors were too blinded by lust to listen to any of the evidence he presented. That could really work in my favor, so I sure hoped it was part of whatever he was planning to spring me from the slammer.

"You don't need angel wings or a halo to persuade a judge or a jury that you're innocent. You need to listen to me and be more believable than him. I think it's pretty obvious he's trying to throw you under the bus. I've seen the surveillance tape the cops took from the bar and this is not a respectable individual we are dealing with."

If he had seen the tape, then that meant he had seen Jared grab the back of my head and slam my face into the dash of the car when I told him I wasn't going to be part of whatever he had planned for the bar. Absently, I lifted up my joined hands and rubbed at the knot that was still prominent between my eyes. I hadn't had a mirror to look in to check out the bump but the paramedics at the scene had declared it a minor injury, even if the headache that had eventually settled in from the blow felt pretty major.

"No, he's not respectable at all. He's an addict."

"It sounds awful to say, but that actually works in our favor." He picked up the fancy pen again and folded the file closed in front of him. He rose to his feet in a lithe movement and I found myself shrinking back in my chair to make myself as small as possible. He had already been sitting on his side of the table when the cops brought me into the room so I wasn't expecting him to be as tall as he was, or as big. "Your bail hearing is in the morning, which unfortunately means another night in lockup for you. However, I'm confident I can get you released tomorrow but it isn't going to be cheap, and I also need to prove to the judge you have a place to go if they do, in fact, grant you bail."

He looked at me expectantly and all I could do was shrug. My dad wasn't here and that spoke louder than any words he had ever said to me.

"I was staying with Jared at his place, but clearly, I can't go back there now. As for bail . . . " I shrugged again. "I don't have any money and I doubt that my parents are willing to foot the bill. I'm not sure that I'm willing to ask them for that kind of favor."

His eyes narrowed a fraction as he reached for the paperwork on the table and slid it into a leather satchel. Even his bag looked expensive and fancy.

"If the judge sets bail and it doesn't get paid, then you stay in jail until we have the preliminary hearing. That can take weeks, maybe even months."

I blew out a breath and felt that bottom I had careened into reach up to embrace me even tighter. "It is what it is. I've let both my folks down a lot over the last few years but getting caught up with a guy that would rob the bar, a guy who could threaten my dad's people." I shook my head. "I deserve to rot."

I was being overly dramatic but that's how I felt. I deserved to sit in jail and so much worse than that. Self-pity was good company down here at rock bottom and I wasn't ready to let go of the warmth it provided just yet.

He gave me a look I couldn't read and headed for the door. "I'll call your parents for you and see if we can have something in place before tomorrow. Working on your case will be a lot easier for both of us if you aren't incarcerated. Remember, you need to listen to me, Ms. Walker. That's the first rule in all of this."

Panic hit me like a truck. What if he called my dad and my dad told him he'd had enough of his problematic daughter and her endless nonsense? What if he couldn't love me anymore? Jail I could survive; losing my father for good, well, it would be the end of me.

Without thinking I jumped to my feet, which had the chains on both my hands and my legs rattling loudly, and two uniformed officers hurried into the room. I was about to make maybe the worst decision to date but I couldn't stop the words from sliding off my tongue.

"Don't call my dad!" Recklessness, thy name was Avett Walker.

The attorney turned around and looked at me like I had grown a second head. He didn't say anything as the officers moved to either side of me and told me to calm down.

"You can't call my dad." The words sounded as panicked and as desperate as I felt on the inside.

His broad shoulders lifted and fell in a shrug like he really couldn't give a shit that he was about to ruin my life . . . which was saying a hell of a lot considering where I was.

"I have to." He sounded bored and impatient with my outburst.

I narrowed my eyes at him, and that vortex of awful, which I always seemed to be smack dab in the center of, started to spin faster and faster around me.

"Then you're fired." I saw the cops exchange a look as my rushed words had the blond man turning fully back around to look at me. "I don't want your help. I don't want anything from you."

Finally, there was something other than indifference in his gaze. There was surprise, maybe a hint of admiration colliding with a huge splash of humor in the pale depths.

"Sorry, Ms. Walker, but you didn't hire me, so that means you don't get to fire me." That grin of his, which should be registered as a deadly weapon, flashed across his face again as he watched me, and then he was gone.

I looked at the cop that was closest to me and frowned. "That's not how it works, is it? If I want a new attorney, I get one, right? The state will give me one, won't they?" I was babbling uncontrollably.

He shrugged. "We aren't here to give legal advice, lady, but there's no way in hell, if I was in your shoes, that I would be handing Quaid Jackson his walking papers. The rumor is that the guy could get the Grim Reaper acquitted of murder if he had to."

Quaid Jackson.

I was struck dumb by him and by the situation. I couldn't

deny that his looks and overall demeanor had sort of left me star-struck. His name, like the man it was attached to, was unusual, sophisticated, and impossible to forget. It rattled around in my head, along with the million and one other things I had done wrong in order to get to this point.

After Quaid was gone and the officers had the shackles off my ankles, I followed them back to the cell and swore softly under my breath when I noticed that gremlin-girl was gone but psycho-wife remained. She was sitting on one of the bunks hunched over and sobbing uncontrollably into her hands. She sounded like a suffering animal and I knew it was only going to take a few minutes for the noises she was making to have my head pounding. It was going to be another sleepless night and not because I was turning over and over in my head what my dad was going to say when Quaid called him.

I shot the cop on my right a look as he opened the door to the cell for me to go through. He shook his head and muttered so that only I could hear him, "The husband served her with divorce papers and a bill for the car and the house. It's gonna be a long night in lockup."

That was putting it lightly.

As the barred door slid shut behind me, I stuck my hands through the slot so the cuffs could be removed. It was all very *Orange Is the New Black,* but far less entertaining. I silently prayed that I wasn't here long enough to draw any more parallels like that one.

I made my way to the opposite wall of the tiny cell and propped a shoulder up against the hard cement wall. I pushed some of my faded pink hair out of my face and winced when my fingers brushed over the bump that was between my eyes.

I hissed out a sound of pain and met the bloodshot and watery eyes of the woman across from me.

I leaned my head back against the wall and stared up at the industrial ceiling transfixed by the fluorescent light as it buzzed above me.

"When I was little, my dad used to tell me that bad decisions made for good stories. He told me that while I was crying in the hospital, getting a metal plate in my arm, after I fell out of a tree he told me not to climb. Again, he told me that when I crashed my first car, which he said I wasn't ready to drive during the winter. He also told me that when he caught me smoking my first cigarette and it made me sicker than a dog." I tilted my head back towards the woman who was still crying, albeit silently now as she watched me intently. "He was right. All those stupid things I did, even though he told me not to, led to some pretty good stories over the years, and I've always appreciated the battle scars that serve as constant reminder that Daddy does indeed know best."

The woman sniffled loudly and wiped a hand across her damp face. "Why are you telling me this? I don't think the fact that I drove a car through my own home will ever make for a good story. I'm sure my kids aren't going to appreciate the fact that my bad decision is more than likely going to result in their mother going away for a long, long time."

I turned my head back towards the ceiling and concentrated really hard until I could hear Brite Walker's deep and rumbling voice whispering to me: *Bad decisions make for good stories, Sprite.*

I hadn't been telling her for her . . . I had been telling myself because I needed to hear it . . . now, more so than ever.

Who would give a law to lovers? Love is unto itself a
higher law.

—Boethius

CHAPTER 2

Quaid

I pulled my already loosened tie the rest of the way off and kicked the front door of my loft shut with my foot. I threw my leather satchel towards the big sectional that took up most of the open living room and swore when it missed the mark by a hair and went careening to the floor. My laptop clattered and slid out of the top flap, taking with it the file from the last case of the day. I pushed my hands through my hair in aggravation and blew out a frustrated breath.

I was home hours before I had planned to be and I was alone, something else I hadn't planned on being by the end of my date. The rejection and subsequent dismissal from a woman that was not only beautiful but as smart and successful as I was had left me edgy and antsy. I was also grumpy and short tempered due to sexual frustration and the unfamiliar feeling of being denied something I wanted.

What I currently wanted was a shot at getting Sayer Cole in my bed.

I was married the first time I was introduced to the stunning family-law attorney but it was a marriage well on its way to crashing and burning. I wasn't married anymore, and as far as I was concerned, Sayer was the perfect woman to celebrate my newfound singleness with. She was gorgeous and she didn't need anything from me. She made the same kind of money that I did. She was already a partner in the firm she worked for, so she didn't need my name or reputation to get ahead in the legal game. She had been unattached the entire time she was in Denver, so I didn't have to worry about her clinging to me. She didn't seem like the type that was husband hunting, which was perfect, because I wasn't going to be anyone's prey. I was much more comfortable being the hunter rather than the hunted and nothing appealed to me more than a woman that had absolutely no reason to bleed me dry. I knew that even though she came across as chilly and reserved, I could warm her up if I got her naked and underneath me.

I should have taken the hint after the second time Sayer rescheduled on me. Women never bailed on me. In fact, more often than not, women chased after me and I had to bail on them because I was busy or because I was bored. After my divorce was final, I went on a sexual bender. I was hurt and reeling from my ex's betrayal, so it was obvious that I was trying to even up the score and soothe my wounded ego with an endless string of willing bed partners. I was trying to screw wasted years, wasted money, and a broken heart out of my system. It became clear from the get-go, that even meaningless one-night stands wanted more than I was willing to give.

One wouldn't leave the next morning until I threatened to call the police. One acted like she was waiting for an engagement ring after one night together. One disappeared with my favorite Tag Heuer watch. One showed up outside of court after an intense day at trial and wanted to know when we were going out again. Then there was the one who called the top partner at my firm, the guy with his name first on the sign, and asked him for an interview claiming me as her reference. That one led to an embarrassing explanation and a ding on my nearly spotless reputation within the firm. I wanted my name as partner on that sign in the near future, and I wasn't going to let my vengeful dick or my anger towards my ex hinder that possibility.

I stopped sleeping around, set my sights on Sayer, and waited for her to get on board with my plan. Only she wasn't interested and sent me on my way, frustrated and at a loss for what to do next. I didn't have a backup plan because I very rarely needed one.

I walked over to the couch and tossed the silk tie in my fist over the back of it, this time hitting the target. I bent to pick up the computer and scowled when I noticed the toss had dinged the corner. That meant I would have to buy a new one even if this one still worked. It wouldn't do to have a damaged Mac. It wouldn't do to have a damaged anything even if it meant throwing good money away.

I scooped up the scattered file on Avett Walker and plopped myself back on the couch. I looked at the expensive watch on my wrist, yet another prop that was nothing more than a waste of money considering I had a cell phone with the time on it, and then back at the file. It was still early enough in the evening that I could call the young woman's father, letting him know that without someone to pay her bail and without a permanent address for her to be released to she was looking at a decent amount of time behind bars until we had a preliminary hearing date. The system didn't take kindly to one of their own being threatened, and since the robbery had involved an off-duty police officer, I wouldn't be surprised if paperwork got lost or misfiled along the way to us getting in front of a judge.

I tapped the edge of my thumb on the black-and-white mug shot photo and couldn't stop the grin from tugging at my mouth.

She tried to fire me.

She was five-foot-nothing, a lifetime younger than me, had multicolored hair that had seen better days, wild eyes that couldn't decide if they wanted to be green, gold, or brown, while dressed in convict orange and obviously scared out of her ever loving mind, yet she still tried to fire me. If it had been any of my other clients— the cop accused of sexual battery, the frat boy accused of manslaughter over a bet on a football game gone wrong, the middle school teacher accused of pedophilia and having an inappropriate relationship with several of her students, or the pro football player accused of domestic abuse—I would have tipped my proverbial hat, wished them luck while I cut my losses, and walked away without a backward glance. People always committed crimes. People always needed a good defense, so it wasn't like I was hurting for clients, but there was something about the girl. Something about the defiant tilt of her chin and the raw desperation in her tone when she begged me not to call her father.

"I don't want your help. I don't want anything from you." She sounded like she meant it when she said it, but I figured she was too young and too scared to know exactly what she wanted or needed. Regardless, it was still refreshing to hear.

Everyone always wanted something from me and my help was usually the least of it.

I tapped the picture again, wondering why I found it so easy to believe that she really hadn't been a part of the boyfriend's plan to rob the bar. She wasn't anyone's idea of a model citizen and she had the shady track record to prove it. She was too young, and frankly too adorable, to have a file this thick. From what I could see, she also had a set of parents always willing to ride to the rescue when she got herself into trouble. She looked like some kind of colorful woodland fairy from a Disney movie with her odd hair and delicate features. None of it added up, but the sincerity in her tone when she said she would never have gone with the boyfriend if she knew his intent and the fear in her eyes when I mentioned her father seemed genuine.

I learned long ago to treat everyone like they were guilty of whatever it was I was paid to defend them against. I didn't want to know the truth. I didn't want to know the circumstances. I wanted my clients to listen to me and let me do my job as I tried to convince the rest of the world they were innocent, regardless if they were or not. But this girl with her faded, rose-colored hair and turbulent eyes oozed innocence through the cracks of her very guilty façade.

Because I was intrigued and actually believed the girl might be innocent, I wasn't going to let her fire me. I was going to call her father and hope that he would help me keep her out of the slammer while I figured out how to plea bargain her charges down or get them dismissed altogether. Again, because a cop was involved in the robbery and because the boyfriend, junkie or not, was offering up a pretty plausible explanation for Avett's involvement in the crime, nothing was a slam dunk, yet. I was going to help her whether she wanted me to or not.

I found the father's contact information in the file and dug my cell phone out of my pocket. If he wasn't willing to help the girl out I was going to call Asa and see what my former client thought the next best course of action should be. I didn't often take on cases based solely on referral, but I truly liked Asa Cross and he was another one of my clients that I actually believed was innocent when I was hired to help him out. If he was willing to pay my admittedly hefty fee to help this young woman out, I knew he would want to know if she was going to end up stuck behind bars if dear old dad didn't step up to the plate.

I pressed the number into the screen while continuing to stare at the grainy mug shot and wondered why I wasn't letting my assistant or one of the paralegals at the firm make the call instead.

A deep voice rumbled a curt hello in my ear and I tilted my head back on the couch so I was looking at the exposed duct-work that crisscrossed the ceiling of the loft.

"Is this Brighton Walker?"

There was a grunt and then, "Who wants to know?"

I almost laughed. It was so far removed from the way the people I usually dealt with on a day-to-day basis interacted with me that it was startlingly refreshing.

"My name is Quaid Jackson, and I'm calling because I am currently being retained to represent your daughter."

There was a beat of silence followed by a heavy sigh that could only come from a frustrated parent. "One of my boys hired you." It wasn't a question but rather a statement of fact.

"I don't know if Asa Cross is one of your boys or not but we worked together in the past on a situation involving the same establishment. He called me as soon as the police read your daughter her rights and told me if I agreed to take the case that money was no object."

A soft curse hit my ears followed by another deep sigh. "I was waiting for Avett to call. She always calls me first when she gets into trouble. They charged her?"

I shifted on the couch and tucked the phone against my cheek. "They did. Accessory to armed robbery, aiding and abetting the commission of a felony involving a firearm, and accessory after the fact. Some of the charges are throwaway charges simply because they wanted to book her fast and hold her in lockup. The fact that there was an off-duty police officer involved in the crime is going to complicate things for the duration."

"Royal." He mentioned the young policewoman's name softly. "I'm so glad that the only person that got hurt was that loser my daughter was hooked up with."

I squeezed the bridge of my nose. "If the police officer hadn't been there that night it might not have been the case. The boyfriend went in armed and pulled a gun on Mr. Cross. This entire situation could have had a much worse outcome."

The man on the other end of the phone went silent again and then muttered, "I am well aware of what could've happened, Mr. Jackson."

I felt like a little kid getting a scolding for speaking before the teacher called on me. That was an impressive feat. I very rarely felt put in my place and this man had done it with his tone of voice and a few carefully chosen words. Again, I wondered how his daughter had trailed so far off the straight and narrow when she seemed to have such a strong support system in place.

"I can't tell you why Avett didn't call you, Mr. Walker, but I can tell you that she is in pretty big trouble. Her arraignment hearing is tomorrow, and while I'm almost certain that I can get her released on bail, it won't be cheap and the judge won't let her go unless she has a stable, safe, and permanent address to go home to. He may even put her on house arrest considering her uncanny ability to find trouble. If that's the case, she'll have to have an address to register the ankle monitor to." I paused to let all the information sink in. "She mentioned she was living with the boyfriend. Understandably, that is no longer an option."

There was rustling on the other end of the line that sounded like he was scraping his hand through his hair, only rougher and scratchier. "So you're asking me to pay my daughter's bail and to bring her home with me, even though she was involved in an armed robbery that could've resulted in people I care deeply about getting injured . . . or worse?"

When he laid it out like that, it sounded like an insane request. It was my turn to sigh. "If it makes any kind of difference Avett didn't want me to call you. I felt that if there was an option to save her from having to spend time behind bars while we wait for the preliminary hearing, we should pursue it. From your reaction, I'm guessing she didn't call you because she knew it would be a waste of time." I didn't know the man, barely knew the girl, but I was oddly disappointed in his reaction. One more thing about this entire case and situation that made no sense. My reactions were totally out of character, but instead of worrying about it, I kind of liked the thrill of it. Being numb was boring.

I paused and as I was about to thank the man for his time there was suddenly a chuckle that sounded like thunder rumbling through the mountains coming from the other end of the call.

"She didn't call me because she's scared and embarrassed. That girl." Even though I couldn't see him, I knew the man had to be shaking his head ruefully. "She's always been a handful, and she's always had a knack for finding the deepest, hottest water to jump feetfirst into. Sometimes I wonder if she's testing me and her poor mother to see just how much we can take. She doesn't realize when you're a parent there are no limits on the love you have for your child. I'll take whatever she dishes out and come back for more. Her mother is a firm believer in letting Avett suffer the consequences of her foolish actions alone—she thinks it's the only way she'll learn—but I'm more of a 'walk through the fire side by side' kind of parent. Tell me what time the hearing is and I'll be there, with bail money or a bondsman and with whatever proof you need that my daughter has a permanent place to stay with me. I've always been her home and regardless of what she's done that will never change."

I wanted to breathe a sigh of relief. I wanted to pump my fist in victory even though the battle hadn't even started yet. Maybe my job and the recent collapse of my marriage had made me too jaded. I was so used to seeing the bad in people, so accustomed to believing the worst by default, that I needed this man to have unconditional love for his child in order to keep some sort of faith in humanity alive.

I ran through what he would need to bring with him for the arraignment proceedings in case the judge needed proof, and warned him that his daughter was going to look worn down and was dressed like a convict. It could be jarring to see someone you loved like that, but the man assured me he would be fine and he would be there to take care of his little girl.

I thanked him for his time and was getting ready to hang up when he stopped me with a quietly spoken question. "Can I ask why you took the time, after what I'm assuming was a long workday, to call me yourself, Mr. Jackson? Don't get me wrong, I appreciate the personal touch and the obvious commitment to my daughter's well-being. I can't say I've had a ton of experience dealing with attorneys, but something tells me this isn't standard operating procedure."

It wasn't, but there was something about the girl so I told him the truth because I had a suspicion that this man would be able to smell a lie or a dodge from a mile away. "It's not and I'm generally not the type to bring a case home with me. I try to leave the law at the office and in the courtroom, but there is something about your daughter." I paused and it was my turn to shake my head. "She isn't exactly blameless, but she doesn't deserve to be lumped in with the kinds of violent criminals I deal with on a daily basis either. She's still young enough to have a shot at something better. I want to help her out."

"Avett's always been special and maybe a little lost. Her mother and I tried to show her the right way, but the girl is stubborn and determined to find the path she's meant to be on in her own way. This is another speed bump, albeit a big one, for her to navigate her way around. I appreciate your help, son. I'll be getting on the phone with Asa as soon as I get off with you. That boy is coming from a good place, but this is a family matter so I'll be taking care of your fees from here on out."

I rubbed a hand over my face and sat up. "I'll let you fight that out with him. As long as I get paid, I don't care who pays the bill."

There was another deep and rumbling chuckle. "You serve in the military, son?"

I blinked in surprise at the offhanded question and looked down at my oxblood Burberry wingtips and the legs of my custom fit, navy Canali suit. I was miles away from the rebellious and untrained eighteen-year-old that had enlisted what felt like a lifetime ago. No one asked me about those four defining years of my life. They asked about finishing my undergrad in record time, they mentioned law school, they talked about passing the bar, and they questioned me about defending a well-known serial killer and getting a sitting congressman acquitted of vehicular manslaughter charges. Most of the time, I forgot about the kid that had been shipped to the desert to fight hostiles and insurgents on endless miles of bloodstained sand. I was too busy being the guy in the suit with a slick haircut and perfectly placed accessories to show how successful, how good at my job I was.

"Why do you ask?" I wasn't going to confirm his suspicions because I hadn't been a soldier or a wide-eyed kid in a very long time and I didn't want to give the man the wrong impression about who I was or what kind of man he was going to be dealing with.

The other man made an amused noise and told me, "I can always tell. Something about the way a man speaks, the way he presents himself, even if it is over the phone and to a total stranger. Like recognizes like. I look forward to meeting you in person tomorrow, Mr. Jackson."

He hung up and left me shaking my head in bemusement. It took a lot to surprise me considering I was intimately acquainted with all the appalling things humans were capable of, but both father and daughter had managed to knock me sideways today.

I hit the Google search bar on my phone and tapped in the name Brighton Walker out of pure curiosity.

Like recognized like.

That may be true but I wasn't sure how alike the two of us actually were. There was plenty of information on the ever informative Google about Brite Walker, including details from his illustrious military career with the Marines, a career that lasted decades rather than the mandatory four like I had served. There were articles about his work with the VA and disabled vets all over the country, news stories ranging from good to really bad about the bar he no longer owned, and several articles that tied him to the largest and most notorious motorcycle club in the Rockies. The man was equal parts hero and outlaw. He was the stuff local legends were made of and the kind of man other men told stories about. He impressed from nothing more than a web search, so I couldn't even imagine how dynamic and enthralling he would be in person. Something told me Brite Walker had never even seen a Rolex and that the things that impressed everyone else who filled my day-to-day would not awe him in the least. For some reason I suddenly felt entirely inadequate, and I started regretting not letting the pink-haired spitfire actually get away with firing me.

Normally, I was a man used to being at the top of my game. I was a man used to getting what I wanted no matter what stood in my path. I was a man used to winning . . . but not lately. Lately, I was a man that had been betrayed, rejected, and drained emotionally and financially. Everything that went down with Lottie, my ex, had left me feeling like a loser, like a failure, like a fool.

We'd known each other since high school, had grown up in the same small mountain town a couple hours outside of Denver. Lottie came from money; I didn't. She grew up in a mountainside mansion that looked like a goddamn ski resort; I grew up in a tiny cabin that only had running water and working electricity half of the time. Her parents worked in the entertainment industry and summered in the Virgin Islands; mine lived mostly off the land, refused to work for "the man," and had bartered and traded for everything we had ever owned.

I hooked up with her at first to prove that I could. Girls had always liked me even though I came from nothing and had a shit attitude about it. Once I sealed the deal, I realized she was sweet, fun, and unendingly kind considering her affluent background. The sex was a stroke to my immature ego which quickly turned into something more. I begged her to wait for me because I had no other choice but to enlist and try to figure my life out. Joining the Army was the only way I was able to afford college, and I was determined to make something of myself, even if it meant leaving my girl and my very disapproving family behind.

Lottie promised to wait, and while I was sent overseas she went to Vassar and started her poli-sci degree. Lottie wanted to be a lawyer long before I did, but only one of us had the dedication and drive to actually get the degree and pass the bar. While I was away fighting a war and becoming a man, she was busy dropping out of school and flitting from guy to guy, all while sending me letters and messages telling me she loved and missed me. I was none the wiser, thought she was still the sweet, innocent girl I had fallen for ages ago. When I got back stateside, I put a ring on her finger, moved her to Boulder so I could attend CU, and spent every dime I made trying to keep her in the lifestyle she was accustomed to while simultaneously paying tuition.

It wasn't enough. I wasn't enough.

The expensive suits, sports cars, the fat bank account . . . none of it had been enough to keep Lottie happy or faithful. At first, I was gone because of Uncle Sam, then I was in school, then I was busting my ass to pass the bar while working full time, and then I got hired at the firm and started working eighty- to ninety-hour workweeks to make a name for myself. She told me I wasn't around. She told me I wasn't present. She told me that she never loved me, and only stayed with me because I was safe and a good bet for her future financial security.

She told me all of that when she was five months pregnant with a baby that wasn't mine. A baby that I knew couldn't be mine because Lottie hadn't let me touch her in close to eight months. The marriage was in the garbage and it wasn't until she really started to show that I figured out why. Even with the evidence sitting plain as day between us, the woman still tried to blame the split and her scandalous actions on me. If I had been better, if I had given more, she would have waited, she would have stayed, she would have been faithful and loved me the same way I loved her.

Lottie had never been faithful, not since high school, but I'd been so blinded by her, so impressed with myself that I had scored someone like her, I'd been oblivious. I'd been trained to observe, honed my natural skills at reading people and being able to tell truth from fiction. I could tell a person's entire life story by the way they moved, the expression on their faces, but my own wife, the person I had always been the closest to, fooled me. Or I had fooled myself because I couldn't believe she would do that to me, do it to us. Now after it was all said and done, I could choke on my own arrogance and self-assuredness. It never even occurred to me she would go looking somewhere else for what she evidently found lacking in me.

I thought I'd given her all I'd had, but it hadn't been enough and she wanted more. She wanted the house. She wanted my money. She wanted my car. She wanted my retirement. Hell, the greedy bitch had even tried to make me responsible for the future school expenses for the baby that wasn't mine.

We'd been together for so long I thought I was going to have to hand it all over, but luckily, Colorado had some pretty cut-and-dry divorce laws considering the high quantity of military marriages in the state, which made it impossible for Lottie to take me totally to the cleaners. I also hired the best damn divorce lawyer I could find and made it clear I was going to fight her tooth and nail for everything. I'd grown up with nothing, and I wasn't about to give up what I had now without a fight. I'd worked too hard for what I had and I wasn't about to let that work and those sacrifices go easily.

I let her have the house in Boulder because I couldn't walk in the front door without imagining who had been in my bed while I was working to keep the extraordinarily expensive roof over our heads and gourmet food on the fucking table. I also let her keep the car. Even though it went with all the trappings of the man I was now, it had never been my style. I preferred my massive, black 4x4 with its monster all-terrain tires and lift kit. Sure it didn't go with my Ferragamos or my Armani, but I didn't give a shit, and if I wanted something fast and sporty I had my Ducati Panigale in storage. The Italian-made street bike may have matched my wardrobe better but Lottie still hadn't approved. She'd never been on the back of the rocket-like bike and I couldn't picture her there if I tried.

In the end, I agreed to a hefty chunk of change for her monthly maintenance fee for five years or until she remarried, which meant that being the coldhearted bitch she was, she hadn't yet accepted her babys daddy's proposal. I told myself Lottie had

CHARGED   35

cheated down instead of up because the baby's father was a struggling artist and not exactly rolling in cash and prospects. I had no doubt she would keep him and his engagement ring at bay for the five years or until someone else with a fatter wallet came along.

It had been a hard and humbling lesson to learn. One that still stung and still made me cringe when I thought about it.

I don't want anything from you . . .

The words danced around in my head along with the image of the young woman dressed in convict orange.

It was a good thing she felt that way because I was pretty sure after Lottie and the string of disastrous women that came after her, I didn't have anything besides my knowledge of the law and my skill at working the legal system to give to anyone.

CHAPTER 3

Avett

It was a sleepless night in lockup and not because of the scorned cell mate. She had actually quieted down some after I told her my dad's words of wisdom. She did spend several hours muttering to herself, questioning what she had done, what her kids were going to do without her, but she eventually fell asleep. That left me alone, in the not quite silent jail cell, worrying about what my dad was going to say when Quaid, the too handsome for my own good lawyer, called him. I turned over every scenario I could imagine in my mind, and none of them added up to Brite Walker being in that courtroom when I went before the judge.

He was going to be so disappointed. He was going to be so hurt. He was going to be disgusted and fed up that, once again, I hadn't listened to him, hadn't listened to any kind of common sense or paid attention to any of the red flags flapping wildly in my face when I decided to hook up with Jared. I wasn't twelve anymore and it was no longer cute when I stubbornly went against the grain. No, this situation wasn't cute at all and there was no way my always supportive, always loyal, and compassionate father was going to condone my behavior when it led to other people he cared about getting hurt. If something had happened to Asa or to the cop, who also happened to be the gorgeous, southern bartender's girlfriend, I wouldn't have been able to live with myself. As it was, I felt the guilt for having any part in putting them in danger weighing me down with every single step I took as I was herded into the courtroom. If I couldn't stand myself for what I had done, how could my dad be there to offer me his massive shoulder to lean on?

The arraignment wasn't like anything I had ever experienced before during all my other dustups with the law. I was hauled there in a van with an armed policeman in the front and back. I was transported with other women, and I learned quickly that the different colored jumpsuits they had us in represented the different levels of offenses that we were waiting to be arraigned on. It was a lot more intense and serious than any marathon of watching *The Good Wife* made it seem. I was forced to sit on a hard wooden bench next to a woman that told me she was waiting to be arraigned on manslaughter charges. She assured me she was innocent but that didn't make me feel any better about the fact I was practically sitting in her lap. We were also placed behind a Plexiglas screen, which I assumed was supposed to be some kind of protection. I couldn't tell if it was for us or for the people in the packed courtroom.

There were so many people, rows and rows filled with curious faces, all with their eyes locked on those of us on the wrong side of the barrier. Some people were crying; some looked furious as they glared at the group of us waiting to learn our fates. I was trying to search out the tawny, perfectly coiffed head of my un- wanted, but very much needed, legal representative in the crowd but I didn't spot him. My heart kicked hard in my chest and my handcuffed hands started to sweat as I curled my fingers into my palms. I was in so far over my head that panic and dread were starting to fill me up as I realized I very well might be stuck in this mess, leveled and flattened on the bottom of rock bottom, all on my own.

I was the idiot that fired him. I told him I didn't need his help because I didn't want him to call my dad. I did what I always did and fucked everything up. God, when was I going to learn to tamp down my foolish and impulsive reactions? Why did I always have to be my own worst enemy? I hadn't ever done myself any favors, and now, it looked like I had gone and shot myself in the foot, all because I didn't want to let my dad down again. When I least expected it, pride and remorse reared up to remind me that I wasn't quite as awful as I made myself out to be. I still had a heart, still had a soul, even though both were tattered and torn.

I sucked in a deep breath and willed myself not to start crying. I really wanted to. I wanted to sob, shake, and fall into a million tiny pieces of regret and shame. I wouldn't though. I was willful and foolish, but I wasn't fragile. I had screwed up, like I always did, and I would take whatever consequences that followed that screwup stoically and silently. I would man-up, take whatever hits I had coming, and maybe finally pull my head out of my ass and start making better choices. That was the only way I had left to let my dad know I wasn't a total lost cause. I could still turn it around if he didn't give up on me.

I didn't realize that I had squeezed my eyes closed to keep the moisture at bay. When I pried them open after I got my emotions under control, not only did I spot that elegant golden head coming through the large wooden doors, but I also quit breathing when I realized it was bent towards a much darker, much grizzlier one as they walked towards the front of the courtroom. Charcoal gray eyes locked on mine and shined so much love at me that I couldn't stop a rebellious and wild tear full of liquid relief from sliding down my cheek. My heart expanded and started beating in a familiar rhythm tapping with hope and warmth as my dad tilted his heavily bearded chin in my direction and took a seat next to the attorney. The chin tilt was a universal signal from Brite Walker indicating everything would be okay, and with him here, with him looking at me like he always looked at me, for the first time since I had been arrested, I actually had a tiny sliver of belief that it would all work out in my favor. Maybe I was on the bottom, but my dad was there to give me a boost up, and this time, I was determined not to immediately fall down as soon as I got my feet under me.

A deep shudder worked through my body and it took me a second to notice that not only was my gigantic and impossible to miss father in the courtroom, but so was my much smaller, much more delicate mother. She had her hand in my dad's, and while I was fighting back tears, she was letting hers freely flow. I knew both my parents adored me, but Darcy had a firm breaking point and I had pushed her to it more than once. I was surprised to see her and wondered if she was here to support me or to support my dad. Even though they were divorced, and often argued like cats and dogs, there was still something between my mother and father that no amount of discord and tension, or even relationships with other people, could kill.

Whoever she was here for, I was glad to see both of them and it was impossible to miss the triumphant look on Quaid's face as

I switched my attention to him. He dipped his very whiskerless, chiseled chin at me, much like my dad had done. With both of them here to silently assure me that things would be okay, or as okay as they could be for the moment, I started to breathe easier and finally unclenched my hands. It wasn't relief that was flooding me, but it was something close.

Since my last name was Walker and *W* was always at the end of everything that went in alphabetical order, I didn't get my turn in front of the judge until well after the possible murderer, who was denied bail, and the drug dealer, who was also denied bail. The longer I had to wait, the more anxious I got. I didn't know the ins and outs of everyone else's circumstances, but I was astute enough to put together the fact anyone going before the judge that had an extensive criminal history already on the books was mercilessly shot down and sent back to the enclosed bench looking at more time in the slammer. I was stunned that it all happened so fast. Each hearing took less than five minutes, which seemed far too quick to decide if someone was worthy of going home or sitting in jail for an undetermined amount of time. None of it seemed to bode well for me when it was my turn, but every time I met the golden-haired attorney's gaze through the protective glass, it never wavered or betrayed any kind of worry. The expression in his light blue eyes never indicated anything but steady assurance and stone-cold confidence.

My dad, on the other hand, was getting just as antsy and just as fidgety as I was the longer time dragged on and the more accused that the judge shot down. Brite Walker was a massive human being. He took up all the available space around him and then some. When Brite was uncomfortable, it made everyone else within his vicinity uncomfortable. I saw the judge shoot my dad a couple of narrow-eyed looks throughout the different hearings, and I watched every single person seated in the same row as my father get up and move the more agitated he became. I kept waiting for Quaid to tell him to dial it down, for him to ask my dad to put a lid on his natural fatherly and protective instincts, but he never did. In fact, every time the judge looked in their direction or another person abandoned their front row seat, a small grin would tug at the man's perfectly sculpted mouth and wry humor would dance in his eyes. My dad typically made a lasting impression on everyone that crossed his path; it appeared Quaid Jackson wasn't immune to my dad's legendary charisma and presence either.

Finally, the court clerk called my docket number and said, "The court will now hear the case of the State against Avett Walker," and it was my turn to go stand at the podium and plead for my temporary freedom—well, let Quaid plead for it. It took a minute to maneuver around the remaining defendants and I almost fell over once without the use of my hands to balance myself. The bailiff shot me an annoyed look as several of the other accused snickered at my clumsiness, calling me a rookie under their breath. I almost melted into the floor in a puddle of gratitude when I was finally standing next to Quaid.

The judge looked at me and surprisingly over my head at what I could only assume was my father. His attention then shifted to the other man in the suit standing off to the left of us.

"Are we waving a formal reading, Counselor? Mr. Townsend has had a long day and I'm sure he would appreciate getting right to the arraignment."

Quaid gave a dry chuckle and nodded his head slightly. "That's fine and every day is a rough day for the prosecution,

Your Honor." The judge grunted and flipped open a file in front of him. I wanted to run up to his bench and snatch it away. Every single mistake I had ever made in my life was there, encouraging him to deny me a chance at freedom.

"What's the people's thoughts on bail in this case, Mr. Townsend?" Across from where I was doing everything in my power not to collapse into Quaid since my knees felt like Jell-O, the other attorney leafed through another folder full of my sins and shot me a frown.

"The charges are serious. The defendant is a known offender and there was an off-duty police officer involved during the commission of the crime Ms. Walker is accused of abetting in. The people can't find a known address, work history, or any kind of solid ties to the community where this defendant is concerned. The people feel that she could be a flight risk, so we are asking bail be set at no less than $500,000."

My knees almost buckled and I couldn't stop the slight wheeze that escaped my lips. Half a million dollars? My dad made all-right money and had a pretty nice nest egg, but he wasn't a millionaire by any stretch of the imagination, and even if he bonded me out that would still be more than he could comfortably afford to give up. Not to mention I would never, ever be able to pay him back. I was going back to jail; even if I knew I deserved nothing less, it still burned.

I turned to Quaid, ready to beg him to do something, to do anything to fix this, but he was looking at the prosecutor with narrowed eyes and a frown. The tip of his elbow brushed against mine. I thought it might was an accident, but then his gaze shifted back to me and the annoyance was replaced with calm assurance.

"Mr. Jackson, I'm sure you have plenty to say about the State's recommendation for your client, so let's hear it."

"I think Mr. Townsend has forgotten that my client is only being charged as an accessory to this crime. There is an actual perpetrator in custody awaiting his own time before the court on actual charges, not just accessory charges relating to the commission, Your Honor. Yes, Ms. Walker has made some unfortunate choices in the past when it comes to following the law, but none of those charges are felonies and none of them resulted in time served. But because I'm realistic and know the court can't overlook those prior indiscretions, I won't push my luck and ask for my client to be released on her own recognizance. As for being a flight risk"—a grin pulled at his mouth, and again I wondered if he used it as a weapon because the damn thing was a killer—"Mr. Townsend was kind enough to point out that Ms. Walker isn't working and doesn't have a long employment history, so I'm not sure how the State assumes she would fund going on the run from the law."

A deep chuckle rumbled from behind me and all I wanted to do was turn around and throw my arms around my dad. The judge grunted and made a "go on with it" gesture with his hand.

"As for her permanent residence, Ms. Walker has and still does keep a room at her father, Mr. Brighton Walker's, home here in Denver. Once we agree to a reasonable bail amount"—Quaid shot the other attorney a hard look that made the man scowl— "Mr. Walker is going to pay it and take his daughter home. He has also given his assurances that his daughter will be present and willing to participate in her own case as well as the case the State is building against Jared Dalton. While Ms. Walker may not have ties to the community, her father has them in spades and I believe him when he says he will make sure Avett is present and accounted for as we move forward."

I held my breath. It felt like an eternity passed as the judge returned his attention to the file in front of him and then once again lifted his gaze and let it settle somewhere over the top of my head.

When he looked back at me I stiffened my spine and tried to make my expression look as innocent as I possibly could. That was a challenge because I sure as hell didn't feel very innocent. Quaid's elbow rubbed against mine again and I realized it hadn't been a mistake the first time. He was letting me know I wasn't alone in this, that my fate wasn't in my own hands. It was barely a touch, barely a connection, but that little bit of pressure, that tiny brush, hit me harder and more deeply than any full embrace I had ever been wrapped up in.

"Ms. Walker." I jolted when the judge addressed me directly. I blinked at him a little stupidly and gulped before I spoke so I didn't sound like a bullfrog croaking.

"Yes, Your Honor?"

"Your counsel is trying to make light of the charges you're facing, but I need you to understand they are serious and that the State has every intention of pursuing its case against you."

I nodded, and when Quaid nudged me, I cleared my throat again. "I understand."

"You seem to be a young woman with a bad habit of ignoring the law. The court doesn't appreciate that attitude but also recognizes that you are young enough to learn from your litany of mistakes. I agree with your attorney that the amount of bail requested by the State is unreasonable considering the circumstances and your prior history." He looked over my head again and I actually felt the air shift along with my dad as he moved on the bench behind me. "Young lady, I also hope you appreciate how influential it has been to know you have a strong support system in place to keep you from making any more foolish decisions as you await your preliminary hearing. The court agrees to release the defendant on bail in the amount of $150,000. The defendant is being released on the grounds she remains at the permanent address of the home of Brighton Walker until the court proceedings are concluded."

I wilted. I couldn't help it. My knees folded and relief blindsided me so strongly I couldn't stand up under the weight of it. Quaid's strong arm was around my waist before I fell all the way into him and he gave my hip a little squeeze before setting me back on my feet.

"Ms. Walker."

I sucked in a breath and tilted my chin up at the judge as he said my name again.

"Yes, Your Honor?" There was a tremor in my voice but I didn't bother to try and hide it.

"My advice to you is to wise up. Stay away from anyone else involved in the situation that landed you here and start using your head."

It was good advice. People always had good advice for me, if only I was wired to take it.

This time around I was determined not to let my father down, so I nodded. "Thank you, Your Honor."

Quaid put his hand on my arm and turned me so that I was facing him. "Your dad is going to post bail and then pick you up from the jail. It's going to take the rest of the afternoon to process you out. I'll give you a couple days to settle in at your dad's and get your head on straight, then we need to have a strategy meeting. The State is going to have a plea bargain on my desk sometime this week and I need to know where we're going with all of this."

I scowled at him and shook his hand off my arm. "I'm not taking a plea bargain, Counselor. I'm not guilty."

He heaved a sigh at me and gave me a look like I was being ridiculous. Before he could say anything else, a man, large enough to block out the rest of the room, was between us. I was pulled into a barrel chest with my face buried in a beard that was as much of a legend in Denver as the man that wore it.

I never wanted to hug my dad so badly in my life. As soon as his tree-trunk-like arms folded around me, I couldn't hold it together anymore. Tears started leaking through my closed lids and my lashes weren't strong enough to stem the flow. My shoulders shook and my cuffed hands curled desperately into his faded Harley-Davidson shirt.

"I'm so sorry, Daddy." I wasn't sure how the words made it out over the lump in my throat as one of his massive paws curled around the back of my head and pulled me closer.

"I know you are, Sprite, but we gotta get to a place where you don't have to be sorry like this any more."

"I know." I breathed the words out and pulled away as someone cleared their throat. My dad dropped his hand onto my shoulder as the bailiff inclined his head towards the doors that led to the prisoner holding area.

"You can have her back in a bit, sir. But right now she has to come with me."

My dad practically growled at the man, which made him fall back a step. He released me after giving my shoulder a squeeze and a kiss on the top of my head. I let the bailiff take my arm and peeked around my dad's broad frame so I could see my mom. She could only meet my eyes for a moment and when she did I saw the heartbreak and disappointment clouding her gaze.

"Thanks for coming, Mom. I'm so sorry for all of this." The bailiff started to guide me away as Quaid ushered my dad back to the part of the courtroom reserved for the families and audience.

"Saying you're sorry and actually being sorry are two very different things, Avett." She got to her feet as my dad reached for her hand with a hard look on his face. She shook her head at me, and even though I could barely hear her because she spoke as they were calling the case after mine, her words hit their mark.

"Sorry" rolled off my tongue so easily and frequently that the words hardly held any meaning anymore. This time around I needed to actually *be* sorry for what I had done, even if what I had done was nothing. I had a lot to prove, a lot to make up for, and my track record for doing the right thing was shit. I didn't want my mom to barely be able to look at me. I didn't want my father to have to borrow against his retirement to bail me out of jail. Saying sorry wasn't enough; this time around, I was actually going to have to change.

I went back into what the bailiff referred to as the "pen" and took my place between the murderer and the drug dealer. They both turned to me with envy and annoyance in their eyes. I was going home at the end of the day; they were going back behind bars.

The druggie lifted her eyebrows at me and stuck her tongue out, licking her dried lips. I cringed involuntarily, which had her giving me a crooked smile that showed all of her yellow and chipped teeth. "That guy representing you is hot. How much does he charge an hour? Are you fucking him? I would fuck him.

I bet he's expensive and good in bed. That hard-ass judge denied us all bail, except for you."

I felt my eyes widen and I looked at the woman on the other side of me; she seemed as interested in my answers as the drug dealer.

I cleared my throat and shifted uneasily on the hard wooden bench. "I didn't pay for him, so I don't know how much he charges, and no, I'm not sleeping with him. I only met him yesterday." Which didn't explain why everything inside of me turned gooey and warm when he unleashed that grin of his. Or why I instantly felt better when his elbow briefly touched mine. It was a totally inappropriate reaction seeing as the man was a decade older than me, noticeably from a different background and social class than I came from, and had only ever seen me in jailbird orange while he was trying to keep my ass out of the slammer. My hormones must have missed the memo that the rest of me was in deep shit and Quaid Jackson was the guy holding the shovel to dig me out.

"I would fuck him." This from the possible murderer on my other side. I wondered if Quaid knew that the entire female criminal population of Denver considered him fuckable.

I clicked the metal snapped around my wrists together to distract myself and muttered, "I don't think we're exactly his type."

I imagined guys like Quaid preferred women that didn't know what real handcuffs felt like when they were used for their intended purposes, and I couldn't see him getting all hot and bothered over a chick with pink hair, even if mine was quickly fading and turning more rose colored as my natural dark brown took over at the crown.

"Girl, I'm every guy's type if the price is right." The druggie licked her lips again and I wanted to curl in a ball and make myself as small as possible to get away from both of them and the way they were talking about my attorney. I didn't like it. Furthermore, I really didn't like that I didn't like it.

Luckily, there were only a couple of cases left and soon enough we were all being herded into the van and heading towards the jail. I was dreading having to sit behind bars again, but instead of taking me back to the cell with the scorned spouse, I found myself in a room similar to the one I had spoken to Quaid in the day after my arrest. The clothes I was wearing the night of the robbery were brought to me and I was told to change and sit tight.

I happily shed the jumpsuit and scrambled back into my own clothes. I never thought torn jeans, a stretched-out cotton T-shirt, and battered Vans could feel like the most expensive evening gown with designer heels. It wasn't haute couture, but man, did it feel luxurious compared to the scratchy jailhouse jumpsuit. There was even a hair tie in my pocket, so I wrestled my thick and colorful hair up into a messy top knot, then did what I was told to do and sat tight.

It was only a few hours, but it felt like days. I counted the tiles on the floor, memorized the pattern in which the flickering fluorescent light above my head was going to flash, and I had plenty of time to go over every single fuckup I had made on my way to this point. The right thing was always there, always right in front of me screaming, "Pick me! Pick me!" and I was always the defiant moron that ignored the best option and went chasing after my downfall. Now that I had officially caught it, I could confidently say it wasn't all that it was cracked up to be. Falling meant I had to land eventually. The falling was scary and endless, but the landing . . . that was where things really got rough. That was what left a mark.

I should have known the second I met Jared that he was no good. There was no reason for him to pursue me. I was a recent college dropout, didn't have my own place, had no job; too much Netflix and junk food had left my tiny frame far rounder and curvier than most twenty-year-old dudes chased after. I needed my dad to come save me when my last boyfriend ditched me, so I knew there was nothing about me that screamed, "She's a good catch." Even with all those marks against me in the girlfriend material department, Jared had pursued me relentlessly.

At first he was sweet and charming. His low-key, stoner vibe worked for me, so did the fact that no one seemed to like him. The more my dad glowered and grumbled about Jared, the more attracted to him I became. My dad was my hero, my idol, my best friend, but the more he disapproved of the men in my life, the more determined I was to hold on to them. It hurt to do that, but the hurt was what I was after. Eventually, Jared and I were sleeping together and I was spending more and more time at his place, even as it became clear he enjoyed more than the occasional marijuana high. I convinced myself Jared was a recreational drug user, that he liked to dabble, but it was a lie, one that I couldn't even tell myself with a straight face as time went on.

I begged Dad for a job at the bar because I needed space away from the drugs and the abuse. Right there, I should have been smart enough to walk away from the man and the situation, but I couldn't and I wouldn't. Jared loved having me work at the bar. It meant free food and booze, and whenever he was short when he had to pay his dealer, he thought it meant an easy place to snatch some cash. I hated stealing. It made me feel dirty and ugly, but I hated having to explain a black eye and a fat lip even more. I didn't have the words to try and justify why I stayed. I sure as hell didn't have the words to describe why I froze and did nothing the night of the robbery.

Eventually, after what felt like eons and eons left alone with my own sour thoughts, a uniformed cop showed up and told me to follow him. I stopped at a desk and was told to fill out a bunch of paperwork. I signed it all without reading it, then took a sealed plastic bag that was pushed my way; it was filled with my belongings from the night of my arrest. My cell phone, as well as my purse, were in the bag, so I took them both out, turning to see my father getting to his feet from where he was sitting in a small plastic chair.

Without a word, I hurled myself at him and wrapped my arms around his waist. He squeezed me back and I felt him rest his furry cheek on the top of my head, squishing my bun down. I inhaled his very-dad scent, which always reminded me of his bike and his bar, letting his familiarity and strength prop me up under the weight of everything pressing down on me.

"You ready to go home, Sprite?"

I hugged him as hard as I could, making a silent promise to myself that I would never put him in the position of having to rescue me from myself again.

"Yeah, Dad. I'm very ready to go home." It was, after all, where my heart, as battered and bruised as it may have been, always was.

CHAPTER 4

Quaid

I was late getting back to my office after court because I'd had a meeting with the district attorney's office that ran long. It happened all the time, but today I found myself irrationally annoyed at the hitch in my schedule and seriously resentful of the wasted thirty minutes that Avett had to spend sitting outside my office while my assistant gave her the side eye from behind her computer. It had been three days since our last encounter in the courthouse, and even though I would never admit anything out loud, she had been on my mind a lot. Her—not her case. That, coupled with the fact that I immediately noticed jailhouse orange didn't do her any favors, and that she was even cuter, even more innocent and fresh looking in her normal street wear, made me approach her more abruptly, even harsher, than I tended to be with my clients.

I jerked my head in the direction of my office door without a hello and didn't look to see if she was following me when I asked, "Where's your dad? I thought he was sticking by your side through all of this?" I sounded like a dick. I was acting like a dick.

I could tell when I rounded my desk and finally turned to look at her that she was very aware of the fact that I was in a mood.

She crossed her arms over her chest, a chest that was ample, round, and far more plush than I would have imagined considering her small stature. And even though I shouldn't have, I had imagined a whole hell of a lot about her over the last few days. Those curves and valleys she possessed were far too enticing and appealing. I was annoyed that I had noticed and was having a hard time landing my gaze on any part of her I didn't appreciate in an entirely unprofessional way. She was more than a handful in a lot of ways and a couple of them had my dick twitching inappropriately. The prison jumpsuit had swallowed her up and what it had been hiding was a curvy little figure currently radiating with as much repressed attitude as I was freely throwing at her.

I shouldn't be noticing her curves, or the way her dark eyebrows snapped into a fierce V over the top of her nose. She was just a kid in the grand scheme of life, but more than that, she was a client. It was my job to help her, to keep her out of jail, not to be enthralled by the irritated pucker of her mouth or entranced by the way her cheeks flushed to the same rosy pink as her hair as she visibly battled for the proper way to respond to my shitty greeting and overall asshole-ish demeanor. I shouldn't like the way she bristled and stiffened but I did.

"Dad wanted to come, but I'm working towards proving that I am capable of doing something right in this lifetime. He'll hold my hand forever if I let him, and frankly, I don't want him to be involved in this mess any more than he already is." She leaned back in the chair and continued to scowl at me. "You're going to offer some kind of plea deal that will seem reasonable and make sense because it will make all of this go away. Dad will encourage me to listen to your advice. He will tell me we're paying for you to look out for my best interest." She shook her head and wrapped her arms tighter around herself like she was giving herself a hug. "And he might be right, but I didn't help Jared rob the bar. I wasn't his accomplice or his accessory. I didn't aid or abet him in anything, so I'm not going to take a deal. Me not taking a deal would probably make my dad worry about what was going to happen to me. I've put him through enough." She finally broke eye contact and looked down at the lush Berber carpet below her sneakered feet. "It might not be the right thing to do, but I'm used to that."

I felt some of the tension that was coiled up inside of me unwind as I listened to her. Most of my clients had their own self-interests in mind when they made decisions about what they were going to do when faced with charges, but not this young woman. It was startling, even refreshing, to have someone in this office genuinely concerned about how their actions and consequences affected someone else, someone they loved. Even if she was a little late to the game, I was glad to see Avett had come to play.

"The D.A.'s office sent over a plea deal this morning. They're willing to drop all the charges except for the accessory charge if you agree to serve ninety days in jail with a two-year probationary period. They also want you to testify against Jared Dalton." I laced my fingers together in front of me and watched as her breathing quickened. The gold on the outer rim of her eyes seemed to blaze as the brown in the center darkened to pitch-black. It was like watching a kaleidoscope shift and change shape and colors.

"I don't want to see Jared." Her voice hitched and her knuckles turned white where she was clutching her upper arms.

"You aren't going to get a choice in the matter. You'll have to testify, deal or no deal. You're a witness and either the state or Jared's attorney will eventually call you to the stand. Jared is trying to use you and the story that you were pissed your dad sold the bar as his reasonable doubt. You're an integral part of his trial regardless of what happens with your own."

She pouted.

I blinked because it should have looked indulgent and petulant. It should have made her come across as spoiled, sulky. It didn't. It made her look adorable and put out. It wasn't the kind of pout Lottie would give me when she wanted to spend an ungodly amount of money on a new couch or some purse that she would only use once; no, this was the pout of a woman that legitimately didn't want to do something and was sullen about it. It was charming in a totally innocent way, and again, I silently berated myself for noticing the tiny gesture at all.

"It's a good deal, Avett. A really good deal. The minimum time served if you're convicted on the accessory charge alone is three years." I lifted my eyebrows at her. "Three years is the minimum, meaning if we do end up at a trial with a jury and they find you guilty, the judge can give you anywhere from three to five years. That's a big chunk of time to sit behind bars if you take a gamble and lose."

She let her arms fall and scooted forward on the chair. She leaned forward and looked at me intently. Her eyes were mesmerizing and I found myself distracted by all the different colors trapped there. I had to ask her to repeat herself when I realized she said something and was waiting for a response from me. I needed to get my head in the game where this girl was concerned . . . *this girl* . . . that was the part I seemed to keep forgetting.

"What did you say?" My voice dipped lower than it normally was and I shifted in my seat as other parts of me started to notice all the interesting and attractive things about Avett Walker as well.

"I said, I Googled you." She swept some of her hair back from where it had fallen over her shoulder, and I literally had to force myself to keep my gaze locked on her face as the motion pushed her chest up higher and tighter against the plain black T-shirt she had on.

"Oh, yeah? How did that work out for you?" I knew what she would find: my service record, my wedding announcement, my work history with the firm, various tidbits on my most high profile cases, and several articles chronicling my divorce. Most divorces weren't newsworthy, but when one of the people involved came from money and the other was as high profile as I was, it made for good filler on a slow newsday. I was curious to see what her interpretation of the snapshot of my life that existed on the Internet was.

She got up from the chair and started to pace back and forth in front of my desk as she talked. "It worked out well enough, I guess. I saw that you were enlisted when you were younger, which explains why my dad immediately liked you." She looked at me over her shoulder and a tiny grin tugged at her mouth. "He doesn't usually like anyone instantly. It takes him a while to warm up."

I listened with half an ear as I watched her brightly colored hair swish around her shoulders. She didn't come across as the girlie or overly feminine type, so I wondered why she had gone with such a delicate and pretty pink when coloring her hair.

"I learned that you're a Colorado native, that you grew up in the mountains, that your birthday is right around Christmas, which means you're almost thirty-two, so you've accomplished a lot in your career in a short amount of time. I also learned that you own a lot of suits."

I snorted out a surprised laugh at that last part, which made her stop pacing. She took a step closer to my desk and put her hands on the opposite edge, leaning forward. The new position made her T-shirt gape at the collar, and even though I refused to look down, I could see the hint of a leopard-print bra peeking out. That hint of something that shoul be forbidden made my mouth go dry and had my pulse kicking. It was a powerful reaction to very little provocation, and I made myself beat it back, forcibly.

"Every single picture you're in, after you got out of the Army, you're in a suit. Blue ones, black ones, gray ones, pinstripe ones. That's a lot of suits."

I grunted. "I spend a lot of time in court. Suits are necessary for that." They also set me apart from that kid running through the forest with exactly one pair of new jeans and one pair of boots that didn't have holes in them. "And I've accomplished a lot because I work hard and I'm good at what I do." I'd been working hard since I was born and I hadn't ever had the opportunity to stop. When I was in high school, I pushed myself academically so that I could take advantage of every accelerated class my school offered. I knew college wasn't going to be an option without the military, which meant I was giving four years to my country, so I was going to lose that time when it came to my career. Luckily, by the time I graduated high school, I had enough AP credits under my belt that I practically had an associate's degree. My undergrad took no time at all, but I'd killed myself academically when I was younger to make that possible.

"Yeah, I got that you are kind of a workaholic from all the stuff printed about your divorce."

Her dry tone made me stiffen. I dropped my hands and tapped the fingers of one against my bent knee in obvious irritation. "I don't discuss my private life with clients, Avett."

A grin pulled at her mouth and her dark eyebrows danced upwards. "Why not? Your clients are probably the only people in a worse position than you were. We're the last people that can judge what's going on behind anyone else's closed door. I'm here because I'm trying to prove I didn't help my ex-boyfriend rob a bar. What's a little infidelity compared to that?"

I shot to my feet before I could control my reaction, shoving my hands through my hair. "She was unfaithful, not me. Not that it matters or that it's a topic open for further discussion." It was the wound that bled and bled, no matter how much pressure I applied to stop it.

Avett righted herself and put her hands on her hips. She looked at me for a second and tilted her chin down a little bit. "Even when someone doesn't want our story, we are still compelled to tell it."

My words to her from the interrogation room at the jail hit me hard when she threw them back at me like a fastball.

She started pacing again and quietly told the room because she was no longer looking at me, "I also learned you are very good at your job. You win more than you lose. You have sent some very guilty people back to the streets, as well as saved some very innocent ones from a life behind bars. If I'm going to gamble on my future, then I couldn't ask for anyone better to be holding the cards. I choose to believe that, for once, the deck is stacked in my favor." She stopped once she was across from me again and we spent a moment staring at each other. "Thank you for not letting me fire you, Mr. Jackson."

Her softly spoken words spurred me on to say something I hadn't said to a client since I started practicing law professionally. "Call me Quaid."

Her spectacular eyes widened a hair and she bit down on her lower lip. "All right, Quaid. I'm not going to take the plea deal and that's my final answer."

We both sat back down with my big desk between us. There was a pulse in the air, a vibration I couldn't name, but it felt electric and more alive than anything that had crossed my path in decades. In fact, the last time I had the same shot of adrenaline, the same thrill racing through my blood, making my heart beat erratically, I had been getting on a plane for the first time in my life, headed to basic training and far, far away from an existence that was a constant struggle and hardship. It was like starting over, being given a second chance at something worthwhile. I understood it then . . . I was baffled by the rush of it overtaking my common sense now.

"The preliminary hearing will be set in a few weeks. The State is going to take that time to dig up every little thing they can on you in order to prove they have enough to make the charges stick if we go to trial. I'm going to remind them that their case against you hinges on a known addict and is nothing more than hearsay. We also have the video from the parking lot that shows the boyfriend manhandling you. Our evidence and witnesses that point the finger at Jared being the sole perpetrator are far more compelling than anything the State might pull out of its hat." I grinned at her and I thought I heard her suck in a breath. "Honestly, if I was in your shoes, I would tell the prosecution to shove their deal, too."

She gasped out a surprised laugh and it made something low in my gut tighten.

"We're in this together, Avett. We gamble together, which means we win or we lose together."

She snorted a little. "Except I'm the only one stuck doing time if we lose."

"True. But I've won cases far more complex, with way better evidence stacked up against my clients. If I lose this one, it makes me look like I'm slipping. I don't slip."

"I gathered from the way your secretary was giving me the hairy eyeball that I'm not your typical kind of client."

"Well, if you called Pam a secretary to her face that might have something to do with it. She prefers to be referred to as my assistant." I gave her a steady look and made sure she could hear the sincerity in my tone when I told her, "And my typical client is anyone that can afford me. I don't care if you have pink hair or if you're the star running back for the Denver Broncos. If you hire me, you will get the best defense I can give, and I will treat your case like it is my top priority."

She breathed an audible sigh of relief. "I'll need to thank Asa for hiring you, then."

I decided not to tell her that her dad was picking up the bill now and instead absently told her, "I like your pink hair, by the way."

She blinked rapidly at me and then lifted her hands up so that the tips of her fingers were touching the rosy ends of her hair.

"You do?" She sounded incredulous.

I nodded. "I do, but you might want to consider changing

it before court. It never hurts to look as respectable and as law abiding as possible." She frowned at me and I lifted my hands up in front of me like I was warding off her ire. "That's the kind of advice your dad would tell you to listen to if he was here. I told you, I spend a lot of time in court, and while your hair might seem insignificant to you, it can have a huge impact on the impression you leave on the judge and the jury. If we get that far." Even though I would be inexplicably sad to see it go. It suited her and I liked the way it and she brightened up my typically drab office.

She fisted a handful of the pink locks and closed her eyes for a split second. When she opened them back up, they glimmered with resignation. Again, her bottom lip jutted out in a pout that not only did I want to bite, but that also made the custom fit of my suit pants much tighter.

"Okay, besides my hair, what else do I need to do before the preliminary hearing? How do I make myself respectable and law abiding?" She sounded so disgusted by the idea, I had to bite down another chuckle.

"The hair, and dress appropriately for court. Something conservative but not too stuffy. You're young and you look fairly innocent. You've got your entire life ahead of you. We want to play that up. Besides that, do what the arraignment judge told you—stay away from the boyfriend and try and keep yourself out of trouble."

She stiffened across from me and whispered, "Ex-boyfriend, and I told you, I don't ever want to see him again."

"And I told you that you aren't going to have a choice." I looked at the watch on my wrist and was shocked to see that I had been talking to her for well over the time I had blocked out in my schedule to meet with her. It felt like it had only been a handful of minutes. "I understand where you're coming from. I wouldn't want to see the person that got me into this kind of mess either, but you're the one that walked in here claiming you want to do something right. That you don't need someone to hold your hand. It's up to you to put the guy that hurt you, the monster that threatened those people with a gun and tried to rob a place that means so much to your family, away for a very long time. It is a huge step in the right direction, Avett." I got to my feet and she followed suit. "I have another client waiting on me, so we need to wrap this up. I'll be in touch. I'm sure the D.A. is going to want to talk to you about their case against the boyfriend. I should have a date for the next hearing soon."

I reached out to shake her hand and almost jerked my palm away when our skin touched. A jolt shot up my arm. It took all my restraint not to rub it like I had brushed up against a live wire.

She pulled back and curled her fingers into her palm, like she was trying to hold on to the vibrant electricity the contact between us had created. When we touched, my blood felt charged, stimulated in a way I'd never felt before.

"I look forward to hearing from you." She delicately cleared her throat, making her way to the door of my office. Once she was there, she paused with her hand on the knob and turned back to look at me over her shoulder. "Quaid."

I looked up from the file I had turned my attention to and lifted my eyebrows at her in question. "Yeah?"

"I'm neither as young nor as innocent as you seem to want to believe I am. If you want to sell that to a judge and jury because you think it will help keep me out of jail, then I'll play the part.

But you need to recognize that's not the reality of the situation." She was out the door before I could formulate a response.

I called Pam to let her know I needed a few minutes to prep before my next client meeting, rocking back in my chair as I tried to recover from Hurricane Avett. She was a tiny whirlwind of destruction and I couldn't seem to keep up with the different directions she was blowing my emotions in. I'd never encountered anyone like her. I couldn't remember ever dealing with someone as real, as open with their faults and failures, as Avett seemed to be. I'd never met anyone as reckless with their own fate as she was. Something about that was really intriguing. So was the gauntlet she threw down on her way out.

Obviously she was technically young, much younger than me at least. When I was twenty-two I had gotten back from the desert and was starting college for the first time. I wasn't as untried as a lot of men in their early twenties but that had more to do with the way I was forced to grow up than it did with fighting for my country. Still, the difference between what I knew then and what I know now was huge, so yes, Avett Walker was young, regardless of her assurances that she wasn't.

As for her being innocent . . . I had her criminal record in front of me, so I knew she wasn't an angel. However, there was something in those wild eyes of hers that seemed so gentle and soft. How innocent she may or may not be was still very much up for debate.

I was getting ready to call Pam and tell her to bring my client in when the phone on my desk rang as I was reaching for it. I knew from the caller ID that the man on the other end was Orsen McNair, the man who had hired me and who was the McNair in McNair and Duvall, the founding partners of the firm. I liked

Orsen, appreciated that he gave me a shot right out of law school and the fact that he had stood by me during the divorce when Lottie had done her best to drag not only me but the firm through the mud. I owed the guy a lot considering my pedigree wasn't as polished and shiny as most of the attorneys hired right out of school. I also recognized I had made it to this point in my career based on my own work ethic and own skills at knowing how to read and work a jury. I wanted my name on the sign along with Orsen's and I hadn't been shy about letting him know that.

"What's up, old man?"

There was a raspy chuckle on the other end of the phone and I could hear his chair creak under his weight. "I hear we're in the business of representing punk rockers now."

I frowned, even though he couldn't see me, and glared at Pam through my closed door. "Where did you hear that?"

"Come on, Quaid. You know the ladies in this office gossip like that's what they get paid to do. Pam couldn't wait to tell Martha about the girl with pink hair, saying she was locked up with you in your office for over an hour. Told her that she seemed flushed and agitated when she finally came out. You have something you want to tell me, kid?"

I closed my eyes and rubbed my temples in vicious circles. "Nothing to tell, Orsen. She's a new client. She was referred by another client. The pink hair is a minor issue, but I already advised her that it needs to go before court. If she seemed upset or worked up in any way when she left my office, it was because I told her she was going to be the State's star witness against her boyfriend. She's not happy about it. Pam has a big mouth."

"Pam is worried about another gold digger getting her claws into you."

The reminder of what I had been through, what I had put the firm through, hit its mark. "She doesn't need to worry about that happening ever again. I've told you a hundred times I've learned my lesson."

Another rusty-sounding chuckle made its way across the phone line. "You need a willing woman that knows how to give a man what he needs and that looks good while she's doing it. In fact, you should find yourself one and bring her to the partners' holiday party that will be here before you know it."

I grunted and forcibly turned my mind away from the image of walking into Orsen's opulent Belcaro mansion with a pink-haired hurricane on my arm. The partners would lose their minds and not just because she was a client. McNair and Duvall had an image to upkeep, a reputation to uphold, which meant everyone that represented them was expected to look and act a certain way. On the outside, Lottie was the perfect lawyer's wife, even though she was corrupted and the worst kind of wife on the inside. It made me cringe that I was even comparing the two women. They weren't cut from the same cloth at all; in fact, I was pretty sure Avett came from some kind of custom textile that only existed to create her. "I'll see what I can do. My case-load is a nightmare at the moment, so that hasn't left a lot of time for much else."

"There's always time for the right kind of woman, kid, especially after you wasted so much time on the wrong kind of woman. Pencil me in for a lunch meeting early next week. You can catch me up on what you're working on, including the punk rocker."

He barked a good-bye, hanging up before I could tell him pink hair did not automatically equal someone being a punk rocker. Orsen was old school and set in his ways. He wouldn't recognize the hair as another facet of Avett's spirited and untamed personality. I wasn't lying when I told her I liked it. It was different and suited her, but I was practical enough to know that it had to go, even if I disliked the idea almost as much as she did.

The entirely unprofessional thoughts I was having where Avett was concerned also needed to take a hike. If there was a right kind of woman for what I currently needed, it absolutely wasn't one that was an almost felon and that seemed a hundred times more comfortable in her skin than I had ever been. I needed a woman I could fuck and forget, not one that was already lingering on my mind and poking holes, without even trying, in the iron façade I had spent years hiding behind.

CHAPTER 5

Avett

"You look pretty, Avett." My dad's gruff voice startled me from where I was still trying to pin strands of pink hair into the tightly coiled bun at the back of my head.

I should have changed it. I'd had almost three weeks to buy a box of dye, to make the pink no more, but I couldn't do it. Every time I thought about it, every time I really contemplated the fact I might have to go to prison for an extended amount of time, the idea of going away as someone that wasn't me, the thought of facing the judge and everyone else slotted to judge me as an imitation of myself, it made my skin crawl. Plus, every time I had a meeting with Quaid in his stuffy office, with its fancy carpet and boring furniture, the first thing he did was look at my hair, then look at me with a combination of reproach and admiration in his eyes. I liked both of those responses from him. I liked any kind of response from him. Getting him to react to me had become a personal challenge, and I was well aware I was pulling on a big, golden lion's tail. The man was a predator, a civilized beast in a designer suit. There was more to the handsome lawyer than met the eye. I was dangerously intrigued by what kind of secrets his killer grin and steely blue gaze kept hidden.

He never mentioned me changing my hair again, so I was secretly hoping he realized it came with the territory . . . one more choice I was making that might bite me in the ass, but like all my other choices, I would face the consequences of my actions. I would own being the type of person that was critically flawed and forever fucking things up. I wasn't hiding any of that, so that meant the pink hair stayed, but I did my best to make it as subtle as possible, and I did concede to part of Quaid's advice, deciding not to dress like a college dropout for the big day. That was why my dad was leaning in the door of the open bathroom looking at me like he hadn't ever seen me dressed up before.

Probably because he hadn't.

My family was casual to our bones. I owned one skirt that dated back to high school. I'd had to go shopping, with my dad, because I didn't have a car or any kind of cash to buy something that was suitable for convincing a judge I would never take part in an armed robbery.

I put my hands on the sink, looking at my dad's dark gray eyes in the mirror. Things had been tough since I'd come home. There was a tension there, a lingering cloud that hovered over us, and I wasn't sure how I was ever going to fix things with the most important person in my whole world. I knew a lot of his unease came from the fact my mother still wasn't happy with me, and when she wasn't happy Brite wasn't happy. I didn't know how to make things better with her either and that meant I did nothing. Doing nothing was always the action that seemed to hurt the worst and, even knowing that, I still found myself doing it over and over again.

"Thanks, Dad. How does the hair look?" The tightly coiled bun had taken more time than I'd spent on my hair in all my twenty-two years. Generally, I let the loose and wavy strands do their own thing. I was all about no-fuss-no-muss.

"Pretty, all of it is pretty. You can't even see the pink from the front." He was trying to be reassuring but I could tell he was nervous by the tense set of his broad shoulders and the down-turn of his mouth within the forest of his beard.

"Good. I'll remember not to turn around in front of the judge. Thanks again for the classy duds." I pulled at the front of the lacy, cream-colored, three-quarter-sleeved, knee-length dress he had actually been the one to pick out for me. It was cute and totally conservative enough when I paired it with black leggings and ankle boots. It wasn't something that made me look like a mom or like some high-class chick I would never, ever be. It was an outfit that made me look like a twenty-two-year-old that should, theoretically, have her shit together. So that's who I was determined to be, even if it felt like I couldn't have my shit less together if I tried.

"I'm happy to help you out, Sprite. Always have been." His frown went deeper into his fuzzy face as his salt-and-pepper eyebrows slanted down over his eyes. "Your mom, too."

There it was. The Darcy-sized elephant in the room that had been hovering between us since he bailed me out of jail . . . or longer. Things had never been particularly easy between me and my mother. I blew out a breath and turned to face him. I leaned back against the sink and met his solemn gaze.

"I don't know what to say to her, Dad. She isn't you. She doesn't forgive the way you do." When I started my downward spiral, when I went from being a simple yet defiant party girl to the girl determined to ruin everything good in her life, my mom didn't understand and she watched me fall with little sympathy or compassion. Granted, she didn't have the whole story but I wanted her to love me enough to forgive me and excuse me anyway. Instead, she forced enough space between the two of us that my guilt and the blame I fostered from the night I learned how tragic doing nothing could be had plenty of room to flourish and grow.

"You have so much of your mom in you, Sprite. I think you're both too stubborn and hardheaded to see it though. She loves you. She will always love you and support you just like I do. She had to find her way just like you did, kiddo. Darce wants more for her baby girl. She doesn't want to see you waste your time on loser after loser like she did, and she doesn't want you tied to a no-named bar. We both know you have so much more to offer. Those aren't bad things to want for your kid."

I sighed and stiffened my spine. "I'll convince Mom I'm innocent and have learned my lesson after I convince a judge. Deal?" He looked at me until I squirmed under his intent gaze. "Dad, I promise I will figure out a way to work on things with Mom. I've let things go for far too long and it's gotten me nowhere good."

Finally, after a beat, a grin that transformed him from surly, grumpy biker badass into a warm, kind, and much more Santa-esque badass broke across his face. "I know you will, Sprite. I have faith in you . . . always. And you might've let go but we're your parents. We've been holding on tight since the beginning."

I pushed off the sink and nervously tugged at the hem of my dress. "Thanks, Dad. Let's do this thing." Quaid seemed so sure the charges would be dismissed, but he never forgot to remind me that we could take the plea deal, that ninety days in jail was a much better option than three years. I was nervous, but there was something about Quaid Jackson, something about the way he handled himself, something about the way he handled me, that gave me unbridled confidence that the situation would go the way he guided it. I honestly believed the man would get the charges dropped, and if he didn't, then I had full confidence he could unleash that dangerous grin and wicked charm of his on a jury and bend them to his will.

My dad moved out of the doorway and followed me down the hall towards the front of the house. I grabbed my purse and was pulling the front door open when my father's heavy hand landed on my shoulder. I turned to look at him in question and was relieved to see his grin was still in place.

"Avett, you need to understand how I got to a place where I learned how to forgive. The main reason I can hang in there until someone that's lost finds their way is because I was a man, not too long ago, that needed that kind of forgiveness and needed someone to show me the way. All the choices we make, good and bad, have a lesson in them. I think it's time you quit letting those lessons go over your head, Sprite."

The lessons weren't going over my head. They were hitting me right in the heart, right in my very soul, and I deserved all of them. Those lessons reminded me every single day what kind of person I was; they reinforced the fact that when you were a bad person, bad things happened to you, and I knew I deserved them all. Every lesson I learned, I held close and let prick at me with sharp barbs over and over again.

My dad pulled the door closed behind him and we walked down the front steps of the beautifully restored two-story Italianate brick home that my dad had lived in since his split with my mom. It was home, as much as the bar had always been, and I loved it and the Curtis Park neighborhood it was located in. We were walking towards his red truck when he stopped by my side and waved at someone across the street. I squinted against the sun to see who he was waving at, but all I got was a flash of rust-colored hair and an arm full of brightly inked tattoos as it disappeared into the driver's side of a beautiful old Cadillac. The guy moved quick and his car sounded loud and mean when he started it. That wasn't a show Caddy; that was a Caddy with some balls and well-maintained guts.

"Who was that?" Dad pulled open my door for me because even the most badass of badasses treated his daughter like a lady, and wouldn't accept anything less from any man in her life.

My dad lumbered up behind the wheel, slapping on a pair of mirrored sunglasses. Maybe Quaid should have given my old man a list of dos and don'ts for proper court wear instead of me. At least he had left the Harley T-shirt at home and had opted for a plain black one in its place. That was totally how Brite Walker dressed to impress. I chuckled a little at the thought as he backed out of the driveway.

"New neighbor. The boys call him Wheeler. He runs a garage down in the warehouse district. Boy has skills when it comes to anything with a motor in it. I keep telling him if he comes across a 1959 Pan-Head, I'll buy it no questions asked and have him rebuild it for me. He's a good kid, and my boys like him."

I lifted an eyebrow. "And he just happened to end up in the house across the street from you?"

My dad chuckled and turned to look at me, but all I could see was my own pale and pinched expression reflected back at me.

Definitely not a chick that had her shit together. I wasn't going to fool anyone.

"The boys may have mentioned he was looking and I may have mentioned there was a for-sale sign in the neighborhood. Kid's got himself a girl and recently got engaged. He's trying to settle down and do right. You know how I feel about a good man trying to do right." He paused and then muttered under his breath so quietly I almost didn't hear, "Even if he's doing right by the wrong girl."

"You don't like his girlfriend?"

My dad shrugged and turned back to the road. In Brite Walker speak, that meant he more than didn't care for her.

"The kid works hard, has raw talent when it comes to what he does. The girl seems happy to sit around and take him for a ride. She's been around a long time and I think the kid doesn't know anything else. Reminds me of my first wife, and my first marriage, and we both know how that turned out."

It turned out bad . . . really bad. Dad had cheated with my mom, knocked her up with me, and left the first wife without a backward glance, even though they had been together since high school and she had waited for him for years while he was overseas with the Marines. He said, time and time again, that he regretted the way things ended with his first wife—she deserved better from him—but he got me out of the deal. I was his great story from that bad decision and I knew he wouldn't trade me for anything in the world.

I chuckled again and looked out the window as we got closer and closer to downtown and to the courthouse. "It's not your job to save every single, confused, twenty-something in Denver, Dad."

He chuckled as well, and wheeled the big truck into a paid parking lot because there was no way to parallel-park the beast on the busy downtown streets. Even badasses hated parallel parking on crowded city streets.

"I'm retired, Avett. What else am I going to do with my time?" I guess he had a point, and as he came around to open my door, I hooked my hand in the elbow he offered, and took a deep breath. My nerves kicked into high gear and my tummy started to tie itself into knots.

"I hope they appreciate you and what you do for them."

He patted my hand where it had gone clammy against his tattooed arm. "Doesn't matter if they do, or don't. I appreciate them and what they do for me." And there it was. He was giant-sized, he took no shit from anyone, he was grizzly, and he was gruff, but there would never be a better heart than the one that beat strong and true inside of Brite Walker. He was amazing through and through. I knew I had never done a single thing in my short life to deserve him, but I was selfish and greedy enough to know I would never, ever let him go. Even if I knew I would never feel entirely worthy of his loyalty and devotion to me.

His voice rumbled over my head and distracted me from my dark musings. "You ready to do this, Sprite?"

I took a deep breath as he pulled open the door and guided me towards the security line. "As ready as I'll ever be, I guess."

We didn't say anything else as we passed through the security checkpoint, the officers giving my dad pointed looks and predictably pulling him aside to run the wand over him before they let us go. We found the tiny room Quaid had instructed us to meet him in outside of the actual courtroom. When we walked in, he was already there tapping away on his phone and looking as sharp and as pulled together as ever.

Today's suit was black and the shirt under was a charcoal gray. The silk tie knotted at his tanned throat was a pretty royal blue and all of it made him look good enough to eat. The man wore a suit well, but I was curious to know what he looked like out of it. There had been one picture Google was generous enough to share with me of him in his Army fatigues, but he was so young then—a boy, really, and not the tall, imposing man that stood before me now. I wondered if he ever relaxed, if he took the suit off when he got home and rocked a pair of tattered sweats and a stained T-shirt. I doubted it, but I would bet good money that he looked as good in casual wear as he did in a thousand-dollar suit.

His eyes roved over me and he gave a quick nod before reaching out to shake my dad's offered hand.

"I see you took my advice to heart, Ms. Walker. This will do, this will do nicely." I rolled my eyes at him when he called me Ms. Walker. For weeks now, I'd been Avett when we were alone in his office, and he had been Quaid. The formal title was a reminder that it was showtime and I better get my act together for the powers that be.

"Thanks. Dad picked it out and I spent forever trying to hide the pink hair. This is the best I could do." I turned my head slightly to the side so he could see the bun, and if I hadn't been standing right in front of him, I would've missed the barely there breath of what seemed like relief that whispered out of him.

"The work paid off."

I nodded my head a little and met his chilly gaze with one of my own. "Whatever happens today is happening to me. I'm going to face the music, own up to the fact I messed up, picked the wrong person. Again. And I'm going to do that as me. Me, who has pink hair and won't be caught dead in a power suit." I let my eyes roll over his long and elegant frame draped in material that cost more than my dad's monthly mortgage payment. "No offense."

Like he would take any. No man on Earth had ever looked as good in a suit as this one did. I mean, I was pretty sure that was an actual fact.

His eyebrows lifted a hint as the edge of his mouth dipped because he wasn't going to let himself smile at me. "None taken and you don't need a power suit. What you're working with is fine and more importantly you seem comfortable. That comes across as earnest and honest. We don't need you in anything that would make you fidgety and uneasy. That behavior comes across as anxious and guilty."

He turned away from me and moved to the table where his computer and a bunch of paperwork was laid out. "Remember the State gets to play their hand first. They're going to bring up every single thing on your record. They're going to bring up the fact you dropped out of school. They're going to hammer the point that you worked at the bar, that you were fired, that you were upset your dad sold it."

My dad stiffened behind me but I didn't turn around. I nodded at Quaid. "I'm ready for it."

"They are going to try and convince the judge you were there to help Jared, that you are a legitimate threat to society, and that you would be better off behind bars, then they are going to try and sway the judge with generosity by offering up the plea bargain." He gave me a pointed look. "I don't get to do my part until all of that is over, so you have to sit there and keep it together while they drag you through the mud. *Both* of you need to keep it together. Am I making myself clear?"

I peeked over my shoulder and saw that my dad was scowling again and that he seemed almost as anxious as I was feeling on the inside.

"I hear you, son." My dad's voice rumbled low and hard through the tiny room.

Quaid nodded. "Good. I'm here for one reason and one reason only, to win this judgment for you. The State has a decent enough case, but mediocre isn't good enough when I'm the opposing counsel. We're in this together, got it?"

He's been telling me that for weeks, saying this was his battle as much as it was mine, but since I was the only one with something to lose, namely my freedom, I'd had a hard time believing him. Here in this tiny room, with my dad practically vibrating with tension at my back and him seeping confidence and talent in front of me, I actually started to believe him.

"Okay. We're in this together."

His eyes thawed just a hint and warm shots of pewter blazed from the depths. That look made my heart beat faster and some of the anxiety that was riding me warmed into something that was heavy and more languid. Even though it was the least likely thing in the world to happen, I realized I would totally fuck my attorney. Exactly like those girls had been talking about at the arraignment. He was hot in a way that was totally foreign to anything I had ever considered sexy before, beautiful even, but it was his steadiness, his indomitable attitude, that pulled at me.

Quaid wasn't reckless or rash. He was a man with a plan, with the kind of fortitude to put that plan into action, and follow it through to the end. He most definitely had his shit together.

While that never appealed to me before, it was suddenly the most desirable trait I had ever seen in a man. He was flawless, and to someone that was deeply and tragically flawed, it was impossible not to be fascinated by that kind of perfection.

I pulled a whoosh of air into my lungs and held it as I followed him out of the room and into the courtroom. Since this was the preliminary hearing, the only people in the room were the court recorder, the prosecutor plus his assistant, and our little entourage. It should be less nerve-racking to have all my mistakes laid out in front of a smaller audience, but since this audience mattered more, and my father was a part of it, my stomach churned and burned as we took a seat on our side of the room.

The prosecutor was the same one from the arraignment. He walked over and shook Quaid's hand before he sat down and let his gaze skim over my attorney's slick attire.

"Nice suit, Jackson."

Quaid gave the other man a smile, but it wasn't a nice one. It was a smile that had too much teeth in it and it didn't make me feel all warm and fuzzy like I usually felt when he grinned.

"Thanks, Townsend. I dressed up for you."

The other man grunted in response and shifted his gaze to me. I wanted to squirm in my seat but repeated over and over again that I was pretending to have my act together today so I needed to sit still.

"You sure your client doesn't want to take the plea deal? I thought the bosses were being generous when it came across my desk."

I opened my mouth to snap that I hadn't done anything, but then shut it just as quickly. Quaid was getting paid a minifortune to defend me, and I knew I would make a mess if I tried to defend myself, so I kept quiet and forced myself not to react to the other lawyer.

"It is a good deal . . . if she was guilty of committing a crime. Having bad taste in men and getting caught up with a junkie loser is not a punishable offense." Quaid's tone was icy and there was no missing that he wasn't in the mood to banter with the other man.

"When that junkie loser robs a bar with an unregistered weapon and threatens the life of a cop, it *is* a punishable offense. She didn't call the cops, Jackson, she didn't do anything."

I cringed and tore my gaze away from their intense standoff. *She didn't do anything* . . . I never did and it forever haunted me. It lingered around me like a black cloud. *Nothing* was just as bad as participating in a crime; at least, that was the way it felt. *Nothing* could linger heavy and thick until you couldn't breathe through it, and I'd been gasping for air for a very long time.

"Again, Townsend, doing nothing is not a crime." It might not be a crime, but the punishment that came with doing nothing might be worse than the punishment that came along with actually committing a crime.

"We'll see if the judge agrees with you or not." The other man skulked his way back to the other side of the room. Shortly after the exchange, the court bailiff told us all to rise and an older man, in billowing robes, entered the room and took his place at the bench. The court recorder read my case number and the charges that I was facing, then we all had to say our names clearly for the record.

The judge said a curt hello to both Quaid and the other attorney, and without any preamble, the other man launched into why the State thought I should be behind bars. Just like

Quaid warned, all my dirty laundry was dragged out and laid flat for everyone to see. The DUI charge I'd recently bargained down, the bar fight that had resulted in a trip to the police station all because I was drunk and thought the other girl was trying to hit on Jared. The trespassing from when I jumped the fence at a resort to go skinny-dipping with some boy in a band that I met at a bar. All of it in its twisted, torn, and ragged glory. Every bad choice and mistake I had ever made there to be judged and weighed. Every instance I had taken the opportunity to do the wrong thing because I didn't deserve to do the right thing. It was rough, but I sat silently, unflinchingly, and refused to look away from the judge, who had his eyes locked firmly on me.

"We also have a witness that will happily testify that Ms. Walker was fired, from the very bar she is accused of helping rob, for stealing. The same witness will testify that Ms. Walker was angry her father sold the bar, the bar she felt belonged to her and should stay in the family, so she concocted the plan for the robbery out of revenge."

Quaid stood up and put his hands on the table in front of him. "Seriously, Townsend? Are you going to disclose to the court that your witness is a known drug user? Do you plan to clue the court in to the fact that you are in the midst of pressing charges against said witness for armed robbery and endangering the welfare of a police officer? What kind of deal did you offer this witness to testify against my client, Counselor?" I finally pulled my gaze away from the impossible-to-read judge and looked at my attorney.

There was a hard line of tension in his arms and along the line of his back. He was angry on my behalf. The little crush I was working on building towards him bloomed into full-blown infatuation. My dad had been the only man in my life to fight for me, so to have this man, this polished, seemingly perfect man, take my back, regardless of the fact he was doing it for a paycheck, still warmed me to my toes.

"Mr. Jackson, you will get your turn to argue against the State's case soon. Please refrain from those kinds of outbursts in my courtroom. You know better."

Chastised and clearly annoyed by it, Quaid sat back down next to me and shot me a look. It was full of heat and turmoil, so it was my turn to tilt my head in reassurance, and even though I'm sure he thought it was an accident, I let my elbow brush against his like he had done at the arraignment. We were in this together, after all.

After the prosecutor was done talking, the judge took his time looking at the paperwork scattered in front of him and then turned back to the other attorney.

"I'm assuming there's a deal on the table since I've seen the tape from the parking lot, and it makes it very clear Ms. Walker was not at the establishment of her own free will."

The prosecutor visibly stiffened and cleared his throat. "The district attorney did offer a deal, Your Honor. Ms. Walker turned it down. We feel like we have a solid enough case to take this to trial."

The judge didn't say anything and looked at Quaid, who climbed to his feet. "Your client is aware of what happens if she turns down the deal and takes her chances with a jury, Mr. Jackson?"

"She is, Your Honor. The fact of the matter is she didn't know Jared Dalton was going to rob the bar that night. She didn't know he had a gun, and when he told her his plan, she tried to exit the car, and we all know what happened." He looked at me.

"Ms. Walker was in the wrong place, at the wrong time, and is paying a remarkably high price for hooking her wagon to the wrong guy. You put me in front of a jury with her and you know as well as I do that they're going to see a pretty, young woman who's made some mistakes but none as bad as sticking around in an abusive relationship with an addict. That video is damning, but so is the witness testimony I'll bring forth. It will attest to the fact she showed up to work with black eyes, and will also state that everyone that witnessed the two of them together knew Jared was bad news. Not to mention the fact, the State's witness is being investigated on trafficking charges, on top of the armed robbery charges. When he was shot during the commission of the crime, it seems he got real chatty while he was in the hospital recovering. Offered the cops a lot of info in search of a deal. Avett Walker is a victim, not a perpetrator."

I wasn't a victim; I was a glutton for punishment and I had my reasons to be that way, but the judge didn't know that. He shifted his attention to me and I swallowed hard.

"Ms. Walker." I got shakily to my feet as Quaid put a hand on my arm and pulled me upwards.

"Yes, Your Honor?"

"What exactly happened that night?"

I felt my knees start to quiver and my heart thudded heavily in my ears. "I, uh . . ." I started to stutter and had to clear my throat. I curled my hands into my fists and told myself to be honest. All the ugly was already out, so it couldn't make it any prettier or any messier with the truth. "Jared had left town for a while. He owed his supplier a bunch of money, which was why I was stealing from the bar. It was stupid. It was desperate, but I did it because I thought I was helping someone that cared about me."

My voice cracked a little and I realized Quaid hadn't let go of my arm because he gave it a gentle squeeze.

"While he was gone, some guys showed up looking for him. They, uh . . ." My voice drifted off again and I had to close my eyes and brace myself to get through the rest. "They broke into the place we were staying and roughed me up." It had almost been so much worse, but thank goodness Jared's landlady was a nosy old bat that had heard the ruckus and showed up in the nick of time. "When Jared came back to town and found me all messed up, he told me he was going to make it right, that he had a safe place we could go. He hustled me into the car, told me he had to make one quick stop, and the next thing I knew we were at the bar."

I felt a sharp pressure in my chest and lifted my hand to hold on to the spot where my heart was kicking against the inside of me like a horse. "I should have known better. He was high—he was always high—and he was angry." I moved my fingers from my chest to the spot on my forehead where the knot had lived for weeks. "I told him to stop it. I told him I was going to call the police. That was when he grabbed the back of my head and shoved me into the dashboard. I was already messed up from the thugs that were looking for him and he nailed me right between the eyes. I think I blacked out a little bit."

I gulped. "I wanted to call the police." I laughed a dry broken sound. "I really wanted to call my dad." I looked over my shoulder at the man that was my own personal rock to lean on and wanted to wither away at the expression on his hard face. I was breaking his heart again, and again. "I didn't do anything though. I sat there with my ears ringing, wondering how in the hell I had ended up in such a terrible spot. I didn't know he had a gun. I never saw it and didn't know until we got to the bar what his plans were. I should have done something, anything, but I didn't, including help him plan the robbery."

It was eerily silent after I said my piece; the only sound I could hear was the rhythmic in and out of Quaid's breathing. He gave no indication if I had been convincing or not. I hoped so, since it was the ugly, unvarnished truth of exactly how broken and imperfect I was.

The judge sighed, an audible sound that echoed throughout the nearly empty courtroom.

"I think we both know, Mr. Townsend, that if the defense puts Ms. Walker on the stand after he coaches her against a junkie that is a proven drug user and with the evidence of the physical abuse, your case is in the toilet."

"Your Honor . . ." The other attorney huffed out an irritated objection but the judge held up his hand.

"Stop, Counselor. I'm not in the habit of wasting the court's time and I'm not in the habit of putting weak cases in front of a jury. I agree with Mr. Jackson that the video evidence is damning and so is the history of your primary witness. Ms. Walker has a history of infractions but none of them prove her to be a menace, just a young lady that needs to grow up and make better choices." His gaze drilled into me. "Do you consider yourself lucky, young lady?"

I blinked rapidly and shook my head in the negative. "No, Your Honor, not typically."

"Well, adjust your attitude and take this as your wake-up call. You are extremely lucky that Mr. Dalton didn't hurt anyone, yourself included, and if he dragged you into his drug activities, which it sounds like he did, you are very fortunate to be here in this courtroom at all." I nodded woodenly. "I'm dismissing the State's case against you, but I'm doing so with the warning that you are expected to make yourself available to both the police and the district's attorney office as they move forward with the case against Mr. Dalton. If I get any kind of hint that you are not being accommodating and cooperative, I will gladly rule on any obstruction of justice charges that are brought up against you. Am I making myself clear?"

I nodded again. "Yes, Your Honor."

"If I were you, I would take a long hard look at the choices that resulted in you ending up in the car with Mr. Dalton and a loaded gun that night, Ms. Walker. Next time, luck may not be on your side."

I blew out a long, shallow breath and told myself I couldn't pass out.

"The charges against Avett Walker are dismissed. Court adjourned." The gavel hit the block on the desk and we all got to our feet as the judge swept out of the room, his robes billowing behind him.

"Dismissed." I whispered the word like it was a prayer and melted into the hard embrace that wrapped around me. My face didn't hit soft cotton and a barrel chest like the last time I won a court battle. No, this time my cheek hit a silk tie and a chest that was rock hard and felt like it was carved of stone. I instinctively wrapped my arm around Quaid's lean waist and inhaled his tangy, expensive scent. I would never tell my dad, but it was a better hug, mostly because it made me tingle all over. It made me feel safe and protected in an entirely different way, a way that was heavy and intoxicating to my already stripped and exposed senses.

"And that's how it's done." He muttered the words into the top of my head and let me go like I was on fire, which I was, on the inside.

My dad cleared his throat and I walked over to hug it out with him as well. His embrace was familiar, warm, and I would give it all up in the blink of an eye to run towards the tingle I got from Quaid's arms around me again. It looked like my addiction to chasing after my ruin wasn't going anywhere anytime soon.

CHAPTER 6

Quaid

I almost kissed her. It was a close call when her face hit my chest and her arms wrapped around me. I wanted to kiss her but I refrained, which was a struggle, so I hugged her back instead.

I never hugged my clients after a win. Usually, it was a businesslike handshake, followed by a tired joke about my bill being in the mail. Not this client. This client I wanted to wrap up in my arms and tell her to start making better choices so she was never in this position again. With this client I wanted to touch my mouth to hers and see if she tasted as wild and rebellious as she seemed. I wanted to find that innocence I knew she had somewhere inside her, hidden under all the debris she piled on top of it. And I knew it would feel as sweet and as soft as I guessed it did. And because I wanted all of that, I pulled back from Avett Walker like her skin was wrapped in thorns, and met her father's knowing look with a guarded one of my own.

Brite didn't miss much. I couldn't tell if the blatant relief in his dark gaze was from the dismissed charges or because I immediately took my hands off of his daughter. Honestly, I wasn't sure which one he should be more relieved about.

I shook hands with the big man and nodded when he offered up a gruff, "Thank you."

"All I did was what I get paid to do." I made sure my voice was flat and devoid of emotion. Maybe if I repeated that it had just been a job, and that she was like any other client, I would eventually make myself believe it. I needed to believe it before I got myself into trouble.

I saw Avett's eyes widen and her mouth pull into that familiar pout that I wanted to nibble on. I bit back a groan and inclined my head towards where Townsend was lingering on the other side of the courtroom. "I've got to touch base with the prosecutor before I head out. If you need anything else, follow up with the firm." I couldn't stop myself from meeting those swirling, colorful eyes as she glared at me. "Good luck with the rest of the case."

She opened her mouth, then snapped it back closed with a shake of her head. Her eyes narrowed to slits as she practically growled out, "Thanks."

Brite took her arm, muttered something to her that I couldn't hear, and then guided her out of the courtroom. I wanted to breathe a sigh of relief that the tiny force of nature was no longer my problem, no longer a temptation I didn't want or understand, but my guts felt hollow and my head started to pound like I'd had too much to drink.

Townsend made his way over to me and set his worn briefcase on the desk next to my much nicer one. He lifted an eyebrow at me and asked snidely, "So, do you think if I dropped a couple grand on a new suit Willis would rule in my favor more often?"

Normally, I would smirk and throw out some offhand quip about clothes making the man, but my sense of humor and typical pride at winning a case was nowhere to be found. I rolled my eyes and didn't bother to mask my annoyance at the other man's petty dig. "Your case was crap and Willis saw it. Even if he didn't, you were never going to get a conviction with the video evidence and the previous criminal history of your only witness. Not even Tom Ford or Ralph Lauren could pull your case out of the crapper. Don't be a dick, Townsend."

I never spoke that bluntly or let my real feelings about a case or opposing counsel show. Spending time around Avett, with her total lack of artifice or pretense, was bad for business. I was supposed to be unaffected, unmoved, by everything that happened in court. That was how I defended the kind of monsters and miscreants that made up my client list. I didn't need the prosecution to see any kind of chink in my flawless armor.

Townsend picked up his briefcase and gave me a smirk. "The hug after the announcement was a nice touch, Jackson. You gonna offer that to all the murderers and rapists you defend, too?"

It was a killer parting shot. All lawyers knew how to give one, which made me even more grateful that this case was won and done. I wouldn't have to go through another arraignment, another hearing, and possibly weeks of trial ignoring my unexpected and inappropriate reaction to Avett. She wasn't on my agenda, and she wasn't someone that I could pretend with. She would see through all the smoke and mirrors that made up my life, and if the charade cracked, if the veil was pulled away, I didn't know who or what would be standing behind it. I was afraid to find out.

I grabbed my bag and made my way out of the building. I

was checking my schedule on my phone when I noticed that Orsen had sent another reminder about the staff holiday party. I groaned. The thing was still months away and he wouldn't get off my case about it. The more he bugged me, the less I wanted to go, and I hadn't put any effort into finding a toss-away piece of arm candy to go with me. I'd been distracted by work, particularly work surrounding a tiny, pink-haired troublemaker that I couldn't drag my mind away from. The same tiny, pink-haired troublemaker that was leaning on the low cement wall outside of the entrance to the courthouse with her arms across her chest and her eyes pinned to the doors, clearly waiting for me. The toe of her pointed boot was even tapping an agitated rhythm against the sidewalk.

I hit the screen to turn my phone off, slipping it into my pocket as she pushed off the wall as I made my way towards her. Her multicolored eyes were riotous with emotion and the heels on her boots clicked against the sidewalk as she kept walking until the tips of our shoes were touching. My hand curled painfully tight around the handle of my bag as she tilted her chin back so that we were looking directly at each other. She barely reached my shoulders but she seemed so much bigger, so much more powerful, than her small frame indicated. The force of her personality and her obvious anger pulsed around us. We stood toe-to-toe, locked in a silent battle that seemed more intense and possibly more important than the one we waged in the courtroom.

"Were you waiting for me for a specific reason, Ms. Walker?" I saw the gold in her hazel eyes blaze when I referred to her formally. I needed the distance mentally because I couldn't make my body move to put the space physically between us. In fact, I wanted to move closer.

She uncrossed her arms from her chest and put her hands on her hips. I tried really hard to ignore the way the new pose pushed her full breasts against the lacy material of her dress. I failed miserably.

"That's it?" Her tone was taunting and sharp.

I narrowed my eyes at her, shifted my weight from foot to foot as her proximity and the charge of her pushing and me pulling thickened both my blood and my cock. I was an attorney for a reason. I never met an argument I didn't like or that I didn't feel compelled to win. The way Avett always seemed to challenge me was as much of a turn-on as her curvy little body was.

"Where is your father?" I lifted my eyes from her penetrating gaze in search of the big biker. I didn't need to try and explain a black eye or a broken arm to Orsen on top of why I suddenly had no interest in searching out a pretty piece of ass to spend time with.

"He's waiting at the truck. I told him I had some questions I needed to ask you about what happens next."

"Do you?"

"Do I what?" She was getting increasingly annoyed and I wanted to groan at the way it made her cheeks flush and her breathing hitch. I bet she looked the same way when she was about to come.

Shit. That was not the direction I needed my thoughts to go, but now that they were there I didn't have a chance in hell of wrangling them back into the safe zone.

"Do you have questions about what happens next?" My voice didn't sound like my own and I knew there was no hiding the wayward direction of my thoughts as they played out in my gaze as I watched her carefully.

Slowly, her head shook back and forth, dislodging the bun at
the back of her head. Pink strands of hair floated around her face,
curling over her shoulders, and my fingertips itched to reach out
and push it off her face.

"I know what happens next, Quaid . . . do you?" Her tone had
dropped to a husky whisper that hit me right in the dick. My entire
body tensed up and I almost, very nearly, leaned down and met
her as she lifted up on her tiptoes towards me. I wanted to kiss her.
I wanted her to kiss me. But over the top of her head, as she moved
towards me, I caught sight of a familiar face. The heady little
bubble of seduction and intoxicating risk that Avett had created
around me popped, dropping me hard, back into reality.

I turned my head as her lips grazed my cheek, and even though
it was as innocent as any kiss had ever been, it felt more erotic,
more forbidden, and more illicit than any of the actual sex I had
ever had. This little slip of a woman could demolish me, waste
me, annihilate me, and if I allowed her to do it, I knew it would
feel better than anything had in a very long time.

"I know that you think you know what happens next, Avett,
but you don't. What happens now is you stop wasting your time
on men that are no good for you, men that have nothing to offer
you and will end up hurting you in the long run. You need to
start making smarter choices for yourself and start living up to
your potential."

She fell back on her heels, rearing away like I had smacked her
across her face. Her pretty flush turned to a furious red, and she
finally took a step away from me, only to lean forward and drive
her finger into the center of my tie. That familiar face was moving
closer and closer. I knew whatever was said next was going to be
overheard, so I needed to keep myself in check and put the armor

back on piece by piece. I hadn't even noticed that Avett managed to strip it off of me. This was why nothing was happening next. I was walking away from her before I was bared and exposed to more than her perceptive gaze.

"You're an asshole, Quaid, you know that. A real dick and a super douche lord." Her eyes flashed at me as her voice continued to rise. "This is me making a smarter choice, at least I thought it was, but I had no idea you were a coward."

I shook my head at her. A coward was the least of what I was, but that was exactly what I didn't want her to find out. "Stop it, Avett. This isn't necessary or appropriate."

She laughed but it held no humor in it. "No, Quaid, *you* aren't necessary or appropriate."

I blew out an irritated breath. We were getting a lot of looks and making a scene. I didn't need the kind of attention we were drawing. I didn't need stories of this little interlude making it back to the firm. I threw my arms up in exasperation and let them fall to my sides.

"I don't know what you thought was happening here, but it was just a job. You are a client, like any other client I represent, Avett. Nothing more, nothing less."

She laughed again and started to back away from me like I had something contagious and she was at risk of catching it. "I guess when you get paid to lie, making a living fooling judges and juries, you get really good at buying your own bullshit. Thanks for your hard work, Counselor. I'll think about you every single time I'm living up to my potential."

She was talking about having sex with someone else. She was talking about getting off with a guy that wasn't me. She was talking about someone else getting ahold of all that wild and sweet and letting them get lost inside of it. She made it sound dirty and cruel. It was the way it had to be, but that didn't mean that it didn't burn and blister when she wheeled around on her heel and stalked off, right as Sayer Cole and a man that could give Brite a run for his money when it came to sheer size approached where I was stuck on the spot.

When they paused next to me, I turned towards them and noticed the big, bearded man's arm where it rested on Sayer's slim waist. It wasn't a casual touch at all, which was surprising. Sayer was so proper, so formal and stiff, whenever I was around her. I knew that her having this man's hands on her meant something serious, something more than a polite touch between attorney and client.

I grinned at her and the man glowered at me like he wanted to take my head off. I thought it was amusing, and I needed the break in the tension left over from my confrontation with Avett.

Sayer made a gentle quip about my skills with the ladies failing where Avett was concerned and I told her honestly, "Yeah, she's one of my more challenging clients without a doubt. She needs to learn to listen to me or she's going to end up in jail." I let my gaze skim over the other man and tried to figure out how a guy that looked like he had just escaped the wilderness of Alaska had won over Sayer and all her reservations when I hadn't been able to make a dent. I wanted to be envious, but I was still so conflicted about doing the right thing versus what I actually wanted to do with Avett that I blurted out, "She's a pain in my ass and a spoiled brat, but I don't think she deserves to serve hard time. I did my damnedest to get her charges dismissed."

The lumberjack scowled at me and growled in a tone that I bet made other men run for the hills, "Avett is a good kid. She fell in with a shitty crowd. She definitely doesn't deserve to end up in jail for what went down at the bar. She has a good family that will look out for her. Obviously, if they're paying your bill."

I reared back in surprise that he knew who Avett was as he offered up an explanation. I was also surprised to know he was connected to Brite, as well as Asa. For being such a metropolitan city, sometimes Denver felt like a really small town where everyone knew everyone else.

Sayer cleared her throat and introduced me to her client. He offered his hand and I wasn't at all surprised by his firm, no-nonsense handshake. The guy wanted to hurt me, wanted to stake his claim on the gorgeous blonde standing between us, and it was there in his grasp.

I made a totally unnecessary comment about him hanging out with people prone to needing legal help and both he and Sayer shut me down, rightly so. I wasn't sure why I was being so antagonistic, maybe to distract them from my blowup with the girl I couldn't get off my mind. Maybe I was looking for a fight, for something to take my mind off the twist of regret and disappointment that was coiling around my insides from watching Avett walk away.

Even though I knew she was going to say no, even though I knew it was going to piss off the giant, bearded behemoth that had clearly claimed her as his, I still blurted out, "I have a dinner party coming up with the partners in a few months. I was going to call you to see if you wanted to go with me, but since we're both here now, I figure it doesn't hurt to throw the invite out in person. I'd love for you to be my date for the night, Sayer." It was a lie. I was never going to call her, even if she was the ideal woman to take to the dinner party. Sayer was beautiful but she was so much more than that. Orsen would get off my case about finding a fuck buddy if I brought a woman around that seemed like she would fill the crater in my life and in my confidence that Lottie had left. My boss was looking for the old Quaid back. The problem being, the old Quaid was make-believe, and the new Quaid was having a really hard time keeping the bits and pieces of the man that wasn't real in place.

The other man let out a low growl and I immediately felt bad for putting Sayer on the spot between the two of us. I was being an ass and it had nothing to do with her. I couldn't blame her for the ice in her tone when she flatly turned me down and put me in my place. "No. Thank you for asking, but I already told you that I'm not interested in pursuing that kind of relationship with you. I'm sorry, Quaid."

I kept my expression pleasant and tried to smooth things over. I ran into Sayer a lot, in and out of court, so I didn't want the easy friendship we'd built to be destroyed because I couldn't keep all the things trying to escape me contained. Avett had dented the shield I kept up and now the protection I was used to having had weakened. All the more reason to stay away from her. "I'm a lawyer. It's my job to try to persuade people to see things my way. I'll see you around. Good luck today."

She mumbled something and hurried away with the lumber-jack hot on her heels. I didn't miss the murderous look he shot me over his shoulder before the doors to the courthouse closed.

As if I hadn't been enough of an ass by embarrassing a good woman that I considered a friend and picking a useless fight with a guy that looked like he could bench-press my truck with one hand tied behind his back, I decided to go all-in on the rashness and scrolled through my phone until I found the email that had Avett's personal information in it.

As I walked towards my truck, I tapped out a quick message and told myself I would do the same for any client. It was a lie. I never texted clients and I very rarely let them have access to my cell phone number. Avett was right; I was extremely well acquainted with believing my own bullshit. I had been doing it ever since I left behind the mountains and the kid that came from nothing, had nothing, was nothing. Only, now buying into it seemed impossible, now that she had burst into my life in a blaze of bad decisions, looming felony charges. She wasn't fooled by any of the falsehoods that made up my life careful piece by careful piece. Her honesty and accountability were contagious and I felt like I was infected.

> Avett, if you need me when you get the subpoena to testify against the ex, let me know. I really am here to help and I know you are nervous about facing him. I'm offering as someone that can be your friend, not as your attorney.

Nothing.

I got nothing back and it made me want to throw my phone out the window as I drove downtown to where my office was located. I wanted to call her and tell her to stop being stubborn, to take the help when it was offered, to ignore the fact I pulled away and shut her down. I wanted to demand that she try and kiss me again. I would let her. I would kiss her back, and I wasn't sure I would stop there. I wanted to touch that wild, to get lost in it. I wanted to taste the sweet, to savor it.

I was pushing through the front doors of the building, mentally preparing for my next meeting, when my phone finally pinged with a message. I literally held my breath as I turned it over to see her reply. I wasn't surprised at her response.

I already told you: I don't want your help.

I sighed and fired back:

Well, you have it, regardless.

I went from being absolutely sure I had nothing to give anyone to feeling a pressing need to give this confusing girl everything I had left.

I don't want anything from you, Legal Eagle. Your job is done and I'm no longer your client and we definitely aren't friends.

A smile tugged at my lips at the asinine nickname she lobbed at me.

My assistant said something to me that went over my head as I completely ignored her, slamming my way into my office. I threw my bag on the desk and swore as my laptop slid out once again, hitting the desk with a thud. I was going to be lucky if the damn thing still turned on since I still hadn't gotten around to replacing it from the first fall.

At some point, between meeting Avett Walker and deciding that I was desperate to kiss her and had to capture some of her tempest, the need for perfection, the drive to keep up appearances had faded to a dull throb at the back of my brain and became nothing more than an obnoxious itch under my skin.

I'm very aware you are no longer my client, Avett. That's why you have my cell phone number. I don't give that out to my clients. Use it if you need it.

She didn't send anything back but I didn't really expect her to. I didn't want to be her friend or her lawyer . . . I wanted to be something else entirely. I also wanted to be someone else entirely, and that scared me more than the fact that I wanted to get Avett naked and under me with every single thing inside of me.

CHAPTER 7

Avett

I pulled the curtains back from the window in my bedroom and peered out into the darkness in front of my dad's house. A single black car was parked at the curb across the street, which wouldn't typically bother me, but this car had arrived only after my dad left for the night, telling me he was going to pick my mom up from the bar and take her home. Which meant he was going to spend the night with her, something he did pretty much every single night she worked the closing shift at the bar that we used to own.

I was alone in the big house and wouldn't have even noticed the black car if the tatted-up neighbor and his shrew of a girlfriend hadn't gotten into a screaming match that rivaled anything I was watching on TV. To be fair, it was the guy's leggy and mouthy girlfriend doing all the screaming, something about the wedding coming up in a few months and him not being invested enough in helping her with the seating chart. It seemed like a conversation that should be taking place calmly and privately inside the cute house across the street, but the girlfriend apparently wanted an audience. The gorgeous, auburn-haired man did a lot of nodding, a lot of placating, and a lot of apologizing, but all his reassurances made the woman louder and madder. I watched the train wreck happening from a crack in the front door, only noticing the car with the two men seated in it after the screaming girlfriend had driven off in a huff and a squeal of tires. I couldn't believe the auburn haired guy gave her the keys to that cherry Caddy after her bullshit, but he handed them over, shook his ginger topped head, and skulked inside. I wanted to go over and tell him to cut and run. He was really cute, and no pussy was worth the kind of headache that chick was going to be for the long haul, but I got distracted by the men that were, very noticeably, staring right at my house.

I slammed the door shut, threw the bolt, and slid the safety chain in place. I tried to tell myself I was being paranoid, that maybe they were waiting for one of the neighbors to get home or something, but it was after ten and any reason I could come up with for them to be sitting across from my house, in the dark, seemed to fall short. I sprinted from room to room, switching on all the lights, until the house was practically glowing. I left the light in my bedroom off as I tiptoed across the floor and made my way to the window. I squinted into the dark to see if I could make out any actual faces on the people in the car, but all I could see was the brilliant red of the lit end of a cigarette glowing in the pitch-black interior of the vehicle.

I snatched my cell phone off the charger next to my bed and scrolled to my dad's number. I was getting ready to hit the call button when I realized he would come running, even if there was a perfectly reasonable explanation for the car to be there. I would ruin his evening with my mom, who still hadn't forgiven me for my most recent litany of poor choices, and they would both be disappointed I interrupted their limited time together, and my mom would have one more reason to shake her head and give me that look of silent judgment and recrimination I felt like she had been directing at me forever. I needed to make things right with the woman that raised me and I needed to let my dad have his time with her. That was the right thing to do. I could figure out a way to handle this on my own.

I bit my lip and tapped the phone against my leg. It seemed like it had been hours but it had only been a few minutes. Still, the car and the men inside of it hadn't moved. I thought about calling Asa. He would also come running as soon as I told him I was freaked out. The blond southerner seemed to have an uncanny ability to show up when things were at their worst, and even if he wasn't exactly my biggest fan, he seemed determined to keep my ass out of the fire since I was so prone to dancing in the flames. I think I reminded him of some of the poor choices he had made when he was younger. He had it in his head he could help me be a better person by teaching me from his mistakes. The only problem with calling Asa was that he would tell my dad. As soon as I got off the phone with him, he would call Brite, then both of them would show up for something that could be nothing, and I would feel like an idiot for wasting everyone's time.

Typically in this kind of situation, I would do nothing, but nothing was what always ended up being the absolute worst choice I could make, so I debated between walking outside and tapping on the window or doing the smart thing and calling the police. I settled on a decision that landed somewhere in the middle, deciding to do what fell between completely reckless and disgustingly logical, and let my index finger hit the call button next to Quaid's name.

I kept my eyes glued to the car and held my breath as the phone rang and rang. I had serious doubts he would even answer, considering the way we left things and at this late of an hour, but he said he wanted to be something like a friend, and I could really use one of those right about now. Besides, he had proven awesome and consistent at offering his help, even when I was convinced I didn't want it.

I was getting ready to hang up and do the really stupid thing by going outside to investigate the situation myself when his gruff, sleepy, and heavy voice finally came across the line.

"Avett? What's going on? Are you in trouble?" I heard the rustle of bedsheets and the sound of something being knocked over. The sounds created images of him tangled up and in bed, images that made my mouth go dry and my palms get damp, but his words had my spine stiffening and my eyes narrowing.

"I'm always in some kind of trouble." And considering I was imagining him naked, which took a little work since I had no idea what he was working with under that suit, trouble was something that never seemed so appealing.

"What kind of trouble are you in?" He was moving around and it sounded like he was pulling on clothes. I wondered if he slept naked and if he was putting one of his impeccably pressed suits back on.

"Um . . . I'm not exactly sure. I'm home alone and there's this car parked across the street. There are two men in it and they haven't moved for the last half hour. I'm probably being paranoid but it's freaking me out. I wasn't sure what I should do."

"Where's your dad?" His question was practically growled at me and I swore I heard the jingle of keys in the background.

"He's with my mom. He only spends the night with her a few nights a week. I didn't want to interrupt them because it could be nothing. I'm trying to be responsible. Do you think I should call the police?"

I peeked out the curtain again and gasped when I saw the glint of the front porch light reflected off of something glass. Someone in the car was peering into the house with a pair of binoculars. There was no denying they were watching the house and me.

"Give me twenty. I'll call the police when I get there, if need be. They'll respond faster to my call than yours. Stay inside. Stay away from all the windows and doors. I'll text you when I get there." I heard a door slam and the sound of him moving but my brain was stuck on the "give me twenty." He was coming. He didn't think I was being paranoid and overreacting, and even if he did, he was still coming and not making me feel stupid for calling him. He was the best almost-friend I had had in a long time.

"Uh, okay . . . It really might be nothing though." Nothing, except two strange men with binoculars parked outside of my house watching me.

"Avett." He said my name with some bite to it and it made me shiver. "You're the primary witness in a high profile case that has ties to drug trafficking. It's very unlikely two men parked outside of your house, in the middle of the night, is nothing. Don't do anything crazy. Just wait until I get there."

"I've retired all my crazy, Quaid. A stint in jail will do that to a girl. Reasonable and sensible are my new middle names." I was trying to make light of the situation but a shiver of unease was making my skin prickle.

I hadn't thought about the men in the car being tied to Jared and the illegal things he was involved in. The last time I had a run-in with his associates I'd been beaten and very nearly raped. I knew the way the men he did business with operated. I could happily live the rest of forever without any more exposure to their handiwork. Suddenly, the original idea I had of going outside and confronting them myself seemed infinitely more than foolish and hasty; it seemed deadly and dangerous. It was a damn miracle that I, with my innate need to screw up and pick the worst option, had managed to skip that choice and jump right into the one that involved the hot as hell lawyer coming to my rescue . . . again.

Quaid grunted at me again and I heard an engine start. It purred with power and rumbled sexily in my ear. "Just stay reasonable and sensible until I get there. Crazy doesn't need to be retired indefinitely. It does, however, need to learn the proper time and place to make its appearance. I'll be there shortly."

I asked him if he needed my address and he told me he already had it from the paperwork he had on me.

He hung up, without saying good-bye, and I stuck my phone in the front pocket of the baggy overalls I was wearing. I looked out the curtain again; this time I was sure the binoculars were pointed right at the window I was looking out. I let the heavy material fall back down and put a hand to my racing heart. I had a bad feeling about all of this.

I should call my dad and let him know what was going on. I should tell him that I was scared and that I wanted to make better choices now so that he didn't have to save me from myself anymore. I wanted to be my own hero for once. I didn't want to be the girl that knew she deserved the worst so she never even attempted to show the world or the people that loved her, her best.

I think I held my breath for the entire twenty minutes as I paced back and forth in front of my bed. I didn't exhale until I heard that same sexy purr that had been in the background of my phone call with Quaid outside my window. I crept along the wall and gingerly pulled the curtains back a hint so I could see what was happening outside. I was directly ignoring the order he gave me, but I'd done about as much smart decision making as I was capable of for one day and my reserves were dry.

A brilliantly red, supersleek motorcycle, which was as opposite as it could be from the massive chrome-and-black Harley my dad rode, pulled to a stop in front of the house. I watched, in shock, as the man sitting on the mini rocket ship swung a leg across the wicked and sexy machine and stared up at the very spot I was standing. I saw the helmeted head shake, and then the black and red protective gear was removed and Quaid Jackson's messy blond hair was revealed as it glinted in the overhead moonlight.

He kept the helmet under one arm and started across the street where the black car was still parked. I was riveted by the way he walked, confident and with obvious purpose. I was also mesmerized by the fact he had on dark jeans, which did wonders for his backside, and the leather jacket he had on seemed to fit him as well, and looked as expensive and designer as his fancy court duds. The man looked like a god in a suit. In jeans and the red-and-black leather jacket that matched the paint job on the motorcycle, he looked much more approachable, more accessible . . . to someone like me. He was still outrageously out of my league, but he seemed less rigid and formal in his after-hours gear.

The bike totally worked for him, too. It wasn't at all like the mean and beastly American machines I had grown up around. That Italian bike was made to go fast and to look good while it zipped around corners and tore up the asphalt. It was elegant and sharp. It purred, instead of growled, and I wondered if the man that rode it did the same thing. I never would have pictured him as a bike kind of guy. He seemed too stiff and serious to be the type to get off on the rush of wind in his hair and the exhilaration of riding free. Most people considered street bikes a hundred times more dangerous than the big cruising bikes that my dad and his buddies rode. Quaid Jackson didn't strike me as a risk taker; at least, he hadn't until he'd shown up at my house in the middle of the night on that gorgeous monster of a machine.

He was halfway across the street, his gaze focused on the car, when the driver started the motor and peeled away from the curb. Quaid had to jump back to avoid getting run over as the car raced away, and he turned to watch it as it disappeared down the street, without turning the headlights on. He stared into the darkness for a long minute, then turned his tawny head in my direction. I wiggled my fingers in a tiny wave that made him scowl. He looked like an angry bird of prey stalking its next meal. It made my body throb and my heart pulse erratically against my ribs.

He turned on his heel and headed towards the front of the house, so I dropped the curtains one last time and raced down the stairs. I pulled open the front door just as his heavy boots hit the top step.

I was heated and flustered and didn't bother to hide my

reaction to him. He let his gaze sweep over me from head to toe, and I had a second of regret that my hair was in a messy topknot and that my overalls were not only two sizes too big, but also a holdover from my high school wardrobe. They were comfy and cute but they had definitely seen better days, and even with Quaid dressed in jeans and a formfitting black T-shirt, I still felt underdressed and seriously outclassed.

"Thank you for coming. I really wasn't sure what I should do or if I should make a big deal out of it." I stepped aside so he could come into the house and watched as his eyes skittered around the well-lived-in and homey interior. He made his way over to the worn couch and tossed the shiny helmet he still held under his arm onto it.

"Considering they took off and almost ran me over as soon as I got close enough to make out their faces and read the license plate on the car, I would say a big deal needs to be made out of it." He turned and faced me, and I stopped being able to breathe as I saw the predatory look on his face. He didn't look like a legal eagle at the moment. He looked like a normal eagle, ready to strike and devour. He was all golden and glorious, his obvious anger and concern making him a thousand times hotter than he normally was. The fact that the anger was on my behalf, that the concern was for my well-being, made me tingle in places I didn't know could tingle. Seriously, the guys that I had been into before Quaid Jackson weren't the type that made a girl tingle, but everything about Quaid had me feeling things I'd never felt before. It was alarming and exhilarating at the same time.

His deep voice distracted me from my body's warm reaction to his close proximity. "I would've taken a plate number down, but there wasn't a license plate on the car. That means whoever they were, they don't want to be found easily. I doubt it's a coincidence. I'm going to call the detective in charge of the case against the boyfriend and see if he'll get a patrol car to swing through the area periodically."

I nodded absently and clasped my hands nervously together in front of me. "Ex-boyfriend." I blurted it out automatically and saw his mouth tighten in response.

"Let your dad know what's going on, Avett. I don't like this. It doesn't feel right. And with you involved in this case still . . ." He shook his head and some of his blond hair fell into his eyes. I wanted to reach up and push it off his forehead so badly that my fingers were twitching. "There is a lot of room for this to go bad on you."

I nodded again, and moved my hands to my back pockets so that I wouldn't reach for that wayward strand of hair and make a fool out of myself.

"I'll tell him. Things with him and my mom . . ." I lifted a shoulder and let it fall. "They're complicated and I don't like to intrude on their time together."

He frowned at me and I noticed his pale gaze was locked on the way my pose pushed my chest up and out. All I had on under the overalls was a cutoff wife-beater that rested well above my navel. In fact, if I turned to the side, there was a clear shot of the hot-pink hipster panties I had put on after my shower this morning. It was an awesome outfit for watching Netflix and eating Jimmy John's while lounging around the house alone, not so much for trying to converse like a grown-up with a man that equally enticed and enraged me.

"They're both your parents. I'm sure your mom would under-stand that your dad needs to be here if something suspicious is going on."

Oh, she would understand, all right. She would understand that my dad was leaving her to rescue me, yet again, because I could never seem to do it myself and it would shove the wedge between us even farther apart.

I cleared my throat nervously. "She would understand, but my mom and I aren't exactly on the best terms and we haven't been for a while. I don't need to give her any more reason to hate me."

He blinked at me and lifted his hands to shove that rebellious piece of hair—I was obsessed—back in line with the rest of the golden strands. When he raised his arms, the hem of his T-shirt hiked up and I was treated to the visual of tight abs and a concave V that cut hard and ripped between his hips. The man was built, and picturing what he would look like out of his fancy duds and wrapped in nothing but his sheets got a whole lot easier. He was tall and lean with wide shoulders that tapered into a trim waist, and now that I knew he was rippling with ropy and taut muscle underneath his hands-off persona, I wanted nothing more than to be totally hands-on.

"Your mom doesn't hate you. I sat next to her at your arraignment and listened to her cry over you." He lifted an eyebrow at me and crossed his arms over his chest. I felt my eyes widen and lock on the way the muscles in his biceps bulged and flexed in the new position. "I told my folks I was joining the Army and I wouldn't see them for at least four years. Neither one of them shed a tear, so I know for a fact that, regardless of what you think, what your mom feels for you isn't hate." His tone was harsh as he dropped the surprisingly personal tidbit like a bomb at my feet.

"Your parents weren't worried about what might happen to you? They weren't sad to see you go, not knowing when they would see you again?" That seemed impossible to me. My mom often acted fed up and had no problem showing her frustration with me, but she was always there; she always worried about my well-being. I knew she wanted better for me, and I couldn't get my head around Quaid having parents that weren't insanely proud of everything he had accomplished, or the man he had become, since enlisting.

"They were mad I was leaving. When I enlisted, they viewed it as a disappointment and a betrayal to everything they taught me and believed in. I know what it looks like when a parent turns their back on you, Avett, and that isn't what you're dealing with when it comes to your mom."

I sucked in a breath at his stark honesty and told myself it would be entirely inappropriate to throw myself at him. He wasn't the tree in the backyard that I know knew enough not to climb, but something told me if I fell because of him, it would do a lot more damage than a broken arm.

"I've never been very good at doing the right thing, Quaid. Years and years of my dad having to pick up the pieces, of him being the one that rode to the rescue . . ." I shook my head at him and gave him a rueful grin. "It took its toll on my mom, not only because I was always into something I shouldn't be, but because my dad never hesitated to dive in after me. I knew I was putting strain on their relationship, knew things were tense and that she was unhappy, but it never stopped me from screwing up. That makes me a pretty awful person, no matter how you look at it, Counselor. The evidence is compelling."

He continued to watch me. Then he was walking towards me and I was walking backwards as he advanced. We kept going until my back was pressed up against the hard wood of the front door and he was all I could see in front of me. He put an arm above my head and I had to tilt my head back to keep eye contact. He was a couple inches away from being pressed fully against me, but every single part of my body felt like it was straining to close that gap. My nipples peaked hard and pointed directly at him; every single inch of my skin pebbled up and practically vibrated as he hovered out of reach.

"The evidence is circumstantial and prejudiced. You say you don't do the right thing, that you can't stop even though you know your actions are hurting the people around you, and hurting yourself time and time again. So my question to the defendant is . . . why? Why do you keep making the wrong choice and keeping hurting yourself and others? What's the motive?" His breath whispered out and danced across my lips.

I let out a startled little gasp at the touch of it. His words kissed me as his eyes devoured me. Even though zero parts of us were touching, I could feel him all over, including deep down inside of me, where all kinds of feelings were starting to boil and pop under my skin. I couldn't hold back the urge to touch him anymore, so I lifted my shaking hands and put them on the center of his chest. Rock-hard muscle tensed at the light touch; my knees went a little weak at the contrasting texture of his soft cotton T-shirt and the cold brush from the unbending material of his leather jacket. He wrapped the hand that wasn't braced over my head around one of my wrists, and for a second I thought he was going to pull my hands off of him. Instead, his thumb found the soft spot on the inside of my wrist, where my pulse was racing, and started to brush back and forth.

"You don't want to hear my story. Remember?" The words squeaked out as he lowered his head a tiny bit, his pale blue eyes raging like a winter storm as we watched each other unblinkingly.

It was a story I never told to anyone, completely. My story was the opposite of a fairy tale, and I knew there was no way a happy ending was lurking somewhere beyond the ever present dead end. I was shocked that I wanted to tell him, wanted to explain to him, why I did the things I did. I wanted him to understand.

His chin dipped down and suddenly that gap that was separating us was gone. The tips of his boots were touching my bare toes. He dropped my wrist so that his hand could fit its way in the large gap at the side of the overalls and sit on my hip. That was a lot of naked skin his palm landed on and I could see the awareness flare to life in his gaze. Considering my small stature and the size of his hands, if he spread his fingers out he would be both under the edge of my tank top and at the top of my underwear at the same time. God, did I want him to put his hands all over me.

"I find myself wanting a lot of things I shouldn't want where you're concerned, Avett." His head lowered until his lips were separated from mine by nothing more than a whisper. "Like that kiss you tried to give me the other day. I wanted it so bad, which is why I couldn't take it. I don't have anything to give back if I take what you're offering. But I haven't been able to stop thinking about how it would feel, or about how you would taste." He exhaled and it made my lips part and my tongue dart out to try and capture his flavor and essence on the tip of it. I wanted to know how he tasted just as badly as he wanted to know how I tasted. His tone dropped lower, his voice rasping across sharp and pointy things deep inside of him as he told me, "I want the story and the kiss, Avett." His lips touched mine in a featherlight caress that made time stand still. Made me wonder if I had been born for no other reason than to kiss this man. "You can decide what order they come in." There was husky humor in his tone, but before he could close the final millimeter of space between us, I pushed on his chest.

"This is a bad idea." I knew it. I could feel it deep in my bones and the allure of letting go, of doing what I always did, and falling headfirst into disaster, was pulling at me hard. But I was supposed to be changing. I was supposed to actually be sorry, not just saying it and turning around into the next catastrophe. I knew kissing Quaid Jackson was going to lead to all kinds of sorry and sorrow. I knew it as much as I knew I didn't care and that I was going to kiss him and chase this bad idea until it crashed and burned, like they always did.

"You made a lot of them lately. What's one more?"

He was right. What was one more? Especially when it looked like him, when it smelled sleepy and expensive like he did, when it felt hot and hard pressed up against me. What was one more awful choice when it came with lips that were firm and demanding as they landed against mine? What was one more impending disaster, when it was attached to rough hands that brushed along my exposed rib cage and paused under the achy swell of my breast? What was one more bad decision on top of all of the other ones that had led this particular mammoth-sized bad decision to my door?

I had plenty of time, tomorrow, to do the right thing, but now I was going to enjoy the hell out of the wrong thing as he pressed his mouth more insistently into mine, taking the choice of which came first—the kiss or the story—out of my hands. Maybe that was why I was so drawn to him, so attracted to everything there was about him. He didn't give me the room or the chance to make any kind of choice, good or bad. He decided and I followed his lead towards victory or towards ruin . . . and this kiss felt like it had both of those things threaded throughout it.

It was the first time in my life that a bad idea felt like the best idea I had ever had.

CHAPTER 8

Quaid

I shouldn't have my mouth on her.

I shouldn't have my hands on her.

My dick definitely shouldn't be hard and pressing painfully against my zipper as she whimpered into my mouth, as her tongue curled around mine.

None of this should be happening, but neither my brain nor my libido seemed inclined to put a stop to it. As my hand wandered even farther up her side and under the hem of her tiny top only to encounter softer, naked skin and the heavy swell of a plump breast, I couldn't be happier that my common sense decided to take the night off. She felt like a dream. Like a dirty, sexy dream that woke me up in the middle of the night hard and hurting. She felt like a dream that made me sweat and shake as I chased down something I couldn't describe, and that I was sure I had never felt before. She felt like the dream that I was lost in and aching from right before she called me and woke me up.

Any kind of logic and rationale had vaporized the instant I saw her number on my phone, and it didn't stand a chance in hell of making an appearance after I heard the nervous tremor in her voice when she told me she felt like she was being watched. I should have told her to call the police, let them handle whatever new kind of trouble that had inevitably found its way to her, but all the things I should do where this woman was concerned got buried under the burning and pressing need to do all the things to her and with her that I shouldn't do. Including running into the night to make sure she was safe and sound. For some reason, I needed to make sure she was okay with my own two eyes, and I needed to be a part of making sure she stayed that way.

I'd been dreaming about her—the way she would feel and taste—when she called me, the panic and passion blended together in a complex mix of emotion that I couldn't untangle or unwind. I knew there was no way in hell I was going back to my industrial-cold loft with its massive, empty bed without knowing, and without taking. She made me careless and greedy. She made me want things that I knew I could never give her back. And with all of that swirling in my blood, I told myself that I had to know if the reality of her was better than the dream.

It was.

Reality was so, so much better. She was sweet. She was soft. She was responsive as hell, and I wanted to devour her in one bite, instead of savoring her like the honeyed treat that she was. She was dressed like she was about to do yard work or maybe like she was going to go work on a car. Her outfit, messy hair, and makeup-free face should have served as a reminder that she was young, that we came from two very different places, but all I could see was the fact that she didn't have a bra on under the bib of the baggy overalls and the hint of lacy pink at her hips. It was all making my blood heat up and my mouth water. She was

teasingly tempting and I wanted to take her up on all the things
I wasn't even sure she knew she was offering.

I pressed more fully into her, careful of her bare feet and
small frame. I towered over her, but the way she made me feel—
breathless and weak with need . . . I wasn't foolish enough to
think I was the one with the upper hand in this situation. I had
her backed into the door and she had to stretch up on the very
tips of her toes to get her arms around my neck. I had to bend
down a bit to get our mouths lined up, but even that made the
way she bowed and arched to reach for me a tantalizing caress.
She was stretched taut all along the front of my body and every
dip and curve of her lush little body was there for me to explore
and memorize. I liked that she had tempting curves to wrap my
hands around everywhere I grabbed her.

I was so used to women that were hard. Hard bodies, hard
minds, hard hearts, and unyielding souls. They pinged and
bounced off my ever present armor, unaffected and uninterested
in the man that lay beneath. Nothing about them ever gave.

But here with this woman, and with my hands full of soft
skin and generous curves, I realized that every single part of
Avett Walker was giving. I liked that she was soft and pliable
against my questing fingers. I liked the way she whimpered
into my mouth and moved closer to me. I liked the way her
fingers pulled at the short hair on the back of my head, letting
me know I wasn't the only one that was greedy and looking to
take. And I really fucking liked the fact that she didn't have a bra
on, so that when I breached the hem of her crop top my hand
was immediately filled with warm and willing flesh. I liked it
so much that I dropped all pretense of keeping this a simple kiss
that was going to be over before I started it, and curled my hand

around the plump weight until her pert little nipple was stabbing me in the center of my palm.

I wanted to see her. I wanted to know if the velvet point was pretty and rosy like her hair. I wanted it in my mouth. I wanted the little nub rolling across my tongue as she gasped my name. I wanted to get my hands inside those hot-pink panties she had on, and feel if she was as turned on as I was. There was no hiding the way my body was reacting to her. I didn't bother to try. As I kissed her more fully, settled into her so that not an inch of her wasn't covered by me, my throbbing cock found a perfect resting place against her stomach. I wanted the rough denim that separated us out of the way so my turgid and overheated flesh could rub against her supple skin.

I never considered myself the kind of guy that had a quick trigger, but her mouth against mine, the heft of her breast in my hand, and the glide of her nipple across my palm, the way she strained to get closer . . . I knew if my aroused dick got to touch any part of her, there was a pretty good chance that that was all it was going to take for me to get off. I hadn't been that responsive or that reactive to a woman since I started having sex back in high school. The way she panted lightly against my lips, the way she tugged me closer so she could kiss me back. All of it was infinitely more potent than any of the one-night stands I had been wasting my time with as of late.

I grunted as her teeth dug into my bottom lip. A second later, the brush of her tongue was there to soothe the tiny sting. It was wild and it was sweet. Both parts of her that I was dying to experience, both parts that I wanted to capture and wrap myself up in. I shifted the hold I had under her shirt so that I had the pointed peak of her nipple trapped between my fingers. I gave the sensitive tip a firm tug to pay her back for the bite and she gave a little cry of pleasure that made my dick ache and had my mouth moving with even more hunger against hers. I wanted to eat her up. I wanted her wild to consume me, to burn and purge all the things that had long since turned sour and stale inside of me. I ached for her sweet to soothe me after we scorched through each other and were left in a heap in our own wreckage, covered in ash and satisfaction. Never had I been so affected or so irrational in my feelings towards another person. She made me forget who I was supposed to be now, and she made me forget the man I had spent a lifetime trying to bury. With her I was someone new, someone that didn't feel fake or forgotten. With my hands on her and my mouth sliding down her neck so I could chase her pounding pulse with the tip of my tongue, I finally felt like a man that was real, a man that existed for more than what he had and what he could do for others.

I swept my thumb over the crest of her nipple again and then pulled my hand out of her shirt. I brushed my knuckles along the ridge of her rib cage, pulling my hand out of the opening of her overalls so that I could tap the little buckle that kept the bib part up with my index finger. My lips were right below the delicate shell of her ear as our chests rapidly rose and fell together.

"How bad of an idea do you want to make this, Avett?" I felt like we were already at the point of no return, that there would be no going back from this now that I knew how good she tasted and how addictive it was to get swept up in the storm that was Hurricane Avett. The rush of her, the urgency in my blood to take as much as I could before this moment was over. I wanted to fuck her, wanted inside that sweet little body more than I could remember wanting anything in a very long time, but I still had enough of my typical smarts floating around to recognize that this wasn't the time or place to make that happen. I wasn't going to have sex with Avett up against the front door of her father's house, but I was going to have sex with her. After tonight, I knew that was a given. I knew I couldn't not have sex with her.

She blinked up at me and the different colors in her hazel eyes warred with each other as she tried to figure out what the right answer to my very complicated question was. It was a tough call because the right answer meant she had to commit to doing even more of the wrong thing, the wrong thing that just happened to feel more right than anything ever had.

Her hands slid from around the back of my neck where she had been clutching at me to rest on my shoulders. The gold in her eyes gleamed and the brown turned to black as it darkened and swallowed the green. "I usually go all in when I make a bad choice. That's why I fail so spectacularly at life over and over again." Her voice was husky and it hitched a little as I popped the fastening on her overalls open and let one side flop open.

I let out an expletive that sounded harsh and raspy when the fabric fell, revealing most of her torso and the gentle curve of her stomach. She was built the way smart men wanted women to be. She was pretty much perfect all rumpled and shoved up against the door. She was luscious and I really wanted to pull the lacy pink that was keeping the rest of her covered from me and discover all the different kinds of pleasure her body had to offer, all the different kinds of pleasure I was sure I could give her.

I kissed her below her ear and lazily let my fingers trace random patterns on the quivering skin of her stomach.

"This does not feel like failing at life." It felt like winning. It felt like a prize I never even knew I needed to claim as my own, which was strange because my entire life had been nothing more than the pursuit of one reward and one accolade on top of the other. I had chased validation and approval since the first time I realized the other kids and teachers knew I came from nothing and had even less than that. My life had been about proving that it wasn't where you came from that mattered, but where you ended up. I couldn't be happier about where I was right at this very minute, even if it was miles and miles away from where I should be.

I hooked a finger under the top of her underwear and rubbed my knuckle in a long, smooth line between her hip bones. The touch made her jerk against me and had her tilting her pelvis closer to my own. I groaned as my stiff cock was pressed even more fully into the hollow of her stomach. She squeezed my shoulders and turned her head so that her mouth was pressed against the tense line of my jaw.

"I thought this was about you taking what I was offering and not you giving. So technically, this is a failure." She let out a very unpracticed and honest-sounding squeak as I dipped my fingers lower and encountered nothing but bare, silken skin. Skin that was hot to the touch and melted into glossy, liquid depths. There was nothing sexier than the sight of that hot-pink lace stretched around my questing hand. There was stretch in the fabric, but not enough that there was a ton of room to move. My fingers were held tight to her most sensitive places and my palm cupped around her like we were made to fit together. It was a pretty pink snare and I had zero desire to escape from it.

I angled my head lower so I could capture her mouth with my own as I let my wandering fingers disappear inside her damp, velvet folds.

"I'm taking your wild and your sweet, Avett. I'm going to know what it feels like against me. I'm going to remember how it tastes and how it moves so that when I'm inside of it, I won't get swept away by it all." A man could get lost inside the storm of feeling and emotion she created and I didn't want to lose my way any more than I already had. Eventually, I was going to have to find my way back to reality, to the life I had spent so much time building.

I used my knee and the leverage I had on her to urge her to spread her legs farther apart so that I could get at all the secret and hidden places that beckoned to me. She complied with a little sigh and arched into my touch. She kept giving me everything I wanted without question, without asking for anything in return, and that kind of openness and generosity went to my head and to my dick faster than any practiced seduction ever had.

She was warm and wet. She was slick and slippery as my fingers moved over her and through her. She whimpered every time the pads of my fingers grazed her excited clit and she moaned breathy little sounds every time my fingers pumped in and out of her drenched channel. Her eyes drifted closed as she clutched at me, as she lifted back up on the tips of her toes to get closer. She was chasing after the sensations I was creating and it was beautiful to watch.

She ripped her mouth away from the endless plundering of mine, tossing her head back so hard that it hit the door behind her with a thud. I leaned forward so that my forehead was resting on the arm that was still bent over her head, and told myself I could do this. I could get tangled up, wound up in her wild, and go back to my own carefully constructed simulation of a life lived well with the best of everything including very little warmth.

It was a lie.

She felt like life. The way she moved on my thrusting fingers, the way her hands pulled at me, the way her body trickled pleasure and gushed satisfaction, uninhibited and unashamed.

She was real.

She was genuine.

She was truth.

She was all the things I hadn't been in a very long time, and I couldn't get enough of it. I wanted to wring all of it from her body, where I had it pinned and held captive by my own. She said my name on a strangled breath as I used my thumb to press down on her clit. The little nub pulsed under my touch and her entire body seemed like it was going to levitate off the ground.

Her eyelids fluttered as she wrenched her eyes open and her tongue danced out to slick across her kiss-plumped lower lip. The wild was there in her eyes as she dared me to keep going, to push her over the edge. The sweet was there, in the way she moved forward to press her lips to the pulse that was hammering at the side of my throat.

She was so close. I could feel her body softening, loosening up around my fingers. I circled her clit with hard strokes of my thumb and pushed off the door so I could put my other hand on the side of her face, holding her still while I kissed her and ate up every single part of her coming apart for me. It was the most decadent and delicious thing that had ever crossed my tongue. She tasted like she felt, turned on and ready to explode.

After she broke and quaked in delicate spasms all across my hand, we panted softly into one another as she fell back down to her normal height. She looked up at me with a million different questions I had no answers to shining out of her eyes and let her hands fall from my shoulders to my waist.

She stiffened when her fingertips landed on the hard metal of the gun I had forgotten I hooked there when I rushed out of my loft. I trailed my wet fingers over the curve of her belly and curled them around her ribs. The weapon added even more questions to her bewildered and startled gaze.

"You have a gun." The bottom of my leather jacket had kept the firearm covered up so her surprise at the deadly discovery was justifiable.

I stepped away from her and reached for the flap on her overalls that I had loosened moments ago. I rubbed the pad of my thumb over the flushed arch of her cheek and shifted so that her hands were no longer near the weapon or near me.

"I have a few. I got used to having one on hand when I was in the service. Your good buddy Google told you all about it, remember?"

She huffed out a breath and crossed her arms over her chest. She was still propped up against the door and I took an inordinate amount of pleasure in thinking that she needed the stability that the door provided because I had done an excellent job of making her knees weak.

"Google told me you were in the Army, not that you were going to show up at my house in the middle of the night, armed and riding a motorcycle. Google apparently doesn't know any of the good shit. You're full of surprises, aren't you, Counselor?"

I grunted and lifted my hands to push back my hair, which was hopelessly tangled, unkempt from sleep, being shoved in my helmet, and her demanding hands.

"I learned how to load and fire a shotgun before I learned my ABCs. I learned how to hunt about two minutes after I took my first steps. When you said you might be in trouble, my instinct was to grab a weapon on my way out of the loft. The motorcycle spends most of the year in storage, but lately it's been calling to me." I lifted my eyebrows at her. "Something has been hounding me to remember what it's like to let go and be uncivilized occasionally."

She snorted and finally pushed away from the door. My ego practically howled in satisfaction when I noticed she was indeed a little bit wobbly.

"That rocket is as far from uncivilized as any one machine can get. And you are as far from uncivilized as any one man can get, so the idea of you as a toddler in diapers with a shotgun in your hand is pretty hard to imagine." She touched her fingers to her mouth and put a hand flat on her chest. "Exactly who are you, Quaid Jackson?"

I snorted. "Nobody. I'm nobody." And that had been the problem I struggled with all along. That was why I set out to be somebody. Why I had left everything I knew behind and created something that looked so perfect, so desirable, from the outside. I never wanted to be nobody again, but with her I also didn't want to be the slick and scheming lawyer, the guy that knew every move I made with her was leading nowhere. I forced myself to grin at her. "Who exactly are *you*, Avett Walker?"

She laughed and threw her hands out at her sides. "I'm exactly who you think I am—Daddy's girl, college dropout, broke and unemployed, a liar and a petty criminal. I'm the girl that can't make the right choice, even when it's the only choice, and I'm the girl that will fall for the wrong guy every single time. There is nothing surprising about who I am, Quaid, so don't try and spin some kind of pretty tale about the woman you had your hands all over. I'm just me. There is no heart of gold or tender soul hidden here. What you see is what you get, and when you're ready for my story, you'll realize that who I am is someone that deserves every single mess I've managed to make along the way."

That was why I couldn't stay away from her or keep her off of my mind. Her authenticity was addicting and so fucking invigorating after decades spent not only living in the lie that was my current life, but also the lie that was my previous life, and the major charade that was my marriage.

I smirked at her and lifted my hand to my mouth—the hand that had played with her, touched her, stroked her, the hand that had coaxed a sharp and piercing orgasm out of her. I licked the side of my thumb and watched the way the action made her eyes bulge huge in her face.

"I like what I see when it comes to you, Avett. I also like what I get and what you give." She made a strangled noise low in her throat and lifted a hand to hold the slender column, like she could prevent the noise from escaping. "And I do want your story, if you want to give it to me. Tell me why you're rushing after the wrong kinds of things, time and time again, when the right kinds of things would die for a shot at getting a taste of all that wild and sweet you have inside of you." By *things*, I meant *men*, but she was smart enough to figure that out on her own.

She moved away from me and reached up to put her hand over her mouth. Her eyes darted away from my propping gaze and it took her a few minutes before she spoke. When the words came, they lacked her typical fire and sass. They sounded strained and forced as she shifted her weight nervously from bare foot to bare foot.

"I was always kind of stubborn and crazy. The more someone told me not to do something, the more I absolutely wanted to do it." She started to pace in front of me as the ragged words escaped her. "When I was little, my folks called me a handful and other grown-ups called me a brat. When I got into my teens, that morphed into me being a bad influence and a troublemaker. I didn't have a lot of friends because I had a wild reputation that I definitely earned, so a lot of girls my age didn't like me and a lot of parents didn't want me to corrupt their kids. I was a party girl, the girl that was always down for a good time, whatever that entailed, and I never cared what anyone thought of me because it was always fun . . . until it wasn't." She shot me a look, but when I didn't interrupt or offer any kind of comment, she kept going.

"I did have one friend, this very sweet girl named Autumn, that moved here from Kansas her freshman year. She was quiet, kind of shy, and had a hard time fitting in. Denver was like a major metropolis to her and she was really a small-town girl at heart. I can't remember how we ended up hanging out, but once we did, we clicked instantly and were inseparable all throughout most of high school."

It all sounded pretty typical to me. I mean, my childhood had been anything but basic, anything but normal, so I wasn't an expert by any means, but what she was telling me sounded pretty much like every teenage girl's trials and tribulations of growing up and growing into themselves. I didn't want to stem the flow of words pouring out of her so I kept my mouth shut as she continued to give me her story.

"I liked to party, and I liked boys. I liked to act older than I was, and had no problem taking the risks that went along with that. Because Autumn was a good friend, and because I was her *only* friend, she often found herself in situations and surrounded by people she was really uncomfortable with. She didn't want to tell me no because she was afraid I was going to ditch her if she didn't participate. I think she was afraid I would find a new best friend to spend time with if she wasn't right by my side. I was selfish. I was thoughtless. I never once asked her if she was okay with what was going on when we went out and partied. I assumed that because she showed up, she understood the unspoken rules and regulations the way I did."

I cocked my head at her and considered her thoughtfully for a long moment. "Do you even understand the rules and regulations now, Avett?" It seemed like a fair question, considering how we had met.

She gurgled out something that may have been a laugh but sounded more like she was choking. She shook her head from side to side and put her hands up on her pale cheeks. "Oh, I understand, but I never seemed to get that breaking the rules might affect someone else and leave me completely unscathed." She made a fist and thumped it against her chest. "I'm the only one that should be hurt when I decide to do something risky and wrong, but it never works that way. Never."

I reached out and put my hands on her shoulders to still her frantic movements and locked my gaze on hers. "So your friend got hurt because she followed you into the lion's den, unprotected, unprepared, and something bad happened to her?" I cocked a knowing eyebrow. "And you feel guilty about what happened, so you've been punishing yourself by making shitty choices ever since."

She gulped audibly and lifted her hands so that she could curl her fingers around my wrists. I wondered if she felt my pulse kick when she softly told me, "She didn't get hurt. It wasn't just bad—it was the worst thing that could happen to someone. She died. I killed her."

I had heard a lot of confessions and a lot of denials in my career, but none of them tugged at my heart and kicked me in the gut like this one did.

"What are you talking about, Avett?" My words were sharper than they needed to be, but I wasn't prepared for that kind of confession out of her.

She squeezed her eyes shut and I watched as her lower lip started to tremble, making her words shaky and hard to follow, but I was good at tearstained admissions, so I had no trouble following along.

"We were at a party, a party in a part of town we had no business being in. I went because some college guy asked me to go and because my mom grounded me for the weekend for failing a test. It was a total 'screw you' and what I thought was normal teenaged rebellion. It was definitely on par with my typical activities on the weekend, but it quickly turned into something else. That night turned into my story, a story I can barely get through because it should be Autumn's story. I feel so guilty that I'm around to tell it and she's not."

She opened her eyes and I could see the horror and tragedy of whatever happened that night clear as day reflected in the glassy sheen covering her turbulent gaze. There was a different storm raging inside of her, and this kind was destructive and hurtful.

"I told her not to take a drink from anyone. I told her not to be alone with anyone, that we needed to stick together. I told her that these guys were older, that she needed to be careful, and keep her wits about her because no one even knew where we were. I thought that was enough. I thought I was taking care of her. It wasn't enough. Not even close." She barked out a sharp laugh and let her head fall forward like she was hanging from a broken marionette string. Unable to resist the urge, I pulled her into my chest and silently urged her to get the rest of the story out, to let that storm howl and rage until it passed.

"She started smoking pot as soon as we got in the door. She was high, had too much to drink, and before I knew it she had disappeared somewhere in the house with a couple of the guys at the party. Her drink was drugged and when I finally found her, she was naked, passed out, and there was no doubt that she had been raped. I wanted to call the police and an ambulance. I needed help, but the guy that invited me to the party took my phone and told me there was no way I was going to narc on his friends. I was so mad and I was terrified for Autumn. She was out of it, but I knew when she woke up, she was going to be in a bad way. She wasn't a party girl, she wasn't like me." Avett hiccupped on a strangled little sob and I felt her hands fist into the sides of my T-shirt as she started to shake. "I took a swing at the guy, never once thinking that he would swing back. He clobbered me. I remember being stunned at how badly it hurt, and I can still summon up how it tasted when my own blood was filling my mouth. I'd never been hit before, and even with the way I liked to go balls to the wall, I'd never felt unsafe until that moment. I couldn't protect my friend, and I couldn't protect myself."

I tightened my hold on her, imagining what kind of animal could possibly attack her when she was so small and vulnerable. It made me feel all kinds of defensive and territorial.

"The guy told me to keep my mouth shut or I would end up just like Autumn and then he hit me again. At some point, Autumn started to come around and puked all over the room they had her in. She was disoriented, scared, and getting sick every few minutes. I thought she was going to die right then and there."

She took a shuddering breath and tilted her head back so she could look at me. "She begged me to get her out of there, to take her home. I tried to tell her that we needed to go to the police, that we had to have a doctor look her over, but she kept crying and telling me that after everything she had done for me, I had to do this for her. She wanted to go home, so against my better judgment I helped her up and out of the house, and took her home. The only reason the guy that took my phone let us go was because it was obvious how scared she was. He knew she wasn't going to talk and he knew I had a pretty terrible reputation, so if I tried to cause trouble it would get shut down pretty easily."

Her next words were bit out and full of so much self-loathing and disgust that I had no problem figuring out why this young woman thought she deserved the worst the world had to offer her. "I did nothing. My best friend, my only real friend, was violated, drugged, taken advantage of at a party I made her go to, and I did nothing to make that right."

She pulled away from me and started pacing in a tight pattern again. "I bugged her for a few days to report the attack, but she kept shutting me down. I told her she needed to talk to someone, to tell her parents what happened at the very least. She pretended to listen, pretended like everything was okay, but she started to drift away. She wouldn't take my calls. She wouldn't look at me in the hallway. She wouldn't sit next to me in the classes we shared. She acted like I didn't exist anymore and what was even scarier is she acted like she didn't exist anymore. She was so withdrawn and remote it was like she wasn't even there. I knew we had no business being at that party and I had no business leaving her to fend for herself once we were there. I knew it wasn't her scene. What happened to her was my fault because she wouldn't have been there if I hadn't been there, if I hadn't been so hell-bent on doing whatever the fuck I wanted to do, so I figured the best thing I could do was let her hate me. It was pretty easy to do, since I was busy hating myself. I was miserable and I figured she had to feel a million times worse because after a few weeks I heard a rumor that she was pregnant."

She put a hand to her chest and bent over at the waist like she was having trouble breathing. She shifted so that her hands were on her knees and she was looking at the floor between her feet.

"I confronted her, asked her about the baby, and when she admitted that she was a couple months along, I told her that she had to tell her parents what had happened. I knew she couldn't go through a pregnancy alone and she had completely shut me out. She told me she didn't plan on keeping the baby, that no one was ever going to know what she had been through. She never once said it was my fault, but I knew. I knew, deep down, that it should've been me. I should've been the one going through what she was going through. I was the one that liked to party. I was the one that liked boys that were no good. I was the one that should be suffering and that should have no future, not her." She sucked in a wheezing breath and righted herself.

I could see the fact that Avett believed the punishment she had assigned herself for a crime she didn't commit was justified, that she honestly believed her story started and ended with what happened to her friend and her inability to do anything about it the night it happened and the carnage afterwards. That was a heavy burden for any soul to bear and was definitely too much weight for a young and wild soul to stand up under.

"That weekend, Autumn's mom called the house and told my mom that she found her daughter hanging from the rod in the closet. Autumn committed suicide. She didn't leave a note, so I was the only person that knew why. I went to the funeral, I watched her parents sob as they lowered her into the ground, and all I could think was, once again, I had done nothing. I hadn't told anyone. Maybe if I had, she would still be here to tell her story. For a minute, I even thought that it should be me in the ground, but I knew there was no way I could ever do that to my parents. I made them suffer enough because I spent every single waking hour trying to." She shrugged helplessly. "I guess I was trying to even the score. I went from being a girl that liked a party and a good time, to being a girl that was on the verge of destruction. I purposely found boys that were no good, instead of stumbling onto them like I had before. I started drinking a lot more, dabbled in drugs here and there, but quickly found out that wasn't something I enjoyed. I wanted to hurt, to feel the pain I knew Autumn went through, and drugs made me numb and made me forget. I stopped pretending to even kind of try in school, and stopped trying with my mom. Before that night I was wild, after that night I was out of control. I wanted to hurt in all the ways I could hurt, but it was never enough. I could never make up for what happened to her, what she lost. Eventually, I went to her parents and told them what happened. I told them about the party and the attack. I told them about the baby."

She lifted a hand to her face and pressed tightly into her temples. "I thought it would help them find closure, that they would have some solace in understanding that Autumn felt trapped." A tear leaked, finally escaped whatever invisible force field that had been holding them back as she spoke. It clung to her dark lashes and then dropped, falling silently, until it disappeared under the curve of her chin. "They told me what I had known from the night it happened. Her mom told me that it was my fault, that it should have been me. Their daughter was a good girl, a sweet kid, until she hooked up with me. I ruined her and then I killed her. They told me I was the one that should be dead, not their daughter. I deserved to suffer every ounce of pain that was filling me up for putting Autumn in that situation in the first place. I couldn't even bring myself to tell my parents what had really happened. They knew Autumn was gone, knew that I felt responsible, but they were already so disappointed in the choices I was making, choices that were so much worse than the ones I had been making before. I couldn't bear the thought of them looking at me like Autumn's parents did. If they blamed me as well, how could I live with myself? I was used to their disappointment but I knew I couldn't survive their disgust."

She swiped at the damp trail the tear had left on her face and returned her tortured gaze to mine. "So I did nothing and it killed my best friend. That's my story and her story, the entire ugly truth of it, Counselor." Her breath shuddered out of her and her watery eyes locked on mine. "Do you still like what you see and what you get when it comes to me, Quaid?"

Her self-loathing was evident, and so was the guilt and responsibility over the tragic event that was hanging around her neck like a leaden anchor.

I walked towards her until I had her backed into the door once again. I put my hands on either side of her face and tilted her head back so that she was looking up at me with wide eyes and an open mouth.

"I've been a defense attorney for a few years now, and if there is one thing that all my clients, whether they're innocent or guilty, have in common it's blame. It's always someone else's fault and it's always someone else's responsibility that they're in the situation they're in. No one wants to be accountable for the choices they made that led to them needing a defense in the first place. All of my clients are like that, except for you, Avett. You own your choices, you take the responsibility, and you don't make excuses for your behavior. What happened to your friend is horrific, and no young woman should ever have to go through that, especially alone, but she made the choice to go with you. She made the choice to take that drink. She made the choice to not say anything to people that could help. Did you force her to go with you that night?" She slowly shook her head in between my hands. "Did you tell her that your friendship was over if she didn't go with you?" Again with a negative response. "Did you do anything different that night than you did any other night the two of you went somewhere you probably shouldn't have been?"

This time she breathed out a soft, "No."

"Then you need to realize that what happened wasn't your fault. Was it awful and avoidable, yes, but the only people to blame are the men that attacked your friend. I don't care if both of you walked into that house naked and ready to party. Consent has to be given and those boys took the option to say yes or no away from her. They are at fault. Not you and certainly not her." I narrowed my eyes as I thought about how devastating that conversation with the other girl's parents must have been for her. "Her parents were looking for someone to hand the blame off onto because they were hurting and looking for a target to land that pain on. No parent wants to think they failed their child, that they may have missed the clues that their kid was hurting and in trouble and that they may have been able to do something to help them. It makes them feel inadequate as well as heartbroken. I see it every day in court when parents are in disbelief that their baby is capable of hurting someone else or themselves so they look for any other reasonable explanation as to how things could go so horribly wrong. It's gotta be someone else's fault. You painted a bright red bull's-eye on yourself and they fired at will."

I bent my head and kissed her softly, comfortingly. I rubbed my lips across her still-swollen ones and let my tongue trace the cute little dip in her top lip. She needed someone to take care with her, and while I didn't think I had any care in me left to give, I was surprising the both of us by doling it out like it was in endless supply.

"Your story doesn't change how I see you, Avett, but it does change how tolerant I'm going to be with your bad decision making because, sadly, your story is one that belongs to a lot of young women. Some even have the same tragic ending as your friend. Your story and her story are not singular and it kills me to tell you that I see similar stories with similar outcomes pass in and out of court all the time. Those stories all have one thing in common—guilt and blame, too often placed on the incorrect person. There is no need for you to be looking for some kind of cosmic punishment—you didn't do anything wrong."

At least, she hadn't that night. Doing nothing wasn't the right choice for either of the girls to make, but sadly, it was the choice too many young women that were victimized made when they found themselves in that situation. Too often the responsibility was taken on by the victim, instead of staying placed on the attacker where it belonged, and that blame did horrific things, like make her friend feel like there was no way out of everything she was suffering through besides ending her own life, and it clearly led Avett to believe she was the one responsible for the actions of those depraved and damaged boys.

She didn't respond, so I pushed back from the door once again and decided it was time for me to go. I had no more wisdom or guidance left to impart on her tonight. Plus, I needed a few minutes to myself to fully comprehend how complicated and deep the waters that ran inside this complex young women were. She fascinated me and captured my attention in a way that was alarming. I'd been focused on work and on moving on from my disastrous marriage so single-mindedly that to have all of that suddenly sidelined by an intriguing pink-haired temptress was enough to give a man whiplash.

"I'm going to see about the patrol unit, but you need to call your dad so that you aren't here the rest of the night alone."

She balked immediately at the order and took a step towards me. "I told you, I didn't want to pull him away from my mom."

I knew that was going to be her answer, so I shook my head before she got all of the words out.

"Call him, because I'm going to be on the phone with him in twenty minutes after I call DPD and ask them about a patrol. If I'm the one that wakes him up and pulls him away from a warm bed and a willing woman, it won't go over as well as if you do it." None of this was the way I typically talked to anyone, let alone a woman I desperately wanted to get naked and nasty with, but all my typical norms and behaviors seemed to have dried up and been replaced with this new incarnation of myself that was a haphazard mishmash of where I had been and where I was now. I let her go and pulled open the door. "This time, actually stay away from the goddamn windows. Whoever was driving that car nearly ran me over, so there is no telling what they would do to you if they get a clear shot."

She shivered a little and grabbed the edge of the door as I exited through it. "Aye-aye, captain." The sarcasm was heavy in her voice and in her actions as she lifted her fingers to her forehead and gave me a little salute.

"Seriously, Avett. You told me you never do the right thing even when it's the only thing to do, so this is me not giving you a choice. Call your dad and keep your head down until we know what in the hell is going on."

She frowned at my harsh tone but relented and gave me a little nod. "All right. I'll call him and stay away from the windows and the doors." Her timid tone halted me when I reached the bottom of the steps. "Quaid." I turned to look up at her and almost ran back up the front steps of the house when I saw how adorable and rumpled she looked propped up in the doorway. To hell with respect and rationale.

"Yeah?"

"Thank you for giving me your number. Thank you for answering my call. Thank you for showing up to make sure I was all right." She paused to catch her breath as the words tumbled out each faster than the other. "Thank you for being here and staying even after I gave you my story. Now you know exactly who I am, and you are so much more than nobody to me, Quaid."

I opened my mouth and let it close. I hefted the helmet up and fitted it over my tousled hair. Before I pulled it down to cover the rest of my face, I told her, matter-of-factly, "I wouldn't have done any of those things if you were anyone else, Avett. Your story doesn't change who you are or how I feel about you. Now, go inside and call your dad."

She gave a jerky nod and then disappeared back inside the house. I walked to where I left the bike parked in front of the house and waited for a few minutes to make sure none of the curtains or blinds twitched. I wanted to make sure that she was doing as she was told. When I was satisfied she had hunkered down and would indeed call Brite, I swung my leg over the bike and cranked the engine on. I decided I would cruise by the closest station house and ask them to send a cruiser through the neighborhood.

It was much harder to deny me what I wanted when I was there to argue my case in person.

CHAPTER 9

Avett

I don't need a babysitter. It's almost been a week and the creepy guys in the car haven't been back. I'm starting to think they were there to take out the bitchy neighbor across the street that won't lay off her poor boyfriend. If I was him, I wouldn't hesitate to order a hit on her mouthy ass. That seems like it would be way less painful than actually marrying someone like her."

I cut a look at the tall blond man next to me and was rewarded by his lips twitching slightly. He looked down at me with glimmering golden eyes and a smirk that I had seen break hearts and then repair them within the span of mere seconds. "I'm sure you have better things to do with your day than chauffeur me around while I look for a job." I was sick of being cooped up in the house, and frankly, I was sick of my own company. I decided it was time to do something, to do anything, to get my life back on track and that meant I needed to get a job. Doing nothing wasn't working for me anymore, and after the purge of all my deepest, darkest secrets and fears I laid at Quaid's feet, I felt a thousand times lighter and not as weighed down by the past. The fog of recrimination and accusation that I lived in hadn't exactly lifted off of me, but I was seeing through the density more clearly than I ever had before.

Doing something meant looking for a job, which I knew would be nearly impossible with a big, bearded biker in tow. After an hour or so of grouching and explaining how important it was to me to get out and be productive, Dad had relented and agreed to let me go on the job hunt, but only if I took one of his boys with me to watch my back should anything happen. In desperation, I acquiesced to his request, and as a result had been gifted with Asa's presence as my formal keeper and résumé holder all morning and afternoon.

The smirk on his ridiculously handsome face turned into a full-fledged smile and I heard the woman I had just handed my application to at the small coffee shop near my dad's house gasp. I was surprised she didn't use the stack of papers to fan herself. Asa Cross was hot enough to warrant that kind of reaction and she didn't seem all that interested in using the application and résumé I'd handed over to offer me a job, so she might as well get some use out of it.

"Believe me, watching you try to be charming and polite to people that you clearly want to strangle is way more fun than anything else that was on my agenda. Besides, your dad asked me to stick with you."

I rolled my eyes and pushed open the glass door that led back out to the sidewalk. "And when Brite asks his boys for something . . ."

Asa chuckled. "We show up and see it through."

I grumbled under my breath and scanned the small neighborhood to see if there was any other kind of shop or café I could stop in and plead my case with, but unfortunately it seemed like I had already made the rounds. I'd dropped my résumé and filled out repetitive applications at every place that had a help-wanted sign or that served some kind of food, with little luck or interest. I was getting frustrated and annoyed and Asa's obvious amusement at the situation made me want to kick him in the shin. I hadn't told him that the reason I was so desperate to find a job, or possibly two, was so that I could start to pay my dad back for bailing me out, and also, so I could work towards paying Asa back the money he ponied up to pay Quaid to represent me.

"I'm surprised he asked the charmer and not the soldier. You come armed with a smile, Rome comes armed—period." I tugged at the end of my braid and looked down at my dark skinny jeans tucked into well-worn combat boots and the long-sleeved flannel I had on with a lacy cami peeking out of the open collar. It was hipster chic and pretty standard wear for fall in Colorado, but I was wondering if I should have dressed a little more to impress. I wanted to groan. I sucked at impressing.

"Rome had a business meeting and an appointment with Cora, for the baby. She's ready to pop. Plus, as much as Rome admires and respects your dad, he's still working on getting over the robbery . . . both of them."

I cringed involuntarily and blew out a breath that turned into a sigh. "Yeah. I can't say I blame him for that." Hesitantly, I reached out and touched the back of his hand where it was wrapped around a to-go coffee. "So, why are you here, Asa? And why did you call Quaid the night I got arrested? You have as much, if not more, reason to hate me than Rome Archer does. Jared could have killed you and Royal that night." My voice cracked a little and I bit the inside of my cheek to keep more jumbled words and useless apologies from falling out. I couldn't even begin to express how devastated I would have been if something had happened to him and his pretty cop girlfriend. Asa had been on my case since our very first encounter at the bar. I played it off like I hated him, resented him for being the boss in the bar my family had always owned, mocked his troubled past and self-sacrificing ways, but the truth of it was, I admired him. I appreciated that he never judged me, never belittled me for finding myself in mess after mess. I'd never had any siblings, but if I did, I would want my big brother to be exactly like Asa Cross, flaws and all.

His amber eyes shifted from where I was touching him to my own and I saw a lifetime of truth and consequences glowing down at me.

"Have you ever heard your dad tell someone that he just met that 'like recognizes like'?"

I nodded absently. It was one of Brite's favorite sayings. He used it a lot when he met someone and could tell instantly that they had served in any branch of the military. He also used it when he was talking about his brothers on bikes. They might not all have been to war, but men searching for something, men looking for that kind of brotherhood, drew like to like.

"I've heard him say it."

Asa nodded and grabbed my elbow so he could walk me across the street towards a small strip mall that had several food trucks parked out in front. Each of the different trucks had a long line queued up in front of it, and the smells coming from them made my mouth instantly water.

Asa paused before we actually became part of the crowd and turned me to face him with a heavy hand on my shoulder. Those gold eyes of his were impossible to look away from, and even though the words he was saying were hard, his lyrical drawl made them feel like feathers when they hit me.

"We are alike, Avett, me and you. The shit you do, the shit you feel, after you do it." He shook his head and his shaggy blond hair fell onto his face. It was easy to see why he had such a potent effect on women and why trouble was so attracted to him. He looked like the kind of man that had being bad down to a science. "I've been there. In fact, before Royal, before Denver, I had a permanent place on rock bottom all picked out and was planning to live the rest of my life there. I knew I was fucking up, knew I was doing shit that would haunt me forever and hold me down, but I couldn't stop. I felt like I had to be the bad guy because I was a guy that had done so many bad things."

I wanted to shake his hand off and tell him he didn't know anything about me. But that was a lie. He did know, and even with that knowledge, he was still here, still trying to make me see that there was more than the next bad decision, and more than making myself feel bad because that's what I was so sure I deserved.

"The thing about rock bottom is that it gets crowded down there because there is always someone out there screwing up worse than you are. You can't see it because your head is so full of your own fuckups that other people's fuckups can't even register. We all have them, and I promise that whatever you think you've done that deserves the dumb shit you've been doing isn't as bad as some of the things happening out there in the big bad world. No matter how long you've been there on what you thought was the bottom clinging to the edge, thinking you've sunk as low as you can, someone else is going to come crashing down and shatter what you thought the lowest point was supposed to be.

They're going to fall right past you and suddenly you're left real-izing you can either fall forever because life is tough and full of pitfalls and there is no actual bottom to hit, or you can get your ass up and start climbing towards the top because a better life is waiting for you up there."

I cleared my throat. "When you started climbing, did you ever reach the top, Asa?" Because that seemed like an awful lot of work if the chances of pulling yourself out of the mire were slim.

He let go of my shoulder and flashed me that smile that screamed good times and trouble because he was full of both. "Not even close. Sometimes I even lose my grip and slip back-wards, but Royal and the life I have with her is always waiting for me at the top, so I never stop climbing, no matter how many times I fall. Every day it feels like I get closer and closer to the top, and whatever bottom I was wasting away on is nothing more than a memory." He lifted a blond eyebrow at me and reached out to tap the bottom of my chin with his index finger. "Start climbing, Avett. It gets tiring and your entire body and soul burns from the effort, but nothing will ever be as rewarding."

I took a step away from him and cleared my throat so I could speak around the emotion that was practically choking me. "You were always really good with words, Opie. But words won't fix all the things I've fucked up lately. That's like sticking duct tape on the cracks in the *Titanic*."

He sighed in exasperation and inclined his head towards the waiting lunch trucks. "I think you would be stunned by how much the right words can fix. Let's grab some food. I'm starving."

I agreed with a nod, thankful that he was going to let the heart-to-heart drop. His words were worthy of consideration because the idea of having another, more polished and proper blond head peeking at me over the edge as I stared up into what could be made a sharp shiver go down my spine.

My dad had been home and all over me since the night I called him home from Mom's. He wouldn't leave my side or let me go out without him, and while his concern was sweet and appreciated, we both had lives that we needed to move on with. That included me finding a job so I could actually be a productive member of society. Dad had mentioned asking Rome if he would consider taking me back at the bar, but I vetoed the idea immediately. I wasn't ready to face down the big, marked soldier yet and I knew there was no way my mom and I could share space in the kitchen right now without killing each other.

The constant vigil also meant I hadn't seen Quaid since the night he appeared like some kind of alternate, motorcycle riding, leather wearing, gun toting, and orgasm giving version of himself.

That orgasm though.

If I closed my eyes and concentrated really hard, I could still feel the way it felt like when he drew that response out of every single cell of my body. It was more than getting off and going about my business. It was something that lingered, that stayed with me, and blindsided me when I wasn't prepared to remember the pleasure and the carnality of it all. I'd had plenty of sex in my twenty-two years. Some of it better than others, but after my interlude with Quaid against the front door, I was realizing that sex was a lot like anything else that someone excelled at. The more practice you had at it, the better you were, and considering all my other partners were around the same age as I was, they were lacking in the knowledge department regardless of how many other women they had been with. Needless to say, I was pretty sure that Quaid was a professional in the bedroom as well

as in the courtroom, and after having his hands on me, I never
wanted to mess around with an amateur or an intern again.

Quaid touched me like he did everything else, confidently,
assertively, decisively, and without any question if I would like
what he was doing because he *knew* I would like it . . . hell, he
knew I would love it and lose my damn mind. If he hadn't put
a halt to things when he did, I would have wiggled the rest of
the way out of my overalls, dropped to my knees right there in
the middle of my dad's living room, and given as good as I got.
I was reckless, but there were lines I didn't cross and having sex
under my dad's roof had always been one of them. Until the sexy
lawyer showed up looking all badass and take-care-of-business in
a totally different way than he normally did.

He'd texted a couple times to tell me the police had no leads
and that the case against Jared was moving along normally. He
told me to get in touch with him if I needed anything but didn't
say anything else, and I figured it probably wouldn't do to text
him that I needed his dick in my hands and in my mouth, even
though I really wanted to. I was learning to slowly but surely
make those smart and appropriate decisions.

After a little debate about what truck we wanted to eat at, I let
Asa talk me into the one promising a modern twist on soul food
and was pleasantly surprised at how good everything looked and
tasted when we got our order. I loved food and I loved to eat.
Being in the kitchen, even when everything seemed terrible and
hopeless, had always been my refuge. I could throw a bunch of
ingredients together and was always impressed with whatever
result I ended up with. When Dad and Mom split I spent a lot
of time alone because Dad was at the bar and Mom wasn't one
to sit down and share a meal with me at the time. I cooked

dinner almost every single night in an effort to feel better about myself and so that I didn't feel so alone with my tragedy and guilt. There was freedom and comfort in creating with food that always soothed the parts of me that felt exposed and raw.

We walked over to a low cement wall and sat down, side by side, as we plowed through our fragrant-smelling lunch.

"So, Wheeler's lady sucks?" He asked the question around a mouth full of grits and I made a face at him.

"Yeah. She's always yelling at him and freaking out. She does it in the front yard and ambushes the poor guy when he gets home from work." I scowled. "There's also a red Honda that shows up in the driveway after he leaves for work, stays most of the day until it's about time for him to come home. I haven't seen who's driving it, but . . ." I shrugged. "She's awful and he seems like a nice guy so maybe one of his friends should mention the Honda." I gave him a pointed look as he grunted and wiped his face with a napkin.

"He's a supernice guy. He goes back with Nash and Zeb a long ways. He works hard, but never says much, and keeps his nose out of most of the drama that pops up. He's never brought his lady around, but I have heard a couple of the boys mention they aren't exactly missing her being part of things. We're all invited to the wedding in January." My dad's boys reached far and wide. They were all a tight-knit circle that seemed to be forever growing thanks to love, and all the rewards it brought with it.

I finished the corn bread I was shoving into my face and brushed my messy hands off on my jeans. "Maybe it's pre-wedding jitters or something."

Both his eyebrows danced up as he took my Styrofoam box

and headed to a trash can. "Maybe, but that wouldn't explain the Honda, would it?"

"No, it wouldn't. Since apparently I am completely unemployable, I will keep an eye on it and let you know if there's something solid you can take back to the car guy."

He chuckled and lifted his hands to push through his hair. I heard a soft sigh and turned my head to see a group of young college-aged women watching him like he was a matinee. I bit back a laugh as he told me he would appreciate it and offered a hand to pull me to my feet.

"You aren't unemployable, but you walk into these places practically screaming the fact that you're overqualified and that slinging sandwiches and pizza is below you. The people hiring realize you're only going to be there until something better comes along, so they don't want to invest the time and money on training you and getting you settled."

I blinked at him in stunned silence as he turned and pointed us in the direction of my dad's house.

"Overqualified? Are you high? I dropped out of college, I barely squeaked my way into graduating high school, and I got fired from my last job for stealing. I think making sandwiches and pizza is exactly where I need to be . . . if someone would give me the chance."

He shook his head and grinned at me. "That bullshit might work on someone that hasn't tasted your food or seen you run a busy kitchen during a lunch rush on your own. You can cook, Avett. You know food and what tastes good. You also know how to operate a line, which is something no college degree can teach you. You would run circles around the kids in these mom-and-pop shops and they know it. You need to live up to your potential, not sell yourself short." Asa had been my boss for the short time I worked at the bar, so it wasn't as easy to brush off his praise and his assertion that I had more to offer than two willing hands as it should be. He had seen me work and he had eaten my food. I was *good* in the kitchen, probably too good to be a short-order cook or a counter jockey. But I needed to do something, and I wasn't afraid to start off with that something being small, and easily managed and maintained.

From somewhere in the not so far distance, the wail of a siren split the air. I turned my head to try and track it and scowled at Asa. "That's what Quaid told me after the charges against me got dropped. That I should live up to my potential." I'd turned it around on him and made my potential sound like something sexual because I wasn't really sure what my potential beyond stirring up all kinds of trouble and chaos was.

"Quaid's a pretty smart guy."

He also was the best kisser I had ever tangled tongues with and had magical hands, but I doubted Asa needed to know that.

"He's also a very expensive guy, which is why I need to find a job, any job, so I can pay you back for hiring him for me." I tugged on the end of my braid as the sound of the sirens got louder and drew closer. "That's the least I can do after everything."

He came to a jerky stop and put his hand out in front of me, forcing me to stop as well. "Avett." His drawl was extra thick as he said my name quietly. "I didn't pay for Quaid. He called me right after he met with you, before the arraignment, and told me your dad was picking up the tab. I told Brite I would cover it, that I got the money from the farm when it sold, but you know what arguing with your old man is like." He shook his head. "You don't owe me anything, doll."

I felt like a ton of bricks had landed on me. I knew Dad had borrowed the money for my bail from his retirement fund, but if he had also paid Quaid's retainer, it meant he must have depleted the entire thing. My dad wasn't going to have anything left to live on; he was going to be flat-ass broke and it was all my fault. I put a hand to my chest as the reality of the fact that even though I had been on a mission to destroy my own life for years, the one that constantly kept taking the hits and kept getting damaged was my dad.

I must have zoned out and gotten lost in my own guilt and sucked into my own vortex of blame, as usual, because the next thing I knew, Asa had my quivering hand in his and was pulling me from my stupor into a flat-out sprint. He had long-ass legs and I did not, so I stumbled after while demanding to know what kind of bug he had gotten up his very fine southern ass.

"Hey, Opie . . . what the fuck?!" I barked out the words as he sped up even more once we hit the block my dad's house was on.

"Don't you smell the smoke? It's so close." He sounded legitimately concerned and as we rounded the corner the acrid and pungent smell of something burning hit me full in the face. I'd been too worried about the role I was playing in running my father's life to notice the sirens were practically on top of us, or that there was a thick cloud of black smoke floating over our heads.

I was short, but I managed to pick up the pace and keep up with him, even as dread settled like a lead weight in my gut. It was pretty clear the closer we got that there was a small army of police and fire trucks parked in front of my dad's house. It was also pretty clear that the cloud of smoke was coming from the beautiful brick building being entirely engulfed in flames that seemed like they were reaching up towards the sky.

The heat was air stealing and intense. So was the spectacle of neighbors and passersby that had gathered to watch everything I owned, everything my father had collected over his life, turn into ash and memory. I was shaking so hard that my legs couldn't hold me up and I fell to my knees on the sidewalk, clutching my chest. I couldn't see anything beyond the blur of tears in my eyes and I felt like the fire was hot enough that it was scalding me all the way to where I had crumpled to the ground. It was going to melt me on the spot, turn me into nothing more than a boiling puddle of guilt and remorse. A police officer came by and told us to back away, that it wasn't safe, and when Asa told him I lived in the home, I saw the pity and an apology on his face.

He helped Asa pull me to my feet and ushered us over to where the fire trucks were parked in front of the house. Waterfalls of water streamed out of high-powered hoses as men outfitted to battle the blaze rushed to and fro. A man that had on navy pants and a crisp button-up shirt with a badge that looked a lot like a police badge pulled me away from the other two men and started peppering me with questions I struggled to answer.

Was anyone home?

No. My dad was at the bar since I was with Asa, and Rome was out for the day.

Did I remember leaving anything on or candles burning when I left for the afternoon?

No. My dad was a certified badass . . . we didn't even have candles in the house.

Was anything unusual when I left the property?

No.

Was it possible I left something on like a curling iron?

No. I always double-checked everything when I left.

Did we have a gas or electric stove?

Gas, and no, I hadn't smelled propane or anything else that would indicate a leak.

Was the electrical in the home up to date?

Yes. Dad had had Zeb redo all the electrical a few years ago, after the toaster shocked him enough to knock him on his ass.

My head was spinning and there were a couple times I thought I was going to throw up on the man, because no matter how much water hit the house, the flames seemed to keep climbing and climbing. The house was being devoured by furious streaks of orange and red and I realized Asa was right. I'd thought being arrested and sitting in jail was as low as I would ever go, but watching everything I had, everything that mattered to my father, disintegrate in front of my eyes, I knew that jail was a false bottom and I was still falling . . . lower and lower. I couldn't even see the top anymore.

The guy continued to drill me, more questions that I didn't have the answers to, and eventually Asa came over and put his arm around me and pulled me to his wide chest.

"Called your old man. Both he and Darcy are on the way." He pressed his cheek to the top of my head and I squeezed him for all I was worth.

"How did he sound?" Heartbroken? Angry? Terrified? That's how I sounded when I asked the question.

Asa muttered something over my head and let me go. He set me away from him but kept both his hands on my shoulders and gave me a hard shake. It made my head snap back and had my teeth clicking together.

"He sounded scared out of his ever loving mind that his daughter might be injured. He sounded pissed as hell that he wasn't here to console you as you lose everything you own right before your eyes. He's worried, like any good parent would be, that this is tied directly to those creeps that were watching the house." He shook me again. "How did you think he would sound, Avett?"

I pulled away from him and buried my hands in my face. "Mad. I thought he would sound mad. If this is tied to those guys that were watching the house and me, then this is my fault. It's always my fault."

He growled a few ugly words at me and then crossed his arms over his chest as he glared.

"Did you start the fire, Avett?" His drawl was usually so silky and sexy; right now it was ragged and mean.

"Of course not. I've been with you all afternoon, and I know I didn't leave anything on. I always check."

"Exactly." The word snapped out like a whip. It was so sharp I jerked my head back like it smacked right across my tearstained cheeks. "And even if you did leave something on, it would've been an accident, so still not your fault. If you think I can't recognize someone actively searching for punishment, for a penance they think they have to pay, then you are sadly mistaken. I saw it in myself and sure as shit can see it in you, Avett. And I can tell you from firsthand experience that whatever it is you are trying to atone for doesn't care how many shitty things you do to make yourself feel bad, and it also doesn't care how those shitty things affect other people. In fact, it doesn't care about you at all, because it's still going to be there, existing in your rearview, and none of the crap you do to yourself is ever going to change the view. What you do now regardless of how good or bad it may be won't change what you did then and that's something you have to live with." His eyes darkened and the gleaming gold dimmed. "That's why I'm still climbing and may never reach the top. That's a heavy weight to haul around."

I wanted to tell him to get the hell away from me. I didn't want his acceptance and comfort to soften the rawness and ravages of what I was feeling. I didn't want him to see through me like I was made of glass. I didn't want to hear from some-one that knew exactly what I was doing, that it wouldn't work. I had convinced myself over the years that if I hurt enough, disappointed enough, lost enough, my penance would indeed be paid, and I could eventually go back to living a life where I didn't feel like I deserved every single bad thing that came my way.

I was going to snap that his lecture was unnecessary, that he had no idea what happened the night everything changed for me. He wasn't around when I realized I was toxic. That night wasn't just where my story started, but where it ended, too.

I never got the chance to say anything to Asa because at the same time my dad's massive truck and another big truck, which looked pretty similar, roared to a stop right beyond the barricades the emergency crews had set up. I thought Rome Archer was going to climb out of the other pickup and couldn't hold in a shocked gasp when it wasn't the scarred soldier that appeared, but instead there was a beautiful blond man in a perfectly tailored suit. Quaid took a minute to strip his suit jacket off and slammed the door to the truck before stalking towards us in his very shiny, very lawyerly looking shoes. I would have preferred the guy in the jeans and boots for this particular situation considering the smoke and soot in the air, but honestly, I would take him any way I could get him.

My mom and dad got to me first. I was wrapped up in a big hug and almost started crying again when my mom also folded me in her arms and whispered, "I'm so glad you weren't home. You scared both of us to death."

I squeezed her then stepped away as Quaid joined our little party.

"Everyone all right? Does the fire chief have any information? Do we know if it was an accident or arson?" He fired the questions at no one in particular as we all gaped at him. He must have noticed that all of us were still shell-shocked at the idea of everything being gone and gentled his tone as he reached out and brushed his thumb over my cheek. "Sorry. I was in court and didn't really have time to shift gears when I got the call. I'm still in cross-examination mode. Are you okay?"

I sighed and fought the urge to turn my face into his palm. "Yeah, other than the fact that everything I own, not that it was much, is now gone."

My mom cleared her throat and snuggled into my dad's side. He didn't seem to notice because he was too busy glaring daggers at Quaid and the spot on my face where his fingers lingered. "I told your dad, on the way over, that you guys are coming to stay with me," my mom said. "I'm taller than you, but I have enough stuff in my closet that you can borrow until we can start to replace your own things."

Shit. I hadn't even thought about that part of it. Where was I supposed to go now that the only place that had ever been home was gone?

Asa must have seen the panic in my eyes because he offered up, "You guys can come crash at the new house with me and Royal. We have the room and my lady isn't just gorgeous, she is also armed. Might be nice to have a cop on hand if this is tied to you testifying against the junkie."

My dad opened his mouth to refuse at the same time I opened mine to accept the offer. I didn't know how Asa's pretty girl-friend would feel about having me under her roof, but I would much rather be the bone of contention between the redhead and the southern charmer than the cause of unease and unrest at my mother's home.

As it turned out the dark horse, or rather the blond horse in the expensive suit, also wanted in on the race. Quaid touched my elbow and, like it had in court, the tiny gesture stilled some of the panic and anxiety that was rampaging inside of me.

"You can come stay with me. If someone is watching you, they'll never think to look for you at my place, and if this is tied to the case against the boyfriend, I can help navigate the legal waters you're going to end up swimming in." He waved at the house. "If this is arson, then it's a clear threat, which is tampering with a witness, and obvious witness intimidation. The police need to be informed about what's going on and how this could be tied to something so much bigger. I can help. I want to help you."

He had been helping from the very beginning, so unsurprisingly I was going to make the only choice that made sense . . . the absolute worst one.

I nodded at him and saw my dad frown as Asa gave me a speculative look.

"I'm going to stay with Quaid." And maybe when I was done letting myself fall in love with him, which would inevitably lead to him breaking my heart, I would finally have hit the threshold of hurt I was willing to put myself through as punishment. Because I was pretty sure when Quaid Jackson was done with me, there would be nothing on earth that could feel as bad or be as painful as that was going to be.

CHAPTER 10

Quaid

The cops grilled Avett for hours. They asked her a hundred different questions about her relationship with Jared, about the guys he stole the money and drugs from, about the robbery, and the guys parked out in front of her house. I was glad they were taking the situation seriously, but I was frustrated beyond belief that there was nothing they could do with the minimal information she gave them. All she could tell them was what the car that was parked out in front of the house looked like, and she had a vague description of what the guys that broke into Jared's apartment and roughed her up looked like. Hearing her halting and jerky words as she went over that evening and the details that she remembered made me want to put my fist through the nearest wall. This girl was a fighter, a tornado full of life and energy, and when those winds died down as she explained how scared she had been, as she told the detective interviewing her how close she had come to being violated and changed forever, the echo of emptiness and fear in her voice ripped at me and fired up possessive and protective instincts that I only seemed to have when it came to this pink-haired hurricane.

The detective told us he was going to speak with Jared, who was still behind bars as he was denied bail, and he informed us that he would be in touch as soon as he heard from the fire department on whether the fire was accidental or purposely set. There was no doubt in my mind the fire was a message, that it had been set for the purpose of intimidating and frightening Avett, but I couldn't figure out what they were trying to scare her or warn her off of. In my line of work, I knew there was always a motive behind actions, and once we had the motive I would feel a whole lot better about her safety. It was impossible to win a fight if you didn't know what exactly it was that the opponent had to lose, if they lost.

I hustled a very somber and very quiet Avett out of the cop-shop and offered to swing by the closest mall or Target so she could grab some essentials, but she shook her head and told me that all she wanted was a shower and a nap. Her normally creamy and rosey complexion was deathly pale and her pretty, pouty mouth was pulled in a tight line as she nibbled anxiously on the inside of her cheek. Her colorful eyes were bleak and rimmed with fine red lines as she blinked rapidly to keep the moisture I could see trapped inside at bay. The finality of the fire, the absolute destruction of everything tangible that she held near and dear to her, was hitting her hard. She was trying to keep the enormity of the loss and the emotions that went with it in check, but the pain she was feeling, the hurt that was swirling around her like a living and breathing thing, couldn't be ignored. I wanted to reach for her hand, to offer some kind of comfort and solace, but she was so close to the edge of entirely breaking that I figured I should wait until we got back to my place. She could shatter once we were there. Truthfully, the place was so sterile, so untouched by any kind of real life, that it could only be improved by the kind of mess that came with someone like this pink-haired handful. Her kind of destruction could be beautiful, if the right person was around to help her clean up the rubble and put the pieces back where they belonged.

I parked the truck in the attached parking garage and took her elbow so I could guide her to the elevator that would drop us off in the penthouse loft. She didn't say a word the entire ride up, and when I unlocked the door and ushered her inside, I was expecting her to be impressed by the high ceilings with their crisscrossed ductwork and the exposed brick that made up the back wall of the kitchen. I was expecting her to let out a little gasp at the three-hundred-and-sixty-degree views that showcased both the sweeping Denver skyline and the soaring mountains off in the distance. It was literally a million-plus view and it often did more to seduce women once they were in my home than anything I could say or do.

I should have known Avett wouldn't respond in any of the ways I was used to. She paid no attention to the expensive leather sectional. The colossal media center, which could rival an IMAX movie screen, didn't faze her. The imported marble floors under her combat-booted feet went ignored and so did the massive king-sized bed that was pushed up against a wall decorated with carefully curated artwork that probably cost more than her tuition for college had been. As a whole, she seemed entirely unimpressed by my meticulously decorated and designed home, but when her eyes hit the kitchen with its shiny, never-used stainless steel appliances and chef-quality range, some of her fire flared in her eyes.

She wandered over to the one part of my home that I never spent time in and caressed the six burner stove like it was her lover. She looked over her shoulder at me and flashed me a weak grin. "This kitchen is beautiful. I could spend a lot of time in here." It was on the tip of my tongue to ask her what she thought of the rest of the place, but considering she had lost everything and no longer had anything, seeking validation for a place filled with useless trappings she didn't even notice seemed thoughtless and adolescent. I wasn't sure why I wanted her approval so badly anyway. I was the one that had to live here, the one that had to have the packaging that matched what I was trying to sell to the world.

"The bathroom is through the door on the other side of the bed. I'll find you a T-shirt and some sweats to hold you over while I toss your stuff in the wash."

She nodded stiffly and walked around the granite counter-top that separated the kitchen area from the living room. She wrinkled her nose and tried to smile but it turned into a grimace that had my heart twisting as tightly as her lips.

"I smell like smoke, don't I?" She picked up the end of her braid and pulled off the tie that held the dusky, pink strands woven together.

I bit back a groan and made my way over to where she was standing, looking lost and so out of place in this overly extravagant loft. She was more breathtaking than anything seen out those expensive-ass windows, and she was far more interesting and colorful than any of the art that hung uselessly on the walls. I pulled her hands away from her hair and tunneled my fingers in the thick and oddly colored strands so I could finish unwinding her hair for her. She looked up at me with a cyclone of emotions swirling in her eyes and I knew all she could do was work through what she was feeling and let the storm rage. For her, I wanted to be impermeable and weatherproof.

"It was only things. You know that, right?" My voice was gruff, and when I had her hair loose and falling all around her face like a wavy pink cloud, I took a step back and met her troubled gaze.

She shrugged. "Only things, but those things meant a lot. All the stuff my dad kept from his days in the service, and the memorabilia he kept from the bar over the years—none of that can be replaced and that sucks, no matter how you look at it."

I grunted a little and moved towards the walk-in closet that lived under the stairwell that led to the upper loft, where my office and home law library were.

"You mean a lot, too, Avett. I'm sure your dad would be willing to sacrifice anything that he had as long as it meant you were safe and sound. You're both lucky."

She made a strangled sound low in her throat and started to move towards where the bathroom was located. I wondered if the slate walk-in shower, with its glass surround and multiple showerheads, would impress her half as much as the kitchen did. I doubted it, but I knew it would be a lot easier for her to let go, to break down in the shower, than it would be over the convection oven.

She paused at the doorway and looked at me over her shoulder and I knew that the tears she had been fighting back were going to fall any second. "Not exactly feeling lucky at the moment."

I wasn't surprised that was her response, but she *was* lucky. She was lucky she was out of jail, and that even though she tried to hide it, her innocence showed through. She was lucky that no one got hurt today and that the fire had eventually been contained so none of the neighbors' houses had been damaged. She was lucky she had two parents that loved her and supported her, no matter what kind of situation she was in. No one blamed her for the blaze today, no one except for her. She was lucky that she was young enough that none of her bad choices would be the be-all and end-all of who she was, and that she still had time to figure her life out. She was lucky that so many people wanted to keep her safe, and be there for her while she finished what was started the night of the robbery. She was lucky she didn't have to face anything that was happening or what was coming down the pike alone.

And I was one lucky bastard that she was here.

She wasn't here for the million-dollar view. She wasn't here because of the zeros attached to the balance in my bank account. She couldn't care less that I was on the fast track to making partner at the firm, and she wasn't here for what I could do for her. In fact, when the shit hit the fan, I had to force her to take my help.

When I got the call from Asa that Brite's house was in flames and that Avett was taking the blow hard, it had been all I could do not to run out of the courtroom in the middle of my cross-examination. I'd had to call a brief recess and debrief my second chair to finish the questioning before I could leave. I'd never left court in the middle of a session. I'd never entrusted anyone else to do the cross-examination because I was always sure no one would get the job done as well as I could. But today I didn't care; all I wanted to do was get to the scene of the fire and make sure that Avett was okay. As soon as I arrived, I knew I wanted to take her home with me.

She looked so small and fragile as the fire roared behind her. I wanted to take care of her. I was so convinced that Lottie had killed any kind of compassion and all the concern I had for other people, but when I saw Avett barely holding on, empathy flooded me. I wanted to make it better for her so badly I could taste it on my tongue.

And she had picked me. She was here with me, instead of with her parents where they could all grieve the loss together. She trusted me to make things better for her and believed that I had something to offer that no one else did. So even though I was convinced I was emotionally tapped out, and that my heart and soul were barren of anything viable to offer, I was going to scrape the bottom of the emotional barrel and offer Avett Walker whatever scraps I had left so I could help her through this.

There was plenty of time to settle into being the angry, bitter, jaded, materialistic son of a bitch I had become since my divorce. With her, and for her, I could simply . . . exist. I didn't have to force anything and life could simply be real. I wasn't sure if I knew what a real life even looked like anymore, but the longer I was around Avett, the better my cloudy vision of what should and shouldn't matter became.

I found an old T-shirt with ARMY scrawled across it in faded letters. The thing had fit when I was twenty pounds lighter and a lifetime less cynical. I knew there was no way in hell her tiny frame could fit into any of my sweatpants, so I rummaged around until I found a pair of soft flannel boxers that Lottie had given me one Christmas that were still in the packaging. I should have known then and there that if the woman I was married to, went to bed next to every single night, didn't even notice that I was a boxer-brief guy that the marriage was doomed. Her lack of interest in me and my underwear should have been the beginning of the end.

I knocked lightly on the door so Avett could hear me over the running water. She left the door open a crack and her smoky scented clothes, in a sloppily folded pile, were next to the sink. The sight made me grin because even when she was trying to be neat and tidy she was still a jumbled disarray.

"Avett, I'm gonna leave this stuff for you and toss . . ." I was going to tell her that her clothes would be in the wash but the words died on the tip of my tongue when her hiccuping sob sucker-punched me right in the heart.

I knew she was going to need a moment, that all her fight had drained out of her and left her depleted and worn, but I didn't expect her to be devastated, on the floor of the luxurious shower like a hurricane that had lost all the wind that kept it raging.

She was lying on her side, naked and shaking as water poured down on her. Her eyes were closed, but even through the steam and the water rushing over her face, I could see the tears squeezing their way out between her tightly clenched lashes. This was what uttered devastation looked like. This was the wreckage that was left behind after the storm passed. Another whimpering sound like that of an injured animal escaped her, and I couldn't stop myself from moving towards her. I'd heard men that had made their first kill and seen their friends and brothers in arms die up close and personal sound less tragic and heartbroken than she did at that moment.

I tossed the clothes that were now crushed in my clenched hands on the sink, and without even a thought as to what the water would do to my Bruno Magli loafers or my favorite silk tie, I walked into the shower and bent down so that the cooling water was hitting me and not her. I reached up to crank the tap off and picked up her quivering form. She was both too hot and too cold as she curled an arm around my neck and continued to whimper and cry into the now-soaked fabric of my shirt. She was shaking so hard that it was hard to hold on to her naked skin, not that my dick was concerned with her volatile emotional state. All it recognized was that she was wet, completely bare, and clinging to me like I was the last thing she had in this entire world. All of those things made the insensitive bastard very happy and very eager to get closer to her.

I flicked my sopping hair out of my eyes and balanced precariously as I juggled to hold on to her and to get out of my soggy and most definitely ruined shoes. I sat on the edge of the bed with her slight weight in my lap and lifted a hand so I could push her tangled and dripping hair away from her face. Water was leaching off of both of us and onto the hand painted duvet cover but I hardly noticed because she peeled her teary eyes open and locked them on mine.

"I'm a mess." Her voice was broken, and in her gaze I could see that her heart was, too. When I was younger, I never had anything, so losing it never even occurred to me. As an adult, I had everything and I told myself I would do whatever it took to hold on to *all* of it, but seeing this vibrant and vital woman destroyed and broken over things that could burn, lost over items that were only belongings, I started to wonder if my effort to acquire possessions of value and prestige had been misguided and focused on the wrong priorities all along.

"I know you are. That's kind of my favorite thing about you."

Her arm around my neck tightened and her chilly fingers found their way into the hair on the back of my head.

"Shut up." She said it without heat, and despite the sorrow in her gaze, a rough grin pulled at her mouth.

I tugged on the slippery strands of her hair and watched as it coiled around the length of my fingers. "It's true. I find the chaos that surrounds you fascinating and intriguing. It seems to be as much of who you are as this pink hair. You're never boring or predictable."

Her dark eyebrows furrowed a little and she shifted on my lap so that instead of sitting across my legs, she was straddling me, with both her arms around my neck and her very bare center hovering right over the damp cloth that covered my dick. Her breasts pressed into my chest and I bit back a groan as she reached for the knot in my tie, not to loosen it, but to pull me closer.

"I don't want to be chaos. I want to be something and someone that doesn't destroy everything that it cares about without even trying." She tugged me until our lips were lined up, and when I stuck the tip of my tongue out to trace the curve of her bottom lip, I could taste the salt from her tears and the tang of her longing.

"Some of us are born into the storm and some of us are born to chase after it, I guess." I breathed the words into her as she wiggled her ass and set herself more fully onto my erect cock. There was no missing the way that it throbbed between us or that the only thing separating me from her entrance was the cage of my metal zipper. I was going to have a permanent indentation from the fastener on the underside of my dick if she didn't stop moving around. I dug my fingers into the curve of her hip and lifted one hand to the side of her face.

She blinked at me and then leaned forward just enough so that her forehead rested against mine. "What happens when the person born to chase the storm finally catches it?"

I chuckled and rolled to the side so that she was trapped

between me and the mattress. "They ride it out. That's the only thing you can do when you're caught in a downpour."

Slowly, the sadness in her eyes started to break and a soft smile that was filled with all of that sweet she was so stingy with started to hover over her mouth and that was worth more than any single item I had fastidiously picked out for this loft.

She used her grip on my tie to pull me down into a kiss that was much softer and sweeter than the one up against the door. She also started pulling on the knot that stubbornly refused to loosen, now that it was wet. While she wrestled with the noose around my neck, I started pulling my clammy shirt off and went to work on devouring her mouth. I wanted to leave no part of her untouched or untasted. I wanted to take away the burn of the fire and loss and replace it with scorching passion and the blaze of desire. I wanted her to forget what she was mourning, for a little bit, so we could revel in what we had. Because whatever this thing was that we had when the two of us were together, it was something that absolutely deserved a fucking celebration.

When I had my shirt off and the stupid tie wrenched over my head since it wasn't coming undone, I leaned over her with one hand braced over her head and used the other to cup one of her breasts. Her skin was warming back up and the delicate, pink tip wasted no time in stabbing into the center of my palm as I gently fondled her. I kissed her lips, the corner of each eye that was still red and a little puffy. I kissed her flushed cheeks and the tip of her wrinkled nose as she made a face at me. I kissed her below her ear and nuzzled her jawline as I moved my hand down her torso.

Goose bumps followed my fingertip as it traced over her ribs, down across her belly, and into the little indent of her belly button. Her legs shifted restlessly on either side of my hips and her hands slid over my heated flesh in a sweeping caress.

Her voice was breathless and a little stunned when she turned her head and muttered in my ear, "I can't believe you have a big-ass tattoo like that."

I was nipping at the pulse point on the side of her neck hard enough to leave a mark. That wasn't my typical style in the bedroom. I liked things orderly and discrete. With her, though, I wanted to be remembered. I wanted her to look in the mirror and see what we had done. I wanted her to feel me when she moved, and I wanted her to remember what my voice in her ear sounded like as I made her come. I wanted her to be as consumed by this thing that raged between us, unchecked and untamed, as I was. So I sucked on the little bite I left and lifted my head as my wandering hand reached the apex of her thighs.

Her belly quivered when she realized where my touch was going but her swirling gaze was locked steadily on the giant image of the eagle I had tattooed across the entire center of my chest. In one talon, the massive bird of prey held a shotgun, in the other, the scales of justice. I'd gotten it on a whim as soon as I passed the bar. The thing took forever to complete since it was so big, and after every single session, Lottie had berated me for ruining my body forever. She hated it and had often asked me to leave my shirt on when we were in bed together.

From the look on Avett's face, she anything but hated the bold artwork that decorated my body. She also didn't hate it when I slid my fingers over her slick folds and found the warm and welcoming entrance to her body. Her hips canted up towards me and her hands fell to the tense muscles across my shoulders.

I kissed the crest of each breast and muttered against her soft skin, "I'm full of surprises."

She laughed a little, but it turned into a quiet moan as I engulfed the tip of one of her breasts in the heat of my mouth. They were so firm and full. So proud and pretty, the way they sat up high on her chest. I wanted to drag my cock between them. I wanted her to let me glide between the soft valley they would create, while she opened her pouty mouth and sucked me off at the other end. I wanted to imprint myself and all the greedy and needy ways I wanted her on every single part of her body. I rolled the pert and pointed nipple around the tip of my tongue as my fingers plowed through her moisture and rubbed against her begging clit.

Her hands fell from my back and worked their way around to my front, where she started to claw at the clasp of my belt. She was panting hard and wiggling underneath me in a way that made my entire body tight. My dick was demanding to be let in on the action but this wasn't about combusting. It was about a slow burn that would warm her up and stay with her.

I let go of the nipple I was torturing with a little pop and moved my mouth to her ear. I traced the delicate shell with the tip of my tongue and told her, "Hold off on that for a minute."

Her legs tried to clamp down around my questing fingers as I used them to pump in and out of her grasping channel, but my hips were in the way. "I want to see what other surprises you have, Quaid."

The little whine in her tone made me laugh. I'd had a lot of women anxious to get at the goods, but usually that was only because they thought the goods could get them something else. I couldn't remember ever being in bed with a woman that pouted because I didn't pull my dick out fast enough to satisfy her. I'd never been with anyone eager to simply be with me because I was me. She was as full of surprises as I was.

I licked across her collarbone, caught her little center of arousal between my fingers, and gave the nub a gentle squeeze before letting go of that secret and pulsing flesh. The motion had her jerking up on the bed, which worked as I stood up between her legs and looked down at her.

"What are you doing?" She seemed bewildered and I liked that, for once, I was the one causing confusion and chaos between the two of us.

I grinned at her and felt it widen as she sighed a little and put a hand to where I knew her heart was racing in her chest.

"Surprising you."

She gasped my name in a shocked cry as I fell to my knees at the edge of the bed so that my face was directly in line with her core. She moved to close her legs but my shoulders were in the way, so she tried to scoot back on the bed but I was faster than she was, and grabbed hold of her hips so that I could pull her to my waiting mouth. I loved that when I put my hands and my mouth on her, there was something there to hold on to. Avett Walker might be as unpredictable and as untamable as the Colorado weather, but everything about her felt substantial and real in my hands.

I kissed the skin of her inner thigh and used my tongue to follow the curve of her leg where it dipped into her shiny and aroused center. I liked the pink on the top of her head an awful lot, but I had to say the luscious and welcoming pink that was begging to be licked and sucked between her legs was, hands down, my favorite and I told her so.

She gave a halfhearted protest when I hefted her up just enough that she had to put her legs on my shoulders to keep her balance as I set about consuming every single part of her.

I feasted on the juices that my mouth brought forth. I inhaled the moisture that my grinding and pumping fingers slicked through. I tasted every quiver, every shake, every flutter that her inner walls made as I fucked her with my fingers and my tongue. I nibbled on that coiled bundle of nerves like it was the finest dessert I'd ever had, and when her hands were suddenly tangled in my hair and pulling me closer as she mumbled my name over and over again, I went back for seconds.

I ate at her, sucked on her, licked her from top to bottom until she was a thrashing and incoherent mess, and when she came across my tongue and her rush of desire flooded my mouth, she did it like she did everything else, wild and sweet. Her chaos enveloped me and I was pretty damn sure that there would be no getting free from it.

I surged to my feet between her now-lax legs and put a hand to my belt buckle. She was lying there limp and quieter than she had ever been in my presence. Her eyes were wide and un-focused, but there was the barest hint of a smile tugging at the corners of her mouth. She looked destroyed again, but this time it was beautiful and sexy. I wanted to pound on my chest and give myself a really douchey high five for being the one to put that look on her face.

My pants hit the floor with a damp plop and her eyes never left me as I peeled my black boxer briefs down my legs. My excited cock bounced at finally being set free and had no trouble aiming itself right at the heart of her. My dick was like some kind of sex- and heat-seeking missile and knew exactly where the sweet spot was.

Her eyes widened a little bit and she sat up so that my cock was level with those glorious tits I was now having X-rated fantasies about fucking. She reached out her index finger and slowly spread the moisture that was gathered at the tip of my aching erection around the tip. I caught her wrist and gave her a pained look.

"I need to get a condom and get inside of you. If you put your hands on me I'm not going to last long enough to do either of those things."

Her eyes widened a little and she let her hand drop. She bit the curve of her bottom lip and I growled. I couldn't stop myself from leaning forward and putting my teeth where hers had been. When I lifted my head, she looked a little dazed and a whole lot turned on. I kissed her again and told her I would be back in a second.

The entire walk to the bathroom I scolded myself for not having a nightstand to keep my rubbers in. Having protection on hand when I needed it most suddenly seemed far more important than the view. I swore under my breath the entire time I walked away, and I swore loudly and desperately the entire time I walked back to her.

While I was gone, she had moved up on the bed so that her head was where it was supposed to be on the pillows and she was lying with her legs splayed, one small hand working between her thighs and the other clutching at her full breast. Her eyes were locked on me as I prowled towards her and there wasn't an ounce of embarrassment or shame in them as she smirked up at me while licking her lips like she was starving and only I could sustain her.

"You took all the fun stuff with you when you left so I had to occupy myself somehow." Wild was fun. Sweet was addicting, and I wondered if I could live inside chaos forever if this was what it looked like.

My hard-on wouldn't allow for any more playtime. My dick demanded satisfaction and my balls felt like they were so tight that they might explode at the first touch of her against my needy flesh.

I crawled up over her and marveled at how much might was packed into such a tiny body. I braced myself over her with one arm, and put my other hand on top of hers, where it was leisurely stroking through the dampness left over from her earlier release. I kept my eyes locked on hers as I slowly started to work my way inside her body. Every inch that gave, every millimeter that accepted me and squeezed around me, felt like the greatest accomplishment I'd ever achieved.

She was pliable from my previous attentions and the dual manipulation of our fingers, but she was still small and I was not. It took more patience and more willpower than I ever used with anything to get my raging erection seated all the way inside of her. Once I was there and I could feel her body start to loosen and liquefy around me, I began to move.

I had every intention of taking my time, of enjoying the buildup and the slow burn I was still trying to stoke. Those intentions went to hell the second she curled her leg around my hip and dug her heel sharply into my ass. She tossed her head back on the pillow and started to pull and twist her nipple between her fingers with more force than I would have ever used on the velvety tip myself, and she abandoned our joint stimulation of her clit to dig her short nails into my side as she told me, "More. I want more." And I wanted to give her everything she had lost and then some.

I'd never been the type to deny a woman anything she wanted in bed, and there was no way I was going to start with this one.

So we rode out the storm. Together.

I bucked into her. I pounded her into the mattress and I rode her hard and long. I kissed her until we both ran out of breath and thrust into her like I was using my cock to tattoo my name inside of her. She fluttered around me and clamped down to pull me deeper and deeper inside of her. It wasn't exactly a perfect fit but it felt real and it felt raw. We had to work together to find pleasure. We had to give and take, to make sure we moved against each other, and on each other, so that we both got what we needed. It was sex that took some work to make it amazing. That meant it was sex that was unforgettable and ultimately rewarding, like no sex before it had ever been.

We writhed together. We pulled and pushed at one another. We left marks. We took each other's air and screamed and growled each other's names. We sweated against each other and we burned everywhere we touched. We ruined each other and we repaired each other. It felt like the beginning and ending of everything I had ever known.

I lost my grip on her slippery center but that was okay, because her clever little fingers were back and every time she brushed across that quivering point between her legs, the back of her knuckles also rubbed along my engorged cock. It was the best caress ever and only better when she started to purposely put as much friction as she could at the base of my cock as I hammered in and out of her.

I felt my balls draw up tightly against my body and a sharp coil of pleasure suddenly tense, hard at the base of my spine. I wasn't going to last much longer, and from the red in her face and the way she was moving under me, neither was she. I wanted her to come with me inside of her, with me riding her rough and hard, more than I wanted any of the useless shit I was so consumed with day in and day out. I wanted to have that unguarded, unfiltered pleasure wash all over me and then I wanted to make her give it to me again and again.

"Avett." I said her name because there weren't any other words that mattered as much in that moment. I felt my cock twitch and my heart start to thunder.

Her eyes locked on mine and she moved her other leg up around my waist and pulled her arm out from between the two of us and curled it around my shoulders so that she was wrapped entirely around me. "Quaid."

My name on her lips as she broke apart underneath me whispered across me at the same time an inferno of pleasure ripped through my insides. I came in a rush that followed hers. I came in a blaze that burned away any memory of any girl that was before. I erupted in a stream of satisfaction and completion that left me empty and drained as I collapsed on top of her.

That hadn't been an orgasm. That had been a reckoning.

I felt the barely there brush of her lips against the side of my face as she breathed into my ear. "I guess at the end of the day it's better to have nothing with the right person than to have everything with the wrong person, isn't it?"

She was absolutely right about that.

CHAPTER 11

Avett

"I still can't believe you have such a giant tattoo." A tattoo that was currently flanked on either side of his flexing and rippling chest by his unbuttoned shirt. He was pulling up a pair of light gray pants, and I wanted to sigh in disappointment when they covered up what was one world-class ass. The man looked phenomenal in a suit and I really appreciated how he looked rough and ready in jeans and leather, but where he really shined was when he had nothing on at all.

Without clothes to conceal him or to define him, the real Quaid Jackson couldn't hide. The tattoo that covered up most of his torso stood out bold and defiant on his lightly tanned skin. I grew up around inked men and had always appreciated a well-done piece. His was something special, maybe because it was so unexpected. I think I liked that he had something so outrageously and undeniably traditional marked on him. It made me feel like maybe there was hope for him not to sink even farther into the designer labels and shiny baubles that consumed his life and his space. I also liked that he had a wicked-looking scar that sat right above his hip and another one that ran lengthwise down his ribs and across his hip. The big one on his side was about twelve inches long, raggedly healed, and made his otherwise perfect body look more normal. He had a flaw, which made me like him even more than I already did. I asked if he got it when he was overseas and all I got was a grunt and a muttered, "I've had it since I was a kid." With the scar and the massive amount of ink, Quaid could easily pass for one of those Instagram guys that had a million followers and had a zillion likes on every image they posted. That much perfection was intimidating, so I was glad that when he was naked every single thing that made him both beautiful and imperfect was on display. And those abs and that ass didn't hurt anything either.

Currently, I was hating that he was covering it all up. All I could do was forlornly watch as he put what I was starting to consider his lawyer costume back on, while I sat on the edge of his bed wearing nothing but his ARMY T-shirt and some seriously tousled-sex hair. He looked down at his bare chest after my outburst and then looked back up at me and shrugged.

"When I was in law school I did an internship for the state attorney general's office. There was this guy there named Alexander Carsten. He had a bunch of tattoo work done that was really impressive. When I passed the bar, I decided I needed to do something to commemorate my life finally going in the direction I wanted it to."

I lifted my eyebrows at him. "The tattoo was your big rebellion before you decided to grow up?"

He shook his head sharply and that wayward lock of blond hair that refused to be tamed fell into his pale blue gaze. "No, my act of rebellion was joining the Army. It was the last thing my folks expected me to do." I opened my mouth to ask him what had happened in his family because it was the second time he mentioned them being disappointed in his choice to enlist but he kept going, apparently not wanting to talk about his bitter break from his past. "I made an appointment with Alex's guy, a kid with a purple Mohawk and a pierced lip named Rule Archer. I told him I wanted something that represented where I had been and where I was going. He knocked the design out of the park, so I didn't care that it was this big. Very few people ever see it."

I laughed a little and reached out to pull him closer to me by the belt buckle he had fastened. I started to work on closing the buttons on his shirt, but I may have spent more time petting his seriously defined stomach muscles than I did actually helping him get ready. "I actually know Rule pretty well. His older brother, Rome, is the guy my dad sold the bar to. Rome's the guy that had to fire me for stealing from the register." I made a face as I got halfway done with the buttons. "He's the guy that's still pretty pissed at me and that I need to apologize to. If there's any way I can make it up to him, I need to figure out how to do that. Rome is like the son my dad never had. I can't have him hating me forever."

I sighed and rose to my feet in front of him so I could finish closing the buttons. When I got to the ones at the base of his throat I lifted up onto my tiptoes so I could press my lips to the strong cords of his neck before buttoning him all the way up. I really did like the suit, but I definitely liked him better out of it.

I tilted my face up towards him as he put his hands on either side of my face and used his thumbs to caress my cheeks. We had weathered the emotional storm that pounded against us yesterday, and the calm and quiet of the aftermath was something entirely new to me. I wanted to bask in it, absorb it, and let some of that tranquillity that had sunk into my bones calm the chaos that always seemed to rage and collide inside of me.

"I doubt he hates you. You need to give people the chance to forgive you, Avett. You screw up, but then you throw up a wall and wallow in the blame, so deep and thick that you never give anyone the opportunity to tell you that yes, you made a mistake but that's not the be-all and end-all of things." His fingers moved to my jaw and I wanted to rub my face against his warm hand and gentle touch like a cat. "You accept the consequences of your actions like a champ, now you need to learn to accept the exoneration as well." He was sexy when he spoke lawyer to me.

I'd never thought I deserved to be forgiven, so it never occurred to me that anyone besides my father, the one person that had always loved me unconditionally, would be waiting with a pardon and an open heart after all the damage I was capable of creating. I cleared my throat and forced a weak smile. "What I need to do is let you finish getting ready for work. Are you sure you have time to drop me off at my mom's on your way to court?"

He had offered to let me stay at his place since it was a secure building with a doorman and a security staff, but there was no way I was going to risk breaking or ruining anything in his swanky pad. I was afraid to touch anything, even though he told me no less than ten times to make myself at home and relax. So, since this was as far from home as I could ever be and considering there was no way I was going to relax, I was going to my mom's house and raiding her closet and hopefully burying the hatchet with her while he went to work. He wasn't thrilled with my decision. I think he really wanted me to like his space and I did, as long as he was in it. Without him in the elegant and tricked-out loft, I felt like an intruder, like the expensive finishes and imported floor knew I didn't deserve the right to use them. It might be entirely irrational but I had no desire to spend the day tucked in one spot because I was afraid the appliances would revolt against me and run me out of the place screaming.

"I told you, I'll make the time to drop you off and I'll make the time to take you shopping afterwards, if you want to go." He lifted a blond eyebrow at me in question.

I'd already told him no. I didn't want him to buy anything for me. Considering how much my family already owed him, the idea of him spending anything else on me made my skin tight and my tummy turn in on itself. It was already going to take a lifetime to pay him back because there was no way I was going to let my dad drain his retirement, on top of losing his home, and all his earthly possessions. I was going to have to figure out a way to pay Quaid back for everything and I wasn't about to add to that tally.

"I told you." I reached out and ran my hand over the front of his pants. I heard him suck in a surprised breath as I palmed his impressive package and gave it a squeeze for good measure. "I'm after what's in your pants, not what's in your wallet, Quaid."

I grinned up at him as the flesh in my grip started to swell and rise into my hand. It was an insanely powerful feeling to know that I could make a man that seemed so collected and controlled react instantaneously to a simple touch. I liked that his composure was nowhere to be found when I put my hands on him. I liked that he didn't think; he simply reacted to me and to how I made him feel.

His thick fingers encircled my wrist and I thought he was going to pull my hand away, but he didn't. He pressed my palm even flatter against the now fully extended length of his cock under the fabric of his pants and rubbed it back and forth.

"I'm offering you both." He virtually growled the words at me and when I looked up at him his eyes were almost silver with the way they glowed and lightened as his desire flared to life deep in the depths. He was offering me both, but he didn't understand why, any more than I did.

We were watching each other intently. There was no veil there, no place for either of us to hide anymore. He knew I was a disaster and I knew he was so much more than he seemed to think he was. I hadn't lied to him yet, so I wasn't about to start now.

I moved my other hand to his belt and told him the truth. "I just want you." And in case my words weren't enough to prove it to him, I had no problem showing him.

Eyes still locked together, I pushed him back a step so that I could get on my knees in front of him. I kept waiting for him to tell me to stop—after all, he was due in court, and we did have a schedule to keep. But he didn't utter a peep as I worked the buttery leather of his belt loose, and he didn't make a sound as I popped the button on his pants or when I pulled the zipper down. He also didn't protest when I rubbed my cheek against his hot, cotton-covered flesh as I reached for his black boxer briefs. He did thread his fingers on one hand through my multicolored hair and exhale a breath that sounded like it had every ounce of control he possessed in it. I told him to keep the tails of his meticulously ironed shirt out of my way as I eyed that intimidating bulge.

I kissed each of his hip bones and tickled that sexy V that cut down towards the cock I was slowly revealing. The end of my nose brushed through the springy, golden hair that arrowed right at his throbbing flesh and his fingers were rough as they scraped impatiently across my scalp. He was impatient and so was his dick. The long and rigid flesh pulsed with its own kind of life and need as it fell into my waiting hands once I had him completely uncovered.

Quaid's cock was a lot like the rest of him, graceful in its length and size; if there was such a thing as a well-made dick, this was it. It was sturdy in the way it bobbed happily away from his corded abs and into my eager hands and it was secure in the way it knowingly pulsed and pearled up in anticipation with the first swipe of my tongue across the sensitive head.

I swirled my tongue around and around as I tasted him and learned him. I wrapped my fist around the base of his erection and tightened my hold until his hips bucked and he shoved himself into my welcoming mouth. I would have giggled at his impatience, but I'd never had an executive cock in my mouth before so I wanted to make sure I had time to savor the experience.

I sucked on him, explored every ridge and detail with my tongue. I bathed the firm flesh in moisture and used my hand to add a different element as he curled a wide palm around the back of my head and started to move my head in the rhythm he wanted. That was the difference between an executive and an intern. An executive showed you what to do; they instructed you in the best and most efficient way to get the job done. An intern showed up with too many questions and inadequate skills.

I'd never had anyone actually fuck my face before, but that's what Quaid was doing and it was one of the hottest things that had ever happened to me in the bedroom. It was unbelievably arousing to have him being the one that was wild and sweet.

He told me to open wider. He told me to suck him harder. He told me to take more of him in and to squeeze him even harder.

But he also told me I was amazing. He told me my mouth felt like a dream. He told me that his hands wrapped up in my pink hair was going to make him blow. He told me he had imagined what I would look like on my knees in front of him for weeks and the reality was so much better. His wild was superhot, but it was his sweet that had me wet and aching between my own legs. If I wasn't so focused on him and so consumed with making this as good as I could for him, I would have slipped my free hand under the T-shirt and gotten myself off while I swallowed as much of him down as I could.

To stay on task and not get distracted by my own sudden and sharp arousal, I skimmed my free hand over the rock-hard curve of his ass and tickled my way between his legs. He swore loudly when I brushed my knuckles across his tautly drawn sac, and because his voice was strained and his hands were getting harder on my head, I could tell he was close. I sucked until my cheeks hollowed out and used the flat of my tongue to lap at the salty moisture that was leaking out of his tip. Even his taste seemed more refined and more palatable than anyone else I had ever been with like this before.

He growled my name above my head as he lost control of his steady motion and began to practically grind himself into my mouth. I cupped the sensitive spheres that hung heavy between his strong thighs in my hands and rolled them lightly across my palms. That was all it took to push him over the edge.

He didn't warn me. He didn't give me the choice to stay or go. He didn't do anything but pull me closer and hold me to him in an almost desperate motion as he pumped into my mouth. He said my name on a long sigh as I moved my hands to either side of his hips and took what he was giving to me.

When he stilled and I pulled back with a smug grin on my face, I thought he was going to tell me that it had been fun but now we needed to haul ass to get back on track for the day. I wasn't expecting him to pull me to my feet or for him to forcibly back me into the bed. His eyes blazed at me with winter-colored fire and I lost all the air in my lungs when he pulled the borrowed T-shirt over my head and made himself at home between my legs.

I was already wet but at the first kiss of his mouth against my tender folds I went torrential. Bringing him pleasure and knowing I was the one that had made him lose control had me at the edge of coming already, so he wasn't going to have to do much to get me the rest of the way there. I moaned at the ceiling and felt no shame in writhing against his working mouth to get some kind of relief for the coiled tension that was tight throughout my entire body. Sucking a guy off had never been such a turn-on. It was my turn to twine my fingers in his thick, blond hair and pull him closer to me as I rode his mouth like it was a carnival ride. When he added his fingers to the party and used his teeth on my already primed clit, I burst across his thrusting fingers with a flood of desire that felt like it would never end.

When the heaving chests and racing hearts started to slow, I pushed myself up on my elbows and looked at him as he pulled himself up so that he was standing between my splayed legs as he tucked his shirt into his pants and refastened his belt. He looked a little rumpled and a little sexed up, but in my personal opinion it made the suit that much sexier. He bent over me and braced himself on his hands so that our noses were almost touching.

"Everything in my life is always about who has what or who is trying to get what from someone else. Every day it's who did this or who did that and it gets really fucking old, Avett. I don't want there to be a set of checks and balances between us."

I gulped a little bit and reached up so I could put a hand on his smoothly shaved cheek. "You know that isn't possible, right? We do not come from the same place."

He narrowed his eyes at me and I shivered at the chill that emanated from them. "Maybe not, but when we're in bed together, we are definitely in the same place. It's not what you have that matters here, and it's not what I have that matters. All that matters is what we have together. Where you've been and what you've done don't exist here and the same goes for me. The only thing that counts is that we're here and what we do while we are in this moment."

I moved my thumb so that I could stroke it across his lower lip. It was still damp and shiny from the very thorough loving he had just bestowed upon me. That was probably the nicest thing anyone had ever said to me, but I knew the truth, and the truth was that everything we did before mattered, and he and I would never be on equal footing, even in bed. He was an executive, and while I wasn't exactly an intern, there was definitely room for upward movement. Whenever I was with him I felt like I was learning something new—about him, about myself, and most definitely about what sex and intimacy could be like, if you weren't using it to hurt.

"You have to get to work and I already made you late." It wasn't what he wanted; I could see that in his eyes as they went a colder shade blue as he pulled himself up and off of me. I didn't have much to offer a man like Quaid Jackson, so the truth was going to have to suffice, even if it made him look at me like he regretted not letting me fire him from the beginning.

"So THE LAWYER? What's going on there?" My mom's voice was curious but also cautious as she asked me the question. I could see her hoping my answer was that I'd finally found a man that would keep me out of trouble, but the more time I spent with Quaid, in bed and out of it, I realized he was the biggest trouble I had ever waded my way into. The fall when things imploded with him might very well be the end of me.

I barely heard her over the disbelief and wonder that had me stunned stupid and stuck on the spot as I gazed at the bounty of stuff that was covering the small twin bed that had been mine whenever I stayed with her when I was younger. I hadn't been inside of this room since I was a teenager and to see it covered in clothing and essentials from top to bottom had me overwhelmed with emotion.

I had a hand to my throat and was fighting really hard to blink back tears as I turned to look at her. "I can't believe they did this. I can't believe they cared enough to do something so nice after I've been nothing but terrible to them."

There was no need to raid my mom's closet for the bare essentials because all of the girls that belonged to all of my father's boys had shown up in full force with every single thing I would need to survive the loss of everything I owned. There were more clothes than I owned before the fire, some new with visible tags and some worn and comfy looking. There were shoes and socks. There were undergarments that ranged from practical to sassy. There was stuff that looked soft and welcoming to sleep in. There was makeup and junk for my hair. There was a brush and hair dryer. There was a toothbrush. I hadn't even thought about the fact I would need a toothbrush, until this morning, when I had to use my finger to brush my teeth at Quaid's place.

The girls had gone out of their way to make sure I had a little bit of everything I lost, and I was so touched, so humbled, that I couldn't even function. My mom put her hand on my arm and I looked at her as she smiled at me.

"Your father has a knack for finding the good ones, and those girls . . ." She spoke about the wonderful women that had done this for me, and I saw something in her face that I never saw when she talked about me or to me—pride. "They have some of the biggest hearts I've ever seen. They have to in order to put up with those stubborn and wonderful men they chose to love."

I cleared my throat awkwardly, and told her, "I'm not sure how I'll ever be able to thank them for all of this. I feel like it's too much. I don't deserve this type of kindness from any of them."

Her hold on my arm tightened and she pulled me around so that I was facing her. Her eyes, the ones where the green and gold in mine came from, locked intently on my face. "They didn't do it because they wanted your gratitude or because they gave a single thought to whether or not you are worthy of an act of compassion and caring. They did it because, to them, it was the right thing to do. Your father has stepped in and helped out so many of their young men when they needed some guidance. To those girls this was simply what had to be done." She grinned at me again. "To be fair, they would probably do the same thing for anyone in a dire situation, but the fact that you're Brite's daughter definitely doesn't hurt matters." Her dark eyebrows shot up and the softness on her face faded back to curiosity. "So, the lawyer?"

She shifted gears, but I was stuck on the fact that I had all this stuff and that I wouldn't have to go without, or struggle to replace the bare necessities, all because a group of women that I hardly knew, that owed me nothing, thought it was the right thing to do. I wondered what that felt like. I wondered if knowing what was right felt as warm and as bright as being on the receiving end of that kind of positive action. I was warm, from my head to my toes, and my heart felt so full that it was a miracle it didn't burst right out of my chest. For the first time in a long time, I wanted to deserve something this good. I wanted to be the kind of person that not only knew what the right thing was without thinking about it, but could also do the right thing, so that I could make someone else feel as appreciated and valued as I did in this moment.

"The lawyer is bound to be another in a long line of mistakes, but until we go down in flames, he makes me feel safe and he makes me think. I don't do enough of that usually, and considering the recent circumstances, thinking is a good thing." I reached up and patted her hand where it was still clutching my arm. "He also knows exactly how screwed up I am and what kind of havoc I can wreak, so I don't feel like I have to warn him or protect him from the inevitable fallout. He's not about to let me ruin the sweet gig he has going on." And maybe that was why I liked him so much. I knew deep down inside that eventually this thing I had going on with Quaid was going to lead to total devastation, but at the end, he would still be standing strong, indestructible, and untouched by the damage I typically caused. To me, the man seemed storm-proof, which meant he could survive me, the typhoon of tragedy I was inevitably going to rain down on us.

My mom sighed and let go of me but only so she could reach up and brush the back of her fingers across my cheek. "Oh, Avett. You have no idea how much you remind me of myself when I was your age."

I couldn't hold back the ragged laugh that escaped my lungs at her words. I was here to make peace with her, to start and bridge the gap that had opened wide over my river of bad choices and faults over the years, but her words stung. If we were so alike, how was it so easy for her to desert me when what I needed was for her to pull me closer and not let go? "Oh, really? Did you alienate everyone that loved you, too? Did you constantly disappoint your mother to the point she could barely stand to be in the same room as you? Did you screw up over and over again, fuck up so many times and so many different things that it seems like all you will ever be is someone else's worst choice?"

I took a step away from her and went to walk around her so that we didn't have to continue the conversation, but I should have known I couldn't throw down the gauntlet and walk away.

She moved around me, and while I got my small stature from her, she was still taller than me and it was obvious from the look on her face that she wasn't about to let me go anywhere. I was tempted to call for my dad, who was on the phone with the insurance company in the office at the front of her house so he could derail this long-coming showdown, but the time had come to own up to all of my sins. Especially the ones that had caused the most damage to the people I cared about most. I wanted to set things right with my mom. I wanted her to know that I was sorry for everything, but I was most sorry for the damage I had done to the relationship between her and my dad. I loved them both, and yet, I had made them both miserable in my quest for self-recrimination.

"Avett," she sighed, and I could literally feel the weight of it as it echoed on the walls around us. "I always wanted you here, but you wanted to be with your father, and considering the way things ended between him and me, well, we both felt like he deserved to have you so much more than I did. Was there tension between us because of the way you suddenly started acting out? Yes, but that wasn't anything we wouldn't have been able to work out if I hadn't screwed up, if I had been a stronger woman and a better wife. Because yes, I disappointed both my parents, not just my mother, and yes, I've often wondered if I was the worst choice your father could've made."

I blinked at her like I had never seen her before and frowned so fiercely it actually hurt my forehead. "What are you talking about, Mom? Things were always fine, great, in fact. We were a picture perfect, happy family, until we weren't." And when they went south it was right around the time I realized exactly how dangerous and life changing doing nothing could be. I took my antics and my acting out to another level as I ran after some kind of celestial payback to make up for what had happened to Autumn.

"We worked really hard to make you believe things were fine, honey. That's what parents who love their children do, even when they are struggling themselves. It got harder and harder to keep our issues from you the older you got. We never saw eye to eye on the best way to handle you, and you and your dad were so close." She made a noise in her throat and shook her head at me. "Your dad was married when we met. I didn't care, but my parents sure did. He was older than me by quite a bit and hadn't quite handled everything he brought back with him from his time overseas. He liked to drink a little too much, and the crowd he ran around with wasn't exactly mom and dad approved. None of that mattered to me, because I was in love with him, instantly. I adored him. I was obsessed with him. I told myself it didn't matter what obstacles stood in our way. We were meant to be together. I didn't respect the life he already had or the woman that already loved him. I met him, decided I wanted him, and was determined to get my way, despite warnings from everyone that cared about me, telling me it was too much, too soon."

None of that was a secret, but the way she spoke about it, the regret in her tone, that was new. She sounded exactly like I did after one of my terrible choices blew up in my face.

"I got pregnant with you before your dad's divorce was final, and while I never had any doubts your dad loved both of us beyond measure, I never could quite get over the fact that I had taken him away from his first wife so easily, especially with everyone always reminding me he had no choice but to leave her once there was a baby. I lived every single day wondering if someone new was going to come along and lure him away from us, exactly as I had done. I wondered if he felt like he *had* to go. I was jealous. I was untrusting. I was possessive, and for a man like your dad, a man with honor and integrity running all the way down to his bones, it wore on him. He loved me, but after a while my insecurity on top of his own demons was too much for him to take. He started spending more and more time at the bar, and of course I convinced myself he was with other women. He cheated before me and then he cheated to be with me so why wouldn't he cheat on me? At the time I didn't recognize that the love he had for me was different than the love he had for the women that were in his life earlier. I didn't realize having a family and someone he loved more than life to come home to every day had made your father a different man."

I scowled even harder because I didn't remember any kind of tension or strain between them. I couldn't recall any fighting or disagreements. All I could remember was happiness and romance between the two of them. Things were sunshine and rainbows until I was sixteen and then things changed, but I was so caught up in how they changed for me, I never considered why and how things changed for my parents as well. Dad left and I went with him, convinced my mom was fed up with my harmful behaviors and fed up with me.

She held up her hand when I opened my mouth to interrupt her and I saw sadness and heart-wrenching grief fill her eyes. "I convinced myself he was seeing someone else, that he was doing what I accused him of. I never listened to him. I never gave him the benefit of the doubt. I let my own fears and everyone else's poison infect me. What I did was something I had done my entire life, I acted without thinking and decided that if he was going to break my heart by being with someone else, then I was going to do the same thing to him."

I gasped and actually stumbled back in shock. "Mom. You didn't." The words came out like they had been run across sandpaper.

Slowly she nodded; and self-loathing was stamped across her face. "I did and I felt disgusting and ashamed as soon as I realized what kind of damage I had done to my marriage and my family. I had a wonderful husband, a lively, independent daughter, and because of the nontraditional way our family came to be, I never felt worthy of them. I never felt like what we had was good enough to anyone else's standards. I never wanted you to know, Avett. I wanted you to be proud of me, to aspire to be like me, and then I went and did the one thing I knew you and your father could never forgive. I never wanted you to think I was willing to risk you and your dad. I was so repulsed by what I had become I started pulling back from you when you really needed me the most. I could tell something was going on with you because of the way you were suddenly acting out and getting into trouble. I knew deep down inside it was because the stress between your father and me was no longer able to be contained and hidden away. I told your dad about my indiscretion immediately, and at first he agreed to try and work it out. But all the fears I had were amplified tenfold, because now, I had given him a legitimate reason to seek out someone else. Eventually, he couldn't handle the pressure of living under the shadow of my distrust and I couldn't blame him. I also couldn't accept his forgiveness when it was offered, because I didn't think I deserved to be forgiven. We were both miserable and it was clearly affecting you. I let you both go because it was my actions and my defective choices that had pushed you both away in the first place. I felt like I deserved to be alone."

"Jesus, Mom." We were more alike than I had ever realized.

She put her arms around herself like she was giving herself a much needed hug and dropped her gaze from mine. "Your father and I had a long, treacherous road to get to a place where trust was no longer an issue and that we could love each other with nothing between us. Part of that was watching him get remarried and loving someone else, and part of it was him being endlessly loyal and supportive of you. He's never wavered with you, Avett. Not ever. There are times we disagree on the way we should support you, but that's because I've watched you be as reckless and careless with yourself and your love as I was. I wanted things to be easier for you."

I let out a strangled and choking laugh. "They haven't been." Because even with the distance between her and me, watching Dad remarry and divorce before my eighteenth birthday hadn't been easy or fun. She was always my mom and she was always the woman I wanted my dad to be with, because she was the person that made him the happiest.

Quaid had told me the night before that some people were born into the storm and it looked like my mom was also one of them. I came by my chaos naturally. My mayhem was, apparently, part of my genetic code. I literally had been born to be wild, and I'd also been so caught up in my own commotion and on my own path of destruction for so long that I hadn't even noticed there was a storm that had nothing to do with me brewing under my roof.

"I know they haven't been, and I blame myself for not being able to teach you from my mistakes . . . believe me, there have been a lot of them."

I slumped back against the wall and ran my hands over my face. "I'm learning that blame is poisonous. Maybe you could have tried harder, and I definitely could have paid better attention, but what's done is done and all we can do is be better from this point forward. Blame has stolen a lot of time and a lot of life from me. I'm really starting to resent it."

I gave her a curious look. "How did Dad forgive you?" My father was a good man, but he was also a badass, and most badasses didn't take too kindly to their woman stepping out on them and not having faith in them.

It was my dad's rumbly and deep voice that answered me. "I forgave her because I loved her, always, even when she made mistakes. I forgave her because she wasn't the only one that screwed up. I could have waited until I was separated from the woman I was married to before getting involved with your mom, but I was impatient and thoughtless as to how our actions might affect our relationship down the road. I forgave her because she was the mother of my child and because we both needed forgiveness to heal and move forward, even if we weren't together. Forgiveness is the only way you can be set free. I forgave her because after a lot of time and a lot of trials together, she finally forgave herself. Our story is still being written, Sprite. We haven't reached the end just yet and there was a lot of editing and revision along the way."

I wondered vaguely if he had talked to Asa and if that was his subtle hint that if I could learn to forgive myself, then maybe some of that dead weight of responsibility and guilt that caged me down on rock bottom would be lifted, and I could start that slow and arduous trek towards something better.

I pushed my hands through my still-unruly hair and blew out a breath. As I exhaled, I felt years of culpability escape from my dense conscience. "I'm so happy you guys found your way back to each other."

My dad chuckled in his thunderous way and he reached out to put his arm around my mom's shoulders so he could pull her to his side. "We are, too, because that story has been a long time coming. We wanted to wait until you were in a place to listen, with your head and your heart. We knew if we told you the truth, at the wrong time, it would have you spiraling even more out of control than you already were. You react, Sprite, and while its honest emotion, it isn't always the healthiest response. Now that all the skeletons are out of the closet, I figure it's as good a time as any for this family to be under the same roof. The house is a total loss. The outside brick is still standing, but everything on the inside is gone. It would cost a fortune to go in and rebuild from the ground up, and I think the money coming from the insurance claim could be put to better use."

I let my head fall back so that it thunked against the wall and turned my face up towards the ceiling. "Yeah. Take the money and use it to replace the money you had to take out of your retirement to pay for my bail, and towards the money you're planning on paying Quaid. I'm not going to let you lose your home and your retirement, Dad. I'm going to find a way to pay you back to cover the bill coming from the Legal Eagle."

Both of my parents chuckled at the silly nickname I had labeled him with, and I couldn't fight a grin at how coincidentally perfect it was now that I knew about the eagle he had inked on his perfectly sculpted chest.

They both started to argue about the money and question how I was going to come up with the necessary funds, but it was my turn to hold my hand up and interrupt them.

"Consider this the first step in the right direction. I haven't done many things that felt right in my life but this" —I pointed between us with my finger— "this feels right. Taking complete responsibility, including the financial part of it, for the mess I made is something I have to do if I'm ever going to be able to get to a place where I can live with some of the things I've done." I took a deep breath and shifted my eyes between the both of them.

"Speaking of the things I've done and not letting blame and guilt control me anymore, I need to tell you guys my story. I need you to know that the reason I kept screwing up and kept hurting myself had nothing to do with you. I need to tell you all of it, and know that you'll still be here and still love me afterwards."

Maybe then I could accept some of that forgiveness everyone was always throwing around.

Knowing what the right thing was did feel warm. It also felt fizzy and exciting as it bubbled in my blood, even as my parents reassured me over and over that they were both there to help me. It felt thick and syrupy as it moved through my veins, pushing out all the recrimination and reproach that lived there.

Knowing the right thing to do felt amazing. Now I needed to break all my old habits and actually do what was right, instead of veering off course and nose-diving into the wrong thing. This time, I didn't want to crash and burn; I wanted to soar to new heights.

CHAPTER 12

Quaid

I exited the courtroom with another not-guilty verdict secured and another very satisfied client. This guy was lucky that the jury bought his innocent and confused act, because I would bet everything I owned that he was indeed guilty of luring the prostitute, who was the complainant, into his home and keeping her there against her will for several days. The court of public opinion held a lot of weight with the average person and the jury took exactly three hours to deliberate and decide that the young woman deserved the horrors she suffered through simply because she made her money on her back and took the risk of advertising her services on Craigslist. It didn't matter that my client had crazy eyes, a previous history of violence against women, and zero remorse on the stand when he was cross-examined. He looked like a soccer dad and drove a minivan. He worked for the local cable company and had an established 401(k), so he was perceptibly the more upstanding and believable of the two of them on the stand. My job was done. I had kicked legal ass and dragged the poor woman even deeper into the mud, and where I would normally want to celebrate a job well done with an expensive Scotch and a more expensive woman, today all I wanted to do was brave the madness of a tiny, pink-haired hurricane and scrub off the film of distaste that covered me in the shower for a hundred hours.

I was sending a text to Avett to tell her I was on my way to get her from her parents' house when I noticed the detective who was in charge of Avett's ex's case waiting for me by the elevators. I slipped my phone back in my pocket without waiting for her response and tilted my chin at the cop in greeting.

"What's up? Do you have any new information on the fire?"

The detective gave a sharp nod and blew out a deep sigh. He lifted a hand to his face and rubbed his chin. "The fire investigator is calling it arson. There was accelerant poured all over the house and the gas line that ran to the stove was cut. The house was purposely burned down."

I wasn't surprised, but I was furious. I hated that Avett and Brite were going through this. I hated that someone was capable of doing something so horrible to another human being.

"That's what we figured. Did the boyfriend offer up any insight as to why someone would be interested in burning down the Walkers' home?"

The cop sighed again. "We questioned him. The kid's a punk. He's the low man on the totem pole and completely willing to sell anyone and everyone out to cover his own ass. We thought maybe he had one of his tweaker buddies go after the girl in order to keep her from testifying, but he hasn't had any contact with the outside since his arrest."

I swore and shoved my hand roughly through my hair, making it stand up wild on the top of my head.

"So where does that leave us?"

The cop frowned. "Well, the tweaker hasn't had any contact with the outside but his lawyer sure has. Do you know who Larsen Tyrell is?"

I grunted. "I do." Larsen was the guy that took the cases the rest of us wouldn't touch with a ten-foot pole. He was the guy that represented drug runners and human traffickers. He was the guy that got child pornographers set free and the guy that reveled in the media attention when he boldly and unashamedly represented cop killers and serial rapists.

"Larsen is the druggie's attorney. He also represents Aitor Acosta. When the kid was picked up the night of the robbery, he was babbling that he had to rob the bar because he owed Acosta a shit ton of cash. The kid was supposed to sit on a stash that he went and picked up from the border, but we all know what happens when you put a junkie in charge of several kilos of coke."

I swore again and pulled even harder on my now out of control hair. "He blew through the stash on his own and didn't have the drugs or the money to give to his supplier."

"Yep. So Acosta sent the thugs looking for the goods. They shook up the girlfriend and that was enough to scare Dalton into robbing the bar so he could go on the run. Aitor has ties to every major Mexican gang operating behind bars. We think the kid told Larsen the girl has the stash, and that Larsen passed that info on to his other client. Dalton is trying to cover his own ass, like he has been from the beginning. He passed the buck to the girl, just like he did with the robbery."

"Son of a bitch." My hand curled tightly around the handle of my bag and I had to breathe slowly and deeply to keep myself from throwing a fist into the nearest wall. "He's going to get her killed."

The cop nodded in agreement and rocked back on his heels a little bit. "Understandably, the lawyer couldn't tell us anything, but the way Dalton clammed up when he was ready to give us everything he had on Acosta and his operation speaks volumes. The D.A. had a pretty sweet deal on the table considering there were multiple felonies involved, but as soon as Larsen got involved, all of that information was taken off the table. We're pretty sure the kid is being offered protection on the inside until the trial is over and until the drugs are found . . . which we know they won't be." He gave me a pointed look. "Since nothing is official, and all we have is speculation, and a sleazy lawyer with zero morals to go on, there isn't much the DPD can do for her. She landed herself right in the middle of a big, fat, dangerous mess."

I pressed down on the corners of my eyes next to my nose as I felt the pounding of a headache start to throb there. "She is way too comfortable being right there. I'll pass along the information to her and her parents so everyone knows to be hyperalert. Thanks for the information."

The cop snorted again as we moved to get on the elevator. "No problem. I usually consider you one of the guys that plays for the opposite team, but that girl . . ." He trailed off and all I could do was silently agree with him.

That girl . . . there was just something about her. She made you want to help her, to heal her, to protect her, even as she blindly chased after the very things that would hurt her, the things that would leave wounds on her mind, body, and soul.

When I got to my truck, I already had my tie off and had

stripped out of my jacket. Avett had texted back that she was making dinner for everyone, so I should be ready to eat when I got to her mom's house. After her reaction to my kitchen in my loft, I figured she liked to cook, but considering her age, I figured I was in store for something simple like spaghetti and meatballs. When I was twenty-two, I lived off pizza and Chinese food. Lottie didn't cook, and when I was in school and working to pay for it, there was no way I had time to be domestic. So even if it was something simple out of a jar and a box, I told myself to pretend that it was haute cuisine because there was no way I wanted to hurt her feelings and run the risk of her deciding to stay with her parents instead of coming with me.

In the twenty minutes it took me to get across town and down into the Baker neighborhood where Avett's mom lived, I decided that with the danger swirling around her and the scales in our relationship tipping into something far more serious than I had planned on, we needed to get away for a few days. She needed a breather from everything that had been tumbling down on top of her since the night she was arrested, and I needed a few days to acquire some peace of mind, where I knew she would be safe and secure. We had to go somewhere that no one would think to look for either of us. I wanted a place that was nearly impossible to get to. It was a place that was hidden and remote. I wanted her to see the area I had come from and to show her the man I had been, so that she would understand that we weren't as different at the core of who we were as she believed us to be. I was going to show her where I called home and where I swore I would never, ever return to. This girl had been bringing me back to the start since the beginning.

Taking her to my mountains meant letting her see a part of me that I had spent most of my adult life trying to cover up. Taking her with me, back into the past, meant there was no more hiding behind the gloss and shine of all the things in my life I used as camouflage. It also meant I was going to have to be as real with her as she had been with me from the very start, and that thought scared me to death. The last time I'd been honest about who I was, where I came from, I was packing my bags and headed off to boot camp a million and one years ago. That much reality at one time was going to be difficult to wade my way through, but the idea of stripping off the façade, of walking through the smoke screen and coming out on the other side as someone of substance, as a man of actual value and worth, instead of one that was nothing more than a disguise, was acutely stirring.

When I got to her mother's house, Avett threw open the door before I even lifted my hand to knock. I fell back a step as she hurled herself at me and I caught her with a soft "Oomph" as her tiny body slammed full force into mine. Her arms twined around my neck and her legs wrapped around my waist as I put a hand under her rear end to hold her up as her mouth slanted skillfully across my parted lips. I wrapped my free arm around her back and pulled her closer to me, enjoying the way her tongue tasted like something citrusy and tart and the way she moaned into my mouth as I deepened the kiss and used my teeth on her bottom lip. More than any of that, I got lost in how good it felt to have her excited to see me, the rush of having someone actually give a damn that I was gone all day. I couldn't recall Lottie ever offering me more than a strained grin when I came home from a difficult day in court.

Avett pulled back and put one of her hands on my cheek as I slowly let her slide down my body. Her eyes sparkled with mischief when her middle dragged across the obvious arousal now tenting the front of my pants. "How was court?"

I rubbed my thumb across the plump and damp curve of her lower lip and looked past her into the house to make sure I wasn't going to have to dodge one of Brite's flying fists for groping his daughter in broad daylight. "Court was court. How was your day with your folks?"

She shrugged and stepped away from me, eyeing the bulge in my pants with a sexy little leer.

"It was fine. I talked to my mom and worked some things out, so that was good. She reminded me that everyone has a story . . . not only me." She looked down at the ground and then back up at me with what I was pretty sure was pride shining out of her colorful eyes. "I told my parents everything that happened with Autumn and everything that happened after-wards. My dad didn't look at all surprised and my mom cried. It was a good talk." Her gaze skipped away from mine and landed on the front of my pants. "Do you need a few minutes before we go inside?" She was laughing at me and while that normally made me feel furious and affronted, coming from her, all I wanted to do was smile at her and indulge her.

"I do need a few minutes, but not for that. I want to talk to you about something." Her eyes widened and her brow wrinkled in an adorable fashion. I reached out to smooth the lines with my finger. "The police determined your house was burned down on purpose, Avett."

She gasped a little and lifted a hand up to cover her mouth. "Really?"

I nodded and brushed my thumb over her winged eyebrow.

"Yeah, and they think the guys that came looking for you when Jared ran off with that last stash are behind it. They're looking for the drugs and if they can't get their hands on the goods, then they're going to come after you."

She scowled and crossed her arms across her chest in a defiant manner. "I never saw the drugs. I knew he was using, but I didn't know how deep in Jared was. I would never agree to participate in something like that."

"I know that, but the guys with the missing drugs don't. Jared is all about Jared, so there is a high possibility he is telling the guys in charge that you took the product and stashed it somewhere. He's buying time while he's locked up, and his story is still that you were behind the robbery. He's put you directly in the line of fire."

Her mouth moved, but no sound came out as cold, stark fear moved into her eyes. "What if they come after my parents? What if they come after you?"

Her voice was barely a squeak and I couldn't resist reaching out and pulling her into my chest. I rested my cheek on the top of her head and told her, "They want the dope and they will go about the most efficient means of getting it. I'm going to tell your dad what's going on so he can keep an eye out, but I think you're the one that needs to be protected. Not everyone else. We should take the weekend and go out of town. We can take a few days off so you don't have to worry about what's next. What's next can wait until we get back, and hopefully by then the police will have a better handle on things. We'll take the bike and go for a ride. I promise to take you someplace safe."

She looked a little shell-shocked but nodded at me as she

bit down on her lower lip. "What happens after the weekend, Quaid? The threat isn't going to go away and it's going to affect the people that matter the most to me."

"Let's get through the weekend and the trial, then we'll figure something out. Once Jared realizes he's facing serious time behind bars, and that his lawyer has a bigger agenda than defending him, the kid might change his tune and we can leverage that to get to his supplier." I didn't have a better answer for her than that, and I wasn't going to placate her with easy words and assurances, because I wanted her to stay alert and ready. The threat to her was very real and it made me want to wrap her up in padding and bubble wrap and put her on the highest shelf so no one could ever get to her.

She bobbed her head up and down under my chin and her arms went around my waist so that she could squeeze me back. "Sounds like you're suddenly working for the prosecution, Counselor. That's the other team."

I let her go and set her away from me far enough so that I could bend down and brush my mouth across hers. "I'm Team Avett right now. That's the only team I'm interested in seeing win. Now, why don't we go in before your dad comes looking for us."

She barked out a laugh and turned to lead me into the house. "He'd be madder about your imported bike than he would that you had your hands on me, Quaid. He's knows exactly how I am, but not buying American . . . well, that's an unforgivable sin to a Harley man."

I'd heard it from more than one motorcycle enthusiast, but I didn't like the idea that her dad, a man I had nothing but respect and admiration for, had a reason to find fault with me. No matter how superficial it was.

"I like to go fast." And I liked the way the Italian bike handled. I also liked that when I rode, I had to concentrate, to focus on the asphalt and the turns. When I rode, there was no room for anything other than the ride. It was the closest thing I had to wildness and freedom in my life. At least it was until Hurricane Avett crashed onto my shores.

Speaking of my tempest, she looked over her shoulder at me with a grin I wanted to kiss off her face. "Don't I know it."

We made our way through the comfortable and cozy ranch-style home and my senses lit up with how normal and welcoming it all was. Brite rose from where he was sitting on the couch, offering me a hand to shake, and Darcy gave me a smile that was missing so much of the tension and strain that had been on her face the last time I saw her. Avett patted me on the arm and told me she was going to finish up in the kitchen and that we could all eat in ten minutes. When she mentioned food, I realized the entire house smelled like something fragrant and delicious. That was no Ragu or Hamburger Helper coming out of the kitchen.

"Smells good." I took a seat on a well-worn recliner and looked at Avett's parents. I was waiting for the third degree or an interrogation. All I got was nods and easy smiles.

"The girl is a natural in the kitchen. She can cook circles around me and I've spent years running professional and not so professional kitchens." The pride in Darcy's voice was evident.

I lifted a hand to smooth down my hair and offered up my own rueful grin. "I was expecting spaghetti sauce out of a jar and maybe some frozen garlic bread."

Brite let out a booming laugh and slapped his knee. "No. When Avett gets it in her head to prepare a meal, it's all from scratch and tastes like you should be paying her for the honor of eating it. When it was just me and her, I wasn't around a lot because of my hours at the bar. She had free run of the kitchen. The leftovers she had waiting for me were better than anything you could get at any five-star restaurant in LoDo. The girl is a natural when it comes to food and I think in her own way that's how she cares for the people that matter to her. She can feed them. Tonight she made chicken picatta and homemade pasta."

No one would ever accuse Brite of not being an observant man. I had wondered where Avett's enthrallment with my kitchen came from and his insight into his complicated daughter made a lot of sense. She knew how to cook and how to do it well. She knew she wouldn't screw it up, so that was how she went about caring for those that she loved. That was her gift and she wanted to share it. My mouth started to water at the same time my heart flipped over in my chest. I couldn't hold back a soft, "Damn."

I pushed my suddenly acute hunger to the back of my mind and filled Brite and Darcy in on what the detective had told me hours earlier. Brite looked furious when I was done talking and Darcy nervously twisted her hands together. I told them my plans to take their daughter out of town for the weekend and was stunned that there was no argument. Brite agreed it was a good idea for her to lay low as much as possible until the trial, and assured me that when we got back to town he would rally the troops to make sure she was never alone. Darcy watched me, speculatively, and simply nodded as she muttered, "You're both going to need to be very careful." I wasn't sure if she was referring to me being in danger because of the situation surrounding Avett, or if she was talking about the way her daughter and I were bound to detonate into an explosion of heartbreak and anguish by the time we were done falling in love with one another.

Avett hollered that dinner was ready and we all moved to the dining room. She wasn't merely a good cook, she was something magical. The food tasted better than anything I had ever put in my mouth, and I couldn't stop telling her how impressed I was. She blushed prettily as easy conversation flowed around the table, and when I got her back to my loft a few hours later, I thanked her for dinner and for sharing her family properly in the shower, several times. The first time I thanked her on my knees, with her leg thrown over my shoulder and my mouth buried in her core as she pulled on my hair and demanded I give her more. The second time I thanked her, I did it with her bent over in front of me with her hands on those slate tiles I couldn't even see because I was focused on the way water sluiced down the sexy curve of her spine, and the way it made her cotton-candy-colored hair stick to her skin as I pounded into her from behind.

Losing myself in her sweet body over and over again did more to cleanse the cobwebs that clung to me from the dirty victory in court today than any amount of hot water and scrubbing could. She made me feel renewed. She made me feel improved. She made me feel like hearing her come on a long sigh, with my name dancing off her lips, was the only victory that was ever going to matter ever again.

After we had the bathroom cleaned up and the things we were going to need to get through the weekend in the mountains packed into two backpacks, I took her to bed and told her I would keep her safe. I told her she had a real gift with food and that I really liked her parents. I told her that I liked the way she told me hello today, and that I really liked going to bed with her. She let me give her the words, she let me hold her close, and she didn't ask for anything else.

She didn't ask about court. She didn't ask about the mountains. She didn't demand attention or validation. She took what I had to offer and snuggled into my side as she traced the wings tattooed on my chest in a lazy caress. She was content to simply be here with me, and what I offered seemed to be enough for her. I liked a lot of things about this young woman, but the fact that she wasn't asking for more than I had to give was at the top of the list. Her unassuming and undemanding nature made me want to dig deep into a well that I was sure had run dry, in order to provide her with more than the bare bones of the emotions I had left. I wanted to give to Avett, as much as I wanted to take from her.

I fell asleep with her head on my shoulder and her hand resting over my heart. I woke up with the sun hitting me in the face and Avett's sassy mouth wrapped around my dick, while her small hand played with my balls. It was the nicest wake-up call that I had ever gotten, and it had me smiling all morning long. I did my best to put a similar smile on her face, and by the time we were done destroying my bed and each other, it was well past time for us to get on the road. The bike was fast, but the drive up to the mountains was still over treacherous passes and the weather was always unpredictable in late fall. I was trying to get the girl out of danger, not put her in more of it.

I had a leather jacket and a helmet that I bought for Lottie and had never been used. Avett made a face when I told her where the gear came from, but she still put it on and climbed on the back of the bike behind me, like a pro. A street bike was nothing like a Harley, but the basics of how to ride on the back of one were the same. That meant she got to wrap herself around me, that I got to have her hands pressed low and tight across my middle, with her legs squeezing me tightly as we moved together around each of the switchbacks that led up to the mountain. She moved like she had been born on the back of a bike, which I guess she kind of had been. But she also moved so in sync and so perfectly with me that all I wanted to do was find a place to pull over so I could bend her over the bike and bury myself inside her, so deeply and fully that she wouldn't be able to remember what it was like to not have me inside of her.

It took several hours as we passed through small mountain town after small mountain town, each one more exclusive and more elite than the last. The tourists were out in force, making their way into the mountains to watch the leaves change and for a last-minute getaway before the snow moved in. We rode hard and fast, zipping around traffic and chasing the wind higher and higher up in elevation, the leaves turning from leafy green to vivid yellow and red the farther away from the city we got. It had been years since I'd been here and I'd spent so much time blocking out the memories that I almost passed the outcropping of rocks that led to the small turnoff where I knew there was a small, flat area where I could park the bike.

I pulled off the road, parked behind the boulders. I waited until Avett climbed off from her perch behind me and then swung my leg over the bike. We pulled our helmets off at the same time, and I loved the way her candy-colored hair floated around her face and down around her shoulders. She looked around the densely wooded area that surrounded us with trepidation and awe stamped clearly on her face. We'd left behind the glitz and polish of the nearest designer ski town miles and miles ago.

"Where are we?"

I rubbed my hand through my hair and pocketed the keys to the bike. "This is the back side of the White River National Forest."

She laughed a little and reached out to put her helmet on the bike next to mine. "Okay. It's really pretty and clearly no gun-toting bad guys are going to follow us all the way up here, but we didn't pack anything to camp with in those backpacks. So I'm officially confused as to where we're going and what we're doing."

I took her hand in mine and started for the trees. There used to be a path worn in the brush, a path I made as I walked over a mile each way every single day through these very woods to get to the bus stop, regardless of the weather outside. The path had long since grown over but suppressed memory and ancient instinct made my steps sure as I pulled Avett deeper and deeper into the thick foliage.

"I told you I was taking you somewhere safe, somewhere you can relax and not worry for a few days. That's exactly what I'm doing. No one knows this place exists."

She was panting a little as she trudged along behind me, doing her best to keep up with my longer stride and to step carefully over fallen logs and hidden rocks.

"If no one knows that it exists, how do you know about it?" That was a valid question and after forty-five minutes of trudging through rough and unforgiving terrain we came into the clearing where my entire past and childhood rested.

I looked at Avett as she came to a stumbling halt next to me. Her pretty eyes widened until they took up half of her face as she turned her head to look at me with questions overflowing in her gaze.

"Quaid?"

I pointed to the cabin and shrugged as I told her, "That's where I grew up."

She breathed out a disbelieving little laugh. "You've got to be kidding me."

I grunted and took a few hesitant steps towards the building as memory upon memory assaulted me, making my steps falter and unsteady. "I'm not. My dad bought this land and a few surrounding acres when he was about your age. He and my mom had a dream of being modern day homesteaders, of living off the land and off the grid. But even when you live strictly off the land, you still have to pay the government for that privilege. My folks owed thousands and thousands of dollars in back taxes on the property. When I got out of the army, I found out that they had pulled up stakes and moved with my brother to some godforsaken part of Alaska, to live on a lake in a roughly constructed houseboat. It sounds like a made-up story, but it's one hundred percent true. They are as off grid as anyone can get, in a place it takes dogsleds and snowmobiles to get to. I haven't spoken to them or my little brother in years. I don't even know if they know about my divorce."

She blinked at me as she tried to process all the information I was giving to her.

"They're like those people on that show *Ice Lake Rebels*?"

I snorted out a surprised laugh that she even kind of knew what I was talking about. "Yeah, something like that."

"You're right, that doesn't sound like a real story, but it also sounds . . . sad? Don't you miss them? How can they not miss you?" She sounded worried as I tugged on her hand and pulled her towards the rustic, wooden structure. "And if they're in Alaska, doesn't that mean we're trespassing right now? I probably shouldn't get arrested again now that I'm finally figuring out how to do the right thing once in a while."

"We're not trespassing. After I started working for the firm, I contacted the man that purchased the land at auction. He was using the cabin as a hunting lodge. I offered him a deal he couldn't refuse and told him he could continue to use the property during hunting season, so he sold it back to me." I cut her a sideways look. "I think I thought my folks would move back if they knew they could have the land with no governmental strings attached to it, but they never did. They like their life the way it is too much to come back, and I think they wrote me off the minute I told them I was joining the military. They never understood why I wanted out, or why I wanted more than the land could provide for me. I haven't been here since the day I left for boot camp."

She whistled softly and squeezed the hand that was still gripping hers. "That has to sting."

I pushed the door open and froze in place at the sight of the barren walls and dusty floorboards. It looked so much like it had when I was growing up. Four walls dotted with cracked windows, a minimal kitchen, a loft with a thin mattress and another one on a cot in the corner. There was a threadbare couch in front of an old wood burning stove and a table made from one of the pines that surrounded the cabin. There wasn't even a bathroom in the cabin. That meant every night I would sprint across the forest floor to the makeshift house that was nothing more than some plywood and a hole in the ground, taking care of business while wondering if I was going to run across a bear or a mountain lion.

"It did sting. It still does when I allow myself to think about it now. When I first shipped out and I had no clue what to expect, no idea where I would end up or if the risk I took in enlisting would pay off or end up getting me killed, it sucked that I didn't have their support or encouragement. My girlfriend at the time, who is now my ex-wife, really seemed like the only person I had in the world. I think that's why I was so oblivious when our marriage started to fall apart. She was my only tie to this life, and she was the only one that didn't leave me when I was my most uncertain. It was all an act, but it was an act that kept me going when I was a terrified and lonely kid headed to war."

The cabin was empty, modest, and bucolic. This was what having only what you needed to survive was all about, and it was so different from the way I lived now I had no idea how either man lived within the same body.

I looked at the girl that had brought me back here, the girl that had made it impossible to pretend anymore. I wanted her to see that we weren't as different as she thought we were, that we didn't come from the same place, but that was because the place I came from was this vacant, humble existence. I came from nothing, and she didn't.

"This" —I gestured with my hand to indicate the sad space around us— "is why I have two thousand dollar sheets and ugly but expensive artwork on the walls. When you have nothing your entire childhood, when you don't get to eat unless you can kill dinner, and when you don't get to be warm unless you've chopped a stack of firewood as tall as you were, you want things. You want comfort and ease. You want luxury and extravagance. You want to be the kid that doesn't get made fun of for being dirt poor. You want to be the guy that gets the girl you should never be able to get. You want to be the kid that gets to see a doctor when you slice your side open chopping wood, not sewn together on the kitchen table and told to toughen up because you cried each time the needle dug into your skin. You want so many things when this is how you live. You want everything, and even that's not enough, because there is always more. So you work your ass off to get those things, and even though you realize that it'll never be enough, you keep working and you keep acquiring. My entire adult life has been about getting enough things to cover all of this up and to show my parents that I made the right choice by leaving and getting out, even though they've never seen and wouldn't appreciate anything about the man I am now."

Avett pulled her hand free, and I thought she was going to make some smart remark about the outhouse or about the fact that I had basically grown up *Little House on the Prairie* style, but all she did was wrap her arms around me from behind and press herself into my back. I felt her cheek rest between my shoulder blades and her voice, even though she spoke quietly, echoed loudly in the desolate space.

"It's so much easier to see you here than it is when you're surrounded by all those things, Quaid."

I sighed and put my hands over hers. "That's because there's nowhere to hide here."

I was done hiding, from her and from the rest of the world.

CHAPTER 13

Avett

It was becoming disgustingly obvious that reaching for the remote and running after the wrong kind of men was not adequate exercise as I huffed and puffed to keep up with Quaid's long-legged stride as he wound his way through the forest surrounding the cabin. Apparently, even the acrobatic and endless amounts of breathless sex I'd been having with the right kind of man wasn't enough in the cardio department because I felt like I was going to die, and we'd only been hiking through the woods for an hour or so. Quaid wanted to show me something on the property. A place that he insisted was worth the burning thighs and collapsed lungs I was sure I was going to have by the time we got there. I couldn't deny the wistful sparkle that lightened his pale eyes even more as he told me about spending hours with his younger brother, climbing on the rocks and jumping off the outcropping into the small mountain lake below. He promised the sound of the waterfall that fed the pool of frigid water was soothing and relaxing, and even though nature was not necessarily my thing, there was no way I was going to deny him this trip down memory lane that he obviously needed to take.

I groaned as I stumbled over a root I didn't see and slammed into his broad back. The noise turned into a soft sigh as one of his arms reached around blindly to steady me. He was always doing that . . . steadying me. It made my heart flutter and the part deep down inside of me that always hurt, that forever pulsed with regret and pain, felt less vast and infinite.

"You okay back there?" Humor tinted his deep voice and pulled at his mouth as he looked over his shoulder at me.

I wrinkled my nose at him. "I'll make it, but you might have to carry me back to the cabin."

He laughed and lifted one of his golden eyebrows at me. "You've got years and years ahead of you before you'll need someone to carry you back, Avett."

I poked him between his shoulder blades and sidestepped something that looked like a pile of wild animal droppings. I still couldn't believe this forest was his backyard and that he knew his way around the rugged terrain like it had only been yesterday when he was running through the trees. It didn't fit with the flawless suits and the meticulously decorated loft. He had a lot going on beneath those silk ties he liked to wear.

"Thirty-something isn't exactly three thousand, and I think it's obvious which one of us needs to spend some time in the gym. Spoiler alert—it isn't the guy with the perfect ass who hasn't even broken a sweat."

He chuckled again, and let his gaze sweep over me from the messy pink topknot to the dusty tips of my combat boots. "I like you just the way you are."

They were simple words, but they mattered so much. The

only other person in my entire life that had liked me just the way I happened to be was my dad. *I* didn't even like me just the way I was most of the time.

"Thank you."

He cocked his head a little to the side and we stared at each other for a long moment before he nodded sharply and muttered, "You're welcome."

We walked in silence for a few more minutes until the trees thinned out and we were suddenly in a clearing at the top of a soaring embankment. The rocks were stacked on top of one another as rushing water spilled over the natural sculpture. It was beautiful, majestic, and so stunning that the last of the breath I had in my lungs was sucked away in awe.

The sound of the water falling and splashing into the pool below was so loud I could hardly hear Quaid as he told me, "This is it. This was my favorite place in the whole world to spend time when I was growing up. When I was deployed and I spent day after day seeing nothing but sand and desert, I used to dream about this spot at night."

He grabbed my hand and tugged me towards the edge of the rocks that jutted out over the crystal clear mountain water. It was probably a forty- to fifty-foot drop and the water was so clear I could see all the way to the bottom of the pond.

"It's beautiful here. I can see why you kept the memories of this place with you when you were trying to forget the rest of this life."

When he turned his head to look at me, he was frowning and his jaw was hard. I wanted to lift my fingers and stroke them across the dark blond scruff but he turned his face back towards the impressive vista and muttered, "I forgot. I spend so much time pretending this life never happened and denying that I was ever the kid that came from here that I forgot that there was this kind of good here, too."

I moved so that I was standing next to his side and inhaled so deeply that it felt like there wasn't any room left inside of me for the guilt and shame that I always breathed in and out, because the clean mountain air invaded every part of me that it touched. It was cleansing and startlingly eye-opening.

I moved to the edge of the rocks and looked down. "Did you ever jump off of here? It looks like a long ways down." A whisper of an idea and the spark of a challenge started to skirt across my skin, and it made my blood pump harder and faster through my veins.

Quaid put his arm around my midsection and pulled me back so that I was pressed against his chest and not leaning precariously over the edge.

"Yeah, my brother, Harrison, and I used to dare each other to jump. Most of the time it's fine if you hit the water right but when the weather changes the surface ices up pretty fast and the runoff is always really fucking cold. Harrison leaped without looking once when we were teenagers and ended up with a broken arm." I felt him stiffen behind me and his arm locked like a vice across my stomach. "My folks refused to take him to the hospital. My dad tried to set the break himself and my mom made a sling out of aspen branches and a torn sheet. It never healed right and Harrison never had full use of his hand again."

I put my hand over his and rubbed my fingers over the tension-laden fingers that were digging into my side. "Harrison and Quaid. You guys ended up with some pretty uppity names for kids that grew up off the land in the middle of nowhere." I was trying to ease some of the rigidity that was coursing through the big body hovering behind mine, but he stiffened even more and laughed without an ounce of humor. In fact, the noise that escaped him almost made him sound like he was in soul-deep pain.

"Quaid isn't even my actual first name. My mom had a thing for '80s movie stars and her two favorites were Harrison Ford and Dennis Quaid." His tenor dropped a little. "I never really felt like a Dennis, so I've always been a Quaid."

I could tell he was struggling with the past and the way it was piling on top of his present, but I couldn't hold back the giggle that bubbled up when he told me how he had ended up with his unusual moniker. "Dennis? You don't really look like a Dennis, but I can be persuaded to try it out the next time we're in bed."

He cut me a hard look and didn't respond at all to my gentle teasing. "I don't know what a Dennis is supposed to look like, but I know that a Quaid is a lot harder to forget. It was always about trying to be more than I was, even with my name."

I leaned back into him and wiggled my backside against the front of his jeans. "Well, regardless if you're a Dennis or a Quaid, I like you just the way you are, too." I felt him exhale a deep breath behind me and his iron grip finally loosened around my middle. Once I had room to squirm free, I moved back to the edge of the rocks and turned to look at Quaid expectantly over my shoulder. "I think we should jump." The idea floated around with all the clarity and lightness the brisk outside air brought with it. I started to pull off my borrowed leather jacket as I looked at Quaid expectantly.

His pale eyes widened and his mouth dropped open as he shook his head firmly in the negative. "No way. It's been too long since the last time I did that. Who knows if the water is deep enough? If something goes wrong we're out in the middle of nowhere, with no help. It's too risky, and I brought you here to keep you safe."

I dropped the leather jacket on the rocks by my feet and bent to pull the laces on my boots. "I want to jump. You wanted to come back for a reason, to remember the good with the bad, and I want to give you that." I wanted to give us both that, because somewhere deep inside of me, I knew that I was a lot like this place and his memories of it. With me, there was also a lot of good, somewhere in there buried under piles and piles of bad. If I could give him this good back, maybe he would remember the good in me the same way when the storm that raged between us passed.

I hopped around on one foot as I got one boot off and went to work on the other. He watched me with disbelief stamped clearly all over his handsome face. "I can have the memories without risking my neck. Stop pulling your clothes off, Avett. This is ridiculous." I was popping the button on my jeans and wiggling the denim down my legs when his hands landed heavily on my shoulders. "You need to stop. This is foolish and unbelievably reckless. I'm not that kid anymore."

I unbuttoned my shirt and let it fall open so that I was exposed to both his probing gaze and the wilderness that surrounded us. "No, you're not, but no matter how hard you try and deny him, that kid is somewhere down deep inside of you and he wants to jump with me." I cocked an eyebrow at him and told him matter-of-factly, "You're also not the guy that needs all the things in order to prove his worth. You are someone spectacular, with or without the things, Quaid."

His brow furrowed, and before he could argue with me further, I slipped out of my shirt so that I was clad in only my underwear and a lot of bluster. His eyes dropped to my practically naked chest and then dipped lower. I saw his Adam's apple bob up and down as his hands curled into loose fists at his sides.

"And you're someone beyond all the careless moves you make, Avett." Was I? Had I finally outgrown the girl that was always trying to punish herself? Had the girl that felt like she had to suffer endlessly for her poor choices made it to a place where forgiveness seemed possible and obtainable? Had I finally, after mistake upon mistake, learned that redemption was possible if you allowed yourself to be forgiven? Had I reached the point where instead of doing nothing or the wrong thing, I could do the right thing without thought, because even though he looked like he wanted to strangle me, I knew taking this leap was the right thing for me to do. It wasn't a leap of faith; it was a leap of life. I was taking my life back from blame and guilt, one step at a time. This step just happened to be off the edge of the cliff where young Quaid had lived wild and rough.

I shifted my gaze from his burning blue one to the serene azure below. I took a deep breath and looked back at the man staring at me like I had lost my ever-loving mind. I smiled at him with every ounce of lucidity and illumination that was now alive and viable inside of me. I felt like I had woken up from a deep slumber and for the first time in a long time was seeing things the way they really were, without the taint of all my faults and failure coloring them.

"Those risks have led to the worst and the best stories, Quaid. And right at this moment, I'm kind of in love with the fact that

I'm here to tell them, because they're mine and I earned every single one of them." I wriggled my fingers at him in a little wave before I turned and hurled myself off the side of the ledge. My name ripped from his lungs, echoed across the hills, and slammed against my own shriek as the wind rushed around and out of me as I dropped towards the water. Everything whirled around me in a green and blue blur as I plummeted faster and faster through the air. It was a thrill unlike any other. The weight-lessness, the freedom, the rush of the water in my ears, and the sting of the breeze against my bare skin was exhilarating in a way that I could only compare to the best sex I'd ever had. That would be the sex I had with the man standing at the edge of the rocks, watching me as I fell. I could hear him cursing me and the pounding of my heart as the water got closer and closer. I barely had time to suck in a breath and clamp my nose closed with my fingers before I hit.

I went instantly numb the second my skin made contact with the glasslike surface of the water. It was so cold that my muscles locked up and my blood froze still in my veins. The impact was jarring and enough to rattle every single one of my bones; for a second I panicked, and because I was so cold, I wasn't sure I was going to get my paralyzed limbs to work in order to push myself back up to the surface. I flailed wildly until I realized that even though it was frigid and my body was pissed off about it, I still had control of my arms and legs. I calmed down and pushed hard at the glacial liquid that surrounded me. It only took a couple of strokes to break the surface and, once I did, I couldn't pull air into my lungs fast enough.

"You're certifiable, do you know that?" Quaid's booming voice bounced through the ravine. I had to crane my neck back so I could see where he was scrambling down from the high point where I had jumped to a lower outcropping that I was going to have to swim to in order to get out of the water.

I raked my shivering hands over my wet hair so it was out of my eyes as I started to make my way towards him with the icy water coating my skin and impeding my progress.

"Weren't you the one that told me that crazy has it's time and place?" I was trembling so hard that I really had to concentrate on what I was doing so that the water and its arctic grip didn't suck me back under.

"I don't think that miles from civilization and hours away from any kind of medical help is the place to pull the crazy out of retirement." He reached the rocks and put down a bundle that I assumed was my discarded clothes. I watched as he lowered himself to his stomach and reached one of his arms down over the side so that I could grab it and he could pull me up.

I was freezing. Colder than I had ever been in my life, and I wasn't sure I was going to have the dexterity to reach for his offered hand when I got to him. I looked up at his too-pretty face set in concerned and annoyed lines and it hit me like a bolt of lightning what Asa meant when he said he always saw Royal at the top so he never stopped trying to climb up from the bottom.

With Quaid looking down at me, worried about me after I made yet another questionable decision, I knew that I wanted to not only keep swimming no matter how cold I was or how hard it got, but that I also wanted to reach for him. I wanted to make my way from the bottom to the top, or as close to it as I could come after years and years of purposely failing and falling.

I finally reached the lower outcropping; all I had to do was lift a hand out of the water, and Quaid had me. He pulled me up and out of the water like I weighed nothing and like I wasn't a quivering mass of uncooperative limbs that couldn't and wouldn't move. My teeth were chattering together so loudly that I didn't try to protest when he took his own leather jacket off and wrapped it around my quaking shoulders. The leather was warm from his body heat and I huddled into it as he ran a hand over my dripping hair and shook off the excess water that was still coursing over my skin.

"I can't believe you used to do that for fun." The words tripped over themselves as he pushed his hands under the opening of the jacket and began to rub them vigorously over my chilly sides. I was covered in goose bumps and I was pretty sure my lips were an attractive shade of blue.

"I outgrew the need to pursue danger for a thrill, and now only chase after it when it serves a purpose or a greater good. The rush lost its appeal when Harrison snapped his arm in half. We need to get you back to the cabin and in front of the fire before you start forming icicles on your eyelashes."

I jerked my head from side to side and leaned into him. "Too cold to walk."

He swore under his breath and pulled me closer to him. I snuggled into his much warmer body and sighed in contentment as his heat started to soak into my frozen skin.

"Was it worth it, Avett? You're ice cold and you're lucky you didn't get hurt. Was the risk worth it?"

He sounded pissed off, so I tilted my head back so I could meet that wintry gaze. I pressed into him further and let out a tiny gasp as one of his big hands worked its way under the clingy lace of the bra I still had on and smoothed over my breast. My skin instantly warmed where he touched, and my already tight nipple pulled even tighter as pleasure pushed past the chill that engulfed me.

"Ask me after."

His eyebrows danced upwards on his forehead as his fingers started to play with the velvety peak that was begging for attention.

"After what?"

I lifted an arm up around his shoulders so that I could get my hand on the back of his neck and couldn't hold back a grin as my icy touch made him squirm. "Just after."

I pulled him towards me so that I could get my mouth on his. The sensation of my icy lips melting against the warmth of his had me shivering for a reason other than the cold. His tongue tangled artfully around mine and his long finger moved to trap the peak of my breast between them. He rolled the sensitive nub back and forth, creating heat and friction that I felt between my legs. One of his hands smoothed down my still-shivering spine and cupped me under the curve of my ass so that he could pull me more fully into the length of his big body. I groaned into his mouth when I felt the press of his stiff erection against my stomach. My underwear was still soaking wet but the skin under it was getting tingly and hot as Quaid worked his big, rough hand under the delicate lace.

"They do say the quickest way to get warm is to share body heat." The dry humor in his deep voice did wonders on its own to warm up my sluggish blood.

I moved a hand to his waistband so that I could start pulling his dark gray Henley out of the waistband of his pants. "Well, sharing is caring, so let's get to it."

He helped me get both layers of his shirts off over his tawny head and when his taut, burnished skin pebbled up in reaction to

the chilly outside air I pulled my mouth away from the invasion
of his and started chasing over those bumps with my tongue.
That majestic eagle once it was revealed looked like it belonged
here, like it was a part of his very essence that had been waiting
for years and years to be returned to its rightful place. I rubbed
my fingers over the impressive design and lost my breath as the
hand that he had wrapped around my backside began to move.

It was a very short trip for his questing fingers to reach their
destination, the soft and slowly melting point between my
legs that lately felt like it was created only for him, but I was
surprised and jolted a little when one of those wandering digits
disappeared into the crevasse that I had never had anyone
venture into before. It was barely the brush of a fingertip, the
barest hint of a caress, but his blue eyes radiated with passion
and curiosity and his unexpected touch on that hidden place
made me vault up on my toes and cling even tighter to him.
He always seemed to find a new way to test me, to spark my
curiosity about things I didn't ever think about before he came
into my life, be they things related to sex or things related to
something deeper and more meaningful, like whether or not I
was the only one solely to blame for everything that happened
the night everything changed. I didn't know I had those kinds of
boundaries and I reveled in the fact that he pushed me to cross
them and to redefine them.

His mouth moved across my cheek and I could feel the tip
of his tongue chasing water droplets that still clung to my skin.
The sensation of hot and cold did wonders to spark arousal in my
still-chilly and sluggish blood. His lips skimmed my ear and my
legs went weak when his skilled fingers found their way to the
one part of me that was most definitely not cold. In fact, it was

scalding, burning, and melting into a liquid puddle of desire, all for him. "I've wanted a lot of things in my life, Avett, and I've spent more time and money than I care to think about trying to get them."

I muttered a useless noise into the side of his neck because he had dipped a finger inside of me and was busy swirling the scorching heat he generated around the stiff point of my clit. The slickness of my own pleasure contrasting with the rough, damp, and chilly fabric of my underwear was enough to have my entire body feeling like it had received an electric charge. I whimpered his name and clung to his broad shoulders uselessly as his fingers moved between my legs, owning and playing with my wanting body while his words worked at fully possessing my head and making their way inside my difficult heart.

"Of all the things I've wanted most, none of them have made me feel as possessive or as desperate as you do. I want to have you every way I can think of, and then I want to invent some new ways to have you so that there is never any question about who you should be with. I want every single part of you to have some part of me inside of it, so that you won't go a single second without thinking about me and about how much I want you." I wondered if that included my heart because even though I knew this wasn't meant to be, there was a pretty big chunk of him in there already, and I didn't really want to pry him out of it.

I tunneled my fingers into his hair as he put his mouth back over mine and leaned heavily into him as he grabbed the back of my thigh, hoisting one of my legs up over his hip so that he had better access to that sweet spot that seemed all too eager to pulse in happy little flutters as he worked his thick digits in and out of the weeping opening. He made me so wet and that wetness was trailing a molten and heated path along the bend in my leg as he hiked me farther up onto his hard body and clamped me in a tight grasp as he started to lower himself to his knees on the uneven surface of the rock we were perched on.

I let out a cry of pleasure as the new position had me straddling his strong thighs and the distended metal of his zipper hit me right in my most tender of places. The scrape of his zipper against the lace that still covered me and the chill of it against the hot bundle of nerves, mixed with the sensations caused by his plundering fingers, took me to the edge of release in almost no time. I heard a bird squawk in irritation overhead but I was too busy trying to get my shaking fingers around his belt buckle to be distracted by the wildlife that were about to get one hell of a show.

I wiggled so that the front of his jacket I still had on was open enough that I could get my breasts up against his bare chest. My nipples stabbed happily into his inked skin and I sighed into his kiss as I dragged the achy tips across his rapidly cooling skin. He growled at the feel of velvet and lace as it dragged across his flesh in one of the most intense and erotic caresses I had ever given to anyone. As soon as I had his pants open and his zipper carefully down around that always impressive package that was waiting for me behind it, he shifted his scissoring fingers from where they were working inside of me to where the fully exposed center of my pleasure was practically begging for their attention. My clit knew his touch, perked up under the rough pads of his fingers, and quivered with so much delight and tightly coiled pleasure I was pretty sure I was going to die from it.

I moaned low and loud and was startled as the sexy sound reverberated around us as the ravine we were in echoed our pleasure and the sounds of our delight as we ravaged each other. I helped him wiggle his jeans down far enough that I could get at the goods, but not far enough that his knees were going to get torn up on the rough surface he was kneeling on. One of his hands found its way beneath the jacket and curled possessively around one of my bouncing breasts as I ground myself against his quick fingers and the hard ridge that was toying with my eager opening. Quaid knew exactly what I was chasing down as I moved on him wantonly and without shame, unafraid of the cold or the nothingness that surrounded our heaving bodies. He worked my clit until I was a blubbering and incoherent mess of need and want on top of him, his touch getting rougher and more firm the more wildly I moved and rocked on top of him.

I grabbed his pulsating cock from where it was hovering right beyond the point I wanted it most, and lifted up barely enough so that I could drag the bulbous and leaking tip through my soaked folds. We both let out a strangled sound at the sensation and his leisurely teasing of my clit intensified to the point that I thought I was going to lose my mind if I didn't come soon. The sensation of his air-chilled skin sliding through our combined warmth had Quaid swearing and me whimpering in desperation.

I dug the fingers of my free hand into the side of his neck and was gratified to see his muscles straining and his veins popping as I continued to rub him through my wetness and tease him with my opening. The tip of his cock was more than wet; it was shiny and covered in both of our excitement. Personally, I thought I'd never seen any man or any man's dick look better. Quaid looked sexy as hell covered in what he did to me. It made me moan out loud and did a lot to chase away the last of the chill lingering inside my bones. My body was doing its best to pull him inside, my inner walls quaking and clenching like they had been waiting for his cock and only his cock forever, like they were bereft and lonely without his powerful shaft to clamp down onto. I lifted up just a little so he was holding me to his chest and let that glistening and slippery rod coast through the crevasse where his curious fingers had been playing earlier. He could tease new and unexpected things, but so could I.

I watched his eyes widen and darken to almost navy blue as I wiggled my hips and rode him with a different, untried part of my body. We both started breathing harder and I could see the speculation and curiosity in his gaze. I liked the way he felt back there, liked the way I felt with him back there, so I made a mental note that executive sex had some really interesting things to offer that I was definitely missing with intern sex. Done with the heated and suggestive manipulation, Quaid tweaked the nipple he was playing with hard enough that it sent a jolt of pain shooting through my nerve endings. I jerked back from trying to eat his mouth with my own and gave him a scowl. His eyes had shifted from denim blue to a stormy slate and I could tell he was as done with the teasing as I was. His nimble fingers abandoned my desperate clit and shifted to the side of the panties that were once again soaking, only this time it was from desire and need and not the mountain water.

"You need to get one of the condoms I put in the pocket of my jacket and put it on me, right now." I heard the sound of fabric tearing and a pop of elastic as the side of my panties gave way to the force of impatient hands and the slide of a chilly blade against my skin. I'd read about men ripping their women's underwear off in the heat of the moment a million and one times, but I never thought I would be on the receiving end of the action or that the

man doing the ripping would be someone like Quaid. He was a
Boy Scout, always prepared, but I doubted getting women naked
in the heat of passion was one of the uses that young scouts
were taught when they were handed their Swiss Army knives. I
admired in ingenuity and shivered at the thought that I was the
one to make him let loose his uncivilized side, that I was the one
that brought him back to his most primal self, almost had me
coming all over the very rigid erection that I still had trapped
between my legs.

My heart was kicking hard and fast in my chest as I stuck a
hand in the pocket of his jacket that I still had on. "You brought
condoms hiking?" I couldn't help the laugh that escaped with the
question.

He grunted a noise at me and put a hand in the center of my
back so that I could shimmy out of the tattered remnants of the
underwear, and so that I could get a grip on his throbbing cock.
I angled his erection away from where I wanted it most, enough
to get the condom on him. His feathery eyelashes lowered as my
fingers rolled the latex down over the stretched and silky skin.

"I went hiking with *you*, so of course I brought condoms. I
would bring them with me if we were going to the grocery store,
or to the post office. I would grab a handful of them if I was
taking you to church. I told you . . ." My mouth fell open and my
head fell backwards as he pushed against my hand and finally
entered the opening in my body that was begging and weeping
to be filled by him and him alone. "You make me desperate and
needy. The time and place doesn't seem to matter. The only
thing that does is that you let me in."

I was sitting on his lap, stretched wide open before God and
country, and all I could think about was how sweet his words

were as they drifted across my now flushed and rosy skin. He said all the right things as his body invaded and took me hard and fast. He spoke sweetly as he fucked me wild, and there wasn't anything I could do to stop him from working his way even deeper into all those places inside of me he said he wanted to fill.

I was perched up on his legs in a way that kept my knees from dragging across the rough terrain he was kneeling on, so all I could do was hold on to his shoulders with one hand as he lifted me up and down on the straining shaft between us. I watched his thick cock, shiny and glistening with our combined pleasure, as it hammered in and out of my body. The deeper he pushed in, the darker the blue in his eyes got, and the wetter I became. It was more than fucking rough and uninhibited. It was a joining, a connection between us that went beyond the way my lower lips parted so prettily for him as he dragged almost all the way out and then used the leverage he had on me to haul me back down so that it was almost impossible to tell where either of us started or stopped. We were one being, intent on bringing each other pleasure. We were one essence, focused on taking what the other person was offering and giving it back to them a hundredfold. We were intent on undoing each other with passion and pleasure, and it really felt like we could mend the holes each of us had within us with the parts the other was leaving behind.

Quaid's other hand held me in the middle of my back, between my now-sweat-slicked skin and the heavy jacket, so I could lean backwards, the ends of my still-wet hair touching the ground. He growled at me to move the front of the coat out of his way as he continued to rock me up and down on his cock like a piston. I felt used and manipulated in the best way possible. He was taking his pleasure and giving me mine and all I had to do was leave myself in his steady hands. As soon as my lace-covered breasts were revealed, his blond head swooped down and engulfed one pert nipple into the scalding heat of his mouth. His teeth scraped none too gently across the soft skin and it made me gasp in a mixture of pleasure and pain. I was lifting a hand to tug at his golden hair when his raspy voice ordered me to "Put your hands on yourself."

Since his mouth was busy licking and sucking its way across my heaving chest, I figured he wanted my hands in only one place. The place that was spread wide around his cock, which pulsed and pounded in a rapid entry and retreat from my quaking core. Every time he pulled out just so, the hint of his swollen tip touched my folds and the frosty mountain air hit the wetness pooled between us, which made me catch my breath at the stunning sensation. Then when he plunged back inside of me, chasing the internal chill with his molten arousal, the sensation from the temperature change on such sensitive tissue was enough to have me screaming so loudly I was surprised flocks of birds didn't scatter from the nearby trees.

He chuckled at my response and repeated the action a couple more times until I got my uncoordinated fingers to obey his repetitive command to touch myself. I loosened my death grip on his corded neck and skimmed my fingers over the nipple he wasn't loving on with his tongue and teeth, then that hand danced across the curve on my belly until I reached the place where we were connected.

The place that was all the best of all the things in this moment. Me and him. Him and me. Hard and soft as it collided with hot and cold. I shivered and my touch tripped through the evidence of how well we were working each other over, and when I got my fingers on that little point of pleasure, it practically vibrated at the first gentle swipe of my fingertip on the sensitive bundle of nerves. I groaned and slammed my eyes shut as pleasure, more powerful than any of the purposeful pain I filled myself up with could ever be, took over.

I felt it move through each of my limbs. I felt it pulse under the bite of Quaid's teeth where they were anchored into the side of my neck. I felt it in the way my nipples hardened to points so hard they physically hurt and I felt it in the way my body locked down on Quaid's surging dick to try and keep him in place. My inner walls milked him, my channel spasmed around him, and every last bit of desire and satisfaction I had left inside of me rushed out and consumed us both. I wanted him with me, forever.

I panted through the orgasm as it ripped me apart on the inside. I was pretty sure the intensity of it had turned my heart upside down and all the garbage that was usually inside of it was now dumped out. I could barely breathe, couldn't think past the fact that this man did things to me and for me that I wasn't sure I would ever deserve, but then he whispered my name against my neck and I realized he was still chasing down his completion. He was always giving to me before he took for himself.

I shifted on his lap, rocked myself up and forward so that I could get some leverage on the ground and began to ride him—hard. I plowed my fingers in the soft hair at the base of his neck, put the other on the side of his face so he couldn't move as I lowered my head to devour his mouth with wet, aggressive kisses. It was my turn to speak to him sweetly while I fucked him wild.

I rocked my hips back and forth and kissed his cheek so that I could get my lips next to his ear. I licked the outer edge and then whispered softly, "You can have me any of the ways you want me, Quaid. I'm happy to let you in, as long as you know what's waiting for you once you're inside."

I wasn't sure if it was the words or the image that went along with them, because even though I'd never let anyone touch me in the places he had hinted at, the thought was intriguing and almost dangerous, so it had my spent and sated nether regions perking up with renewed interest as his hips bucked up hard to meet my final downward thrust. He roared into the wilderness like the primitive, animalistic man he was here, in this place with me, and I felt his entire, big body shake as his orgasm rolled over him. I could feel his cock kick and jerk inside of me as his hips stopped moving and as his eyes quit burning.

His chest was billowing in and out like he had run a mile, so I grinned up at him as he slowly lowered me the rest of the way to the rocks, making sure the heavy material of his jacket protected me as he settled into the cradle of my hips where we were still joined.

He lifted a hand and used it to push my now hopelessly tangled and snarled hair off of my face. He brushed the pad of his thumb over the crest of my flushed cheek and breathed, "My mountains are still standing after my hurricane blew through them."

I shivered and felt my heart squeeze tight at the possession in his tone. I lifted my arms up so that I could hold him to me. "At least, this time, there was minimal destruction." We both knew I was capable of so much more.

When he lifted his head to look at me, his eyes had shifted back to the unusual grayish-blue and there was an emotion in them that I didn't recognize.

"Don't be so sure about that, Avett."

Not liking the seriousness on his face after what had been some of the most astounding sex in the world, I kissed him softly and rubbed the end of my nose against his.

"For the record"—I lifted an eyebrow at him and used my body to squeeze him where we were still connected on the inside— "I'm always going to jump and think the risk is worth it. That's part of who I am."

I couldn't tell by his expression if he agreed with me or not about the risk, but when I mentioned that I was on the pill and had gotten myself checked out as soon as I realized how deep into his addiction Jared was, his head jerked up and he seemed a whole lot more interested in the different kinds of risks we could take that involved having no kind of protection between us at all.

CHAPTER 14

Quaid

I was surprised how easily I slipped back into the role of the guy that knew how to do without and how to make the most out of very little. The two days spent in the tiny cabin with nothing more than a roaring fire and Avett for entertainment were some of the most peaceful, relaxing, recharging days I'd had in . . . I couldn't remember how long. I thought she was the one that needed escape from the commotion of her life but it turned out I was the one that really benefited from the forced unplugging and isolation. The quiet used to haunt me and taunt me with the emptiness and memories; now it soothed all kinds of ragged edges that I thought I had ruthlessly polished off. Plus, the way my name sounded when Avett screamed it or whispered it was so much better with nothing around for it to get lost in.

I felt like two parts of my soul that had always been ripped apart were slowly being stitched back together, but Avett seemed no different than she was deep in the heart of the city. She went fishing with me without complaint and didn't even balk when we had to clean and cook our own dinner. She tromped through the woods with me, her pink hair getting tangled with pine needles and bark as the trees reached out to touch her like I felt compelled to do. I took her out to the makeshift firing range that had been an integral part of my youth and was shocked and, admittedly, impressed that she handled my firearm almost as well as I did. She laughed and told me that when you were the daughter of a badass, things like spot-on aim and not being squeamish at the sight of blood came with the territory. The only thing she complained about was having to use the bathroom in the middle of the night and it wasn't even that she had to use the rickety outhouse; it was the fact that she was afraid of mountain lions and bears that made her grumble. All we had with us was what we packed into the backpacks the Ducati forced us to use and still she didn't seem to be missing a thing. She was content with me and the woods for company and that did something fundamental to all the truths I had been holding up as my reality for so long.

I wanted possessions to matter because I'd had so few of them growing up. I wanted stuff to make me important and to fill all the empty voids my childhood, the fallout with my folks, and the sham of my marriage had left in my life. I wanted to have so many things and obvious material objects so that no one could ever doubt my success or my worth because I lived in a constant state of fear that someone, like my ex-wife, would decide I wasn't enough. I was smart enough to know it was a deep-rooted fear that came from growing with parents that were more interested in teaching me how to survive than they were in teaching me how to love or how to be a good man. Because I wanted an education, because I wanted a way out, because I wanted more than they thought I needed, they always considered me the weakest member of the family. I wasn't strong enough. I wasn't resilient enough. I wasn't solid enough or brave enough to be the man they wanted me to be. So I chased after a girl that I knew would never settle for the kind of life I came from. I threw myself into a fight for a government my family abjectly disapproved of. I went into a career that was all about rules and order and I took up on the side that was guaranteed to put me in the press and in the crosshairs of ethics and morality. And I got the stuff. Submerged myself in the things because I had something to prove.

Only now, I wasn't sure who in the hell I was trying to prove any of it to.

The girl that currently had every single piece of me tied in knots and broken me down to my most basic, my most pure self, apparently didn't care about any of the shiny and opulent things I was surrounded with. She was happy with me wherever I happened to be, so there was no need to kill myself trying to show her the finer things in life.

My parents hadn't bothered to reach out to me since I let them know I bought back their land for them, and even then, other than to let me know that they weren't coming back to the lower forty-eight. Harrison and I used to be close, but when he left and my parents followed, I lumped them all into the category of what was. I never gave my little brother the benefit of the doubt. He might not know about my marriage ending, but I didn't have a single clue what he was up to, and how his life was going either. I felt like my folks abandoned me, but I'd never done anything to bridge the gap as I got older and maybe not so wiser.

If Lottie had been impressed, maybe she wouldn't have cheated or been so callous about how she treated the life we built together. I'd wanted to give her everything, and had tried, but there was always more, so I knew that no matter how much I worked or spent I was never going to have her look at me like I had done a good job. To her, I was always going to be the kid from nothing, doing his best to hold on to the girl that was out of his league.

There was Orsen and the guys at the firm. I worked my ass off, took cases other lawyers were scared of, and I won far more often than I lost. I made them money. I fit the mold that was set out for me to crawl right into when I was hired, and I did it all with determination and my eyes set firmly on the big picture. But the reality of the situation was that no matter how nice my home was or how expensive my suits were, they still hadn't made me a partner, and I had more than earned the right to have my name on the sign. I don't know if it was because I didn't have an Ivy League law degree like the rest of the partners did, or if it was because my messy divorce had made the news, or if it was simply that they knew underneath the veneer I was a guy playing at being civilized and refined. I wondered if those jagged edges that were so apparent here in the wild and with this girl were blatantly obvious to people that hadn't been born with them. I wondered if who I had been born to be was keeping me from being the man I was so sure I wanted to be.

After waking up with dawn in my face and pink hair tangled in my hands, I woke Avett up by kissing her, and touching her, and warming her up in front of the fire. I hated that I had to take her back to a place that wasn't safe and hated even more that I was going to have to put her into the hands of other men to keep her protected and out of the trouble that so effortlessly found her. I could tell she was nervous when we stopped for a late lunch, and I tried to reassure her that once her ex went to trial and saw that his lawyer had a bigger interest than his at play, Jared would do whatever he could to cover his own ass. I had a feeling his first night in jail without Acosta's protection would have him singing a new tune.

She nodded, but I could tell she was still worried about what came next and it made my heart throb because I was worried, too. My job was typically to put guys like Jared back on the streets. I never wanted the story and when the story was staring me right in the face, terrified and trying not to show it, I understood why I'd kept myself so separate from my clients. Emotion and personal attachment meant I couldn't do the job I was hired to do. The reason I had been so off-kilter and unsteady with her from the beginning was because she had managed to tell me her story without words. It was in her eyes and in the way she sat there, locked up, devastated, and forlorn over her circumstances, knowing she was the one that had orchestrated her own downfall. She was never a client. She wasn't a job or another victory I could put in my cap and tote around as I searched for validation that I shouldn't need or want. She didn't merely see past my personal façade to the man underneath; she had managed to slip under my professional one as well.

When we got back to the city I wanted to take her home with me, but she insisted that she should spend some time with her parents since they were all back under the same roof for the first time in too many years. I had to work early in the morning, and since I wasn't at the office on Saturday, I knew I was going to be drowning in paperwork so I reluctantly agreed. I also didn't miss the warning look that Brite sent me when I pulled up in front of the house with her on the back of the bike. To be fair, I wasn't sure the glare was for the fact I had his daughter plastered to me and wrapped around me or the fact that my bike wasn't American made. Either way, I nodded, acknowledging that he had his eyes on me, and lifted the dark visor off my face so I could stare at the tiny hurricane of a woman that had blown past all my defenses and turned my well-ordered and structured life upside down as she climbed down off her perch and moved to my side.

She leaned up on her toes and kissed me on the end of my nose and told me she would text me later.

I went back to my sterile and lifeless loft and took a scalding hot shower so I could get my head back where it needed to be before I went into work the next morning. It didn't work. All I could see was eyes with every single color of the woods we had left. All I could feel was soft skin and silky hair moving across my body. I brushed my teeth before getting in the shower but all I tasted was sweet chased by wild. Every single one of my senses had been corrupted by her, and by the time I shut the water off and climbed naked into bed I knew I was in for a restless night of sleep. My dick was hard and my brain was scrambled. It made for a particularly uncomfortable and annoying situation.

I had the lights off and was scrolling through emails for the morning on my phone when a message from Avett popped up. I was expecting a good-night text or a see-you-tomorrow text. What I got was:

> I miss your dick. I wanted to send you that text after the first time you kissed me, but I refrained.

I blinked at the glowing screen and then read and reread the message to make sure what I was seeing was accurate. No one sent me messages like that . . . no one except for Avett Walker. Sexting wasn't something I had much practice with and, frankly, wasn't sure I was any good at, but I was game to try.

It misses you, too.

Is it hard for me?

I looked at the dark sheet that was tented in front of me and let out a snort, suddenly glad I hadn't taken care of the discomfort the thoughts of her created while I was in the shower.

Unbelievably.

I want it in my mouth, or in my hands. Not picky. Where do you want it, Quaid?

I groaned into the darkened room and looked at the glittering lights of the city as they watched me wrap my fist around my now throbbing dick like curious voyeurs. I could feel my blood pumping under my fingers and tension coiling at the base of my spine.

I'm good with either of those places.

Lol. No . . . where do you really want that cock that's so hard for me, Quaid?

So many places. I wanted it between her legs where she was always so wet and ready for me. I wanted to bend her over and take her where I was positive no one had before. I could die happy with her sassy mouth so full of my cock that she couldn't wrap me up in her words and tell me her stories that broke me. I could get off with her small hands twisting and turning around my length. Her soft palm caressing me and holding on to my balls as she whispered in my ear of all the ways she wanted me. But since it was dark and I was rubbing myself off to my fantasy, I told her the truth. I told her where I wanted to ride her from the first time I got an eyeful of her spectacular breasts.

I want to fuck your tits. I want to kiss them and suck them until your slippery and wet . . . everywhere.

I panted a little as divulging it to her made my blood rush loud between my ears. I kicked the sheets off and squeezed the base of my dick—hard—as pleasure started to leak from the tip. Typing one-handed while I was jacking myself off took more skill than I ever would have imagined.

I want you to lay back, wrap those fantastic tits around my dick, and let me ride your chest while you open that pouty mouth and lick and suck the head until I come down your throat.

There wasn't a response for a long minute but the little ellipsis was flashing showing me that she was working sending a response back.

I've never done that before. And considering how wet you made me by telling me that, I'm assuming it's moving up on the must-try list.

I swore as my cock jerked at her words.

I'll be happy to show you everything I know, Avett.

Lucky me. Are you getting close? Are you picturing me touching myself, thinking about you, imagining you and all the delicious things you can do with that executive cock of yours?

I narrowed my eyes at her terminology for my junk. I needed to ask her what she meant by that, but right at the moment I got distracted as my balls started to ache, letting me know I was close.

Growling under my breath I shifted my thumb on my phone to her number and hit the call button so that I could FaceTime her. It was dark and when she answered I couldn't see more than her gleaming eyes and mischievous smile in the little box.

"Took you long enough." Her voice sounded thready and thin like it always did when she was about to come. "I was sure when I told you that you made me wet you were gonna call."

"I'm going to come and I figured you would want to witness the fruits of your labor." It was so out of character for me, so different from the sex I typically had, but it felt good. It felt right and totally freeing.

She whimpered a little and I watched as she moved so that she was lying down and holding the phone up over her face. I could see her shoulders shift and move as she worked herself over on the other end of the call.

"I'm close but I'm trying to keep it quiet. No noisy orgasms under Mom's roof."

I laughed a little and then groaned as I rubbed the flat of my palm over the weeping head of my cock. Moisture swirled around and as good as it felt it still didn't compare to her mouth or her gentle touch.

"Avett, hold the phone up higher. I want to see more of you."

It was dark and I wouldn't get a great view of all of her pretty, pale skin but she obeyed my gruff command almost instantly. I watched her chest rise and fall rapidly, her nipples puckered and raised in pleasure as her body moved in time with whatever her hand was doing out of the frame.

I exhaled her name and told her gruffly, "I swear those tits are going to be the death of me."

Her face was flushed and her breathing was getting erratic. "I didn't know you were such a breast man."

She licked her bottom lip and whispered my name as she tossed her head back on the shadowy pillows behind her. "I wasn't until yours."

"That's nice." Her eyes fluttered closed and the end of "nice" got drawn out into a long *s* sound. She started to pant in earnest and I barked her name to get her to look at me.

"Are you going to come, Avett?"

She nodded. "Yes."

My hips bucked at the word and my hand started to rock rapidly up and down the length of my shaft far more aggressively than I typically handled myself. Desire pounded furiously through every part of me and pleasure howled from somewhere deep inside of me to be released.

"I want you to come with me, so keep your eyes on me."

She nodded jerkily, and while I knew I could tell her to move the phone down so that I could watch her fingers moving through her slick folds and playing with all that pretty pinkness that puffed up and bloomed so sweetly for me, it was her face I wanted to watch as she broke apart. I wanted to know that it was me that did this to her, even when I was across town. I wanted this thing between us to be powerful enough and important enough that it should sweep both of us away no matter how we were connected.

"Quaid." It was my name uttered like it was the sweetest thing she had ever tasted that sent me over.

I growled her name in return and let out a satisfied hum as ropy streams of satisfaction spurted from the end of my very happy cock and landed on my abs.

I watched as her eyes snapped back shut and as her chest lifted up off the bed as her head tossed side to side. Her teeth bit down into her bottom lip hard enough to leave marks and every single part of her turned the same rosy shade of pink as her head. I wanted to lick her like she was my own cherry-flavored lollipop. She was gorgeous and the pleasure she found while thinking about me, while imagining us, was the most valuable gift anyone had ever given to me.

I waited for a few seconds for her to come down from the sex high, and when she did, she did it with a throaty chuckle and zero shame in coming for me in such a spectacular way.

I sighed and shifted so that I was sitting on the edge of my bed. I was going to need another shower.

"That was beautiful, Avett, and so are you."

She blinked at me and settled herself back into the bed behind her. "You're the beautiful one, Counselor."

I huffed out a breath. "As fun as that was, it's got nothing on watching you get off up close and personal. I've never been that great at looking but not touching. I want things, remember."

She yawned and gave me a sleepy grin. "I'll let you touch whatever you want next time we have a sleepover. I'll even let you try out those dirty, sexy things no one would expect a guy like you to be all about. I'm going to bed. Good night, Quaid."

A guy like me thought them but he never told anyone about them until the right someone came along. Who would have ever thought the right someone would be a tiny dynamo with pink hair and an appetite for self-destruction and trouble. "Night, Avett. Be safe tomorrow."

She nodded loosely. "Will do." She blew me a little kiss and the screen went dark.

I got to my feet and made my way to the bathroom. It wasn't until I was halfway through my second shower of the night that I remembered I wanted to know what she meant by my executive cock. The idea made me chuckle and as I washed the evidence of how she affected me off of my stomach. I wondered if the person that had coined the phrase "trying to capture lightning in a jar" had ever met Avett Walker.

THE NEXT DAY I was bogged down in client meeting after client meeting. A couple were cases I had already agreed to take on but a couple were new clients. New clients that I vetted way more carefully than I would have in the past. I asked questions. I wanted details beyond bank account balances and ability to pay my fees. I turned down a guy that was out on bail for suspected arson. He was a friend of Orsen's and told me the partner had sent him to me and that I couldn't come any more highly recommended.

I thanked him for the praise, but the more I talked to him, the more his inflated confidence and sense of entitlement filled my office, and the more I knew I couldn't and wouldn't take his case. The guy was accused of burning down his girlfriend's house after she left him for someone else. It was a brutal and unnecessary crime, and when he mentioned that the girlfriend, her new boyfriend, and the child that he shared with the woman were home when the blaze started, it took every ounce of self-control I had not to leap across my desk and hit him in the face. He had no remorse, no basic human decency to pretend like he was sympathetic to what was lost. Considering how devastated Avett had been after the fire that took her home I couldn't stomach the thought of helping this guy out.

I told him I wouldn't be able to take his case and got the expected reaction.

He was pissed. He called me a hack. He told me he would take it up with my boss. I told him that if he and Orsen were such close friends he should ask the partner to represent him at his trial. The guy huffed out of my office, leaving a slammed door and the stench of guilt and wrongness behind.

I knew my refusal to take the case and the paycheck attached to it would have Orsen in my office, so when my receptionist told me I had a visitor the last person I expected to walk through my door was Avett.

She had on leggings covered in a spray of colorful roses that clung to her curvy legs like a second skin, with her ever present combat boots and long black top that was fitted with a scoop neck until it flared out at her hips like a tutu. She looked like a hipster ballerina with her Technicolor hair piled up on the top of her head in a messy bun and bright red lips painted on her smiling face.

Before I could ask her what she was doing in my office downtown when she was supposed to be under lock and key, she shoved a Styrofoam container in my hands and bent down to give me a hard kiss on my mouth, which went slack with surprise.

"Asa is on Avett babysitting duty today and he had a property around the corner he wanted to look at. He's opening his own bar. He wants to do some kind of upscale speakeasy. He asked me if I wanted to run the kitchen for him." She barked out a laugh. "He's insane." Her eyes glowed at me as she propped her hip on the edge of my desk. "I told him your office was around the corner, so he walked me to the entrance, but then I saw that there was a Greek food truck parked across the street and bet you hadn't had lunch yet, since you were with me all weekend, so I thought I would say hi and feed you." All the words tumbled out each faster and more hurried than the other. She smiled at me and I felt it take up so much of the empty space that was inside of me. "Food trucks are like my new favorite thing. They have so many different kinds of food in them and they can go all over the city so you're not in one location. Freedom and food, they speak to my soul." She finally ran out of breath. "So hi, here's lunch."

I reached out and put my hand on her knee and crooked my finger at her so that she bent down enough that I could touch my lips to hers.

"Hi."

It was a sweet kiss. It was a kiss that had more than our mouths touching. I was pretty sure with the brush of her pouty lips against mine that I felt her heart bang against my own.

She put her hand on the side of my face and was rubbing her thumb across my cheek when she told me, "You look tired."

I snorted and ran my hand up her thigh until it was resting against the lush curve of her backside. I wanted to pull those ridiculous leggings off of her and put her in my lap on my dick.

"I wonder why?"

She snickered and bent so that her forehead was touching mine. "I have no idea."

I was going to kiss her again but as I was getting to my feet so I could grab her face and tilt her head back, my office door swung open and clattered against the wall hard enough to have my diploma and credentials shifting and sliding out of alignment.

I knew Orsen was going to be upset that I turned his friend away, but I didn't expect the red-faced, squinty-eyed, chest-billowing kind of mad that stormed into my office. Avett let her hands fall away from me and I took a step away from her and closer to Orsen as his furious gaze swept over us. I saw him take in her unusual hair and her colorful outfit before a nasty sneer twisted across his angry mouth.

"If you wanted to take on charity cases and get paid by getting your dick sucked, then you should have joined the D.A.'s office, Jackson. We are not a pro bono firm, we are a firm that takes clients that can pay . . . with money. Not with whatever else they may be offering." I heard Avett suck in a sharp breath and saw her whole body go stiff out of the corner of my eye.

I put my hands on my hips and gave Orsen a hard look. "That's enough. I've been picking and choosing my own cases for years, Orsen. I've earned that right. The one today was no different."

His angry gaze swept back over Avett and then bored into me with warning and threat obvious between each blink he took.

"No, but her case was different. Did you even bother to send her a bill, Quaid, or did you decide it was okay to waste your time and the firm's valuable resources because you wanted to get your dick wet?"

I opened my mouth to tell him he needed to shut the hell up when he held up his hand before I could even begin.

"If you want any shot at being made a partner you will take the case like you should have done this afternoon. You will tell your little playmate good-bye, send her an invoice, and get on with finding a proper"—the sneer on his face was so ugly that if I hadn't spent years perfecting a stone-cold poker face for jury trials I would have recoiled from him— "and suitable companion to bring with you to the company party. I don't know where your head or your priorities are at, Quaid, but this behavior is not becoming of the young man I hired. I'm starting to wonder if your ex took more than half your bank account with her when she left. Your common sense seems to have gone missing."

With another disparaging look he turned on his heel and stormed out of the office with as much bluster as he'd entered.

I ran a rough hand over my face and turned to look at Avett. She was staring at the place where Orsen had left with wide eyes and her lower lip was trembling.

"I'm sorry about that." The apology seemed so minimal for what my boss had said to her. "Orsen is kind of old school when it comes to things. He isn't very . . . progressive."

She cleared her throat and I could see how shaken the encounter had left her. I put a hand on her arm when she refused to look up at me and meet my eyes.

"Asa sent me a text. He's done looking at the space and he's waiting for me out front."

I bit back a bunch of dirty words and slid my hand up to her shoulder. "Avett, don't let what Orsen said get to you. You are different and your case was different, but it didn't have anything to do with me wanting to get you naked."

She finally lifted her eyes up to mine and I could see it so clearly. Disaster and destruction clashing bright and hot in the swirling depths. My hurricane had reached the shore and it was about to lay waste to this fragile thing that was starting to grow roots and take shape between us.

"Avett." Just her name but it was a plea, a promise that I didn't think like Orsen, a pledge that I would never discount her or devalue her the way my boss had done.

She shook her head at me and took a step to the side. A lopsided grin twisted her pretty mouth and it made me want to break every single thing in my office.

"Send me the bill, Quaid. I'll get it paid somehow. I know you mentioned not wanting checks and balances between us but they were always there."

I growled at her and took a step towards her but she held her hands up in front of her like she was trying to ward me off. "I don't care about the fucking bill, Avett. I care about you and keeping you safe and that you stop trying to destroy everything good in your life to make something up to a dead girl." I motioned between us with an angry sweep of my arm. "This is good between us, better than good, and you can't abide by it. You've been looking for a way to twist it into something else from the inception."

My words were harsh, accusatory, and I knew better than to go after someone feeling vulnerable that way. I'd seen too many witnesses shut completely down after similar tactics used by the prosecution.

"Maybe I have been waiting for it to go bad because—let's be honest with each other, Quaid—how many good things really come from the bad decisions we make?" She blinked at me and her eyes narrowed. "I'm never going to be proper or suitable. I'm never going to be the kind of girl you can take with you to some fancy office party . . . a party you never mentioned to me." I cringed because she had a point. I'd never mentioned the event because it was still a month away and her current situation with the loss of her house and the unknown bad guys after her seemed more pressing than some snotty shindig I didn't even want to attend.

She shrugged at me and headed for the open door. "I grew up in the back of a bar. My dad's half biker and half saint. My mom is a short-order cook with almost as many issues as I have, and I look supercute with pink hair, so I'm not planning on changing it, or me, anytime soon. I like where I come from and I'm finally starting to like who I'm coming to be." She cleared her throat and if I hadn't been watching her like a hawk I would have missed the sheen of tears that covered her eyes as she tossed over her shoulder, "I'm not trying to atone to a dead girl anymore, mostly because of you, but there are still a lot of people in my life that I do owe apologies and repentance to. I'm not interested in adding you to that list, Counselor."

She moved to the door and shut it behind her with a soft click as I stalked back to my desk and picked up the lunch she brought me and tossed it in the trash with more force than necessary. I kicked the side of my desk, which only led to my wingtip getting scuffed and my mood getting sourer. I threw my big body into my leather chair and glared at the crooked achievements that looked like they were barely hanging on to their place on my office wall. I'd worked so hard for all of those pieces of paper. I was so sure that they were going to ensure me the life I wanted and guarantee me everything that I thought would make me happy.

I saw them for exactly what they were, pieces of paper that

meant nothing unless the man that possessed them did some-thing worthwhile with his time and his talent.

It wasn't until I left for the day after ignoring more than one email from Orsen demanding that I take on his friend's case that it occurred to me that Avett hadn't left because she was hurt about what Orsen said to her; she left because she was hurt about what he said to me. She would weather blow after blow that landed on her because that's how she operated, but she couldn't stand to see someone she cared about, maybe even loved, in the line of fire. She didn't want me to put my job and possible promotion in jeopardy because of our relationship. I'd made no secret about how important my career was to me. She was protecting me the only way she knew how . . . by destroying the good and forgoing her own happiness. She would blame herself if my position at the firm was threatened because we were together and she was cutting off that culpability at the pass.

I called myself every kind of idiot I could think of for not recognizing her motivations sooner. I was too busy formulating my counterargument and dialing in my cross-examination that I fully planned to level at her that I'd forgotten that the girl I was falling for was equal parts whirlwind and martyr.

CHAPTER 15

Avett

It took a few days of moping around my mom's house and refusing to take Quaid's calls for my parents to ask what had happened with the handsome attorney. My mom didn't ask so much as give me pleading looks every time our eyes met that indicated she thought I should do whatever it took to fix the situation. I wanted to tell her for once I broke things for the right reasons and not because I purposely wanted to feel like I had ripped my heart out and left it resting at Quaid's feet. I wounded myself but I did it so that the man I was pretty sure I was in love with didn't have to hurt, and hurt he would if we stayed on the course we were on. Quaid deserved more than being caught circling a ceaseless dead end because he wanted to be with me.

There was no mistaking the disdain or judgment on his boss's face when he saw the easy affection that existed between the two of us and his hostile words were as true as they were painful to hear. I wasn't suitable or proper to the lifestyle Quaid lived and I wouldn't ever fit in with the kinds of people he worked with and longed to impress.

I'd finally felt the level of pain and agony that I had been hunting since the night everything went wrong. My heart felt like it wouldn't ever work right again and everything on the inside of me ached and throbbed like it had taken the worse beating imaginable. I would never feel like I had paid my dues to Autumn, and I would always carry around blame and responsibility for what happened to her, but Quaid had helped me to see that we were all responsible for our own actions and the only thing we could control was ourselves and the person that our choices molded us into. Making bad choices, repeatedly, hadn't made me into a bad person, but the way I handled those bad choices and let them twist into something worse had made me into a person that was desperately out of control and in need of guidance.

Walking away from Quaid and the goodness he offered didn't necessarily feel like the right choice, but I knew I was making the decision for all the right reasons and that was leaps and bounds ahead of where I had been before meeting him. I finally met the right guy; it was a shame I would always be the wrong girl for him.

My dad was more direct than my mother. He always had been. He waited until Mom went to bed one night and then sat down with me on the couch when I was deep into an *Archer* marathon, wishing I could be as kickass and as strong as Lana was. It was a pretty sad state of affairs and a pretty clear indication that my heart was hurting that the hilarious superspy hadn't managed to make me laugh once in the two hours I'd been zoned out in front of the TV. It wasn't my heart that was broken in this fall; it was all of me.

My dad threw a beefy arm around my shoulders and pulled me into his side so that my head was resting on his chest. I let out a quivering sigh and let my eyes drift closed so that the tears that had been threatening to fall since I walked out of Quaid's office once again gathered behind my eyelids.

"You want to tell me what happened?" My dad's voice rumbled deep and soothing over my head as I breathed in his comforting Dad scent. "Despite his terrible taste in motorcycles, I liked the guy. I liked him for you and we both know that never happens."

I laughed a little and sniffed as it tried to turn into a sob. "Right guy, wrong place and wrong time. Not to mention, I don't think I was ever really his type."

My dad harrumphed and I felt the hair on the top of my head move with the disgruntled sound. "He tell you that?"

He sounded offended on my behalf, so I lifted my head so I could look him in the eyes to make sure he knew that I was the one that had walked away, not Quaid. "No, Dad, he never said anything like that but I knew the end was coming before things even really got started. We don't live in the same kind of world." I laughed bitterly and laid my head back down. "One of his suits cost as much as my entire wardrobe."

My dad made another noise in his throat and curled his fingers around my shoulder so he could give me a squeeze. "You know better than to judge a man based on what he puts on his back. All that matters is that it's a strong back, one that can carry whatever load is stacked on top of it. I know I taught you better than that."

"It's not the clothes, it's everything. Where he lives. Where he works. Where his future is headed. We have common ground but we only seem to find it when we're naked."

His big body stiffened under me. "Don't want to hear about my baby girl being naked with anyone, ever."

I chuckled a little. "Sorry, Dad." It was rare he was uncomfortable about anything, but I guess the thought of his only child being anywhere near any kind of sex still had the power to make him squirm.

"Avett, I don't know much about your legal eagle, but he helped you out time and time again and refused to let you go about all that *Law & Order* business alone. He stepped in when he thought you were in danger and he showed up when you needed him when the house burned. That's some pretty solid evidence that the man is the right one in your old man's opinion. Those are the kinds of traits a father appreciates in the man his baby girl has her eyes on."

I snuggled in closer to him and muttered quietly, "I can't believe you're trying to convince me to keep a boy around. You never do that. You're always shoving them out the door and telling me to do better."

I felt his beard move against the top of my head as he sighed. "That's because Quaid isn't one of your boys, Avett. He's a man with his own life and a whole history that he had before you came along. It sounds to me like he's willing to share both of those things with you, and instead of taking him up on his offer you ran away. The boys were throwaway—this man's one you might want to consider holding on to, Sprite. Not sure anyone will ever be good enough for my little girl but this man comes pretty close."

I frowned at the TV and pushed off my dad so that I could sit up and cross my arms over my chest. "I didn't run away. I left because one of us was going to have to leave eventually."

My dad's bushy eyebrows lifted up and I saw his teeth flash within the forest of his beard. "Why? Why would one of you have to leave eventually?"

I opened my mouth to tell him that we didn't fit, that we didn't work, and that Quaid needed someone more elegant and refined that would suit his polished and pristine life. I wanted to argue that our backgrounds were too different, that what we valued and held dear were on opposing pages, in completely different books, on opposite sides of the library. I couldn't get the words out because they weren't really true. I'd spent my time trying so hard to feel as badly as I possibly could while Quaid spent his trying to feel as good and as successful as possible. Neither one of us had obtained our goal until each other. Right at this moment, I knew I felt as bad as I ever would and I had seen it in Quaid's eyes when we made love on his mountain that he had never felt that good and that worthy.

Like recognized like. And while we had both been lost and floundering on our own, when we were together it felt like we were exactly where we were supposed to be.

I heaved a sigh of defeat and slumped back into the couch. "I was at his office and his boss came in and made a bunch of shitty comments about me. He accused Quaid of only taking my case because he wanted in my pants and then told him he needed to find someone acceptable to bring with him to some office function. Quaid was pissed but all I could see was him trying to take me with him to something like that and it going horribly wrong. He's done so much for me in such a short time. I don't want him in hot water at work or at odds with his boss. He wants to make partner and I doubt if we stay together that will happen. I don't want him to sacrifice his plans or his dreams because of me."

My dad narrowed his eyes at me and it was his turn to cross his arms over his barrel-like chest as he glared at me consideringly.

"Why not? He's an adult and if he wants to sacrifice anything, including his career for the woman he cares about, that's his choice. It's not up to you to make it for him, Avett."

I poked a finger at my own chest. "I don't want to be a mistake he makes and suffers from. He's already lost enough." I wasn't comfortable giving my dad Quaid's story. It was his to tell and if he wanted my father to know the ins and outs of his child-hood and his divorce he could share those details, not that I was expecting them to get any bonding time in the near future.

My dad swore softly and lumbered to his booted feet. He bent over and dropped a soft kiss on the top of my head and I felt those damn tears threatening again. "I understand where you're coming from, Sprite, and I get that it's coming from a good place in your too-big heart, but that's still not your call to make. If the man wants to rearrange his life for you, that's his choice to make, be it good or bad. You don't get to corner the market on making risky decisions, Avett. Nothing is guaranteed, especially love, but only a coward doesn't roll the dice and take a chance on it when it's right there in front of them. Giving the man that has been there for you, that has shown up time and time again, the benefit of the doubt that he knows what he wants is far braver than tying yourself to all those losers that have been dragging you down for years. You were destined to fail with them, so when everything went south you knew it was inevitable." His eyebrows lifted and a knowing grin pulled at his mouth. "Look at me and your mom, kiddo. We lost before we won but we wouldn't have you or each other if we didn't pony up and gamble on each other in the first place."

I groaned. "Thanks for encouraging heartbreak and insanity, old man." But his words settled around me and taunted me with their wisdom. I was beyond defying his good advice because I knew it was the smart thing to do and I wanted to live unfoolishly. Now I wanted to live the best life possible and be the best Avett possible and that meant no more blowing off dad's sage wisdom and hard-earned insight.

He laughed. "Anytime. By the way, I'm meeting Zeb Fuller at the old house tomorrow. He wants to walk through it and see how much damage was done to the foundation and the outside brick. He thinks if there are enough bones left he'll make an offer and rehab the place."

I gaped at my dad in shock. The house looked like a total loss the last time I saw it. But he wasn't done.

"If he offers on it I'm making him give half that money to you since the house was half yours."

I shook my head in an automatic denial. He'd tried to do the same thing with the insurance payout but I wouldn't let him. "No, Dad. That money is yours. My name wasn't on the house and I want you to put all that money back into your retirement or maybe you can take Mom on a tour around the world. I haven't done anything to deserve that kind of generosity from you."

He swore at me again and narrowed his eyes in a way that I knew meant there was no more argument. "It's half yours, Avett, not because you earned it or deserve it but because you are my daughter, you lived there, and you lost as much as I did. I watched you grow into a young lady that has my whole heart there. It was always as much your home as it was mine. My retirement is fine, not that it's for you to worry about. I repaid the money I borrowed for your bail, and I haven't seen a bill from your man, so maybe you can use the money and settle up with him once it comes . . . though I doubt it ever will. I don't care what you do with the money, but if Zeb offers on the house, then that's what's happening. End of discussion."

I sighed in defeat but I couldn't deny that the idea of writing not only Quaid but also Rome a check for the actual, physical amount I owed them was tempting.

"Well, the house was a wreck so I doubt he'll make an offer. Night, Dad."

My dad chuckled. "You don't know those boys like I do, Sprite. They seem to be able to breathe life into anything that needs a second chance. Come with me tomorrow when I go to meet him and you'll see for yourself."

Since I wasn't spending much time on my own with the baddies still floating around, it was hang with him or at the bar all day and I still wasn't one hundred percent ready to have a showdown with Rome. I agreed to go to the house with him and spent the next hour in front of the TV letting his words really soak in.

He and my mom had both tragedy and triumph woven throughout their story. They both had some seriously bad decisions under their belts but the best choice for both of them was to be together. Neither of them seemed to regret allowing themselves to love one another even when that love had led to terrible heartache. I cared about Quaid enough to let him go, enough to let my heart hurt as it struggled to beat through the pain I had inflicted upon it.

I could love him and knew I could easily get lost in him and in the goodness he offered. What I wasn't sure of was if I was strong enough to weather the blizzard of the errors we were both bound to make trying to be together and the consequences that would rain down upon us. I survived my own mistakes and missteps by some kind of miracle. I didn't want to leave Quaid's fate and future happiness to that same kind of chance. I was the one who jumped; he was the one that stayed warm and dry. I didn't want my love to ruin him and I was scared that's exactly what it would do.

My dad thought the answer was right in front of me . . . I wasn't so sure we were looking at the same thing.

THE NEXT DAY I was standing in the driveway of my old home staring listlessly at the charred mess of brick and wood. I couldn't believe the beautifully restored home was nothing more than a scorched shell of its former glory. I couldn't believe my dad had the emotional strength to tromp through the ashes with Zeb as the big, bearded contractor knocked against walls and crawled all around the debris. The entirety of my father's earthly possessions were now nothing more than ashes that could be swept up and discarded, and when I said as much he gave me a hug and told me the things that mattered: me and Mom, his memories and experiences. Those were the things that he would be sad to lose . . . everything else was simply stuff.

I took a couple steps inside the front door intending to follow the men into the blackened depths and say a proper good-bye but the minute the total loss and wreckage hit me I turned around and walked back out. My dad didn't want me out in the open by myself so when he saw the flashy Cadillac parked across the street he marched over and knocked on the door. Moments later, a sleepy-looking Hudson Wheeler was standing at my side rubbing his eyes and stifling a yawn.

He was even more attractive than I thought he was up close. I liked his mahogany-colored hair and the way his blue eyes crinkled up with sympathy and anger as he looked at the nightmare before us. His eyes were a couple shades darker than Quaid's and far less world-weary and sharp but they were a pretty, clear blue and that made my heart kick hard when they turned my way. I was used to being around heavily tattooed men, but this guy had most of the guys I knew beat hands down in the ink department. Both sides of his neck sported swirling designs and the back of each of his hands were marked with impressive art-work. When he cocked his head to look at me questioningly, I noticed he even had ink etched into his skin behind his ears. He was colorful, beautiful, and softly spoken. His mellow demeanor was at serious odds with his tough-guy exterior and it made me like him even more than I thought I would. I decided then and there that I hated his bitchy girlfriend even more for all the times she kicked him around for the entire neighborhood to see.

"It's such a bummer. I hate that this happened to you guys. Brite is the best."

I nodded absently and looked over my shoulder where a non-descript sedan had pulled up to the curb in front of his house. There was a lone female driver that seemed to be looking at something on her phone and nothing about her screamed bad guy so I turned my attention back to my attractive and tattooed companion.

"How's the wedding planning going?" I was secretly praying that he was going to tell me that the she-beast had been abducted by aliens but no such luck.

He shrugged and muttered, "It's going. No one told me that it was going to be so hard. I feel like there should be a handbook or something. We've always been together, so it seemed like the next logical step for us to take. I didn't know it was going to be more like taking a leap out of a plane without a parachute."

I coughed to clear my throat and gave him a look out of the corner of my eye. "Do you ever stop and think that if planning the wedding is so hard, how difficult the marriage is going to be?"

He stiffened next to me and I saw his tattooed hands curl into fists by his sides. "We've been together since high school. Things weren't like this until we got engaged." He looked at me almost to see if I thought his words were convincing. They weren't.

"Most of us aren't the same people we were in high school. Hell, I'm not the same person I was a couple months ago. We grow and we change. I think the key is that if you're with someone you do that growing and changing with them." Kind of like Quaid and I had been doing with each other the last couple of months. He had definitely opened my eyes to things I needed to see in a different light but I knew I had done the same for him. I knew that he had to know that he was completely lovable and worthy regardless of how big his TV was or how much money he had invested. He was so much more than his possessions, and I hoped that instead of resenting where he came from, I helped him realize it was a part of him that had enabled him to accomplish all the things he had. Without him, I would still be clinging to the ledge of guilt and blame, refusing to let go. Because of him, I was climbing and had my eyes firmly on anyplace that wasn't rock bottom. I was trying to reach the top.

Wheeler didn't comment but he did look over his shoulder at his house and then back at me with his rust-colored brows furrowed.

"Kallie used to be the sweetest girl in the world. She never had a mean thing to say about anyone and she was always happy. I had it really bad at home so her cheer and her infectious attitude was my escape, not to mention her folks took me in even when they knew what I was doing with their daughter when her bedroom door was closed. I needed her. I don't think I would have survived high school or gotten to where I am today without her. She never minded that I spent more time with my cars than her and she was always my biggest supporter. We moved in together and I put a ring on her finger and it seemed like overnight all of that changed. We're getting married in a few months and all I can hope is that the girl I fell in love with shows up to meet me at the altar."

I cringed because I was pretty sure that girl didn't exist anymore and this very nice boy was going to make the biggest mistake of his life if he tied himself to the shrew he currently shared his life with. It wasn't my business and I wasn't sure that it was my place, but I couldn't do nothing. I wasn't ever doing nothing again; that was one lesson learned. So I put a hand on his arm and told him solemnly, "I know you don't know me and that my reputation with the people we both know probably doesn't inspire any kind of trust in me, but I have to tell you that every day you leave for work a red Honda pulls into your driveway and stays until about an hour before you get home from work. I don't know if you have a cleaning service or if your girl has a friend over all the time, but to me it's shady as hell, and you seem like a really nice guy so regardless if you believe me or not, I'm telling you that the chick that lives in that house with you is not the girl you are describing."

I thought he would balk or laugh off the accusation but instead his shoulders slumped and his head dropped forward like it suddenly weighed a thousand pounds. He lifted his hand and rubbed the back of his neck while staring at the concrete between the toes of his battered checkerboard Vans.

"Every day?"

I nodded even though he wasn't looking at me. "Every day."

He heaved a deep sigh and then turned his head to look at me. "I caught her cheating on me once before. We broke up and she spent six months promising me it would never happen again and she did everything to convince me that the girl I loved was back. As soon as I proposed all of that went down the drain, and we were back to how it was when we were broken up." He swore and tossed his head back so that he was looking up at the sky. "How hard do you think it is to cancel a wedding?"

That surprised a chuckle out of me. "Probably easier than planning one with that human nightmare has been. Look, I don't know who the car belongs to or what is actually going on under your roof when you're not there. But I have heard the way she talks to you and how unappreciative she is, so regardless if she's been unfaithful or not, I promise you can do better."

He sighed and I really wanted to hug him. He totally had the moody, broody thing down and it really, really worked well for him. Once he ditched the she-beast, he was going to be single for exactly zero seconds. The women of Denver knew a catch when they saw one, me and my own terrible taste in men obviously excluded from that group. Though my body had no trouble knowing that Quaid was an absolute keeper, it was my head and my heart that needed to figure their shit out.

"Is there better than the girl that you've loved since you figured out how to love?"

I patted his arm and dipped my chin in a nod. "There is better than the girl that doesn't know how to take care of that love. That, I'm sure of."

His eyebrows dipped down over his eyes and his mouth pulled into a tight line. "I sold a car to this girl yesterday. She came in with one of my friends and she was so sad, so quiet and shy. It was obvious she didn't want to be seen, but I saw her. I mean I really saw her, and when I was looking at her and trying to figure out what could have possibly happened in her life to make such a pretty girl look so scared and so lost, I wondered if I would have noticed any of it if things were the way they were supposed to be at home. Other girls were never on my radar in any way before Kallie and I started having problems."

"My dad seems to think that the answer to all of those kinds of questions are staring us right in the face." He gave me a sad grin and I almost died when I noticed he had dimples, one adorable little indent in each of his cheeks. Like the tattoos and the pensive persona weren't enough to get him laid on the regular? Those damn dimples would seal the deal for sure.

"Your dad would be proud that you're doling out his advice. You need to perfect his 'listen to me or else' look."

I laughed. "If you tell him I'm quoting him, I'll deny it. He has enough 'I told you so' stocked up to last a lifetime."

I jumped when a voice from behind us called, "Avett Walker?"

Even though Wheeler hadn't gotten the full rundown of what was going on in my chaotic life at the moment, he still stepped in front of me and made sure I was completely covered by his much bigger body as the woman that had been in the car across the street slowly approached us.

"Are you Avett Walker?" Her tone was serious and so was the way she stared at us without blinking.

"Who are you?" Wheeler was the one that barked the question

as I peeked around his muscular back to peer at the woman. She had a folded piece of paper in her hand and I felt my blood go cold.

"I'm from the sheriff's office. I have a subpoena for you."

Wheeler stiffened in front of me, and while every single part of me wanted to refuse the paperwork in her hand, I knew I had to take it. I scooted around the tattooed wall in front of me and snatched the folded papers out of her hand. She nodded at me and told me, "You've been served. Good luck."

I held the papers to my chest and couldn't keep my fingers from shaking.

"What was that all about?" Wheeler's voice was curious but not prying, so I sighed and tapped myself on the forehead with the court documents. I didn't want to open them because I knew once I did I was going to have to call Quaid and ask for his help and my heart wasn't ready to go back into battle with him or for him yet.

"That was one of my bad decisions. I can't seem to shake them and they continue to bite me in the ass. My dad insists bad decisions lead to great stories but so far all this one has led to is my heart being confused and mile-high legal fees."

There was a soft chuckle next to me and this time I didn't bother to hide the sigh that escaped when those amazing dimples appeared on his face.

"Messed up hearts and legal fees sound like they should make for a pretty good story."

They should, but I was hoping it was a story that was going to have a happy ending and I couldn't see that happening right now.

I could see my dad and Zeb walking towards us with their bearded faces set in satisfied lines. They both had grime and soot streaked all over their clothes and in their unruly hair but I could tell by the matched set of their shoulders and steady strides that they had struck some kind of deal.

I should've known not to bet against one of my dad's boys. Even if the house was a total lost cause, Zeb would never throw in the towel. Because the house mattered to my dad and my dad mattered to Zeb.

It looked like the legal fee part of my story was indeed going to have a happy ending. I crossed my fingers and closed my eyes and wished and hoped to any silent being that was listening up above that the bewildered heart part would straighten itself out as well.

CHAPTER 16

Quaid

I looked at the man that was seated at the other end of the long glass table from me and Avett and tried not to let my irritation show. She was stiff as a board next to me and I couldn't tell if the tension coming off of her in waves was from having to confront Jared's attorney during this deposition or if it was from the fact that we were close enough to touch. She wouldn't look at me, but I could see her unease and anxiety in every delicate line of her face. Technically, she wasn't even my client anymore because the charges against her had been dropped, but when she texted me that she had been subpoenaed and asked what "discovery" meant, I knew that I wasn't letting her walk into the legal lion's den alone. Much to Orsen's obvious and much vocalized displeasure, I had cleared my morning so I could sit with her in this sharply modern conference room located at the courthouse as her ex-boyfriend's attorney tried to pick her apart and break her down. I knew the deposition was pretty much a dress rehearsal for what he had planned for her when she took the stand, and I could see the calculating intent in the other lawyer's demeanor as soon as he ushered us into the room.

Larsen Tyrell was dressed better than I was, his shoes were more expensive, and the watch on his wrist was just as ridiculous and pricey as the one on my own. Before Avett crashed into my life and turned everything upside down and sideways, all of that would have rubbed me the wrong way and put me automatically on the defensive. I would have come out swinging and aggressive, trying to make it clear we were on equal ground; now all I could think was that having drug traffickers and clients with ties to the cartel noticeably paid well, but wondered how Larsen could enjoy his posh surroundings knowing that it came from blood money. His suit was perfectly tailored and clearly imported but I couldn't stop myself from wondering how many people had had to die at the hands of the people he represented in order for him to be able to afford it. There wasn't an ounce of envy or desire to have any of what Larsen had to be found anywhere, and that was how I knew the woman sitting rigid and unblinking next to me had done as much to save me as I had done to save her. She was a wake-up call I had desperately needed. My eyes were fully open and the man I had been striving to be with such single-minded focus was nowhere to be seen, and instead the man that now looked back at me was one that didn't feel fake or forced. He also wouldn't fight over frivolous things, but he would fight for the things that mattered. Right now, nothing mattered more than the pink-haired young woman at his side. The one he knew without a doubt he loved beyond measure and wanted to keep forever.

I leaned back in my chair and moved my elbow over so that

it was resting against hers where she was gripping the arms of the chair like she would float away if she dared let go. At the brief contact, she finally let out a long breath and turned to look at me with wide and intimidated eyes. I dipped my chin to let her know everything would be okay and she returned the small gesture and finally started to relax by fractions.

"We finally have a trial date and the jury selection done. It's in a little under two weeks and you're the prosecution's first witness. I'm surprised Townsend didn't want to sit in on this discovery session." Larsen flashed an artificially polite and whitened smile at us and I didn't miss the dig that I was here instead of the D.A.'s office.

"I'm the attorney of record on this case. I'll pass along anything I think Townsend needs to know before the trial." I narrowed my eyes at the other attorney as his shark-like smile widened.

"So, is it professional interest in your client's participation in the upcoming trial that brought you here today?" I stared at the other man without answering him. I wasn't representing Avett in court any longer so there was no conflict of interest now that our professional relationship had turned personal, but Larsen was making it no secret that he planned on twisting those facts to however they best suited him. The guy was as slippery and shady as the people he represented.

"I'm interested in my client's interests—period. Get on with it, Tyrell. All this flash and showmanship might impress the prosecution and the jury, but frankly, I'm bored, and both Ms. Walker and I have better things we could be doing with our time."

The man's eyebrows arched up as he laced his fingers together and gave me a smile that made my skin crawl. "I bet you do. I also have a full day and a court appearance, so I'll get right to the point. Ms. Walker, were you upset your father sold the bar that he owned to someone that wasn't you, the bar he had been grooming you to take over since you were old enough to work legally?"

I felt her body tighten next to me and as much as I wanted to comfort her I knew if I reacted in any way that Larsen would use it against her when he had her on the stand.

"I was upset, but not with my father. I was upset that I was such a mess, that I had never given him a good enough reason to hold on to the bar for me. He never told me that his plan was to turn the bar over to me when the time was right. I think it was an assumption that a lot of people, myself included, jumped to as I got older."

Her body was stiff and tight but her voice was light and clear. She wasn't hiding from the truth and I could see that Larsen knew, as well as I did, that her honesty and earnestness would come across clear as day to any kind of jury that was selected.

Larsen scribbled down some notes and then looked back up at us with that creepy smile that I really wanted to rearrange with my fist. "Were you upset when the new owner of the bar, Rome Archer, fired you for stealing from the cash register?"

She shifted a little in her seat and out of the corner of my eye I saw her full mouth pull into a hard line. "Again, I was upset, but only at myself. I knew there were cameras. I knew it was wrong, but I did it anyway because Jared insisted we needed the money. When you convince yourself that you're in love, you can justify doing a lot of rash things." I wanted to look at her to see if she was talking about the incident at the bar or something a little closer to home, but I wouldn't give the observant man at the other end of the table that kind of leverage.

"So you are telling me you knew you would get caught?"

She nodded and we exchanged a look. "I did."

He jotted down some more notes, and I could practically see the wheels in his head turning.

"Do you often do things that are illegal knowing you'll get caught?"

"I've made some mistakes in the past. I'm sure you have most of them in that file in front of you. Everything I've done is public record."

He was trying to rile her up, but she wasn't giving in to the bait and I couldn't be any prouder of her and how she was handling herself.

Larsen made a noise and moved forward in his chair. "The security cameras at the bar show that my client got physical with you before going inside the establishment. Was that an isolated incident?"

She lifted her fingers to her face and touched the smooth skin below her eye as she shook her head. "No. Jared got rough with me a couple times previously. Normally, when he was coming down off a high or freaking out about how he was going to get his next fix. He hit me once because I was supposed to bring beer to a party and I didn't and my mom and some co-workers noticed the black eye. One of the guys that works at the bar told Jared if I ever showed up with anything other than a smile on my face, he would make sure that I was the last woman he ever raised his hand to. He left me alone after that."

"So you knew Mr. Dalton had a substance abuse problem

and a history of violence and yet you went with him that night. Why?"

I felt her balk a little and couldn't resist the urge to look at her. Her eyes were wide in her face and she was very pale. It was obvious she was trying to think of a way to answer that question that explained her convoluted reasoning at the time without giving too much of her story away.

"Because I was scared and he told me he was taking me somewhere safe. I went with him because he was my boyfriend, and as I mentioned earlier, I was pretty sure I was in love with him."

"Not so sure of those feelings anymore?" The snide question had me narrowing my eyes threateningly at the other end of the table, which made the man smirk at me knowingly.

"Spending a couple nights in jail really does wonders for clarity. I could never love a man that threatened someone I care about with a weapon. Jared was desperate and dangerous that night."

"And why is that, Ms. Walker?"

She shrugged a little. "Because he stole drugs and money from bad people and they were looking for him."

"How do you know this?"

"Because before they found him, they found me." Her tone was cutting and it was obvious that Larsen was starting to get to her.

"Is that so? There are no police reports from you or from anyone else that indicates you had a run-in with these supposed bad people that were after my client."

"I didn't want to get Jared in trouble so I didn't call the police, but you can contact Asa Cross. He came to see me the day after the attack and he can tell you what I looked like. You can also question the landlady from Jared's apartment complex. She's the one that scared off the guys that attacked me."

Larsen leaned back in his chair and tapped his fingers on the file in front of him. "Well, you see, Ms. Walker, that's where we run into some problems with your account of the events that led up to the robbery. The landlady doesn't recall anyone being in the apartment besides you and my client, and Mr. Cross has an ax to grind considering he was the one at the bar the night of the robbery. The woman he is involved with is also the police officer that shot my client, so his interest in seeing my client incarcerated makes him biased in so many ways. The only person claiming there was an attack prior to the robbery is you, so isn't it much more likely that you were mad about the bar being sold out from underneath you and coerced your drug-addicted boyfriend to rob it? Knowing he couldn't say no to money for a fix or to the woman he loved?"

My skin crawled when he mentioned the landlady because I was pretty fucking sure her current memory loss only came about after fistfuls of cash exchanged hands. This guy wasn't above bribing a witness to get his way and that let me know that this was going to be as ugly and as dirty as it could get.

A broken laugh wheezed out of her as she turned her head in my direction and then jerked it back towards Larsen. "You've got to be kidding me. Even if I was mad, which I told you I wasn't, I would never risk the lives of the people that worked there. I was stupid enough to stay with Jared after the first time he hit me, but I would never inflict him on anyone else. I knew how dangerous he could be when he was high."

"Is that so?"

She heaved a deep sigh and shook her head. "Yes, it's so. I mess up and I get myself into bad situations, but I do my best not to let that bleed on to anyone that I care about."

"So, what happened with Autumn Thompson a few years back?"

She and I both stiffened when he mentioned the girl's name that had been so instrumental in leading Avett down the path full of self-inflicted wounds and purposeful pain. I heard her breath wheeze out of her in a tortured sound that had my heart cracking right down the middle.

"Autumn took her own life, as I'm sure you are well aware." I couldn't keep the razor sharpness out of my tone or the warning. I could typically play these dodge and parry games with the best of them, but with Avett caught in the middle and her composure as the prize I was barely keeping all the things I knew about brutality and violence leashed.

"Ms. Thompson's parents feel very differently about the matter. They have a lot to say about Ms. Walker and her influence on their daughter. It seems your client is very good at leading other people into trouble and then ducking out while everyone else suffers some very dire consequences."

"I think my client has a knack for finding lost souls and trying to help them out in her own way and we both know if you put the Thompsons on the stand that Townsend is going to pull them apart. Why would you question the parents and not the boys that actually hurt their daughter? The only people guilty of committing any kind of crime that night were the boys that attacked Autumn. Townsend's going to ask the parents why they let Autumn spend time with Avett in the first place if they were so concerned about her influence. He'll question their parenting ability and all the jury is going to see is you bringing up a dead

girl and rehashing bad memories. People don't like being manipulated, Tyrell. It doesn't go to probable cause at all, and the
judge won't let it go beyond one question. Your sole purpose for
bringing that part of my client's past up is because you wanted
to rattle her."

His eyebrows went up again and that slick-as-shit smile was
back on his face. It took every ounce of self-control I had not to
let my hands curl into fists where they rested on the arms of the
chair.

"You would do the same thing if you were in my position,
Counselor. I'm obligated to give my client the best defense
possible."

It irked me because he was right. That was a huge, open,
gaping wound that festered and seeped into pretty much every
aspect of Avett's life. It was her major weak point and every
attorney, no matter what side of the law they were on, learned to
go straight for that spot when dealing with anyone on the stand.

Suddenly, Avett straightened up in her seat and she reached
out to grab my forearm. Her head turned in my direction and
her multicolored eyes popped open so wide they seemed to take
up half of her face. "Asa wasn't alone when he came to see me
the day after the attack. His sister was in town visiting and she
was with him."

"My client is accused of robbing her brother at gunpoint. Her
testimony would be as suspect as Mr. Cross's." Larsen's tone was
sharper than it had been and his gaze had narrowed at our end
of the table. It was the first time since we entered the room that
some of the smug satisfaction that surrounded him slipped.

I snorted and leaned forward so that I could put a forearm
on the glass tabletop. "Right, the brother and the sister and my

client are all conspiring to set your client up and to send him to jail. Sounds like there is witness testimony available that backs up my client's story that your client ripped off his suppliers and was desperate for money, leading to my client being shaken down and roughed up. The robbery was clearly his idea."

"This witness isn't on the prosecution's list and hasn't been vetted."

It was my turn to smirk and flash some teeth. "It's called discovery for a reason, Tyrell. I'll be sure to send Townsend this new information, as soon as we leave."

We had a vicious stare-down for several long minutes until Larsen moved forward and closed the file in front of him with more force than the task required. "I think that's all for me today, Ms. Walker."

Avett let out an audible sound of relief, but I could see by the predatory look in the other man's eyes he was far from done with her or with me.

"Thank you for your time. I want to remind you that when you are on that stand, nothing, and I do mean nothing, is off-limits. I can ask you about your past, including the men in it, and I can ask you about your current circumstances. I'm sure McNair and Duvall will be thrilled to have their firm's name tied to a felony robbery case when it hits the press that one of their top litigators is sleeping with one of the witnesses. I can discredit both of you, with the right innuendo and the right wording. We both know exactly how to do that, don't we, Jackson? You'll have no chance of making partner when this trial is over. That's a promise."

The other attorney swept out of the room and before I could tell Avett not to give a second thought to his idle threats she was on her feet and moving out of the conference room after him. I called her name but she didn't even look back as her small body artfully moved in and out of the rush of people coming and going in the busy courthouse. She hit the glass entrance doors without slowing down and only stopped when I caught up to her a few hundred feet from the entrance. I put my hand on her elbow and spun her around to face me and felt my heart had split open when I noticed she was crying and that her lush bottom lip was quivering.

I didn't think. I didn't deliberate the pros and cons. I didn't rationalize that it wasn't the time or place. All I could do was react. My girl was hurting and I wanted to make it stop, so I pulled her to me and put my lips over hers and tried to kiss the pain away.

At first, she yielded soft and sweet, her return kiss a delicate surrender. Unfortunately, it quickly turned from something warm and comforting into something that felt more like combat. She jerked her head away from mine and then her hand cracked across my cheek with enough force to have my head snapping to the side. She gasped in shock at the same time I barked her name. She lifted the shaking fingers of one hand to her mouth and put the others on what I was sure was a violent red welt that was rising on my cheek. I could feel her shaking and remorse all the way through my body.

"I'm so sorry, Quaid. Oh, my God, what is wrong with me?" She took a step back and I saw fresh tears start to spill out of her wild and terrified eyes.

"Avett." I said her name with patience I wasn't feeling, especially when I caught sight of a familiar blonde woman watching our interaction with open curiosity as she talked on the phone pressed to her ear.

"No, Quaid. I'm super sorry I hit you. I'm shaken up and heartsick but that isn't an excuse. I never seem to be able to do the right thing or react the right way, even when I really want to. I feel terrible but maybe it's for the best. It looks like we're having an epic breakup and that means your bosses won't get on your case and maybe it'll keep that viper of an attorney off of your back. Walk away from me, Quaid. Walk away from this entire mess before it's too late and your entire future is gone."

I reached for her again but she evaded my grasp and shook her head violently from side to side. "I'm serious. I'm always going to be the girl that jumps, Quaid. I'm going to jump not knowing what's below. I'm going to jump even when I know the water is cold and that it's dangerous. I'm going to jump when I know the risks and when I don't know them. I'm going to jump even when I know the landing is going to hurt. You said yourself that you're not the kid who jumps anymore because it lost its appeal. You know better and maybe I do, too, but I'm still going to jump because that's who I am. Who I am is not going to ruin you, Quaid. I won't let it."

She looked like she was ready to bolt after she tossed her revelations at me. I put my hands in my pockets and studied her thoughtfully. "Did you ever think that I was ruined when you found me and that you've been instrumental in reconstructing me? I wasn't living any kind of life before you blew into it, Avett. My wife left me after starting a family with someone that wasn't me, even though I gave her everything I was capable of. My parents practically disowned me because they didn't approve of the way I wanted to live my life. I have a job that is getting increasingly difficult to stomach, and all I have to show for it is a nice wardrobe and a killer view. Everything was all for show and there wasn't a single real thing until you. I told you that your chaos doesn't scare me." But her wild terrified me because I knew there was no way to harness the wind and she looked like she was getting ready to blow out of my life as quickly as she had careened into it.

She put a hand to her chest and pulled her watery gaze away from mine. "But it scares me. There are very few people in this world that I want to protect from the kind of mayhem I bring with me and you are one of them. I love you, Quaid. I didn't want to but I do, and that means I'm going to let you go."

I wanted to shake her and hold her to me and never let go. I wanted to throw every argument I could think of at her to keep her from making this mistake. I wanted to pick her words apart and put them back together into ones I wanted to hear. I wanted to focus on the fact she said she loved me, not the fact that she was leaving, but she turned around and started moving away from me, which made that impossible to do.

"Avett." She pulled up short and shot me a look full of sorrow and sadness over her shoulder. "This is a bad decision you don't have to make. You don't have to protect me from you or anything that comes with being with you. I'm a big boy."

She gave a shuddering sigh and I saw the finality of her decision stamped all over her expressive face. "That's the thing, Counselor. This feels way too much like the right decision. And I'm not protecting you from me. I'm protecting you from yourself, and the things you'll lose if you love me back."

Her words hit me hard, and all of the feelings and emotions

she had stirred to life inside of me got so big and so out of control that I felt like they were going to consume me. I wanted to give her so much, everything I had, and none of it had a dollar sign attached to it. I knew I could tell her that, throw words at her until I was blue in the face, and that I could lawyer-speak my way around her argument and fear that she would hurt me by being with me, but words felt like they were too simple and could be too easily misconstrued. I was going to have to show her she was worth everything to me and then some.

I'd worked hard at my education because I knew it was my ticket out. I'd worked hard to distance myself from my child-hood and from having nothing because I knew I wanted more out of life than the basics. I worked my ass off to establish myself in my career and to be considered a force to be reckoned with in the courtroom and in the bedroom because I wanted to be the best and I wanted everyone to know it. I put up a reasonable fight to save my marriage before I realized it was all a sham and I battled through my divorce so I could keep all the things I thought were the most important to me.

Watching Avett walk away from me for my own good, I real-ized I needed to work and fight like I never had before because I wasn't willing to let her go. This was a battle I wasn't going to lose because to do so meant losing her. She was everything I wanted and all that I never knew I needed. I could put in all of my effort for her because she was more valuable than anything I owned and worth more to me than how many wins in the court-room I could brag about. She finally managed to show me what was really important in life and what I had been missing from what felt like the very beginning. I needed someone to love me for me and for what I had or didn't have. I needed someone to support me because what was important to me was important to them since they cared about me. Avett did all of that without a second thought and I knew, deep down into the fibers that made me the man that I was, that she was the only person I was capable of giving my all to, because she deserved everything I had to give . . . even though she never asked for any of it.

I knew if I wanted to keep her I was going to have to show her and prove to her that she wasn't my ruin. She was my salvation.

She jumped, and I was going to have to show her that I was willing to be the guy that jumped after her.

CHAPTER 17

Avett

I was glad I had refused to let anyone go with me to the deposition even if digging in my heels about it had made my dad extragrouchy and my mom supernervous. I knew I was going to be shaky and off balance after the interrogation from Jared's lawyer and I knew that I was going to be a total mess after being around Quaid. I was right on both counts and it was taking everything I had not to crumple into a useless ball of broken heart and rivers of tears on the sidewalk in front of the courthouse. I made my way to the street while wiping ineffectively at the mascara that I was sure was running over my cheeks like sad war paint and hailed a cab.

My dad was home waiting for a status report and surprisingly my mom had opted to take the day off and wait with him. Her wanting to be around for moral support and to offer a hug after what was undoubtedly going to be a bad day was a testament to how much our relationship had changed and improved now that both our stories were out there in the open. We would never have the typical mother/daughter relationship and

I would always very much be my father's daughter, but it was nice to know that my mom and I had been able to find a way to a better relationship, despite the roadblocks we'd both thrown up. Getting to a place where I could let my mom love me and love her back was instrumental in me finding my way to forgiveness and understanding myself and both of our past misdeeds.

Walking away from Quaid for good had me feeling lower than I ever had, and knowing there was nothing on this Earth or beyond that could make me feel any worse than I did at that moment, I decided it was finally time for me to try and make amends with the one person I hadn't been able to face since I put the wheels of this entire debacle in motion all those months ago. It was time to put on my big-girl panties and try to make things right with Rome Archer. I knew I was going to squirm and falter under that unwavering blue gaze that cataloged and weighed every single move I made, but it was time. Because even if he refused to accept my apology, even if he didn't want my story and the honest compunction that came along with it, I would walk away knowing I had done the right thing with one less anchor tied to my soul. Rome was important to my dad, which by default made him important to me, but I knew now that even if the big, scarred man couldn't forgive me, I couldn't carry that around for the rest of my life. I needed to have my hands free to catch any of the good stuff that I was fortunate to have come my way, and that meant I couldn't keep my hands full of the garbage and negativity I had been clutching like a lifeline for so long.

I had the cab drop me off at the bar and barely noticed that the driver was giving my tear-streaked face a very concerned look in the rearview mirror for the entire ride. I took a deep breath and pushed through the doors like I was walking into an old Western gunfight completely unarmed. I had to blink to let my eyes adjust to the dimmer light inside the bar, and as I was getting reacquainted with a place that had always been in my blood, a deep and gravelly voice colored with tones from the deep south rumbled my name and drew my attention.

Dash Churchill, or Church as he was more commonly known, had been hired as security for the bar right about the time I lost my job. He was a strikingly attractive man. He was also the man that had stood up for me with Jared even though he hardly knew me and what he did know was nothing to write home about. I had a soft spot a mile wide for the beautiful former soldier and it had very little to do with the fact that he also had hazel eyes that were a crazy swirl of blue, brown and yellow that stood out like beacons in his golden-skinned face. Church never said much of anything to anyone so I wasn't sure where he was from other than someplace down south and I had no clue what his heritage was, but wherever his parents had come from they sure as hell had succeeded in making one amazing-looking son. He was unforgettable and that was saying something because all my dad's boys were pretty impressive in their own way.

"Hey, Church. Is Rome in his office? I want to talk to him real quick."

"Long time no see, kiddo." I could listen to him talk all day with his Johnny Cash–style rumble and that twang that wouldn't quit, but I was on a mission and I needed to accomplish it before I chickened out.

"I know. I wasn't sure about my welcome and, well . . . I need to make sure the boss knows how sorry I am for everything. He might not want to hear it, but I need to tell him anyway."

For a big man Church moved quick and light on his feet. That was one of the reasons he was an asset to the bar; he could be in the middle of a fight or disagreement and have it broken up before the combatants knew what hit them. He was also stoic and seemingly immune to any and all the womanly charms that were constantly being shoved in his direction, but I secretly thought that had more to do with the adorable Dixie Carmichael than it did with any actual disinterest in women on his part. Dixie had worked at the bar for as long as I could remember. She was as much a part of the place as my dad was, and for as long as I had known her she had been unlucky in love. She and Church danced around one another, which had been both entertaining and frustrating to watch.

I jolted when his heavy arm landed on my shoulders and sucked in a surprised breath when I was folded into a chest that felt like it was carved of stone for a rib-cracking hug. Church wasn't the most affectionate man I had ever met, so the hug not only caught me off guard, but it tugged on the heartstrings that were currently tied in knots and frayed at the ends because of Quaid.

"The boss knows this place is as much yours as it is his. You've always been welcome and you've been missed. He'll listen to what you have to say and then you'll listen to what he has to say and that'll be the end of it." He tilted his head in the direction of the back and gave me a hint of a grin, which was as close to a smile as I had ever seen him come. "He was working on invoices and bills for the month so I'm sure you'll be a welcome distraction."

I nodded briskly and stiffened my spine as I pulled out of the hug and headed across the battered wood floors towards the closed office door. I knocked and it felt like an eternity before a gruff "Come in" was issued. I pushed the door open and expected a scowl or a glower when Rome looked up from the messy desk in order to see who was behind the interruption. What I got was a smile that showed pearly white teeth and turned his harshly handsome face with the fierce scar that bisected one of his eyebrows and his forehead into something that was breathtaking and hard to look away from.

"Avett. What brings you by? Is your dad here?" Rome spoke a lot like he was still in the military. He didn't waste words or time and his laser-like baby blues pinned me to the spot with almost no effort on his part. He cocked his shaved head to the side and gave me a narrow-eyed look when I didn't immediately answer him. "Have you been crying?"

I laughed nervously and made my way over to one of the shabby chairs that sat across from his desk. I flopped down into the worn fabric and met his curious stare with an unfiltered one of my own. I was feeling raw, open, and stripped down to my most basic elements after that horrible confrontation with Quaid outside of the courthouse and there was no way to hold back the flood of honesty and admission as it rushed out of me.

"I came by because I wanted to tell you that I'm sorry. I'm sorry I was a shitty employee. I'm sorry that I didn't respect you or what you did with this place, and I'm so, so sorry I didn't say no when Jared asked me to take the money from the cash register. I hate that I put you in a position where you had to fire me and it makes me so mad at myself that I purposely did things that made it impossible for me to ever come back here. You're a good man, Rome. My dad wouldn't have done what he did with the bar if you weren't. I spent a lot of time ruining everything that was good in my life, which is why I self-sabotaged every opportunity you offered me. I can give you the long explanation as to why I felt like I deserved to be kicked around and why I kept inflicting wounds on myself to bleed from, but the moral of the story is that I know now that punishing myself never got me anywhere, and those actions hurt other people far worse than they ever hurt me." I blinked at him and bit my lip. "Like you, and Asa."

He tossed the pen he was holding onto the desk and leaned forward on his forearms so that he was peering intently into my eyes.

"You know, when you come home from a war zone and have to settle into a normal, everyday kind of existence, no one ever tells you how to deal with all the things that you bring back with you. When you're in a situation that calls for you to make life and death choices, you do so knowing those decisions affect so many more than just yourself." I was mesmerized by his words and by the sincerity and depth with which he gave them to me. "When you come home you're full of things like regret and doubt. You can't sleep some nights because you wonder what-if, and guilt feels like it's going to bury you alive. But eventually you realize all you can do is come to terms with the choices you had to make, for whatever reasons you had to make them. You can't take those choices back, but you can learn from them and let them make you a better person. I'm almost jealous that you get the opportunity to apologize, Avett. There are some days I feel like I would give everything I have to be able to say I'm sorry for the things I may have done wrong. And I'm not talking about when I was overseas."

I exhaled and felt some of the dread and trepidation that was fueling this little meeting fade away. I lifted my hands to my face and rubbed them over my messy eyes. "Thank you for understanding. I also plan on paying you back every single cent that I took from you."

"I understood before you walked in here. I have a little brother that was all about self-destruction for a while. You actually pulled yourself out of it much sooner than he did."

I wrinkled my nose and sighed. "That's because girls mature faster than boys."

Rome chuckled. "That's true, and just so you know, you always have a place here. That kitchen belongs to your mother, not to me, so if you ever want to come back, she's the one you need to make amends with."

"We're good . . . well, better than we were. There's been a lot of apologizing and accountability since I got out of jail. Realizing you're on a crash course with prison is surprisingly enlightening."

"Are you sure that enlightenment didn't come from the guy that kept you out of prison? After Brite finished bitching about the fact the guy rides a crotch rocket, he had nothing but good things to say about him. It sounded like he was shipping you and the lawyer pretty hard."

I lifted my eyebrows at him. "Shipping?"

He rolled his eyes and I grinned when I noticed he had pink heat filling his cheeks. "Blame Cora. She watches all that stuff on the CW Network and is always shipping this and shipping that. She's corrupted me."

Cora was his pint-sized, very pregnant, soon-to-be wife. The two had an adorable daughter that was proving to be as much of a handful as her mother was. Cora was also the only person fierce enough and stubborn enough to put up with the moody former soldier on a permanent basis. On the outside the two of them were as different as night and day but when anyone saw them together it was obvious that they were perfectly matched and deeply in love. They were the epitome of relationship goals in my book.

I laughed for real this time and let it drift into a sigh. "The lawyer may have had something to do with the enlightenment and he most definitely had everything to do with this." I pointed to my tear-streaked and makeup-smeared face. "Some things aren't meant to be."

"And some things are meant to be even if they seem like they shouldn't be." He sounded so much like my dad that it was eerie and I told him as much. He gave me that heart-stopping smile again and replied with a firm, "Good."

I rose to my feet and couldn't stop myself from circling the desk so that I could wrap my arms around his neck for a quick squeeze.

"I'm glad this bar and my dad found you, Rome. I really am."

He patted my arm awkwardly and stood so that I really had to crane my neck back to look up at him. "I'm glad you finally found you, Avett."

I swallowed back the emotion that crawled up my throat and threatened more tears. I'd never been so weepy or quick to cry but all this being in touch with my emotions was wreaking havoc on my well-worn barriers.

"The trick is staying found, I think. It's easy to get lost when your life is constantly in a state of disarray. The right path gets obscured as quickly as you make it."

He put a hand on my shoulder and told me solemnly, "That's why you find something or someone that guides you, someone that won't lose you, and someone that you don't mind getting lost with when that inevitably happens."

I winced involuntarily because I'd walked away from the guy that I was pretty sure was my magnetic north, the guy that hadn't let me wander or get off track since the moment I met him. Quaid didn't lose his way in the storm; he rode it out.

"I'll keep that in mind, big guy. Thank you for making this easy on me. We both know you didn't have to." My voice was scratchy and I could feel the tears threatening again because I couldn't pull my mind away from my legal eagle.

He didn't reply as he followed me out of the office and back into the mostly empty bar. Church was leaning against the long bar top talking to one of the regular daytime patrons and a bartender I didn't recognize.

"Where's your dad?" It took me a minute to realize he was looking around for whoever was supposed to be on Avett babysitting duty for the day.

"I had a meeting at the courthouse about Jared's trial. I went alone because I wasn't sure how long it was going to last. He's at home waiting for me to check in with my mom. I should call them and let them know where I'm at. I need to call a cab and head that way before they worry."

Rome grunted and crossed his arms over his muscular chest, which was covered in a faded Eagles T-shirt. "It's slow. I can run you home since Church is here to keep an eye on things."

I was getting ready to agree when my phone flashed and I saw my dad's number on the screen. I held up a finger and told Rome to hold on as I put the phone to my ear.

"Hey, Dad. Sorry I didn't call sooner. That lawyer Jared hired was a real piece of work, a total slimeball. I needed a minute. I'm at the bar with Rome. He offered to run me home."

"Tell him you have a ride waiting for you outside." The voice definitely wasn't my father's. I didn't recognize it at all, and before I could ask who in the hell had my dad's phone the person on the end snapped, "You better make whoever you're with think everything is okay or your parents are going to experience what it's like to lose everything from the inside."

Rome was looking at me curiously, so I forced a shaky smile and took a few steps away from him. I put a hand to my churning stomach and whispered, "I understand." I had to lock my knees because they felt like they were going to buckle right out from underneath me.

"Do you? To be clear here on what's going to happen, you're going to walk out front and get into the black Yukon that's waiting. You're going to tell my associates where you stashed the drugs your boyfriend jacked from my boss, and then you are going to take them to the location. If you call the police, if you alert anyone as to what's going on, this cute little house where you've been staying will go up just like the other one did, only this time your parents will be left inside to burn."

I cleared my throat and looked over my shoulder to see that Church had joined Rome and that both of them were staring at me intently. I shivered and fought to get out quietly enough so that I wasn't overheard. "How do I know you haven't hurt my parents already?"

There was some rustling, the sounds of an obvious struggle, and then my dad's strained voice came on the line. "Don't you go anywhere with these people, Avett! You hear me! Call the police and keep yourself safe. Do not worry about me . . ." There was a sickening crunch and a heavy-sounding thud that made me gasp and had me putting my hand up to my mouth.

"If I were you, I would ignore your father's advice. If the police show, this place goes up like a tinderbox and we'll go after the lawyer. We want the product. Once we have it, we'll be on our way. Your freedom and your parents' safety for our drugs. Seems like an easy decision to make if you ask me."

Maybe it would be if there were drugs and if I didn't already know how these men did business. I still had nightmares from my last run-in with them and it looked like this time around a baseball-bat-wielding landlady wasn't going to be enough to save the day.

"Don't try and call the lawyer for help either. We have people watching him in case you decide to be difficult. He's our plan B."

At the reminder that Quaid was in as much danger as my parents were, I suddenly had an idea. It wasn't the best plan in the entire world but it was the best I could come up with given the circumstances.

"All right, I'm headed out to the SUV. I'll give you what you want."

"See how easy that was? And to think everyone told me you weren't a smart girl."

I squeezed my eyes shut and tightened my fingers around the phone. "Not smart enough to keep everyone I love out of another one of my fuckups. I'm leaving now."

I hung up the phone and whirled on Rome and Church. "I need you guys to head over to my mom's house. My dad really needs your help with something."

I felt guilt threaten to choke me as words shot out at them. I couldn't call the police, but I could send two highly trained former military men to the rescue. I had to do it without alerting them to what was really going on because there was no way they were going to let me out the door if they discerned what was waiting for me on the other side of it.

"Um, yeah, he's run into a situation and he needs you both there. I have to go back to the courthouse. They have more questions for me. Jared's attorney even sent a car. I have to go." I rushed towards the front door with both of them calling my name and moving after me as I did so. I looked over my shoulder and told them, "Also, you need to hurry and don't try and call him because he won't be able to answer."

"What in the actual fuck just happened, Avett?" Rome officially lost his patience and I had to dodge out of the way as he reached for me.

"Go to the house . . . and you both need to be very, very careful. It's a bad situation and you're the only ones that can help him, so promise me you won't call the police. If you do, his situation is going to go from bad to worse. Do you understand what I'm trying to tell you?" They both gave me hard looks, accompanied by angry and confused scowls. "When you get there tell him I'm sorry. So sorry."

I pushed through the door and hit the parking lot at a run with both of them hot on my heels. I saw the big, black SUV idling on the street and made a beeline for it as my heart crawled into my throat. I grabbed the back door handle and looked back at Rome and Church, both of whom had their phones to their ears as they paced the asphalt like uncaged predators. I should've known they wouldn't listen to me after my less than subtle freak-out and all I could do was hope they didn't call the police before going to check on my dad themselves. As I was getting into the

SUV I screamed, "Stay safe!" and hurled myself into the backseat and the unknown. I would never forgive myself if something happened to either of them but I had to do something.

A guy that couldn't be much older than me sat in the seat next to me and I tried not to throw up when my gaze landed on the wicked-looking gun that he held in his hand. The driver turned around to look at me through mirrored sunglasses and the passenger turned around to smirk at me. I recognized him from the attack at Jared's apartment and everything inside of me froze and went startlingly numb.

"Where to?"

The driver pulled the big vehicle into traffic as I gulped and tried to make my unresponsive body respond. I curled my shaking hands into fists on my lap and kept my eyes locked on the gun that was trained, unwavering, right on my side.

"Do you have a full tank of gas?" I finally got the words loose and they had both the men in the front seat turning to look at me.

"Why?"

I exhaled and could taste terror and panic bright and crisp across my tongue.

"Because we're going to the mountains."

Not just any mountains. We were going to go to Quaid's mountains. I was going to take these thugs on a wild-goose chase so I could hopefully buy Rome and Church time to help my parents out. There was a pretty good chance I wasn't going to see tomorrow, and if that was the case, I was going to spend my last moments in the place where I fell in love and felt more loved than I ever had.

It was the easiest decision I ever made.

CHAPTER 17.5

Church

S he told you not to call the cops."
    I shot Rome a look out of the side of my eye. It had been a long time since the big man had been my CO but some habits were hard to break, and ever since I came to Denver to work for him I often found myself looking to him for direction and guidance. The man had saved my life more than once, so it was a rare occasion I questioned him. That's why I was sitting next to him in his big-ass truck as he raced across town towards Darcy's house based on nothing more than Avett's cryptic words and odd behavior. He thought something was wrong and I hated to think he was probably right.

He tossed his cell phone on the seat next to him and met my look with one of his own. The scar that bisected his eyebrow and slashed across his forehead always made him look fiercer and more terrifying than he actually was. Rome had settled into full-on civilian life since leaving the Army. The man had a forever kind of girl and a growing family, not to mention he was pushing paper and paying bills like an average Joe, instead of doing things that a man trained to kill in a variety of ways could be doing with his time. Maybe I should envy him. It was clear Rome had found not only peace but his place since getting out, but none of that was for me.

In fact, speeding towards the unknown, handguns stealthily tucked away as we tossed around various hostile situations that could be waiting for us when we reached the house, was the most alive, the most invigorated, I had felt in way too long. I wasn't sure what kind of sick fuck that made me—the fact that I missed dodging bullets and the sounds of bombs going off way too close to where I was trying to sleep, but I did. What I didn't miss were my friends dying and fighting a war that felt like it would never end. If I never had to make another phone call to a surviving wife and family again, I would be a happy man. A bored man, an unfulfilled man, but a happy one. I was pretty sure I wasn't hiding that the only part of bouncing at the bar I liked was knocking heads together when idiots got out of line and the daily back and forth I had with Dixie.

The job was simple—I could do it in my sleep—but Little Miss Sunshine with her strawberry blond curls and her "I don't believe in bad days" attitude was anything but. I'd never met anyone that was so . . . happy. The woman acted like the world wasn't going to shit and like her go-nowhere job handing out drinks and smiling at drunks was the best thing to ever happen to her. And what really got to me was the fact she wanted to be my friend. What in the actual fuck? I only had a handful of those and sure as shit none of them were women. I wasn't friends with people I wanted to fuck, and even though she wasn't my type, her optimism alone was enough that my dick had no business getting hard when she turned her pretty fawn-colored eyes in my direction. Big doe eyes that were so soft and warm that they made me want to believe in things I knew weren't real. I'd left anything that looked like hope and faith in the desert when my last platoon had been attacked and I'd buried pretty much every single man I'd been in the war with for the last eighteen months. It didn't matter; Dixie spread her sunshine around, tried to get the rays to break through the perpetual black cloud that hovered around me, and I wanted her. I wanted to show her how rough and ugly the world and the people in it could really be, and since I wanted to tear apart what made her who she was, I stayed away while everything inside of me ached to get as close to the sunny little cocktail waitress as I could.

My being able to kill time and lay low at the bar was running out and not because I was bored and restless. My time was up because it was getting harder and harder to stay away from the girl and I refused to be the reason any of her pretty and infectious light went out.

"I didn't call *the* cops, I called *a* cop. Royal said she would wait for my call but would have guys ready to roll as soon as we give her a status update."

I tapped my fingers on my knee and nodded. "You really don't miss this?"

Rome turned his head towards me and the edges of his mouth pulled down. "No. I have people I need to be around for now, and I want to see my kids grow up. Catching bullets and putting myself in danger are two things that are so low on my list of things I want to be doing with my time they don't even rank." He lifted the ruined eyebrow at me. "You do?"

I shrugged a shoulder and turned to look out the window as he pulled the truck to a stop around the block from where Darcy's modest home was located. "I was in for a long time, longer than you. Sometimes I think the fight and the fear changed my blood. It doesn't seem to move through me the way it used to. I can only feel it when the adrenaline kicks in."

His dark eyebrows snapped down in a deep V and his mouth pulled tight. "That's not any way to live, Church. You shouldn't have to chase after things that can kill in order to feel alive."

No, I shouldn't, but I did, which meant I was a dangerous man, far more dangerous than I had been when I was working for good ole Uncle Sam.

We climbed out of opposite sides of the truck and I cocked my head at Rome as we rounded the back. "You take the perimeter and let me go inside."

"We don't know what we're dealing with. We should both take the perimeter and then work our way inside together."

I shook my head at him. "No way, brother. There is more un-known happening inside the house. Brite's a big fucking dude. It woulda taken more than one guy to get him down. You've got those people you need to be around for, so there is no need for you stick your neck out any more than it already is. I'll go inside—you make sure the outside is clear."

He scowled at me and I could see the argument in his eyes before he said anything. "I don't like this plan . . . at all."

I chuckled drily and clasped a hand on his beefy shoulder. "Well, you aren't my CO anymore and I've got more tactical strike experience than you, so this is how it's going down."

He blew out a breath of resignation. "Let's hope we don't need your tactical experience."

If I was able to hope for anything anymore it sure as hell wouldn't be that. "Let's do what we do so we can focus on figuring out where Avett went because we both know that wasn't any kind of hired car she jumped into. This situation is a full-on shit show and we're in the stink neck-deep."

He grunted his response as we split up and maneuvered our way around the block from opposite directions. Rome had changed since leaving the service but one thing that was ingrained in the man regardless of his situation in life was his need to protect those that needed it. Brite wasn't only Rome's mentor and savior; he was the man's friend and there were no lengths the former soldier wouldn't go to in order to make sure his friend was safe. I considered it my job to make sure that no one that mattered, no one that had someone to lose, got hurt. I would storm the castle and I would take the shot of adrenaline, the surge of fire and focus, that the first action I had seen in over six months brought with it.

I cut through the backyard of the house behind Darcy's and dodged a barking German shepherd as I scaled over the privacy fence that separated the two yards. Luckily, Darcy's yard had plenty of big elms scattered throughout the landscaping so I ducked behind one as quickly as I could in case whoever was in the house with the captive Brite and Darcy went in search of what had the dog going nuts.

I waited a beat to see if anyone was going to come out of the house guns blazing, but when nothing happened, I moved my way closer to the house using the trees and then the deck at the back of the house as coverage. I made sure to keep my head below the window lines since I was tall and would be easily spotted by anyone looking out. I crept along the side of the house and found my way to the back door. I didn't think I would be lucky enough to find it unlocked, but fate apparently wanted Brite out of harm's way as much as I did because the knob turned easily under my palm. The interior of the garage was dark and I could clearly make out the outline of Brite's Harley and the bulk of Darcy's Chrysler 300 parked next to it.

My heart was thudding in my ears, but outwardly every single part of my body was focused on the possible threat that was waiting for me behind the door that separated me from whatever was happening inside the house. I didn't hear any noise coming from outside but Rome was good like that. If there were bad guys protecting the perimeter he would take them out without making a sound, even if it had been years since he'd had to put those particular skills to use.

I didn't get as lucky with the interior door. It was locked up tight and I knew all my stealth and covertness was about to be blown to hell. I wasn't going to waste time picking the lock when a shoulder and some muscle could get me in so much faster. I pulled out the gun that I had tucked in the back of my waistband and made sure the safety was off. I took a deep breath and reared back so that I could shove my way into the house, knowing I was only getting one shot to get through the door and take whoever was on the other side unawares. It felt like the good ole days and there was no denying that I could feel my blood rushing through my veins and the way the thrill of the action had me feeling alive in a way I seriously missed now that my life wasn't about war and carnage anymore.

The flimsy wood gave way easily enough; it was the body on the other side that proved difficult to get through. I took a man to the floor as soon as I broke through and wasted no time in cold-cocking him on the side of the head with the butt of the weapon in my hand. I jerked my head back as blood spattered up at me and rolled to the side as gunfire erupted over my head. A bullet tore into the floor right next to where my face had been only moments before, and I swore as I aimed from my back and fired off a return shot that it hit its target dead-on, if the sound of the man shooting at me screaming was any indication.

I scrambled to my feet with my weapon clutched in both my hands and made a quick sweep of the room. The guy I hit was out cold and the guy I shot was lying on the floor clutching his leg as blood pumped steadily out of the hole I put there. I made my way over to him and kicked his gun to the side. I cocked my head as I looked at him and asked, "How many more?"

He looked up at me with glazed eyes as his pallor turned from white to gray. I may have hit his femoral artery with my shot, but I didn't have time to feel bad about that. I nudged him with the toe of my boot and asked again, "How many more of you are in the house?"

His head lolled to the side as his eyes drifted closed and I knew I wasn't going to get an answer from him any time soon. I swore under my breath and pressed my back to the wall so I could make my way down the hallway towards the front of the house while being as small of a target as possible. I couldn't believe I missed this . . . but I did. I was operating on instinct and years of training. It felt good to be doing something, anything, that felt useful and purposeful again. I needed the charge. I needed the threat, and like Rome said, that was seriously no way to live the life I was lucky to still have. I so easily could have been one of my fallen brothers that didn't even get a chance at anything more.

When I got to the end of the hallway, I caught sight of a reflection in the glass of one of the pictures Darcy had hung on the wall. Brite was on the floor on his side and his hands were tied behind his back. He wasn't moving but that could be because there was a man in a dark suit, also reflected in the distorted image, who had a nasty-looking revolver pointed at Darcy where she sat crying on the couch.

"Fuck me." The situation took on a whole other level of seriousness when it wasn't insurgents taking hostages, but thugs threatening an innocent family. I wasn't sure which was worse but I knew I couldn't stand by and let Darcy and Brite get hurt any more than they already were.

"I heard the commotion from the back of the house and my spotter out front hasn't radioed in. I know you're there and if you don't want this pretty lady's brains splattered all over the couch you'll throw your gun out so I can see it and then get your ass in here."

I swore again, this time loud enough that he could hear me. I never liked to give up my weapon, but in this case I didn't really have much of a choice. I threw the gun down and kicked it across the floor so that it went skidding well into the living room. I shook my head at how quickly things had gone south and lifted my hands up in front of me in the international gesture of surrender as I rounded the corner. I glanced down at Brite and was instantly relieved to see the man's massive chest moving up and down in even breaths. His eyes were open and furious as he gazed at me with blood dripping down his face from a wicked-looking gash that ran the length of his forehead. I knew the badass biker wouldn't go down without a fight.

The man with the gun shook his head back at me and gave me a grin that made my skin crawl. "I can't believe you actually tossed the gun away. That's an amateur move and I'm gonna make sure the girl pays for not following orders."

I heard Brite growl from his position on the floor and Darcy started crying harder.

I dropped my hands so that they were hanging loosely at my hips and lifted my brows up at the cocky intruder. "No, an amateur move is bringing a single weapon into an unknown situation with an unknown number of hostiles."

Before he could fire off the shot that I knew was coming as his finger twitched on the trigger, I pulled out the other pistol I had stashed behind my back and fired first. I hit the guy in the shoulder and the gun he was holding fell uselessly to the ground. I hurried across the room and tackled the man to the floor before he could regain his wits about him and reach for the weapon again. I punched him in the face hard enough that I heard my knuckles crack. He gurgled a trickle of blood out of the side of his mouth, and let out a pitiful little moan. Satisfied he wouldn't be going anywhere anytime soon, I climbed to my feet and asked Darcy where I could find some rope to tie all the intruders up with.

She was a blubbery mess and couldn't respond but Brite barked out that he had a whole stash of zip-ties in the garage. I made short work of the guy in the back hallway and bypassed the one that I was pretty sure had bled out. When I jerked the guy's arm with the bullet hole in it he screamed in agony and called me a lot of really colorful names. By the time I had them all situated, Rome burst through the front door followed by a pretty redheaded woman dressed in police blues.

They both gave pause as they took in the bloody but handled situation as Rome visibly shook himself back into action as he made his way over to Brite to work on getting him free.

"I'm calling this in. Ask the guy that's still conscious if he knows where the guys that grabbed Avett are going."

The redheaded cop disappeared back out the front door while she was talking into the radio pinned to her shoulder.

Brite leaped to his feet and went to work untying his lady. His dark eyes shifted between us with an intensity only a person that had been to war or a parent that had a child in danger could manifest.

"I need to call Quaid. He might know where she would take them. I have to get her back."

Rome put his hand on the other man's shoulder and told him solemnly, "We will. There isn't any other option." Brite nodded and started frantically poking at the phone that he had clutched in his hand.

Rome turned to me with narrowed eyes and asked in a voice so low that only I could hear him, "You really fucking miss this?"

I looked around at the blood and smelled the acrid scent of spent gunpowder that lingered in the air. I flexed my bruised hands and shifted on my feet.

"I do." And that was why I had to get the hell out of Dodge, before I did something stupid like fall in love with a girl that didn't have any idea what I was really like.

CHAPTER 18

Quaid

Orsen was staring at me from across his desk with an expression on his face that I had never been on the receiving end of. He looked frustrated and disappointed, but more than that he looked resigned. He had his hands resting on the slight roundness of his belly and his mouth was drawn in a line so tight it made the rest of his face look like it was stretched too tautly across his bones.

"What do you have to say for yourself, Quaid?"

I lifted an eyebrow as he bit out the words and settled back in my chair. I felt a lot like a kid getting pulled into the principal's office. Where I would normally be doing everything in my power to placate Orsen and fix the situation, now that I had a better understanding of what was really important to me and what I really wanted to fight for, it was all I could do not to roll my eyes at him and his exaggerated bluster.

"Nothing." I leaned back in the chair and crossed my ankle over my knee. I wanted him to know I wasn't intimidated by this little meeting and that I was done letting him yank on my chain.

"I have nothing to say for myself, Orsen. I told you I wasn't going to represent your friend, so even if I had been in my office when you brought him back by this afternoon, my answer would have been the same."

Orsen's bushy eyebrows rose until they almost disappeared into his snowy hairline. "Have you forgotten that you work for this firm? The firm you have been chomping at the bit to be made partner in, I might add."

"I haven't forgotten because it's this firm that has dangled that partnership in front of me like a golden carrot for years, while I jump through every single hoop you've put in front of me. Answer me honestly, Orsen, are you and Duvall ever planning on offering me a full partnership?"

He huffed a little and I watched as red filled his puffy cheeks. It was no wonder Orsen had me handling all the trials for the big-name clients; he had no poker face and was as easy to read as an open book.

"You have to prove yourself in order to be made partner, Quaid." His tone was firm but his hands were fidgety, telling me all I needed to know. They were going to work me like a dog, put my face and my talent out there in front of the entire legal world with their title behind it, but they were never going to let me be one of the shot callers. They were never going to consider me their equal.

"I've proved myself, Orsen. In fact, I've more than demonstrated what an asset I am to this firm and to the legal community in general. I've earned the right to pick and choose the cases and the people I want to represent, and if you don't agree with that, then I think it's time we go our separate ways."

I watched the older man balk and some of the arrogance that

surrounded him waffled. "You won't quit. You've got too much time and energy invested in your career here."

He sounded so sure and he was almost right. Before Avett, the thought of quitting would have never crossed my mind, but after you survived a hurricane your perspective on the things that mattered most in life changed and I no longer needed or wanted to impress Orsen McNair. I was pretty sure I didn't want to work for him any more either.

"That's the thing, Orsen. It was time and energy invested in the wrong thing. If I hadn't been so focused on you finally seeing me as an asset, maybe I would have noticed my marriage falling apart sooner. If I hadn't been convinced that being made partner would finally make me happy and give me the kind of self-worth I was sorely lacking, maybe I would have realized the people I was fighting for, the people I was giving my all to, were the kind of people that absolutely didn't deserve the best of me and would never, ever appreciate what I gave. I've been searching for the good life for as long as I can remember, Orsen. This sure as shit isn't it."

Orsen held his hands up in front of him and his face went from accusatory to cajoling. "Now, son, don't make any rash decisions. Where else do you think you're going to get the kind of opportunities and money you've had access to here? We have a wait list a mile long of young attorneys right out of law school that are dying to be let in the door. You're lucky we offered you a position at all considering your less than stellar credentials. I handpicked you because I saw the fire and the drive in you, Quaid. Don't forget that."

I snorted at him. "I'm a good lawyer. Fuck that, I'm a great lawyer, and I'm the one that has handled every ugly, sticky, complicated, tangled case this firm has profited from since I signed on. You really think anyone wants you or Duvall representing them in front of a jury when you haven't left your goddamn office in all that time? I go and the media and the high profile cases are going to go with me. So don't pretend I don't know who is doing who the favors here. Day in and day out, I persuade people to go against their better judgment. I lie for a living, old man, so here's a word to the wise . . . you're out of practice when it comes to bluffing your audience so don't try and outmaneuver me—it won't work."

Orsen dropped all pretense of this being some kind of friendly office chat and leaned forward so that his hands were resting on the desk in front of him. The red in his face turned a furious maroon and his words sounded like each one was being bitten off and spit out in my direction.

"If you leave this firm, I will ruin you, Jackson. I will make sure no other law firm touches you and that you never get the opportunity to represent another client."

This time I didn't bother to stop the eye roll. I also decided Orsen and his precious firm had taken up enough of my time and my personal investment. I rose to my feet and leaned over so that my palms were flat on his desk. I narrowed my eyes at the man who I once thought gave me everything and told him flatly, "I don't want to represent the kinds of people you think need a solid defense, Orsen. I'm no longer interested in setting free the kind of man that could start a house on fire knowing his own child was inside. I don't want a reference or a referral from you. I want to get as far away as possible from the man you helped me become." I saw fear flash in his gaze and felt a kick of satisfaction that some of my old roughness and intimidation was starting to rise back to the surface. "I'll have my office cleaned out by the end of the day."

I pushed off the desk and was headed for the door when I heard his quiet, "This is all that girl's fault. You were on the fast track to success until you took her case and let her get to you."

I looked at him over my shoulder and frowned when I pulled my ringing phone out of my pocket and saw Brite's number on the screen. I figured he wanted to chew me out for making his daughter cry. I was willing to face his wrath so I could tell him I was working on a way to show Avett that she was the most important thing in my entire world. A way that she couldn't misinterpret or ignore. Brite seemed like the kind of guy that appreciated actions over words so I was sure I could smooth things over with the right words.

I told Orsen matter-of-factly, "You're right that she made me realize that I need more in my life than the next big case, and the next paycheck, but you're wrong about the path I was on, old man. That path led to nothing more than high blood pressure and more useless shit that never impressed anyone anyway."

I touched the face of the phone and expected to get an earful about how to treat women; what I got was Brite's breathless voice that was made even rougher by panic.

"Quaid, Avett's been abducted."

I slipped out of Orsen's office and pressed the phone more fully to my ear as my fingers reflexively tightened around it.

"What? What do you mean abducted?"

My feet of their own volition carried me away from Orsen's office and down the hall towards the elevator. My blood started to rush between my ears so loudly that I could barely hear him when he told me in a rush, "These guys broke into the house and held me and Darcy captive while they called Avett. They think she knows something about the drugs that loser ex of hers took off with. I told her not to leave with them, but do you think she listened to me? She got into a black SUV and they took off with my little girl."

"Did you call the police?" My heart was pounding and my palms were slick with fear-sweat.

"Of course we called the police, and we have the plate number on the Yukon, but these guys are armed and they mean business. We need to figure out where she would lead them to. I know she would want them as far away from Denver and us as possible. Do you have any idea where she would go?"

"Wait, if you were being held captive how do you know all this? How did you manage to call me?" My brain was going a million miles a minute but the need to have as much information as possible was ingrained in me and I couldn't keep the questions from spilling out as I practically ran towards my truck.

"Avett was taken from the bar. Before she got in the car, she told Rome and Church I needed them at the house. Armed thugs have nothing on former special ops guys. We called the police as soon as the situation here was under control, but it's been an hour so that's one hell of a head start the bad guys have."

Where would she take them? Where would she go so that she could buy time for everyone she cared about to get safe?

I put my hand on the door handle and swore long and loudly. "I know where she's taking them." It was the exact same place I would go if I wanted the rest of the world to be unable to find me. "I own a cabin out in the woods in the middle of nowhere. That's where I took her when we dropped out of sight for the weekend. I'll call the state patrol and tell them to haul ass there but the woods are thick and there aren't any real landmarks, so the chances are I'll find her before they do."

"These guys are dangerous, Jackson. They were armed and had every intention of taking both Darcy and me out and setting the house on fire as soon as they heard from the guys that have Avett."

I stiffened as I heard something behind me. In the reflection of the glass on the driver's side window, I saw the man dressed head to toe in black moving up behind me. I let out a slow and steadying breath through my nose and told Brite, "I'm aware how dangerous the men are and how critical the situation is, Brite. I'll text you a general location as soon as I'm on the road."

I ducked and spun out of the way as the man behind me reached for me. I slid to the side and caught the arm he had raised to grab me by the wrist and used his surprise and my leverage to my advantage. I wrenched the wrist up behind his back and between his shoulder blades with enough force that I heard the distinct pop as bone slipped out of the socket. I slammed his face against the window on the side of my vehicle and leaned in close so that I was talking directly into the assailant's ear.

"You better hope your buddies don't touch a single hair on her head. If you hurt her in any way, jail will seem like a vacation compared to what I'm going to do to you and your friends."

The man gasped as I put even more pressure on his arm. "I wanted to ask you to use your phone. I have a flat and I forgot mine at home."

I grunted and leaned farther into him. I used my free hand to give the man a quick pat-down and turned out the pockets on his coat; I wasn't surprised when a switchblade fell out of one and when I found a gun in the other. I took the snub-nosed revolver and tucked it into the back of my pants, under my suit jacket, and shoved away from the man, who turned around and immediately groaned and listed to the side as his injured shoulder was released.

He blinked at me through a scowl as I kicked the knife under the truck.

"I thought you were some kind of suit. The guys said you were an attorney, not a fucking commando."

I pushed him out of my way and reached for the door handle once again. "I wasn't always an attorney. The guy that pays you should have done more research." I wanted to tell him that he could pass that message along to his co-workers, but I didn't want the men that had Avett to have any kind of heads-up that I was coming after my girl and that I would do whatever needed to be done in order to make sure she was safe and returned to her parents unharmed.

The truck started with a growl and I was pleased that the state patrol already had people on the highways and interstates looking for the SUV. I gave them directions to the turnoff and tried to explain the best way to get to the cabin, but I knew that it would eat up too much time as they combed the dense wilderness that surrounded the homestead. I was the only one that was going to get to Avett before something unthinkable happened.

I sent a haphazard text to Brite giving him the general vicinity I was sure that Avett had directed the men to take her and wasn't surprised at all when he told me the men that had freed him were already on the road. No one was going to let Avett fight this battle on her own, even though that was what she had set out to do. Her actions might seem brave and heroic to some, but I knew her well enough to know that she was once again surrendering herself when she didn't have to. Avett wasn't planning on leaving those mountains alive if that meant the people she loved were safe. I wanted to throttle her for being so noble and so stupid. When I got my hands on her, she would never again be able to doubt that she was the most valuable thing in my life and that if she sacrificed herself for the greater good I would be left with nothing.

A car honked at me as I drifted lanes because I was focused on my phone instead of my driving. I put the device away and floored the big truck, making it jump and speed up to miles per hour the big beast wasn't ever made to see. The body vibrated around me as the engine roared. I kept my eyes locked on the road as I weaved dangerously in and out of city traffic on my way to the interstate that would take me out of town. I hoped no one called the cops on me, and if they did, I had no intention of stopping until I hit the turnoff that led to the cabin. The cops were going to have to follow me into the mountains, that was all there was to it.

The drive typically took a little over three hours. I made it in two and was amazed I didn't get pulled over. The truck was screaming and my nerves were shot when I rounded the last turn with gravel kicking up and the tires barely sticking to the road, but I saw the turnout and the black Yukon. I also saw the guy that was sitting behind the steering wheel perk up and take notice as I came to a skidding halt in a cloud of dust and exhaust in front of him.

It was a less than subtle entrance, but when he reached for his phone, presumably to call in a warning that I had joined their party, my foot found the gas pedal and before I could fully think about what I was doing the truck lurched to life again and raced hard and fast for the front end of the Yukon.

Metal shrieked against metal, and the air bag knocked me stupid when it deployed, but when I was able to shake the fuzzy from my vision, when I adjusted to the ringing in my ears, and the tang of blood on my tongue, I noticed that the entire front end of the SUV had crumpled up like an accordion up to the windshield and the driver was slumped over his own deployed air bag and steering wheel, limp. His face was covered in blood, and he didn't appear to be moving. Smoke billowed up from the front end of both the vehicles and it was obvious that neither was going to make it back down the mountain without some help.

I was wobbly on my feet as I climbed down from the cab, and when I touched my fingers to my forehead where something was burning, I wasn't too surprised they came away smeared with crimson. I'd knocked my own head pretty hard in the collision but not hard enough that I was going to go into the woods without making sure the driver couldn't get away, in case the state patrol showed up.

As I walked to the mangled vehicle, I made sure to tuck the gun I took from the thug back into my belt, because I wasn't taking any kind of chance when I knew I was the only hope Avett had of getting out of these woods alive. It took a bit of effort to pry open the door, considering the way the front was smashed in; the driver flopped to the side without the metal there to prop him up. He definitely wasn't going anywhere soon, but I still pulled my tie off of my neck and used it to lash the man's wrists around the steering wheel several times. The silk pulled tight and I knew it would be impossible for him to work his way free unless he ripped the steering wheel loose and, considering his current state, that seemed highly unlikely.

I shook my head—hard—to get my focus back and cringed

as the motion sent blood spattering to either side of me. I looked down at my wingtips and swore I would sell everything I owned to be dressed in jeans and hiking boots. If I'd ever needed a sign that all the expensive and luxurious stuff I surrounded myself with was absolutely useless when it came right down to it, this was it. Right now, I needed to be the man I tried so hard not to be in order to be someone worthy of the girl I was trying to save.

I pulled my dress shirt out of the top of my pants and took off my suit jacket. I was going to have to shred the thing in order to leave a trail of bread crumbs to follow for whatever type of backup that arrived. I was falling back on survival instincts and training that came from both my life lived in this wilderness and the tools Uncle Sam had imparted on me. I'd never thought I would have to use them again after I passed the bar, but at this moment I'd never been so glad to have the kind of knowledge I did at my disposal.

I popped all the buttons off with my teeth. I applied a little muscle and yanked each of the sleeves free and worked at shredding the silk lining. Once I had a decent pile of scraps, I headed off into the woods. I kept my eyes peeled and scanned for any sign of movement since they had evidently left the guy behind to prevent anyone from following. I veered in the direction of the cabin and glanced up at the sky. This close to the end of fall, the night crept into the sky pretty early and there wouldn't be much daylight left soon. That could work to my advantage if the guys that had Avett weren't aware that I was coming for them. But if they did know I was on their tail because my pal with the dislocated shoulder or the driver had managed to get a warning sent out, I knew they would randomly fire into the darkness hoping to hit something and that made the situation more dangerous than it already was.

As I dodged trees and slipped on the foliage that was wet and slick with almost-frost, I decided I was never wearing Italian-made shoes with no tread on them again. I made sure to space out the bits of fabric and metal I scavenged from my coat so that even a blind man or the most ill-equipped city slicker could find their way to the cabin. When I got to the clearing where the ramshackle building rested, I breathed a sigh of relief that there wasn't anyone out front waiting for me with double barrels pointed in my direction.

I worked my way around the outhouse and crouched down low so that I could use the pile of logs that I'd stacked only a few days ago as cover. I pressed my back flat to the rough logs that made up the structure of the cabin and crept my way along the side of the house, careful to make as little sound as possible so that the woodland creatures that were bound to be watching didn't alert anyone to my presence.

So slowly that I was hardly moving, I inched my way up so that only the top of my head and my eyes were visible as I peered into the grimy window that looked into the vacant cabin. I let out the breath I was holding and lifted myself to my full height so I could get a better look inside. The cabin was empty, completely barren, and it looked as sad and ramshackle as it had when Avett and I left it.

She wasn't here. She hadn't been here, which meant the only other place she could have taken them was the waterfall. My girl wasn't just fearless; she was also clever as hell. The men that had her wouldn't know about the drop-off or the cabin. She could lead them around the woods for hours, and maybe if she was

lucky, she could create an opportunity to catch them unawares
so that she could jump.

My girl always jumped. It was one of the things I now realized
I loved most about her.

I changed my game plan and my direction and started off for
the falls. When I hit the crudely worn path that was barely obvious
from our last visit, it was clear that people had recently used it.
There were several pairs of footprints in the moist earth, including
a set that had to be Avett's because they were tiny and the tread
matched the heavy soles of her ever present combat boots. Plants
were bent and hanging askew from impatient bodies moving by
them and there was a tuft of dark hair caught in the gnarly bark of
one of the pine trees that sat off to the side of the trail.

I rolled my sleeves up even though the temperature seemed
to be dropping with each minute that passed. I was so frustrated
with the way that my shoes slowed my progress that I kicked
them off and pulled off my argyle socks. I hadn't ran through the
woods with bare feet since I was a kid and there was something
about having my toes sink into the mud and the undergrowth that
immediately took me back to a place that was purely primitive
and wholly primal. I wasn't simply a worried man going after the
woman he loved; I was part of the woods, part of the mountains,
part of the place I came from and that had formed me.

I made pretty good time considering the cold and the
impending darkness. I was used to the altitude and the strain it
took on the lungs and the rest of the body, but I doubted the men
I was hunting were. Avett wouldn't have taken them directly to
the drop-off either. I figured she would have done her best to
wear her captors out, to buy herself some time so that her folks
had a fighting chance to get free.

When the roar of the falls hit my ears I slowed my pace and ducked off the trail so that my arrival wouldn't be as visible to the two men that were standing with Avett right at the edge of the falls. Even in the dwindling light, I could see how pale her face was and the black lines that still marked her cheeks from earlier. She was shaking and had her arms wrapped so tightly around herself that she looked even smaller and younger than she normally did. Her terror and vulnerability was being broadcast loud and clear even through the distance that separated us.

One man was facing her where she had her back to the drop-off. He had a handgun pointed directly at the center of her chest, and he was so close to her that if he pulled the trigger, there was no way he was going to miss a vital part of her. There was another man that was clearly the lookout standing with his back to them as he faced the rapidly blackening woods and scanned the trees. He also had a weapon in his hand, but he was clearly nervous because he kept shifting the gun from hand to hand and his weight from foot to foot. Every time a bird squawked or the squirrels made the trees rustle he looked over his shoulder at his partner and told him to hurry the hell up.

"We walked two hours through the fucking forest to get up here so there better be some kind of secret pirate cave behind that waterfall, bitch." The guy with the gun pointed at Avett took a step towards her and she took one back. One more and she would go over the edge, which I was pretty sure had to be her plan all along.

Slowly, she shook her head from side to side. "I told you, there are no drugs. I told you the night you tried to rape me and I'm telling you now. I had nothing to do with Jared ripping your boss off."

Rage, unlike anything I'd ever felt, boiled furious and thick in my blood. The man that was threatening her was the one that had hurt her previously, and all I wanted to do was tear him apart and scatter the pieces into the wind.

"You need to hurry the fuck up and get over the hard-on you have for that stupid bitch. I think I heard something move out there."

The other man swore back at him and waved the gun around. "Stop being paranoid. You need to get your ass out of the city more."

"You're the dumb fuck that believed her when she told you that the drugs were in the woods. What kind of junkie would ever hide drugs out here? Stupid fucker. We don't even get cell service this far out, so how can you check to see if the guys took care of her parents? You blew it and Acosta is going to have both our asses."

I held my breath as their argument escalated. I waited and watched because I needed the guy with the gun pointed at Avett to turn around. I didn't want to make a move until I knew she was totally out of the line of fire. I couldn't bear the idea of her catching a bullet on accident.

"I'm telling you something is out there."

"Well, go check it out, then."

"Put a goddamn bullet in her and then you go check that shit out. I don't fucking work for you."

The other man turned his head and looked over his shoulder as I eased my way even closer to the rock outcropping.

"I'm not putting a bullet in her until I finish what I started all those months ago. I hate being denied after I got a taste of something that I know is going to be so sweet."

"We don't have time for that."

"We're making time."

My teeth clenched together so tightly I was shocked my back teeth didn't crack. I watched Avett's arms fall and I saw her face shift from scared and shaken to serene and calm. I knew what she was going to do before she started to move. I took aim at the guy that was facing the woods and knew there was no more waiting for the right time, because the time was *now*.

Avett took a step backwards and the ground disappeared under her as her body vanished over the edge of the rocks. I screamed her name because I couldn't stop myself from doing so. The crack of gunfire echoed loud and furiously through the gorge as I fired at the same time as the guy aiming at Avett did. Gunpowder was acrid in the air as the guy who was the lookout crumbled to the ground and the other one turned to fire wildly in my direction. I dashed across the clearing, returning fire as bullets whizzed by me but didn't land. My mountains echoed with the sounds of war and fury as I ran faster and faster until I hit the man that was shooting at me full force. I grabbed for the hand that had the gun and we struggled as I pushed him back and back, going for the ledge he had forced Avett over.

Another round was fired as he swore at me and tried to kick me, but I had rage and love on my side, so he was no match for me. It took another heave and my shoulder in his gut to send both of us sailing through the air. Even in the darkness that was now all around us I could see him lose his grip on the weapon as we free-fell through the crisp mountain air. He screamed so loud that it hurt my ears and I was almost thankful as the frigid water engulfed me.

The shock of the cold was enough to make my entire body

stiffen painfully, and I had to really work to get my lethargic arms to cooperate to push myself to the surface. When I broke through, I sucked in lungfuls of air and frantically searched the inky water for any sign of Avett. I didn't know if the man I'd taken over the drop with me had managed to hit her before she jumped and I couldn't immediately see her.

"Avett!" I screamed her name at the top of my lungs and started to thrash around as the cold threatened to suck me back under the surface. "Avett!" Her name and my fear bounced off the stone faces that surrounded me but she didn't answer and I couldn't see that unmissable pink hair shining anywhere in the darkness.

"I can't swim. You have to help me! I'm going to drown!" The gunman was suddenly visible a few hundred yards away, splashing and thrashing against the water like he was doing karate against an invisible appointment.

"Avett! Goddamnit, I can't lose you when I just found you. Where are you?" An owl hooted from somewhere overhead and I jerked my head around.

There, floating right under the surface, was that spray of Technicolor hair. I screamed her name again and cut through the water as quickly as my numb limbs would allow.

She was floating facedown and there was an obvious gash that decorated the side of her head, right above her ear. She felt like a lifeless doll in my hands as I pulled her frozen body to my own and muttered her name over and over again, and I struggled to keep the both of us afloat.

The other man in the water with us was making so much racket I couldn't hear if she was breathing or not but her lips were blue and she wasn't responsive to my touch.

I thought my heart had fractured when I realized my parents were never going to be proud of me and everything I accomplished. I thought I had lost everything when Lottie left me after telling me she was pregnant. I was so sure I had absolutely nothing left to give to anyone after everything I thought I knew to be true was proven to be a lie, but with this woman that was everything in my arms not drawing breath, I knew I had no clue what heartache felt like and that I had more than enough to give her if it meant she would still be here with me.

I tilted her head back as far as it would go without dunking her back in the icy water and started to breathe into her mouth. I breathed in all the love I had for her. I gave her air flavored with my confidence that we were meant to be, and laced with the knowledge that she made me a better kind of man. I breathed out and filled her lungs with the future I wanted to share with her and all the memories I wanted to make with her.

It took far longer than I was comfortable with, but after a few breaths and some desperate kisses on her frozen lips she finally started to cough and sputter in my arms. Those wild eyes slowly opened, and her teeth started to chatter as she looked up at me, unfocused and visibly confused.

"You found me." Her words were raspy and barely audible over the noise the gunman was still making as he faltered and floundered in the water behind us. He might not be able to swim but he was doing an all right job of keeping his head above water.

"You found me first, Avett." I closed my eyes and squeezed her as tightly as I could. "I love you."

One of her arms moved sleepily up and around my neck as her legs started to kick so that she was helping keep us afloat.

"I know you do, Quaid."

"I will always come after you. You know that, right?"

She nodded and winced as she put her fingers to the oozing wound on the side of her head. "You didn't only come after me, you jumped."

I rasped out a shaky laugh and rubbed my frigid nose against her cheek. "Yeah, I jumped and I always will, when it matters. You matter more than anything, Avett."

She opened her mouth to respond when her name, called by a voice that sounded as frantic as I felt, split through the darkness. He father had found us. He had come for her, like he always did. Her eyes widened as I hollered back to Brite, "We're in the water! You have to climb down and help us out. Avett is hurt."

She wrinkled her nose at me as I started to float us towards the lower outcropping of rocks. "I hit my head when I jumped."

I breathed a sigh of relief that she hadn't been hit with a bullet. "Good thing your skull is rock hard and you're the daughter of a badass."

I huffed in exertion and wondered if hypothermia was close to setting in. I was so cold I couldn't even shiver anymore, and I was pretty sure my lips were as blue as hers.

"You saved him and your mom. You saved everyone, including yourself. That makes you your own hero, Avett." I couldn't keep the pride out of my voice, even though I was pretty sure I was going to black out if we didn't get out of the water as soon as possible.

She let out a shaky laugh and her arm tightened around my neck as her dad and two men I didn't recognize suddenly appeared on the rocks. Brite called Avett's name, again the fear and panic that only a parent could have when their child was in danger reverberating from one side of the ravine to the other.

She looked at me and then back at our rescuers with a faint smile touching her quivering lips. "I might be able to save myself now, but it's still nice to know that the people that love me will show up when I need them to."

I kissed her hard and fast as I finally got us to the rocks.

"Always." I'd told myself I needed to show her that I loved her. All I had to do was jump.

CHAPTER 19

Avett

3 weeks later . . .

I used the key Quaid had given me a couple weeks ago to let myself into his loft and simultaneously wrinkled my nose and covered my ears as I walked into what looked like a culinary massacre.

When he texted and told me that he would take care of dinner tonight, that he wanted to cook for me, I was surprised. The only person that ever got any use of that amazing kitchen in his loft was me, and the delivery guy who brought in packages of carryout and set them on the counter. Quaid wasn't exactly comfortable amidst the pots and pans, but the gesture was sweet and I knew the reason he was doing it was because I had been beyond anxious the last few days about what the future had in store for me.

Jared's trial had been pushed back because of all the new charges and empirical evidence against Acosta and his goons. His attorney had filed a motion for continuance while he tried to figure out how to argue against the new kidnapping, attempted murder, attempted arson, tampering with a witness, and coercion charges that his client was now charged with. Quaid was sure the feds were going to step in now that there was enough evidence to put Acosta away for a long time, but so far everything was still happening on the state level. Realizing he was very much the low man on the totem pole, Jared had swung back the other way on the legal pendulum, and fired Tyrell, and was singing at the top of his lungs to the D.A.'s office. He missed his shot at a deal, but in exchange for his testimony against Acosta, the D.A. had agreed to move him to a secure facility where Acosta's reach on the inside couldn't get to him. Quaid thought my ex was hoping for a federal deal that would move him into witness protection, but he assured me that wouldn't happen. Jared was going to do jail time, and I didn't feel bad about it at all.

I was still going to have to testify at Jared's trial when he finally went to court, and now I was looking at having to be involved in the other trial against Acosta as well, but I was no longer scared or hesitant to face either my ex or the men that had made me run for my life. I wanted to see them all behind bars and I wanted justice served. I was ready and willing to do the right thing and I knew that I wouldn't have to do it alone. My parents and Quaid would be right by my side as I told my story and that gave me all the courage I needed.

I watched with wide eyes as Quaid swore and wrestled a pan with something black and smoldering in it into the sink as he wrenched on the water and swore like a biker. I shut the door behind me before the smoke from whatever he incinerated could set off the fire alarm in the entire building. He gave me an exasperated look as he climbed on top of the marble countertop with a towel and started to fan the shrieking alarm.

"Hey."

"Hey, back." The words came out on a laugh that quickly turned into a sigh of appreciation as his T-shirt rode up when he lifted his arms and exposed the ridged slats of his tight stomach. I'd had a lot of casual Quaid time since he wasn't working right now, and I was getting used to him in faded jeans and T-shirts. I knew it wouldn't last because he was already fending offers left and right from other law firms that wanted him, but I planned on soaking up as much of the softer, gentler Quaid as I could get. It was so much easier to get him out of jeans and a T-shirt than it was a three-piece suit, and ever since he jumped after me, and proved beyond a shadow of a doubt that he loved me and whatever kind of chaos I came with, I hadn't been able to keep my hands, mouth, and the rest of me off of him. It wasn't merely celebrating the fact that we both made it out alive and reaffirming the life we had together; it was a desperation to have as much of him, the need to make as many memories, and the desire to have as many stories that surround him and me as I could. Nothing was guaranteed, and I wanted to make sure the time I had with this man was spent in goodness, and a big part of that was getting him naked and inside me as often as I possibly could.

It was a bonus that the guy who jumped for me also happened to be smoking hot and a serious professional in the bedroom.

The smoke alarm finally quieted as I waved a hand in front of my face and made my way over to the counter. He climbed down and pulled me to him for a quick and biting kiss. His fingers brushed over the section of my hair that was shaved off and currently sporting a raised and pink scar from where my head and the rock collided. The other side was wound together in a long, rosy braid that he yanked on the end of as he leaned away from my greedy lips. Initially, the hospital had only buzzed a tiny section, but it was right above my ear and impossible to cover so I took the whole side of my head down in a buzz cut and was rocking a seriously asymmetrical and edgy haircut. The pink was back, bright and vivid, but Quaid seemed to like all of it and didn't blink an eye at any of the drastic changes.

"How did it go today?" His voice was curious, but also supportive. I knew that if I was bringing bad news in with me he would not only be there to help me through it but also to help me come up with an alternate game plan. One amazing side benefit of dating a man that was as sharp and as smart as Quaid was that he never saw anything as a dead end. All he saw was a way that was blocked for the time being, which meant an alternate route was needed. Because of him, I had finally found my new course and the dead end I was stuck in was no more.

"It went okay. My grades aren't really good enough to enroll for this semester because of dropping out before. I need to go back to community college and get the basics out of the way and get decent grades for a year, then I should be accepted into the culinary program at the arts institute. I can afford the classes at the community college, no problem, and if I take Asa up on his offer to work in his new bar, I should be able to save up enough money over the next year to pay for at least the first semester of culinary school when I get there. I want to do it all the right way and I think I'm on the right track."

It was scary to have such serious plans so far out in the future and I'd never been a very good student but I wanted to cook and I wanted to be the best at it that I could. I wanted to not only prove to myself that I could commit to something that mattered to me but I also wanted to prove to my parents and even to Quaid that I wasn't falling anymore. I was climbing my way up and they didn't need to worry about me slipping back down like they used to. I could still see rock bottom when I looked down, but after everything I'd been through in the last few months, I knew it wasn't a place I ever wanted to be again. Rock bottom no longer felt comfortable or necessary.

"Sounds like a plan. Whatever you need holler at me and I'm here for you." He put his hands on my hips and backed me away from the still-smoky kitchen towards the massive leather couch that took up the entire center of the living room.

I put my hands on his shoulders when my ass hit the back edge of the sofa and parted my legs so he would press himself right into the notch that I swore was designed to fit around him and only him. "You can help me with my math homework . . . naked."

He chuckled and bent his tawny head down so that he could brush his lips across mine. The soft caress made me catch my breath and the hitch quickly turned into a sigh as he pressed me back even farther so that my feet were no longer touching the ground and I had to wrap my legs around his lean waist to avoid falling backwards. I curled my hands around his biceps and watched with heavy lidded eyes as he shifted his attention to my combat boots—pulling one off and tossing it over his shoulder, where it landed with a heavy thud.

"Homework won't get done if either of us is naked. I can't even boil water when I start thinking about you in my bed, under me, and calling my name. I almost burned the fucking loft down trying to toast bread when my mind wanders and all I can picture is you on your knees in front of me, with that pouty mouth wrapped around my cock. You are the best and worst kind of distraction, so really it's your fault dinner is in the trash."

I let out a strangled laugh as he slid his hands under the waistband of the black-and-white leggings I had on underneath the plaid shirtdress I had worn to meet with the advisers at the arts institute. The stretchy fabric was down my legs and thrown over his shoulder within seconds, and the abrasive scrape of his jeans against my inner thighs as he pressed right into my center made me groan and shift against that prominent bulge that was making its presence known.

I lifted my eyebrows at him as he put one hand on the curve of my ass and used the other to slowly start opening the front of my top. "Sorry about dinner." The dry humor in my tone made him grin at me and the lightness in his expression, the pure, unfiltered happiness that now shone out of him on a regular basis, made me love him harder than I already did. Quaid finding his balance, his place between who he was and who he thought he was meant to be, was a beautiful thing and it inspired me to always try and be the best me I could going forward.

"You can make it up to me by offering to be dessert." He finally had all the buttons free and pushed the fabric to the side so that I was sitting before him in nothing more than dark red panties and the matching bra.

He hooked a finger under the leg of my lacy underwear and I bit out a gasp as his knuckle brushed delicately across my outer folds. "Are you calling me dessert because I look like candy?" The words were harsh because his finger found its way into the damp cleft that never failed to quiver and tremble for him.

"You're dessert because you're sweet, Avett. So very sweet, and you would be that way whether you had cotton-candy-colored hair or not."

That made my heart swell and my body go liquid and loose around his probing finger. I went to pull him closer so I could kiss the shit out of him for being so sweet himself, but instead I yelped as he suddenly tugged the lace down and off of me right before he lowered himself to his knees in front of me and moved my legs so that they were resting on his wide shoulders. I had to wrap my fingers in his thick, golden hair to keep my balance as he pushed my legs open wider and moved his head to the side so that he could place a sucking kiss on the inside of my thigh. My flesh pebbled in anticipation and I saw his eyes narrow and his nostrils flare as my sex started to glisten in eagerness.

His face was covered in golden scruff, and the rasp of it against my most tender of places had my toes curling and my mouth watering as he traced lazy patterns with the tip of his tongue against my skin.

My hips rocked towards his face involuntarily and I made a noise as I almost toppled backwards on the couch. He grunted as I pulled on the fistful of hair I was still holding on to for balance and looked up at me with humor and desire clouding his pale gaze. "Careful."

"I can't be held responsible for my actions when your mouth is that close to my vagina." I forced myself to loosen my hold on his hair, but my entire body tensed when his low chuckle hit all the aching and exposed nerves right at the heart of me.

Both of his hands settled on the outsides of my hips to hold me steady as he tugged me closer to his mouth. I muttered his name as his tongue darted out and swiped at my slit from the top to the bottom, sending chills and desire scattering all across my skin.

I instinctively parted my legs even wider and arched into the elusive touch of his mouth. His stubble scraped across my skin as he settled in and used his mouth to fully devour me like I was, indeed, the sweetest dessert he had ever tasted.

The tip of his nose dragged through my folds and brushed across my clit; it made me jerk and had his hands tightening on my hips to keep me upright. He laughed again, and the puff of air and the vibration from his mouth had me whispering his name and letting my eyes float closed as pleasure wrapped its way around every nerve ending and cell in my body. The flat of his tongue dragged its way through my sensitive valley and then circled my clit playfully. The rough scrape of his teeth across the sensitive bud followed and I threw my head back with a loud moan.

He barked at me to hold on to the back of the couch so he could let go of his hold on me with one hand, and the next thing I knew his fingers were filling me up as his hungry mouth worked its way over and around that taut bundle of nerves that pulsed and throbbed at his every stroke. My body bent and bowed towards him and my thighs shifted restlessly next to his ears as the slick sound of sex and pleasure started to fill the loft. He had no problem making my body respond to him in the most delicious and obvious ways. There was never any hiding how turned on I was, or how much I wanted him when he put his mouth on me.

My spine stiffened and my entire body thrummed in anticipation as I rode his pumping fingers and moved my desperate center against his biting and sucking mouth. I moved my hand from his silken hair to his bristly cheek and shivered when I felt it hollow out under my palm as he sucked my overly sensitized clit between his teeth for an artful nibble.

"Quaid." I muttered his name and rocked my hips up as he added another finger to the mix and I whimpered when I felt my own wetness start to trickle down the inside of my leg. He didn't act like he heard me or if he did he was ignoring me, so I tapped his cheek with my fingers and said much louder, "Dennis, I need a minute."

At the use of his given name, Quaid's head jerked back and I wanted to groan at the sight of his too-pretty face flushed, damp, and shiny with all the amazing things he did to me. His brows pulled together in a tight V over his faded blue eyes as I scrambled over the edge of the couch so that I was on my knees facing him as he rose back to his feet in front of me. I reached out a hand and ran it over the delineated lines of his abs and up the front of him until I had his sculpted chest and all that marvelous artwork visible to my greedy gaze. He shrugged the shirt the rest of the way off over the top of his head and took a step towards me as I grabbed the top of his jeans and popped the button loose so that I could circle the tip of his cock with my thumb where it peeked out over the edge of his dark boxer briefs.

"Dessert is meant to be shared. You got your bite first, and now I want mine." I'd been salivating to have him in my mouth ever since he told me it was the image of me on my knees in front of him that had made him ruin dinner in the first place. Getting when Quaid was the one giving was amazing, but giving when he was the one receiving had its own kind of heady power and was its own special kind of thrill. I liked that I could make him as weak in the knees and as needy as he made me on the regular.

I forcibly tugged the denim down around his hips, taking his underwear with the rough fabric so that I had unfettered access to his long, thick cock. It jutted out at me, ready and willing for whatever I had in mind. I grinned up at Quaid and used the tips of my short nails to rake through the tuft of darker blond hair that his happy trail led to. All of him was so golden and glorious I was sure there was no way I would run out of ways to revel in touching him. Being with this man was always the best decision I could ever make, and the rightness of it all made things between us even better than they already were.

I bent my head down so I could swipe my tongue across his rigid length from root to tip, pausing when I got to the leaking slit and spending extra time savoring his taste and his desire. Quaid grunted and moved one of his hands to the top of my head as I worked my mouth up and down in combination with a circling and gliding fist around the base of his shaft. His other hand slid down across my spine and rested in the center of my back as I leaned over on the couch so that I could swallow as much of his insistent direction as I could.

I could hear his breathing shift as I squeezed him tighter and sucked him harder. I felt his nails drag across my skin and watched as his muscular thighs tightened as I hummed my appreciation of all his masculine glory along the unyielding flesh that was riding my tongue like it was a carnival attraction. I was struggling to breathe as he started to move against my face but I wasn't complaining. I liked him out of control, crazy with lust, and lost in his own pleasure and taking for himself. As long as I was the one giving him what he wanted, he could be as selfish and as greedy with me as he wanted.

But this was Quaid. This was the man that loved me and had made it his mission to bring goodness back into my life, so right when I was sure he was going to come down my throat with a shudder and a shout, I was suddenly left sucking in lungfuls of air as he wrenched his now glistening and wet cock out of my mouth and with a dirty word groaned loudly and desperately.

Before I could ask him what he was doing, he had his hands under my arms and he was lifting me over the backside of the sofa and turning me around so that my back was to him as he bent me over and told me to put my hands on the edge. The back clasp of my bra was undone and my breasts fell heavy and full into his waiting grasp as he stepped up behind me so that his heart beat right against my spine. He used his feet to spread mine wider and I felt the steely probe of his erection as it slid through my soaked folds as he rocked his hips against my backside.

His lips hit the back of my neck as his talented fingers plucked and rolled my eager nipples. "How 'bout we feed each other dessert?" His warm breath made the tiny hairs that were exposed by my braid dance and had my entire body shivering.

I nodded weakly and put one of my hands over the top of his as he continued to fondle me with equal parts gentleness and roughness. "Sounds like a plan."

He chuckled as I used his earlier words, but we both stopped being able to make any noises beyond a gasp and a moan as his tip hit my begging opening. I canted my hips a little to help him slide in, and as soon as we had the position right, he slipped all the way in and I felt the stretch and burn of his body overtaking mine through every single part of me.

He pulled back and rocked forward with more force, which had my teeth clamping down on my lip and made me lift up onto the tips of my toes so I could take even more of him inside of me. My channel spasmed around him and I could feel my body pulling on his, asking for more. Begging him to go farther, to push deeper, and because he was an executive he knew what I wanted without my having to ask.

He put a hand on my back and bent me over even more so that

my ass was in the air and my hands were on the seat cushions in front of me. It wasn't exactly comfortable, but he was in me so deep and thrusting so hard and wild that I could have been bent in half and I wouldn't have cared, and when he wrapped the end of my braid around his hand and used it to pull my head back and ordered me to look at him while he fucked me, I was pretty sure I was going to explode on the spot. The sounds of our hips slapping together, and the slick sounds of his body thrusting and filling mine, was making me hot and squirmy where I was impaled on his hammer cock. And the sight of his tattooed chest heaving and slick with sweat as he worked us both to the point of incoherent pleasure was so animalistic and sexy that I had to squeeze my eyes shut again to avoid losing it all simply from watching what he was doing. I loved all of Quaid and all the different types of men that were housed inside his gorgeous body, but this version of him was undoubtedly my favorite. When he fucked me raw and untamed, when he owned me, the sensations he brought to life in me—that was when he was the most authentic and the most honest. He knew what he wanted and he knew how to get it. He also knew what I wanted and knew that he was the only man that was capable of giving it to me. It made sex with him a memorable and an exciting experience, every single time.

The hand that wasn't wrapped in my hair rubbed across my hip, skated over the lifted curve of my ass, and expertly dipped and played in that darkened valley I had yet to let him explore. Quaid liked to play and liked to explore every single inch of me but I wasn't quite at his level yet and he never pushed me past what I was comfortable with. That didn't mean that he didn't tempt and tease with erotic and dangerous touches that hinted at the pleasure and surprise that was waiting for me when I relented and put myself in his very skilled hands. His palm slipped down the front of me where I was leaning against the back of the couch. I knew where he was headed so I sucked in a breath and let it out slowly at the first brush of his fingers across my clit. Everything swirled and spiraled into a vortex of sex and pleasure as my orgasm hit with the force of a tidal wave and I couldn't stop the shriek that tumbled across my lips. I fisted my hands on the couch cushions and let my head fall forward as he finally released my hair and he shifted his hands to my hips as he pounded into me jerkily, frantic in search of his own release.

His breathing was harsh and rustled through the fog of satisfaction that engulfed me. He mumbled my name and it was the sweetest sound I'd ever heard, so I found my balance and lifted the knee of one of my legs up on the back of the couch so that he could go even deeper and get even closer to the edge of his own completion. He growled something dirty and sexy as the new position opened me up even further to him, and it didn't take long before I felt his big body tense where it hovered over mine and felt the heat and rush of his orgasm fill me as his cock jerked and his movements stilled.

We stayed that way for a minute as he worked to catch his breath and as I floated around in a happy bubble of fulfillment and languid love. I muttered a soft protest as his strong arms were suddenly wrapped around my middle and pulling me upright so that I was pressed all along the front of him, the tattoo of the eagle so close to me I could swear that I could feel each and every single one of the feathers on its massive wings. Quaid's arms wrapped around me in a tight hug and his lips rested on the top of my head as he whispered, "Now you really look like dessert, pink hair all tangled and wild around your head and covered in cream. If anyone besides me thinks they get a taste, I may have to murder them."

I snorted at the filthy words and lifted my arms so that I could hold on to the hands that were holding on to me so tightly. "You may suck at dinner but you've got dessert handled, hotshot."

He kissed the top of my head again and I leaned back into him with a sigh as sex and love covered both of us from head to toe.

"Hey, Quaid." My voice was soft and so was my heart.

"Yeah?"

"You're the best bad decision I ever made, and you are, by far, my favorite story to tell."

He pulled out of both the embrace and where we were still joined and turned me so that I was facing him. He put his hands on either of my cheeks and bent so that his mouth touched mine in the lightest kiss he could give me and still have it be considered a kiss.

"You're the *best* decision I made period, Avett. Our story is only at the beginning so I hope you want to tell it for years and years to come."

I laughed and pulled him in for a real kiss, and all I could think was, Of course my dad was right about everything.

Bad decisions did lead to great stories and, in my case, great love. I'd make every single crappy choice and foolish error again if it meant I would end up exactly where I was right now. Every mistake was a piece of me, a part of my story, and without each of them there was no way I would be starting my own happy-ever-after in his perfect, stormy, blue-gray eyes.

EPILOGUE

Quaid

Christmas Day . . .

She was everything I ever wanted and then some.

Her multicolored eyes sparkled up at me with humor and knowing as I braced a hand on the wall in front of me and used the other to roll her velvety nipple around with my thumb. When she told me she had a Christmas present for me, I assumed it would be a new tie now that I was back at work or some home-made sweet treat that she made now that she had taken over my kitchen as thoroughly as she had taken over my heart.

What I wasn't expecting was for her to lead me to our bed, strip, and tell me she wanted to give me my biggest sexual fantasy for Christmas. She was always open and giving in bed, but I was aware that there were some things I wanted from her and to do to her she wasn't ready for. So, when she laid back with those spectacular tits all oiled up and waiting for me, I was pretty sure I'd died and gone to sexual heaven.

I could never take from her without giving everything I had to give first, so before I took advantage of the gift she was giving I kissed my way up her body, making sure I spent plenty of time to stop and savor her where she was already wet and willing. She looked like a pretty confection, so colorful and covered in a hard shell that she needed to keep her soft center safe, but she tasted like dreams and promises. There was no actual definition for the way she tasted when she blossomed and went slick against my tongue, but each time she did, I swore she tasted better than the last time I had my fill of her.

I circled the tiny indent of her belly button with the tip of my tongue and used my fingers to tweak and tug on her clit as I worked my way up her delectable body as slowly as I could. When I got to the valley between her glistening breasts, I chuckled and whispered, "Cotton candy," against her slippery skin.

"Your favorite." Her voice was thready and tight with anticipation and desire. Her legs shifted under me and her hips lifted and dropped with each thrust and retreat of my plundering fingers.

I bent so I could nibble on her candy-flavored nipple and told her, "You're my favorite— period."

She muttered her appreciation and wound her fingers through my hair as I started to circle her clit with my thumb. My dick was harder than it had ever been and I couldn't resist wrapping my fist around it as I simultaneously worked her and myself to the breaking point. Her tongue darted out and swiped at her full lower lip and I was a goner. Knowing I wouldn't last much longer, I maneuvered myself the rest of the way up her body and swallowed a flood of dirty words as she pressed her pillowy flesh around my dick. Her plump breasts, tipped with those luscious and pointy nipples engulfing my cock so that all I could see was her and the tip, which was even better than my fantasy.

The position wasn't quite right for her to get her mouth around the leaking head as I rocked my hips carefully across her chest, making sure I didn't crush her much smaller frame with my weight or my overzealous reaction to how good what she was doing felt. My balls dragged across her slick skin and my dick throbbed where it was trapped in the best vice ever. She couldn't get the head in her mouth but each time the tip moved towards her mouth she managed to stroke the flat of her tongue across the slit, and each time she cleared away the evidence of how good this felt only to have another pearly drop rise up to replace it. She cased my pleasure with her wet tongue and I rode her breasts with a cock that felt like it was made of stone. I'd never been so hard that it hurt before, but leave it to this little hurricane to take me somewhere else I'd never been and leave me disoriented and so fucking happy I could hardly stand it.

I felt the desire coil tight at the base of my spine and felt my balls start to ache in a way that let me know it wasn't going to be long before those flushed and thoroughly worked-over tits were going to have more than cotton-candy-flavored oil covering them.

In my mind, marking her and claiming her in all the ways I possibly could was sexy and appealed to the need I had to completely make her mine. The reality of it was that nothing felt better than being inside her tight, wet heat. There was no place that made me feel more like the man I was supposed to, the man that deserved this woman and all the wildness and sweetness that she offered than when I was seated all the way inside her.

When my heart touched hers and when she breathed me in, as I breathed my love for her out, that was the sexiest thing that could ever happen between the two of us.

So even though I was mere seconds away from blowing all over her, I pushed off the wall where I was bracing myself and scooted back down her body, dropping a kiss on her surprised mouth as I hovered over her in a one-armed pushup as I lined my now very angry erection up with her opening. I could see confusion in her eyes but it was quickly replaced by passion as I pushed my way into her with a contented sigh. Her body welcomed me with quivering muscles and featherlight pulses.

"You feel better than anything ever has, Avett."

She sighed and wound her arms around my shoulders as I lowered myself to cover her fully. She wrapped her legs around my hips and her heels dug into my ass as she whispered into my ear, "So do you."

She didn't only feel better, she felt right. The way she moved against me, the way she responded to me, the way she took and gave with equal passion, the way she said my name, the way she came for me . . . wild and sweet . . . every single time. She never held back and every single time I took her to bed I found something new to love about her; this time it was the way she shifted below me and urged me to roll with her so that we could switch places and she was the one doing the fucking.

I complied and immediately put my hands on her breasts. The soft flesh was still shiny and slick from the oil and she moaned in pleasure as her nipples slipped and slid in and out of my fingers as I tried to catch them as she bounced vigorously up and down on my shaft. I loved watching her ride me. I couldn't tear my eyes away from the place where we were joined, the way her body pulled me in and released me as we both glinted with sex and passion.

When she dipped her fingers between her legs and started to circle her clit as she rocked even more quickly on me, I knew she was close. I let go of her breasts and shoved my hand behind her head so I could pull her down for a kiss as she stiffened above me and let out a little whimper of pleasure. She always came beautifully, but when she was above me, I could see the rose-colored flush flood her entire body. I could watch her odd colored eyes spin out in a tie-dye of satisfaction and completion. It brought my own orgasm racing forward when I watched her sex flutter and flex so delicately and prettily around my much more aggressive arousal.

I bucked into her wetness as she planted her hands on my chest and rode out the rest of the storm with me. It only took a few more thrusts and her telling me that she loved me for me to find my own finish, and once I did, she collapsed on top of me and used her fingers to lightly trace along one of the eagle's wings. I swear I was so far gone for this woman that the feathers ruffled and fluffed up under her touch.

"Best present I ever got." I turned my head so I could kiss her cheek but ended up kissing her nose as her head jerked up so that she could look down at me with wide eyes.

"I got you something else. When I get the feeling back in everything below my vagina, I'll get it for you."

I twisted her long, colorful hair around my hand and used that to pull her down for another kiss. "I told you that we didn't have to exchange gifts. I get you in my bed every single night and that's all I want. That's all I'll ever want."

I'd asked her to move in with me over a month ago and she

said no. She said she was still working on trying to do the right thing without thinking about it and she wanted to keep working on her relationship with her mom. Plus, Brite hadn't quite gotten over almost losing her so the bearded giant wasn't exactly ready to let his little girl go yet. I'd given her a key to my loft and told her she was always welcome and luckily she spent more nights than not in my bed. But apparently, a couple of days ago she had come home early after a meeting with the D.A.'s office and found her mom and dad in a fairly compromising situation on the kitchen table.

Avett laughed it off and told them she was glad they couldn't keep their hands off each other but the run-in had finally convinced her to move in with me, which meant I got to put her in a compromising position on *our* kitchen table . . . twice.

She wiggled loose and we both let out a moan as our bodies separated. She was glossy from head to toe, covered in all kinds of sex and good times, and all I wanted to do was wrap my arms around her and tumble her back underneath me on the bed.

She lifted her hands up and tried unsuccessfully to unstick her hair from her still-oiled-up chest and made a face at me as I licked my lips. "Lofts don't really offer much in the way of hiding places, but luckily you've avoided the kitchen like the plague since that disastrous dinner incident."

She made her way over to where the fridge was and I saw her wiggle and shake, her naked backside making my tired dick take notice. She let out a triumphant sound and came back towards the bed with something as big as she was wrapped in brown paper covering her almost completely up. She hefted the burden onto the mattress and pushed it towards me with a mischievous grin.

"Merry Christmas, Quaid."

I grabbed the edge of the giant package and started to care-fully peel the corner back as I picked at the tape holding it shut. She watched me with wide eyes and the longer I took with the wrapping, the more impatient she became. By the time I had one side of the tape free and opened, she had her arms crossed over her bare breasts and was tapping her foot impatiently. The fierce look was ruined by her lack of clothing but I didn't tell her that. Instead, I took hold of the big flap I'd worked free and ripped the front of the packaging off with a quick jerk of my arm.

I blinked and lost the ability to breathe when the image waiting for me on the massive canvas was revealed. The bed sank down a little as Avett crawled back up next to me. She reached out and touched the eagle on my chest as I traced the identical image that was staring up at me from the painting in my hands.

"Remember I told you that I knew the guy that did your tattoo? Well, he and his business partner have branched out and are doing all kinds of things beyond tattoos. Custom artwork happens to be one of those things. I thought you could hang it in your new office. That way you can have a little bit of wild Quaid around even when you have to be civilized Quaid."

I couldn't look away from the painting and I couldn't get my heart to stop beating her name over and over again. No one had ever done anything as thoughtful or as personal as this for me. No one understood me the way Avett did, which proved even more how right she was for me.

She reached out and peeled more of the wrapping away and I whispered, "Those are my mountains."

She nodded and reached up to pull on the ends of her hair. "I wanted to you to be able to have your favorite place with you even when you were having a bad day."

I let out a deep breath and moved the big painting to the side of the bed so that I could pull her to me. I arranged her so that she was straddling me and lowered my forehead so that it was resting on the center of her chest. She smelled sugary and decadent. I wanted to eat her up all over again, but it was the steady and sure beat of her heart that made me tell her, "The mountains used to be my favorite place. Now that's anywhere you are."

She hummed in appreciation and scraped her fingers over the short sides of my hair. "Well, you shouldn't have too many bad days anyway now that you're working for yourself."

Instead of taking any of the numerous offers that had come at me fast and furiously when I walked away from the firm, I decided that I had worked too hard for other people and all the wrong reasons for far too long. The only person I wanted to impress and to prove myself to was currently wrapped around me and I knew there was nothing I could do that would make her love me any less so I decided it was time to jump again and go into private practice. I already had more clients and more inquiries than I knew what to do with and I wasn't even officially back in business until after the first of the year. I was planning on being more selective and more discriminating in who I invested my time and legal knowledge into. I still believed everyone deserved the best defense possible, but now I wanted to give it to the people that really needed it. There would be no more putting bad people back on the street simply because they waved a wad of cash in my face and were guaranteed to get their names in the press.

I'd wanted some time to settle into life without the smoke and mirrors, and I'd wanted time to spend with Avett before she started school and went to work for Asa. I was being selfish with my time and my talent, but at least I knew I was doing it for something that mattered, something that was beyond value.

"I got you something for Christmas, too, but it's too big to hide in the loft."

She jerked back and looked at me with her brows puckered and her mouth set into that pout I couldn't resist. "I told you not to spend a lot of money on me, Quaid. You better not have bought me a car or something else that's going to make me fight with you on our first Christmas together."

I shook my head against her soft skin and chuckled. My little hurricane was full of fire and independence, something she never let me forget. I could love her and support her but she wouldn't let me coddle her or indulge her. She insisted that was part of us doing this relationship right. There were times when I wanted to spoil her for her simply being so unconcerned with material things but then she would remind me that I gave her my heart and the real me and that was worth more than any trinket she insisted she would lose or break anyway.

"It's not a car . . . exactly. Let's take a shower and clean up and I'll take you by the bar so you can check it out before we head over to your parents' house for dinner."

She was still looking at me through narrowed eyes but she didn't offer even a peep of protest when I scooped her up and started walking towards the bathroom. If we were taking a shower together, that meant we were going to have to get very dirty before we got clean, so it was a good thing her parents wouldn't mind if we were running a little bit late.

Going to Brite and Darcy's for Christmas dinner was the kind of holiday gathering I was actually excited about. I was looking forward to spending time with a family and a close-knit group of friends, where it was actually about enjoying each other's company and spending time together, not about having the appropriate date or the best gift for the boss in order to gain brownie points and accolades. Being taken into the fold by Brite Walker was a profound experience, and knowing that the burly man not only approved of me but more importantly approved of me for his daughter was the greatest validation I had ever been given. I finally felt like I was reaching the potential I'd long been chasing after and it had nothing to do with things and everything to do with one special girl that whipped through my life like a cyclone.

Being around Avett and her family had even inspired me to reach out to my own estranged brood. I'd sent my folks a Christmas card, one that had a picture of my mountains on it, and mentioned that I wouldn't mind taking a trip up north to see them. I didn't even know if they had a way to get mail out on their frozen lake or if they were interested in seeing me after so much time and bad blood, but I tried and figured that counted for something.

After a very steamy shower that had nothing to do with the water temperature and everything to do with me trying to lick all of the cotton-candy flavoring off of Avett, we got dressed and grabbed the gifts she had picked out for her parents—a new knife set for Darcy and a picture of her sitting on a Harley when she was still in diapers with Brite holding her on the massive machine, a smile brighter than the sun splitting his bearded face. The picture was yellowed and there were burn marks around the corners but the damage was hardly noticeable where it sat in the silver frame that looked like it was made of spokes. Avett had cried when Zeb called her and told her he found a box of pictures in one of the closets of the destroyed house. The box had been under the remnants of a leather jacket so the damage was minimal but the effect something so simple had on my girl was profound.

We got dressed and bundled up in defense against the winter chill that was thick in the December air. Snow had fallen over-night, leaving a light dusting on the ground that crunched under our feet as we exited the truck when I pulled to a stop behind the bar. Avett huddled into my side and rubbed her bare hands together as I led her towards the big metal vehicle that was taking up a good portion of the back parking lot.

"Is that an ice cream truck?" She sounded bemused. "Why does Rome have an ice cream truck in the parking lot in the middle of winter?"

I gave her a tight squeeze where she was pressed into my side and reached out with my index finger so I could draw a heart in the frost that had accumulated on the side of the big vehicle.

"Not an ice cream truck—a food truck, and it's yours." I shifted her so that she was facing me, her wide-eyed look of shock and her slack mouth making me chuckle. "Merry Christmas, Avett."

She looked at the truck over her shoulder and then back at me, disbelief and astonishment clear in every line of her small body.

"What did you do, Quaid?" Her tone was breathless and filled with awe as she moved out of my grasp and towards the towering truck. She traced a heart next to mine and then trailed the rest of her fingers through the frost like she was petting the side of the monstrous vehicle.

"It wasn't all me actually, and I can't take credit for the idea— that was all Asa. When I mentioned that I wanted to get you something that you would have forever, no matter what happens between you and me, no matter what choices you make in the future, he was the one that brought up the idea of giving you your space to cook in." I rubbed the back of my neck sheepishly and looked down at the crisp white blanket beneath my feet. "I may have suggested trying to buy a restaurant and it was quickly pointed out to me how ridiculous and unrealistic that kind of undertaking would be, not to mention how uncomfortable it would have made you. Asa mentioned the food truck, and your dad and Rome immediately decided that they wanted to pitch in as well. This is from all of us, Avett. We wanted to give you whatever kind of future you want to have for Christmas because we all believe in you and we all love the passionate, talented woman that you are."

She spun around and threw herself at me, which made me stumble because of the slick ground. I struggled to keep us both upright as her arms wound around my neck in a stranglehold.

"I can't believe you guys did this. I haven't even started school yet. I don't know what to say."

I kissed her because she was happy and because she didn't automatically tell me that she didn't deserve something like this. We'd come a long way from that day she sat across me dressed in convict orange, looking like every bad thing that happened in the world was her fault and her burden to bear. I kissed her because she was mine to kiss and that was what made me happy.

"That's the thing . . . this truck is yours, so you can do whatever you want with it. You can let it sit until you finish school, you can run it on the weekends, once you figure out what you want to do with it, you can hire someone to run it for you, or you can even sell the damn thing and invest the money back into your education. The options are endless and the choice is yours to make."

She buried her face in the side of my neck and I shivered as her icy nose rubbed back and forth below my ear.

"You trust me to make the right one?" There was laughter in her voice and an alluring glint in her eyes as she pulled back and smiled up at me.

I grabbed her face between my hands and lowered my mouth back to hers. "Right or wrong, think of the stories you'll have to tell after you make it." I couldn't wait to be a part of every single one of them. She was the beginning, middle, and end of the best story I had ever been lucky enough to be a part of. She always made for interesting plotlines and dramatic twists. Whatever story we were living was never going to be boring or predictable, and there was no one else I ever wanted to reach the climax, or a climax, with. The silly analogy made my lips twitch as hers rubbed softly against them in a whispered thank-you.

As long as my story and her story ended the same way and on the same page, with her and me together at the end of it, I didn't care about the decisions we were going to have to make along the way, good or bad, because I knew all the important ones we would be making together.

AUTHOR'S NOTE

I was reading the introduction Joanna Wylde puts in the front of all her Reaper books as I devoured her latest book. (I'm obsessed with her words, people! She is so, so good!) She says she never lets reality get in the way of the story and I kind of love her for putting that out there like that because I feel the same way.

Quaid is a lawyer so there is a lot of court and legal jargon thrown around in this book. I made sure most of it was as accurate as I could, but there are some parts and some time frames that have been manipulated to fit within the confines of this particular story. The real legal system moves much slower and has more moving parts . . . I am aware . . . but the gist is on-point and I've said it before: sometimes truth makes for really boring fiction.

So to any real legal eagles out there I apologize for any liberties I may have taken with your profession. I sure hope you enjoyed the end result!!!

AVETT AND QUAID'S PLAYLIST

Riders on the Storm - The Doors
Tornados - Drive-By Truckers
Hurricane - American Aquarium
Ain't No Sunshine - Bill Withers
Blackhole Sun - SoundGarden
Have You Ever Seen the Rain - CCR
Like a Hurricane - Neil Young
Lightning Bolt - Pearl Jam
Only Happy When It Rains - Garbage
Rock You Like a Hurricane - The Scorpions
Set Fire to the Rain - Adele
The Sun and the Rain - Madness
After the Storm - Mumford and Sons
Butterflies and Hurricanes - Muse
Crying Lightning - Arctic Monkeys
Dust in the Wind - Kansas
Hurricane - Thirty Seconds to Mars
Look Out Sunshine - The Fratellis
She's a Rainbow - The Rolling Stones
Snow Falls in June - Ryan Bingham
This Is a Low - Blur
Thunder Road - Bruce Springsteen

ACKNOWLEDGMENTS

Truthfully this book may not have been written and definitely wouldn't be as fun as it is if it wasn't for Kristen Proby, Jennifer Armentrout, Jen McLaughlin, Karina Halle, Cora Carmack, Lindsay Ehrhardt, Heather Self, Ali Hymer, Debbie Besabella, Denise Tung, and Stacey Morgan. I needed a break. I needed an escape. I needed to decompress and to whine about life and words and all the things that were tangled up and confused in my head, making it a pretty unpleasant place to be. The story wouldn't come and in my line of work that's a pretty terrifying thing to be facing. I took a few friendcations and a few mental health days where I ran away from being an adult and responsibility for a while because clearly my coping skills were lacking. But I needed that space and I needed that time. I also needed to hear that I wasn't alone and that things would be okay.

These ladies all had a hand in helping get me back on track. They kicked my ass when I needed it and all around forced me to pull my head out of my ass . . . where it was pretty firmly lodged, I must admit. I have good friends who are good people and manage to keep me and themselves grounded and true when this business feels like it might swallow you whole—frankly, they are the best—and it's nice to know that they won't let me wander too far off the path I have been steadily carving out for myself since I started this journey three years ago. I owe them a lot and I am forever thankful that books brought them into my life. I'm not giving them up for any of the stuff and things.

This book is lucky (I mean, the book is finished and I think it's awesome so that makes it lucky by my standards . . . lol) number thirteen!

I can't believe it. So many words, and so much work in such a short amount of time, and it never gets old or boring to unleash my own special kind of crazy and magic on the book world. Thank you so very much for being here . . . regardless if this is your first book of mine or if you've been here for all thirteen. I can't thank you enough for giving me the opportunity to tell my stories and to live out my biggest dream. Every single reader, blogger, author, professional, friend, and family member that has been here for this ride has had a hand in making something that seemed unbelievable and unrealistic my reality. That is so special and so important that there are never going to be enough ways to share my gratitude with you.

Thank you . . . a million thank youz . . . and a million more . . .

Amanda (and Martha all the way across the pond), Jessie, Caroline, Molly, Elle, KP, Stacey, and Melissa . . . thanks for never wavering, for staying on course, for navigating the waters no matter how choppy and treacherous they may get. Thanks for your faith and belief when I have none of my own. Thanks for reminding me this is a team sport when I often feel like I'm playing, winning, and losing solo.

Thanks to the best folks a girl could have . . . if you see them at an event with me give them a squeeze and tell them Jay loves them. You might want to buy them a drink while you're at it because traveling with me and my bad juju is no picnic!

Hey, Mike, you rock, and I wouldn't have made it through this year without you, no joke. Thank you for always being rock solid, for being there, and for being my go-to guy for all the things.

To all the authors who are so disgustingly talented and so inordinately gracious with their time and gifts, thank you for being my inspirations and my friends. You are all brilliant and who you are as people as well as storytellers is unparalleled. This huge thanks and virtual hug goes out to Jennifer Armentrout, Jenn Foor, Jenn Cooksey, Jen McLaughlin, Tiffany King, Tina Gephart, Tillie Cole, Joanna Wylde, Kylie Scott, Cora Carmack, Emma Hart, Renee Carlino, Penelope Douglas, Kristen Proby, Amy Jackson, Nichole Chase, Tessa Bailey, J. Daniels, Rebecca Shea, Kristy Bromberg, Adriane Leigh, Laurelin Page, EK Blair, SC Stephens, Molly McAdams, Crystal Perkins, Tijan, Karina Halle, Christina Lauren, Chelsea M. Cameron, Sophie Jordan, Daisy Prescott, Michelle Valentine, Felicia Lynn, Harper Sloan, Monica Murphy, Erin McCarthy, Liliana Hart, Laura Kaye, Heather Self, and Kathleen Tucker. Seriously, I admire every author on this list, and what they add to this business and to my writerly life. If you are looking for a solid book to read, I promise one of theirs won't disappoint.

Last but not least, thanks to my furry little entourage for being my heart. Woof!

If you would like to contact me, there are a bazillion places you can do so!

Check my website for updates, release dates, and all my events: www.jaycrownover.com

I'm also all over the interwebs!

Please feel free to join my fan group on Facebook:
https://www.facebook.com/groups/crownoverscrowd/
https://www.facebook.com/jay.crownover
https://www.facebook.com/AuthorJayCrownover?ref=hl
Follow me on Twitter: @jaycrownover
Follow me on InstaGram: @jay.crownover
https://www.goodreads.com/Crownover
http://www.donaghyliterary.com/jay-crownover.html
http://www.avonromance.com/author/jay-crownover

ABOUT THE AUTHOR

Jay Crownover is the *New York Times* and *USA TODAY* best-selling author of the Marked Men and Welcome to the Point series. Like her characters, she is a big fan of tattoos. She loves music and wishes she could be a rock star, but since she has no aptitude for singing or instrument playing, she'll settle for writing stories with interesting characters that make the reader feel something. She lives in Colorado with her three dogs.

EVEN THE HARDEST OF HEARTS CAN BE *RIVETED*
BY THE BLINDING LIGHT OF LOVE WHEN THE
RIGHT PERSON COMES ALONG AND SHINES
BRIGHT AND BRILLIANT IN THE CENTER OF A
LIFE LIVED DARK AND DREARY . . . CHURCH
AND DIXIE'S STORY COMING SOON . . .

When Honor is on the line, nothing else matters.
Keep reading for an exclusive excerpt to *New York Times*
bestselling author Jay Crownover's

HONOR

A BREAKING POINT NOVEL

Don't be fooled.

Don't make excuses for me.

I am not a good man.

I've seen things no one should, done things no one should talk about. Honor and conscience have no place in my life. But I've fought and I've survived. I've had to.

The first time I saw her dancing on that seedy stage in that second rate club, I felt my heart pulse for the first time. Keelyn Foster was too young, too vibrant for this place, and I knew in an instant that I would make her mine. But first I had to climb my way to the top. I had to have something more to offer her.

I'm here now, money is no object and I have no equal. Except for her.

She's disappeared. But don't worry, I will find her and claim her. She will be mine.

Like I said, don't be fooled. I am not the devil in disguise . . . I'm the one front and center.

COMING FALL 2016

I walked into a disgustingly gaudy strip club, offended by its crass ugliness. I was expecting to meet the ruler of the land, state my intentions, and let him know I would bow to no man here or anywhere else ever again. I was expecting a shakedown and maybe some strong-arming since I was obviously foreign and undocumented. I was technically legal since my mother had been an American citizen before she fell in love with an extremist, but I hadn't really existed on paper since she handed me over to killers and radicals when I was just a kid. Mossad didn't want me to be anything other than their trained attack dog, so they hadn't offered up any proof of identity for me during my time at the end of their string. What I wasn't expecting was that my cause, my reason, my purpose for living, and my something to believe in would be dancing nearly naked on a horrifically ugly stage, looking like she was going to cry at any second. She was so much more than freedom.

She was Honor.

She was beautiful, young, innocent, and so obviously resigned to her fate. It pulled at a heart I was stunned to find I still had buried somewhere deep underneath the brutal history that filled up the inside of me. It was the first time I felt it beat, and the pulse of its yearning scared and electrified me in equal measure.

I started to move toward her like all those invisible gods I spent my life killing for were leading me directly to her when suddenly a man twice her age and triple her size leaped from his seat next to the stage and hurled himself up onto the platform directly at the girl. In the blink of an eye he was on the top of her, rough hands all over her naked flesh. I heard her scream. I saw her long limbs flail and thrash under him. A red haze filled my vision and I forgot all about staying quiet and laying low. I forgot all about being a ghost, and realized that I could channel the fight that had been forged into my very soul, the fight that was slumbering restlessly inside me at that moment, into protecting something so innocent. She woke the fight up and she kept it alive.

I was on the stage before my mind even registered that I had moved across the room. I pulled the hulking man off the dancer and offered her my hand. Pretty eyes the color of an overcast sky glimmered up at me. She looked at the hand I'd offered like it was her lifeline out of this place, out of this vicious world, and clutched it ferociously as I pulled her to her feet.

We stared at each other in silence and I knew in that instant that this young woman would mean more than anything in my life had ever meant.

"Are you okay?"

She blinked at me like a terrified animal and I felt all the dead things inside me roar to life with new purpose and passion.

"Yeah. I could've handled him. He just surprised me."

She was so young and her words pounded into me so hard they hurt. She shouldn't have to handle him at all. I was the opposite of innocent and suddenly all I wanted was to keep her as different from me and my life as I could, keep her that way forever.

I squeezed the hand I still held and told her, "I'm Nassir Gates." I gave her the name of the man I had decided I was going to be, half Middle Eastern, half American, one hundred percent lie. All the things I had done, all the things I had been, were no more. I was just a man that was going to make this new place his home. I didn't know at the time it was going to require as much blood and warfare to survive here as it had in the desert.

As the guy who attacked her started to make noise on the floor behind me, I turned to regard him. I was far from done with the bastard, but I wanted a proper introduction before I did what was inevitable the instant I watched the brute put his hands on her.

She smiled at me softly and returned the squeeze like we were going to be friends or something. "Keelyn Foster." Her eyes widened and she bit her plush lower lip, and I wanted to put my own teeth there more than I wanted anything in life. She was almost completely naked but I couldn't look away from those eyes. "I mean, Honor. Around here I'm Honor."

I smiled at her, and I was pretty sure it was the first time I had smiled. *Ever.* "How about I only call you that here in this club. I'm new in town but I have a feeling we'll be bumping into each other. Keelyn is a pretty name."

She blushed. She was gyrating for the pleasure of strangers, but giving her a throwaway compliment had her turning hot pink. And at the sight of her smile, everything suddenly made sense in my world.

"Thank you," she whispered, but I heard the words as loud as a thunderclap.

I inclined my head at her and turned around to the man trying to crawl his way back off the stage. I could be civilized. I could be restrained. I could be calm. But when I thought about those meaty paws all over, I didn't want to be anything other than what I had been born to be . . . a killer.

I was on him between heartbeats. His face disintegrated under my hands. His bones turned to dust. His breath was stamped out under my feet. His life was nothing to me until I caught sight of stormy gray eyes looking at me like I was evil incarnate. Now they were the color of charcoal, and full of fear . . . fear *of me*. I shook the blood off my knuckles and walked away from her before I inflicted more damage.

The man in charge watched the whole thing go down. Instead of asking me for money to stay in his city, he offered me papers that were fake but good enough to make me legalish. He asked me if I could get my hands on some armor-piercing rounds. I said yes to both the papers and the ammo, and my plan for laying low swelled up like a balloon and popped right over my head. I would never be able to run from who I was, or what I was, so I figured I might as well make the most of it in this place that was eager to embrace it. This place was a different kind of war zone, where every man seemed to be fighting for himself. It was familiar enough that I knew I could thrive here, could find a place where I fit. I could absolutely work with what made the Point tick, and while here, I could watch the girl. I could wait for her while she realized this was hell on earth—and when you make your home in hell, you want to have the devil in your corner.

I could fight for her even if she thought I was a monster. After all, I already knew all about chasing a lost cause.